BUCKET'S LIST

BUCKET'S LIST

A Charley Field Victorian mystery

Gary Blackwood

This first world edition published 2017
in Great Britain and the USA by
SEVERN HOUSE PUBLISHERS LTD of
Eardley House, 4 Uxbridge Street, London W8 7SY.
Trade paperback edition first published
in Great Britain and the USA 2018 by
SEVERN HOUSE PUBLISHERS LTD.

British Library Cataloguing in Publication Data
A CIP catalogue record for this title is available from the British Library.

ISBN-13: 978-0-7278-8738-2 (cased)
ISBN-13: 978-1-84751-851-4 (trade paper)
ISBN-13: 978-1-78010-911-4 (e-book)

Typeset by Palimpsest Book Production Ltd.,
Falkirk, Stirlingshire, Scotland.

For my Muse

ONE

Before we begin, a word of warning.

A novel is like a police informant, or a witness at a crime scene. Even the best ones can't be trusted to tell the truth all the time. And the worst ones are wholly unreliable. This one, I think you'll find, falls somewhere in between.

I can say with some confidence that it comes nearer the truth than the so-called penny bloods. If you've read even a single installment of *The Mysteries of London,* for example, or *The String of Pearls*, you know how you come away feeling slightly soiled and more than slightly disturbed, convinced that every lodging house in the city harbors a fiend in human form who butchers a victim a week at the very least. Or perhaps a swarthy foreigner who snatches helpless women and children and delivers them to a fate worse than death.

But in fact killings and kidnappings are relatively rare these days. According to police records – and if we can't trust the police, who can we trust? – the city has seen a mere twenty murders in 1853, plus forty or so cases of manslaughter, and the year is nearly over.

Those sensational serials would also have you believe that around every corner lies a hell on earth whose residents are consumed not by everlasting fire but by ever-present filth. The tenements there teem with ragged urchins, folk dying in droves from typhus and cholera, others wasting away from consumption – consumption of gin, that is – and the lot of them engaged not in useful work but in all manner of vice and depravity.

Naturally a canvas the size of London can't possibly be painted with a single color, or a single brush. As the newspapers and members of Parliament declare at every opportunity, we live in the largest, most populous city in the world – in fact, the largest that has ever existed. Not that you can put much stock in either the papers or the Parliament, but even so.

It's no good denying, of course, that London has its share of squalor – perhaps more than its share. But it also boasts posh paradises such as the likes of Arlington Street, Park Lane, and Piccadilly, plus any number of neighborhoods that, though they may not be very models of morality and industry, are nevertheless quite respectable.

Mrs Bramble's introducing house is in such a neighborhood. Forgive me for not divulging the actual location; as I say, you can never expect the whole truth from a novel. I wouldn't like to advertise her address to the police commissioners or the magistrates; the coppers on the beat already know it, of course. Let's just say it lies (both geographically and economically) somewhere between Knightsbridge and Millbank, not far from Belgrave Square – but not too near, either.

I don't suppose that, strictly speaking, the establishment itself can be called respectable. Though a polished brass plaque next to the entrance reads *Madame M'Alpine's Seminary for Young Ladies*, there is no Madame M'Alpine – at least not here – and the place is nothing more nor less than a molly house. But it is a very well kept, very clean molly house. The same may be said of its occupants and, for the most part, its visitors. There's always the odd exception, of course, and we'll be meeting some of those later on.

Another exaggerated feature of those penny dreadfuls is the wooly fog that always seems to swathe the city, no matter what the season or time of day. In real life, there are days on end when a breeze from the river leaves the air almost as clear as in the country – especially summers, when no coal fires burn. And there are many nights when the gaslights don't flicker for want of oxygen but glow brightly, like lighthouses for weary workers and wandering wastrels alike, guiding them safely home.

This is not one of those nights. This is a swathed-in-fog night, a guttering-gaslight night, a night when no one is abroad without a compelling reason. The gonolphs and bug hunters are always on the prowl, of course, but tonight they will have very slim pickings.

From a lace-curtained window on the third floor of Mrs Bramble's introducing house, Charley Field surveys the street below, or what he can see of it, which isn't much. It's an old habit, this street-surveying of his, carried over from his early years as a police constable. Coppers are generally well regarded and respected these days, but it wasn't always the case. Back then, you never knew when a costermonger you'd chased off for obstructing traffic might heave half a brick through your window, nor could you tell where a cove on whom you'd been forced to use your truncheon might lie in wait, itching to return the favor.

Though his policing days are officially over, Charley knows there's no shortage of men out there, and a few women, who wouldn't mind caving his head in, now that it's not protected by a constable's reinforced chimney-pot hat. But it works both ways: The city is also full of old acquaintances that he wouldn't mind seeing put away for a while, or at least spooked so badly that they take their business elsewhere. In fact, just before his retirement – almost exactly a year ago – he compiled a list of the ones who got away, the ones he knows are guilty as sin but somehow managed to escape punishment.

Now that he's his own man, he intends to remedy that.

'Charley?' says a drowsy voice from the bed behind him. 'You ain't leavin' yet?'

He regards the curry-colored mist that presses against the window pane like a burglar looking for a way in and sighs at the prospect of going out into it. 'I don't want to overstay my welcome. You'll have other customers to see to – paying ones.'

Rosa props herself against the wrought-iron head of the bed, a sheet held modestly over her bountiful breasts. 'I don't get so many as I used to. And if I do, Mrs Bramble will let me know. Come lie with me a little longer, won't you?'

Charley turns from the window with a sly smile. 'I've never been able to refuse a lady's request.'

She laughs softly. 'I don't often get accused of bein' a lady, neither.' She pulls back the blankets for him. 'You might turn up the lamp just a bit, love. I like to look at you sometimes.' When he passes by the coal-gas sconce without adjusting it, she shrugs. 'Only maybe you don't like lookin' at me so much.' She doesn't sound offended or hurt, just matter-of fact, as though she's well aware that she's no beauty.

'You know that's not so,' says Charley. He slides in next to her and places a noisy kiss on her plump cheek. In truth, he delights in her well-rounded body, which turns so rosy during their lovemaking, as if she's living up to her name. It's his own well-rounded body he doesn't care to display. Though he still has the thickly muscled arms and shoulders and neck of a bare-knuckle boxer, his midsection, from years of indulging his taste for good food and drink, has taken on a distressingly overstuffed appearance, like one of his wife's old-fashioned armchairs.

And then there are the scars. Every so often, Rosa runs her fingers over them lightly, and asks how he came by this or that one. He doesn't mind recounting their stories – at least the ones in which he acquitted himself well – but he sees no reason to show them off, as if they're a source of pride. If he'd been a better bobby in those early years, one who relied more on persuasion and less on pugnacity, he wouldn't have so many scars.

Charley is sure he has more aches and pains, too, than most men of forty-eight. But again, it's his own fault. He was foolish enough to spend his youthful years pounding on other prize-fighters and being pounded on in return, all for a chance at some paltry purse of a sovereign or two. It seemed like a good idea at the time; he didn't consider the price he'd be paying a couple of decades down the road. Well, you never do when you're twenty, do you?

His body is showing its age in other ways, too. He's finding lately that he can usually manage only one turn among the cabbages in his weekly hour or two with Rosa. It's not as if he feels cheated – not in terms of money, anyway. After all, he enjoys her favors for free. And it's not as if Rosa minds; she's said enough times how pleasant it is to share her bed with a man who is more like a companion than a client. It's just one more reminder that, contrary to what he thought at twenty, he's not immortal. Im*moral*, perhaps, but that's never bothered him much. He's less concerned about Morality than about Right and Wrong.

Rosa turns to him and casually wraps one soft leg around him, as though to keep him here a while longer. 'Charley?'

'Hmm?' He buries his face in her wine-colored hair – the one feature of hers that any man would concede is quite beautiful.

It smells a bit like wine, too – a warm glass of negus, with plenty of sugar and spices.

'You never have said what you done to make Mrs Bramble so kindly disposed towards you. I ain't complainin', you understand. Havin' your company is better than any amount of money. I'm just curious, is all.'

'I know. And maybe someday I'll tell you. But for now, it's between her and me.'

She walks her fingers playfully across his chest, down his belly. 'Oh, now, can't you give me a little hint, even? Just a teeny, weeny hint?'

Charley feels his wilted *arbor vitae* coming to life, pressing against her leg. He laughs and shakes his head. 'You're incorrigible, you are.'

'I ain't certain what that means, but I'm sure it's a compliment.'

When he was a bare-knuckle boxer, Charley prided himself on always being able to go another round, no matter how battered and exhausted he was. A pale, ghostly version of that pride returns as he finds himself able to go a second round with Rosa – a far more pleasurable experience than being pummeled by some bruiser's brine-soaked fists. What's more, it keeps Rosa's curiosity in check – for the time being, anyway.

There's nothing really shameful in his past history with Mrs Bramble, and she's never specifically asked him to keep it a secret. But one of the first things Charley learned about policing was to be discreet, not to discuss a case with anyone who wasn't directly involved.

Back when he was a Bow Street Runner, he encountered a six-year-old in a pawnshop, attempting to fence no less than four elegant pocket watches. He should have run the boy in, but he looked so scrawny and pitiful that Charley didn't have the heart. His real mistake, though, was relating the incident to an amiable drinking companion over a pint of grog. As it turned out, the fellow was not so amiable after all. He was, in fact, a kidsman, and the boy with the watches was one of his gang of young thieves. Instead of handing over his take to the kidsman, the enterprising lad had decided to keep the profits himself. Charley learned the truth only when he came across the boy again that same night, curled up in a doorway, dying from internal injuries from the beating he'd received.

Mrs Bramble's story had a happier ending. She'd been accused of poisoning her husband, a landlord with half a dozen lodging houses that earned him a good deal of money. Charley, who by then was chief of the detective branch, sensed that the matter was not nearly as simple as it seemed, and began poking about.

Poking about was his favorite part of police work, because you never knew what you might turn up. In this case, he turned up the fact that Mrs Bramble's husband, who suffered from stomach distress, had lately resorted to a popular patent medicine, Dr Benjamin's Panacea. Charley visited the families of other recent poisoning victims and found that a good – or rather an unfortunate – two-thirds of them had bottles of Dr Benjamin's in the house. When the contents of the bottles were tested, they proved to contain a very unhealthy proportion of arsenic.

There was no Dr Benjamin, of course; the stuff was concocted in a factory. Charley got hired on there and, after only one day, collared the cove responsible for adding the arsenic – an employee who had asked for a raise and been refused.

Mrs Bramble gained her freedom, and Inspector Field gained a good friend and a valuable source of information. Though London may be the world's largest city, the underworld it harbors can seem incredibly small, especially to those who are trying to hide within its confines. The criminal class – the *residuum,* some call it – are in many ways a community unto themselves, not unlike one of your rural towns where everyone knows everyone else's business. Though Mrs Bramble occupies a place on the outskirts of that community, its rumors waft to her on the wind; she crosses paths with its natives and observes their comings and goings.

In his quarter-century of policing, Charley has built up an impressive collection of such friendly informants, most of whom owe their freedom to him, and sometimes their lives. It was a running joke among the New Police that Constable (then Sergeant, then Inspector) Field had far more acquittals than convictions to his credit. Charley didn't mind; to his way of thinking, bringing a man to justice doesn't necessarily mean locking him up. If those penny bloods are to be believed, criminals are a sort of separate species, driven by evil desires and motives unknown to ordinary men. But in Charley's experience, the vast majority of wrongdoers have one simple motive: to put food in their bellies. Where's the justice in punishing them for that?

Technically, prostitutes like Rosa are part of the criminal class, but of course they ply their trade for the same reason everyone else does: not because they are depraved, but in order to provide clothing and food and shelter for themselves – and, in Rosa's case, for her young daughter. Still, it can be a dangerous trade, and Charley would like to see her take up a safer one – even if it means he can no longer visit her.

As if preparing for that eventuality, he pries himself away from her warm embrace and retrieves his clothing from the wooden valet at the foot of the bed. Once he's donned his union suit, he turns up the gas a little. He glances at the small watercolor that hangs, unframed, next to the bed – a fairly accurate representation of a bottle of wine, two plums, and an apple. 'This is a new one, isn't it?'

'Aye. I did it only yesterday. D'you like it?'

'I do. Looks good enough to eat.' He gives her a lecherous glance. 'Much like yourself.'

She guffaws and throws a pillow at him. ''Tis what they call a still life, y'know. I seen them at the museum.'

Charley sits on the edge of the bed and takes her hand. 'You've got talent in those fingers, Rosa. You should make use of it.'

'Well, that's what I'm doing, with the paintin', ain't I?'

'Of course, but I meant use it to make money.'

She gives him a startled look. 'Like counterfeit banknotes, y'mean?'

'No, no,' says Charley, laughing. 'A photographer I know is looking for someone to hand-color portraits for his customers. I told him I'd ask you about it.' He doesn't bother to tell her that the photographer is, in fact, a reformed counterfeiter.

Rosa smiles ruefully and squeezes his hand. 'I appreciate you thinkin' of me, Charley, truly I do. But we've been through this afore. You know yourself I make more here in one night than I could make in a week at that sort of a job. I figure that, if I can stick with this for another two years, and don't lose too many clients, I'll have enough saved up to start my millinery shop.'

'But you worked in that line before, my dear, and couldn't make a living at it.'

'That's because the scrawny shrew as owned the shop paid us by the piece – half a bloody crown per hat. Do you know how long it takes to make a decent hat? And of course she turned around and charged the customer at least a guinea.'

Charley throws up his hands. 'All right, all right. I'm not telling you what to do, I'm just concerned about you, that's all.'

'I know y'are.' She flings the sheet aside and gives him a hug around the neck that fairly strangles him. 'Not to worry; I'm careful. I have a little girl to think about, after all. If aught happened to me, heaven knows what'd become of Audrey.'

Charley disentangles himself and pulls on his trousers. 'Well, I suppose Mrs Bramble won't let in anyone too unsavory. I know *I* wouldn't care to try and get past her if she didn't approve.'

'No,' says Rosa. 'She's always looking out for us.' Though she's smiling, there's something in that smile and in the tone of her voice that sets off a tiny warning signal inside Charley. It's not a fire alarm sort of signal, or even a constable's rattle sort of signal, more like a whispered warning in his ear, hardly worth noticing – except that Charley has spent his whole career learning to listen for those whispers and to heed them.

'But . . .?' says Charley.

'What?'

'There's something you're not saying. "She's always looking out for us, *but* . . ."'

Rosa sighs. "'Tis nothing, most likely.'

'Why don't you let me decide that?' He sits on the bed again, lifts her chin, and looks into her eyes. The eyes, he's learned, seldom lie.

'Well, 'tis just . . . 'tis just this one client. He came earlier this afternoon. There were something about him . . .'

'What sort of something?'

'Well, he were a bit odd-looking to begin with. I mean, he dressed like a swell, and he were flashing a big bundle, but he talked more like a scroof or a street-sweeper. His voice were odd, too – all rough and gratey, like a hand mill grinding grain. And there were something wrong about his neck.'

The faint warning in Charley's ear becomes more like a stage whisper. 'Wrong? How do you mean?'

'It were all stiff-like. Like it hurt him to move it.'

Charley's eyes narrow with suspicion. 'Were there any sort of scars on his neck?'

'I can't say. He never did take his shirt off. There were a nasty scar on his buttocks, though. I could feel it.'

Charley nods grimly. 'I know how he came by it, too.'

'You do?'

'Yes,' says Charley. 'I shot him. With his own revolver.'

TWO

C harley takes a small bound notebook from the inside pocket of his tweed frock coat and flips it open. The information he's looking for is on the very first page. 'This fellow you entertained – was he a tall, skinny cove with bulging eyes and coal-black hair?'

'Aye. And mustaches.' She puts a hand to her mouth, as if recalling how they prickled her skin. 'I don't like mustaches.'

'He was clean-shaven when I met him, but that doesn't signify. No doubt he's trying to change his looks. He can't change that neck of his, though.'

'Who is he?'

'His name, you mean? He has more of those than the Devil does: Thomas Twitter. Tom Twit. Mickey McAdoo. Mike the Mutcher. As best I can determine, he was born Thomas Tufts, but us coppers just called him "Neck." They say he killed a man in a jealous rage some years back, up in Yorkshire, or it might have been Lancashire, and was hanged for it.'

Rosa stares, open-mouthed. '*Hanged*? But – but—'

'Don't worry, he's not a ghost or a vampire. The coroner pronounced him dead, and they gave the body to an anatomy class to dissect. But the moment the first scalpel broke the skin, he coughed a few times, sat up, looked around, and rasped, "This don't look like Hell to me."'

'Laws! I hope they make sure I'm good and dead before they cut *me* up!'

Charley runs a hand over her rosy skin. 'I don't want to think about that. Anyway, the long and short of it is, they let him go free. You can't hang a man twice for the same crime, they said. Of course, he's committed enough crimes since then to be hanged ten times over.

'When I caught up with him, he was setting fire to a boot shop in Burlington Arcade; a rival boot maker had hired him to burn the place down. He pulled a Colt's revolver, but I *knocked* it—' Charley demonstrates, with an imaginary walking stick, and Rosa gasps – 'to the ground. Well, he hooked it – meaning he fled – and I had the choice of running him down or putting out the fire. So . . . I snatched up the Colt's and I shot him.' He displays his stiff, crooked trigger finger; he broke it once, or perhaps more than once, while boxing and it never healed properly. 'I'm not good with handguns, and my aim was a little off. By the time I got the flames under control, of course, he was long gone.' Charley taps the notebook. 'He's at the top of my list. If he shows up here again, you send for me right away.'

Rosa doesn't reply. She pulls the blanket up to her neck, as though she's taken a sudden chill.

'Rosa? You'll send for me, if he comes back?'

'Yes,' she says. 'I will, Charley.'

'Is there something more you're not telling me?' He tries to lift her chin again, but she pulls away.

'He just – he just frightened me, that's all. The things he talked about.'

'What sort of things?'

'I – I can't remember, exactly. I know he were bragging about how much money he's going to make from some scheme or other. Us whores, we're a bit like priests, y'know – when they're with us, men will confess just about anythin', and then later wish they hadn't done. I've learned not to listen too close.'

And Charley has learned when not to push too hard. Some coppers will try to force a witness or a victim or a perpetrator to talk, but Charley has seen too many of them just close up tight under duress, the way an oyster will when you try to pry it open. 'Well, if you remember anything more, you write it down, and I'll come back and see you in a day or two.'

She nods silently. As he's putting on his greatcoat, she says softly, 'Are you going home?'

'No, not in this fog. Besides, it's too awkward, after coming here. I'll just go to the office. I often sleep there; I've put a cot in the storage room.'

'I feel a bit sorry for her – your wife. I suppose she must miss you.'

'I suppose not. Anyway, she doesn't need me. She's got her mother for company. When I'm not there, they can discuss all my shortcomings without even having to whisper.'

It wouldn't surprise Charley if his wife and mother-in-law had their own little notebook, in which the catalog of wrongdoers consists of a single name – his – followed by a list of all the things he does to infuriate and annoy them. At the top of the list, no doubt, is his pipe-smoking habit.

Standing on the steps of Madame M'Alpine's Seminary, he pulls his meerschaum from the pocket of his greatcoat and fills it from a leather pouch. Then he fishes out one of the paper twists he carries about for this purpose, ignites it from the gas lamp – which, unlike those outside many brothels and intro-ducing houses, has discreet panes of clear glass, rather than red – and lights his pipe.

For a time, he tried using phosphorus matches, but found them a nuisance. Sometimes they failed to light at all, other times just their rubbing against each other was enough to set them ablaze. What put him off them altogether, though, was meeting Mary, another of Mrs Bramble's girls. For three years she had worked days in a match factory, and the fumes had eaten away most of her jawbone – phossy jaw, they called it. She had been a pretty girl, and she still attracted a few clients – as long as she kept a scarf wrapped about her lower face.

There's a cab stand not far off, in Eccleston Street, but he can't really spare the money. Business has not been good of late; though people trust the police for the most part, private enquiry agents are still looked upon with some suspicion. And anyway, Charley prefers to walk. You can see more that way, even in the fog.

The streets and pavements are slippery with a damp layer of licky – a mixture of soot, dirt, and desiccated horse droppings – but not a trace of snow or ice. It's been one of the warmest Decembers he can recall. A person would scarcely guess that Christmas is only a fortnight away if it weren't for the shop windows.

Most are shuttered at this time of night, but he passes a grocer's shop with windows that are protected by an iron grating. Through it, he can view an embarrassment of edibles, many of which make an appearance only in the weeks leading up to Christmas: great heaps of St Michael's and Maltese oranges, apples, winter pears, pineapples; edifices constructed from tins of caviar and mincemeat; gemlike jars of raspberry jelly and preserved ginger; boxes overflowing with walnuts and figs, currants and sultanas, bonbons and biscuits.

Charley could live without such stuff – roast beef and beer are more in his line – but he'll have to present Jane and her mother with a basket of Yuletide delicacies soon, or he'll fall even farther from grace. No doubt they'll want a tree as well, to hang the oranges and the candies on, as is the fashion. And good lord, they'll be expecting gifts; he hasn't even begun to look.

He walks on. Street lamps are sparse in working-class neigh-borhoods like this one; there are times when he has to feel his way along, swinging his walking stick to and fro like a blind man, to avoid colliding with walls or with the palings that separate the pavement from the street. The lighted window of the Cat and Fiddle emerges from the fog, like the yellow moon rising behind a bank of clouds. Charley is surprised to find the public house still open; he'd thought it was well past midnight. It turns dark so early this time of year, it plays havoc with a man's sense of time.

When he steps inside, a dozen heads turn in idle curiosity. Most stare at him blankly, but in every tavern in the West End there are always a few who recognize Inspector Field, for better or worse. Some of those who've spotted him quickly duck their heads, not caring to be recognized in turn. Others raise a hand or a pint in greeting. A red-faced, white-haired fellow cries, 'Blow me, it's Inspector Bucket!' Charley grins and waves, not unhappy with the minor celebrity lent him by Mr Dickens' serial, which concluded only a few months ago.

Sitting at the bar is a uniformed constable whose baby face is unfamiliar, and Charley has a good memory for faces. When the red-complexioned fellow calls out to Charley, the young copper turns, looking startled and clearly embarrassed at being caught neglecting his beat, then quickly downs his drink. Charley notes that it's not porter or stout he's having, but an egg flip – minus the brandy, something tells him. Despite the rules, coppers have been known to drink stronger stuff while on duty, especially on a night this raw and damp, but the boy just strikes him as a teetotaler.

Charley prides himself on his ability to read people and to notice details that most people would overlook, even other detectives. Though his years of policing have helped him hone this skill, he first learned it when he was a lad in Chelsea, sitting in the back room of his father's public house, watching raptly as his mother told fortunes for sixpence a go. Sometimes she used a tarot deck, other times she read tea leaves or palms, whatever the customer preferred.

The method didn't matter, for the underlying strategy was always the same: It wasn't truly the tea leaves or the tarot that she was reading; it was the customer. Some things she observed with her eyes – what the person wore, the state of her health, the way she carried herself, how she responded to questions and hints. Other things, his mother simply sensed somehow. But often there was nothing particularly skillful or uncanny about it; she was simply relying on gossip she had gleaned while pouring glasses of gin in the tavern.

By the time he reaches the young constable and lays a hand on his shoulder, Charley already knows half a dozen things about him. First off, he's from the Midlands somewhere – Derbyshire, most likely, from the way he says to the publican, 'Thank 'ee, but I mun be up and off.' He's no laborer or tradesman, though, as the coppers from that area tend to be. His hands are too soft, and his speech, despite its regional flavor, is more schooled than most. A parson's son, would be Charley's guess; that would account for the liquorless egg flip, which he's even more certain about now that he can smell the boy's breath. As further evidence, there's a gold chain visible inside the lad's coat; he's unbuckled his collar in the warm room. Charley is willing to wager that, at the nether end of the chain, there's a crucifix.

He'd also bet any amount that the fellow is neither quite old enough nor quite tall enough to meet the criteria for joining the force; that means he's clever enough to have got in anyway, and determined enough to have made the effort. The number on his collar – B62 – tells Charley that he's fresh fish, probably just out of training. That number formerly belonged to Aloysius Egg, who was dismissed a few weeks ago for having the gall to marry what his superiors called a 'common prostitute' – though Charley has met the woman, and there's nothing common about her.

When the boy feels Charley's heavy hand on his shoulder, he turns again and slides off the stool, hanging his head sheepishly. 'I was just returning to my beat, Inspector Field.'

'You know me?' says Charley, unused to strangers calling him by his real name and not that of Mr Dickens' character.

'Eh, everyone knows you, Inspector. You're a bit of legend, actually.'

Charley laughs. 'A legend, eh?'

The boy nods, more eager than embarrassed, now. ''Twas hearing about your cases and how you solved them that made me wish to join the force.'

'You're not confusing me with Inspector Bucket, now?'

'No, sir.'

'You've read *Bleak House*, though?'

'Yes, sir. 'Tis a ripping tale, and Bucket is a gradely fellow. But I want to be a *real* inspector.'

'Good for you. First, though, you need to get out there and haul in your quota of drunks and pickpockets.' He gives the boy a slight shove in the direction of the door. When he's gone, Charley bellies up to the bar. 'Good evening, Samuel. A pint of purl, if you'd be so kind.'

The publican warms a glass of beer over a spirit lamp, adds a shot of gin, a spoonful of sugar, and a slice of ginger and plunks it in front of Charley. 'Good to see you, Inspector. It's been a while.'

'Well, I don't get around like I did when I was with the force. I have to stick close to the office, you know, on the slim chance that a client might find his way there.' Charley takes a swig of the purl and smacks his lips appreciatively. 'So far, I've been hired to find a ten-year-old boy's missing dog and to spy on a cove who threw himself under a carriage and then sued the rig's owner.'

'What did you find out?'

'About the dog?'

Samuel laughs. 'About the injured bloke.'

'He did the job a bit too well. He can barely move, even when he thinks no one's watching.' Charley finishes off his drink, wipes his mouth on his sleeve, and places a shilling on the bar. Samuel waves it away.

'Your money's no good here, Inspector.'

'I'm not a copper any more. I'll pay for my drinks.'

The man shrugs. 'If you insist.'

'I do.' Charley jingles the few coins remaining in his pocket. 'Can I ask you a sort of a personal question, Samuel?'

'Is this an interrogation, Inspector?'

'I told you, I'm retired. I'm just a private enquiry agent now.'

'Well, then, is this a private enquiry?'

'Not exactly. Only I want to know: What are you getting your wife for Christmas?'

Before Charley can leave he's obliged to make the rounds, greeting old friends, reminding old foes that he still has his eye on them. By the time he emerges from the Cat and Fiddle, the bells of St Peter's are tolling midnight – though the fog makes it seem as if the sound is coming from some other quarter altogether. At the same time, his ears catch another, shriller sound from somewhere closer by – the muffled piping of a policeman's whistle. It's true, then, what he's heard: the commissioner is phasing out the heavy old wooden rattle, which never did fit comfortably in a fellow's pocket and which more than once was seized by a perpetrator and used to bludgeon the arresting officer.

Though the whistle is meant to summon coppers from neighboring beats, Charley knows it won't carry far in the fog. He plunges into the murk, heading in the direction of the sound, or as nearly as he can tell. He hasn't gone more than a dozen strides before he collides head-on with someone coming the other way and traveling far too fast for conditions. Charley is a big man, and solid; running into him is no better than running into one of the sides of beef you see at Smithfield Market.

The other fellow lets out a whooshing sound like a blacksmith's bellows and staggers backward, clutching his chest. Charley catches him by the arm and props him up with very little effort, since the man is about half his size. 'Sorry, sir; I didn't see you coming. Are you all right?' The man gives him a look of alarm, as if he takes Charley for a robber, and tries to pull away. 'There's nothing to fear, sir. I'm a detective.' Not strictly true, of course, but more reassuring than saying *I'm a private enquiry agent.*

The man doesn't seem reassured, though; he struggles even harder to break free. 'I ain't hurt,' he groans. 'Just turn me loose, would you?'

'Of course, sir,' says Charley. 'Of course. Just as soon as you open up that coat of yours.'

'My – my coat?'

'Well, we have to make certain you're not bleeding, don't we? You might need to be taken to hospital.' Charley guides the little man, not very gently, toward the nearest street lamp. The fellow has clearly been in this sort of situation before, and knows it's no use resisting. With a sigh, he unbuttons his coat, revealing an ornate, gilded mantel clock. 'Don't tell me,' says Charley. 'Your wife said to be back by midnight, so you took the clock along, just make sure. And you were running because you've outstayed your curfew.'

The man can't help chuckling. 'You got it right in one guess, guv'nor.'

'Well, I'm afraid the little lady is going to be sorely disappointed. You're not likely to be going home for a while.' From the inside pocket of his greatcoat, Charley retrieves a set of cast-iron 'D' handcuffs, one of the few mementos – aside from all the scars – of his policing career, and shackles the thief to the lamppost. 'You just wait there, while I fetch a real officer.'

'A real officer? You said you were a detective!'

'Did I? Sorry. Old habits are difficult to break.'

As Charley walks off, carrying the mantel clock, the man calls after him, 'Listen, if you let me go, I'll split the take from that timepiece; it'll bring at least two guineas!' His pleas are swallowed by the fog.

Within a block, Charley comes upon the young constable from the tavern; he's sitting on the steps of a small and slightly run-down town house, his head in his hands. 'Lost your man?' says Charley.

The copper glances up, then buries his face in his hands again. 'My first chance to catch an actual criminal, and I make a hash of it.'

'Not entirely.' Charley hands him the clock, which, aside from a cracked crystal, seems to be no worse for the ordeal.

'Where did you— How did you—'

'I just ran into the cove who took it – literally. If you want to take him in, he's cuffed to a lamppost up the street, the one advertising M. Claudet's Photographic Portraits.'

The boy springs to his feet, all wide-eyed and eager again. 'All right! Why don't I do that, then? Thank 'ee. Eh, I hate to ask, but would you – would you mind watching yon residence until I come back? The door isn't secure. I tried to summon another constable, but I dunnot think this whistle carries well in the fog.'

'No, I don't mind. Always happy to help a fellow—' Charley lets the sentence drop. He still hasn't quite got used to being a plain citizen. He takes the constable's spot on the steps and sits there humming 'Hark, the Bonny Christ Church Bells' under his breath. He gets through three full choruses before the young copper returns – alone, and looking even more dejected than he did earlier.

'Didn't you find him?' asks Charley.

'I found the lamppost, sir, but not the thief. Nobbut these.' The boy holds up Charley's handcuffs, their toothed jaws dangling open like those of a rabid dog someone has shot.

THREE

'Well,' says Charley, with an ironic grin, 'the little man has made fools of us both, hasn't he?' Ruefully, he regards the open cuffs. 'He's very adept at picking locks.'

The constable regards the open town house even more ruefully. 'Eh, 'tis how he got inside, as well, I suppose. The family's gone for the holidays and asked that we keep an eye on the place. I was about to try the door when a young lady come hurrying up to me, sobbing, saying she'd been manhandled by some stranger and wanted him arrested and that. I'd have gone with her, only just then I heard a noise from inside the house. Before I could investigate, the door flew open and the thief flew out. I started after him, but the young lady mun have tripped me up, for I went sprawling.' He rubs his bruised knees. 'By the time I got to my feet, the man had vanished in the fog and the lady nearly so; I could've caught up with her, only I didn't like to leave the house hanging open. She mun have been in league with the thief.' The boy shakes his head sadly. ''Tis a sad shame; such an attractive young lady.'

'Yes,' says Charley, 'it's a pity Mr Lavater's theory of physiognomy isn't more reliable. We could just lock up all the ugly folk, and be done with it.' He gives the constable a sympathetic pat on the back. 'You're not the first copper to be gulled by a canary, son, nor likely to be the last.'

'A canary?'

'That's what we call the maiden in distress who draws your attention away from the real crime.'

'Oh.' The boy lets out a discouraged sigh. 'Eh, I can see I've a lot to learn about policing.'

'No doubt. But you *want* to learn, so that's half the battle.'

The young constable gives him a puzzled look. 'You sound as if you know me.'

Charley shrugs. 'I know a few things about you. Though

physiognomy may not be reliable, you can still tell a good deal about a person just by observing. For example, I'd bet you're from Derbyshire.'

'Then you'd win.' The boy considers this a moment. 'No doubt my speech gives me away.'

'And you're a clergyman's son, I believe?'

'How did you know *that*?'

'Lucky guess. And you've been on the force for . . . I'd say . . . three weeks.'

'Right again. 'Tis obvious that I'm new, given the way I handled myself. But why three weeks?'

'Well, it's clearly been more than a week, or you'd have a partner walking the beat with you. And yet—' Charley points his crooked finger at the boy's feet. 'You're still wearing your own boots. Most recruits wash out in the first fortnight, so the force don't bother ordering boots for you until they're fairly certain you're going to stay around, and it takes another week to get them made.' He examines the boy's baby face. 'There is one thing, though, that I've not been able to deduce about you.'

The copper shifts uncomfortably under his gaze. 'Whatever is that, sir?'

'Your name.'

'Eh, I'm sorry, I should've said. Constable Mull, sir.' He salutes, then hesitantly holds out a hand, as if unsure which greeting is proper under the circumstances.

Charley grips the hand so firmly that boy winces. 'Do you have a first name?'

'Of course, only I thought—'

'No need to stand on ceremony; I'm not your superior any more.'

''Tis Lochinvar, sir.'

'*Lochinvar*?' Charley stifles a laugh. 'Sorry. It's an unusual name. Your mother must be a great admirer of Sir Walter Scott.'

'That she is.'

'I may be good at deducing things, but I'd never have hit on Lochinvar. I had you down for a Matthew or a John, something biblical.' He claps Constable Mull on the back again, and the boy nearly stumbles. 'Well. I'm playing the canary now, distracting you from your duties. You'd best resume your beat, and I'd best get to bed. You never know; tomorrow may be the day a wealthy client turns up.'

'Yes, sir. But – eh – what do I do about the house? 'Tis still not secure.'

'You leave that to me.'

'I've no key. How will you—' He breaks off as Inspector Field pulls, from yet another pocket of his greatcoat, a ring of twirls, screws, picks, and rakes of various shapes and sizes.

'If a lock may be picked,' says Charley, 'it may also be unpicked.'

The vicinity of Ebury Square, where Charley's office may be found, is an even more respectable neighborhood than Mrs Bramble's. In fact, according to one of his more reliable sources, until recently Mr Tennyson, the celebrated poet, lived nearby. Though the rent is really more than Charley can afford on his pension, he's taken to heart the advice of Mrs Bramble, who maintains that, if you set up shop in a poor area of town, the only clients you'll get are poor ones. She's fond of quoting the old Scots maxim, 'Doan't thou marry for munny, but goa wheer munny is.'

So far, he's attracted scarcely any clients – rich, poor, or middling. It almost makes him long to change places with Constable Lochinvar Mull, to be out on the street where the real policing happens, not cooped up in an office, waiting impatiently for some case that needs solving. He wouldn't really care to be a young copper on the beat again, of course – not unless he could somehow take with him all the things he's learned since then.

Thinking of the earnest Constable Mull makes him smile. The boy reminds him a little of himself at that age. Not in his background – Charley grew up in the rowdy atmosphere of a Chelsea public house, not some quiet parish in the Midlands – but in the way the young copper thinks he can make a real difference in the world by bringing wrongdoers to justice. Charley still believes that same thing. In fact, he knows it; he's seen at first hand how the streets have become a bit safer every year since the New Police appeared on them. But he's no longer making much of a difference; he's just marking time.

He's had bills posted; he's advertised his agency in the papers; he's told everyone he knows – and he knows a lot of people. But it seems that those who need his services can't afford them, and those who can afford him don't need him. Still, Charley is by nature an optimist, so this morning and every other morning he shines his shoes and brushes his frock coat, builds up a nice fire, puts a kettle of water on the hob so he can offer tea to whoever might walk through the door. Then he tidies up his little office, which occupies the garret of a narrow brick building in Flask Road. On the ground floor is a cigar shop; the second floor is let to a musician – a violinist who, judging from the quality of his playing, must have some trouble paying his rent as well.

The only part he doesn't tidy up is his desk, an imposing pile of oak that belonged to his wife's first husband, who owned a distillery and could afford such things. It takes up a good tenth of his floor space; in order to hoist it into the garret, it was necessary to remove a window. But Charley learned long ago how important appearances are; a client – supposing one ever appears – can't help feeling that a man with so solid and dependable a desk must be solid and dependable himself.

It's just as important to appear busy and in demand, so the desktop is as snowed under with documents and correspondence and memoranda as that of a Doctor's Commons lawyer. If you look closely, however, you'll find that, like his handcuffs, they mostly date from his days as Detective Inspector.

So does his habit of getting up early. Like his pipe-smoking and his fondness for singing and whistling music-hall tunes, it's a constant source of irritation to his wife and her mother, both of whom consider it uncivilized to arise before ten. By the time he puts the finishing touches on his stage set – *The curtain rises on the small but well-furnished office of a successful and distinguished private enquiry agent* – it's barely gone eight o'clock. There's plenty of time to nip down to the coffeehouse next door for toast and bacon and a lovely cup of Mocha; at his wife's house it's always tea, tea, and more tea.

To his astonishment, no sooner has he returned to his desk and cleared a space for his little repast than he hears a rapping on his office door – the head of a walking stick, would be his

guess. A good sign; it shows that the visitor is a man of means
. . . Unless, of course, he's wrong and the sound is made by a
cosh or a set of knuckledusters, which would indicate that one
of his old nemeses has sought him out. But in his experience,
that sort don't bother to knock. Charley scoops the toast and
bacon in their greasy wrapper into a drawer, snatches up pen
and paper, and calls out in a genial yet businesslike voice,
'Please come in!'

The man who enters is clearly one of means – in fact, quite
a dandy, from his brass-headed ebony walking stick to his
voluminous white greatcoat to his flowing silk cravat, which
matches the blue of his large, striking eyes. 'I am told,' says
the visitor, in a voice too loud for the size of the room, 'that
you can read a man like a book, just from his appearance.' His
large mouth is set in a disarming but rather supercilious smile.

'Well, sir,' says Charley, 'I'd say that depends upon the book.
I believe I can offer more insight into a man's character than,
say, *Spring-Heeled Jack*, but perhaps not so much as you'd find
in, say, *Nicholas Nickleby*.'

'Indeed. I assumed it would depend more upon the man.'

Charley shrugs. 'I've found that the majority of men make
for pretty easy reading.'

The visitor raises his eyebrows. 'A brave boast, sir.' He
spreads his arms and his lapels wide, revealing a flamboyant
striped waistcoat. 'So, then, let us see. What can you deduce
about yours truly?'

Charley looks him carefully up and down. 'You were raised
in Mongolia by a troupe of high-wire artists – which accounts
for your taste in fashion. You are four feet five and a quarter
inches in height and weigh fifteen stone – though your girdle
keeps the weight well hidden. You work days as a trotter scraper
and nights as a pure finder. You have one wife in Bow and
another in Barstow, and eight children by each. It is your life-
long ambition to play the part of Hamlet upon the stage or,
failing that, Varney the Vampire—' He can go no further with
his portrait, for the visitor dissolves in a fit of mirth. Charley
sits there, grinning modestly, until the man finds his voice again.

'Oh, Charley!' the fellow gasps. 'That's the best description
of me I've ever heard! Particularly the part about wanting to play

Hamlet! So true! So true!' Still chuckling, he pulls a silk hand-kerchief from his sleeve and wipes at his eyes. 'Oh, dear; I should write all that down. It will afford me with a standout character for my next novel. Why bother creating one from whole cloth, when you may get such an excellent one ready-made?'

'I believe I've missed my calling,' says Charley, rather glumly. 'Perhaps I should open an author's advice agency. I couldn't possibly do any worse.'

Mr Dickens sobers. 'Business is that bad, is it?' He removes his overcoat and hangs it carefully on the coat rack; then, tugging fastidiously at the knees of his trousers, he seats himself on the special client's chair, which is more comfortable than Charley's own.

'Can I get you some tea?' asks Charley.

'No, no, I can't stay long. But do go ahead and drink yours – which I deduce from the aroma is, in fact, coffee.'

'You'd make a fine detective.' Charley takes a gulp of the Mocha and makes a face. 'Good lord. This is at least one-fourth chicory.' He sighs and sets the cup down. 'It's getting harder and harder to find bona fide coffee that isn't bulked up with burnt acorns and horse peas and sawdust and the devil knows what else.'

'Well, you see; there's a case for you to solve, my friend. Find out who's adulterating the stuff, and expose them. I'll even print an account of your investigations and pay you a few shillings for the privilege.'

'Not a bad idea. But I'll need more than a few shillings to pay the rent on this place.'

'Then why don't you place an advertisement in my magazine? What are you calling yourself?'

'Mr Field's Private Enquiry Agency.'

The great author throws up his hands dramatically; Mr Dickens is nothing if not dramatic. 'Well, there, you see, that's your problem! You need a name that will *intrigue* and *excite* people, make them say to themselves, "Why, that's precisely what I need! A private enquiry agent! Why didn't I think of it sooner?"'

'But that's my name; I can scarcely call myself something else.'

'Why not? The name Field means nothing to most people – unless they happen to be coiners or cracksmen. Even if they've read my piece about you in *Household Words*, that was two years ago, and people have very short memories, believe me.'

'All right, what do you suggest?'

'Well, *Inspector* Field would be some improvement . . .'

'But I'm not an—'

'Wait!' Mr Dickens' wide eyes grow even wider; he leans forward in his chair and says, in a hushed, dramatic voice, 'I have it! *Inspector Bucket's* Private Enquiry Agency!' He sits back in the chair with a triumphant grin, arms smugly crossed. 'Bucket is – and I say this in all modesty – a household name in at least half the households of London.'

'Well, yes, but he's not an actual person—'

Mr Dickens lets out a laugh. 'Try telling that to the reading public. Commissioner Mayne tells me that, at least once a week, some distraught man or woman comes into one of the station houses demanding to speak with Inspector Bucket, convinced that he's the only man who can help them. In any case, I modeled Bucket after you, so you're certainly entitled to use the name.'

'And you wouldn't mind?'

'Mind? I'd be delighted! Life imitating art imitating life. It's perfect!'

'Well, I suppose it's worth a try. I've got nothing to lose. Except my real identity, of course. But I know my wife won't mind if I turn into someone else altogether. She's reading your novel now, and is quite taken with Inspector Bucket. Ironic, isn't it?'

Mr Dickens' face turns suddenly somber. 'Yes. Men in books are far easier to get along with than the real thing. Just as books themselves are so much more pleasant than their authors. And if they do become tiresome, you can always put them aside.'

Charley wouldn't have to be much of a detective to deduce that Mr Dickens and his wife, whom he invariably refers to as 'poor Kate,' are unhappy together; he's been seeing evidence of it for as long as he's known the man. And though it's his business to ask questions, Charley senses that this is one of those cases in which it's best not to press the victim too hard.

Or is Mr Dickens the victimizer? It's hard to say which; both, most likely, as is usually the case.

His visitor shakes himself out of his gloom and, like the sometime actor he is, puts on a practiced smile. 'You know, with all this commiserating about the vagaries of business and marriage, I nearly forgot what brought me here to begin with. This is not a purely social visit – though it has been a while since we raised a glass together. As it happens, I have a job for you.'

FOUR

Since its publication ten years ago, Mr Dickens' tale *A Christmas Carol* has become something of an institution. It has gone through at least two dozen printings and nearly as many dramatic productions – most of them tending toward the *melo*dramatic, actually, but wildly popular despite that. Or perhaps because of it. One might assume that its success would have made Mr Dickens a wealthy man – and in fact he is quite comfortable, but it's no thanks to *A Christmas Carol*, which costs nearly as much to print as it does to buy. Though Mr Dickens is an artist, he is also a man of business, and he's determined to wring a decent profit from his creation.

'I've decided that the best way of accomplishing that,' he says, 'is to produce my own dramatic version of the story.' He holds up both hands, as if expecting Charley to make some objection. '*But*! Not in the form of a play. I will present it as a *reading*. Oh god, you're thinking, not another of those endless, monotonous recitations that have you wishing you'd stayed home, or the author had, or better yet that someone would garrote him before he can read another sentence, nay, another word.'

'I wasn't thinking that.'

'Well, you should have been. In any case, my presentation will be far more than just a reading. It will be an interpretation, a *realization*, complete with sound effects and a variety of voices

– all of them provided by me, of course. *Bong, bong, bong! Clank, clank! Dreadful apparition! Why do you trouble me?* Well, you get the idea. My first engagement is at the Birmingham Town Hall on the twenty-seventh.'

'And you want a bodyguard, in case you're threatened with garrotting.'

Though Charley is only jesting, Mr Dickens nods in agreement. 'Something like that.' He rises and paces back and forth on the small amount of floor not taken up by the desk. There is a long hiatus before he speaks again, but Charley is a patient man. He takes out his notebook and jots down the details of the reading. At last Mr Dickens says, 'Have you ever seen an actress named Julia Fairweather?'

Charley makes a note of the name. 'I have, at the Adelphi. Quite a stunner, as I recall.' Though he doesn't say so, he recalls a lot more than that about her: her honey-like voice, how gracefully she moved, how spirited she was, how seductive, how amusing. For weeks afterward, he couldn't get her out of his mind. And now she's back.

'Oh, yes,' says Mr Dickens. 'She's also quite clever and ambitious. A year or so ago, she formed her own company, which performed at the Royalty Theatre. She asked me to review one of their plays for the papers, and I was happy to do so – that is, until I actually saw the thing. I don't recall the title or in fact anything else about it except that it was utterly dismal, as were most of the actors. Even the presence of the lovely Miss Fairweather couldn't salvage it. Well, she played the part of a consumptive beggar or some such, dressed in rags, with matted hair and dark circles around her eyes; you would scarcely have recognized her.

'I tried to find something to praise about the production, but the best I could do was to say that it was blessedly short. Only later did I learn the reason for that: the male lead muffed his lines and they ended up skipping over most of one act. Well, two days after my review appeared, the show closed, and shortly afterward the company dissolved. Miss Fairweather has never forgiven me. The word in theatre circles is that she means to take her revenge by sabotaging *my* show somehow.'

'And you want me to stop her.'

'Exactly.' Mr Dickens takes out his wallet, an enormous, bulging affair of buff leather. Unless he also uses it to carry cigars or spare handkerchiefs, it must contain at least a dozen banknotes. 'I'll give you an advance, and I'll tack on a bonus if you manage the feat without her creating a scene – she is an actress, after all. What's your usual retainer?'

'Fifteen bob a day, plus expenses. But see here, I don't want your money. You're letting me use your character's name; that's worth far more to me. Just give me a couple of crowns for train fare, and we'll call it even.'

'Nonsense.' He thrusts three one-pound notes into Charley's hand. 'There's your advance. If you can't think of anything else to do with it, buy Jane a Christmas present.'

'Well . . . thank you. I'll do my best to keep your Miss Fairweather under wraps.'

'Good. You'd best be on your guard, though, Charley. As I say, she's a very clever lady, and she's used to getting her way, by whatever means necessary.'

'Yes, well, so am I.'

'Speaking of ways, I should be on mine; Mr Ollier has turned in a piece on pantomimes that's going to need some major rewriting.' He shakes his head. 'It beats me how you can write about something as entertaining as a pantomime and be so deadly dull.'

'Before you go, Mr Dickens, there's an urgent matter that you may be able to help me with.'

'Indeed?' says Dickens eagerly. 'What is it? Forgery? Murder?'

'Worse. I haven't the vaguest notion of what to get for my wife. Any suggestions?'

The Great Man grimaces. 'Oh, dear. I was about to ask you the same thing.'

The rest of the morning and all of the afternoon are, like most every other morning and afternoon, totally devoid of clients. His only other visitor is Wink, the young ticket porter who is the most recent addition to Charley's cadre of reformed criminals.

When Charley made his acquaintance, the boy was only ten

or so – he was so undernourished it was difficult to tell – but
he had already perfected a slick con that involved delivering
messages to self-important merchants and businessmen. Though
the messages were entirely bogus, by the time the recipient
realized this he had usually tipped the boy a ha'penny, at least.
The beauty of the scheme was that the lad took the trouble to
learn his target's name beforehand and print it on the outside
in admirable penmanship. He even sealed it with wax, thus
giving himself more time for a clean getaway.

Charley figured that so enterprising a lad deserved to be given
a chance at a real job. He managed to obtain a license and
badge for Wink, and got him work delivering authentic messages,
documents, and packages. First, of course, Charley had delivered
his own message to the boy: *Cross me up, and I'll make you
sorry you were ever born.*

'If you're back this way around teatime,' he tells the boy
now, 'I may have something for you. In the meantime, would
you fetch me a beef sandwich from somewhere?' He forks over
sixpence. When Wink returns with the provender, Charley says,
'One more thing. Do you ever have call to deliver a package
from a gentleman to a lady?'

'Only all the time. P'tic'ly this time o' year.'

'Do you ever see what's in them?'

'Oh, aye. As often as not, the lady rips it open right afore
your eyes.'

'What sort of thing?'

'Joolery, mostly. Sometimes a music box. A bird in a gold
cage, oncet.'

'Hmm. Those sound expensive.'

'I believe it. A nice necklace or a bunch o' pearls can fetch
a guinea or two from a good fence. Last week, though, I delivered a fancy mull to a lady, and it couldn't 'ave cost more'n a
crown, but she seemed wery pleased wiv it.'

'A *mull?*'

'Some calls it a snuffbox.'

'I'm afraid I don't know many ladies who take snuff.'

Wink laughs. 'Oh, they don't put *snuff* in 'em, Hinspector,
just *stuff*. Pins, buttons, smelling salts, rooge, comfits, that sort
of fing.'

'You certainly seem to know a lot about the ladies, my boy. *How* old are you, again?'

He lets out another laugh. 'Old enough to like huggin' 'em, young enough to get away wiv it.'

While Charley eats his sandwich, he tries his hand at writing a new advertisement, something more – in Mr Dickens' words – *intriguing* and *exciting*. He prints the words large, so he won't have to use his spectacles, which are yet another reminder that he's not getting any younger. It's just as well that he has no clients, since the task occupies the entire afternoon and two pipes of tobacco. Lucky thing he didn't want to be a novelist; at this rate, a book would take him ten years to write, and even then it wouldn't be worth reading.

At some point, the fiddler in the flat below begins to play, which wouldn't be so bad except that he's practicing a music-hall tune, 'The Dog's Meat Man,' and Charley can't help humming along. By the time Wink returns, he's managed to come up with nothing better than this:

INSPECTOR BUCKET's
PRIVATE ENQUIRY AGENCY

Twenty-five years policing experience.
Six years Chief of the Detective Branch.
No case too large or too small.
All investigations conducted with the
utmost discretion and confidentiality.

Confidentiality? Is that an actual word, or did he just make it up? He doesn't want to seem a nincompoop, but neither does he want to sound like a professor of law. Well, it's not exactly intriguing or exciting, but at least it sounds as if he knows his way around. And perhaps the reader will find the prospect of hiring the original of Inspector Bucket exciting enough. As an afterthought, he adds, *Reasonable rates*. Though he's hoping to attract at least a few wealthy clients, he's found that it's the people with the most money who are the most reluctant to part with it.

He makes four copies of the advertisement – three for the

newspapers, one for Mr Dickens' magazine – and gives them to Wink, along with enough money to pay the papers and then some. 'Keep whatever is left over for yourself, lad.'

'Y'know, Hinspector, you could put these in a postbox; they'd get there almost as quick.'

'I know, but I don't trust the Royal Mail. Besides, you need something to do, to keep you out of trouble.'

'T'anks.' Wink tips his cap and, grinning, juggles the coins in one hand. 'I'll eat well t'night.'

'Just make sure it's good food you buy, and not gin.' You'd think that a boy of eleven or twelve would have no interest in liquor, but Charley has seen too much evidence to the contrary. And after all, Wink had a good teacher; his mother drank herself to death.

'I will, Hinspector, I promise.'

Charley doesn't bother reminding the boy that he's no longer an inspector. How can he, when he's just reclaimed the title?

When four o'clock comes and there's still no sign of a client, he shuts up shop and sets out in search of a suitable present for Jane. Of course, he'll have to find something for the mother as well, or he'll never hear the end of it.

It's a tricky task, buying things for those two. When Mr Munge, his wife's first husband, passed away so conveniently only a few years into their marriage, he left her well provided for; she's never divulged an exact figure, but Charley has deduced that it's somewhere in the neighborhood of £500 a year – more than twice what he earned as a detective inspector. As a result, her interpretation of the phrase 'living within one's means' is considerably different from Charley's.

Before he and Jane tied the knot, Charley made it clear that he wouldn't accept a grey groat from her, that in fact he would contribute his share toward the rental and upkeep of her house, which might be tolerably roomy and pleasant if it weren't for the overabundance of easy chairs and squab sofas and tables and chiffoniers and carpets and drapes and doilies and knick-knacks.

At first, he welcomed the comforts offered by Jane and her home, after years spent surrounded by bachelors in the spartan confines of the Holborn station house. She was a decade older than he was – sedate, conservative, almost motherly, and at the time that appealed to him. Her place was like a refuge from the hard, harsh world of the streets. Nowadays, he can bear it for only an hour or two before he feels as though he's suffocating.

It's difficult to know what to give a person who has so much already, and at the same time avoid running himself into debt. Though Charley prides himself on his ability to fit in almost anywhere – aside from his wife's home, that is – he's always felt out of place in the fancier shops, even when he's there in an official capacity, to investigate a break-in or apprehend a thief. He's more comfortable in the markets and the pawnshops – the legitimate ones, not the dolly shops whose goods are mostly ill gotten. Often a pawnbroker in the right neighborhood will have the same quality of merchandise as the stores, at a fraction of the price. And if he boxes it up and wraps it nicely and lies a little, his wife and her mother will be none the wiser.

Though Mr Popper, who owns the pawnshop in Elizabeth Street, is a Hebrew, he is as keen to capitalize on the Christmas season as any grocer or gift emporium. His front window is practically aglow with gilded geegaws that some swain gave to his sweetheart when their love was young and strong; when it grew old and infirm, the memories provided by the object were less important than the ready cash it provided.

And there in the front is an array of elegant enameled snuff-boxes. Though Charley feels a bit sheepish having to rely on the advice of a ticket porter, Wink's idea is better than any he's come up with. For a mere half a crown, he walks away with two of the nicer boxes; one is hand-painted with flowers – no better than Rosa could do, really – the other is printed with a scene of Eliza crossing the ice, from *Uncle Tom's Cabin*, one of his wife's favorite books. Mr Popper would gladly have given him the boxes; after all, Charley once broke up a gang of demanders who were extorting protection money from Popper and other local merchants. Charley has always preferred, though, that people display their gratitude not in the guise of gifts or money, but in the form of information and favors, and the policy has proven very profitable.

Mrs Bramble or Rosa will do a far better job of wrapping

the snuffboxes than he could hope to, and the Seminary for Young Ladies isn't far off. He's anxious to talk to Rosa again, anyway; perhaps she's recalled something more about the stiff-necked man, or is more willing to share what she knows already.

When he rings the bell, it takes Mrs Bramble an unusually long time to answer. When she finally does open the door, she scarcely looks like herself. Normally, no matter what the hour, she is impeccably coiffed, carefully made up, smiling in a warm and welcoming way – unless, of course, you've done something to displease her. But now she looks disheveled, distracted, distraught.

'Charley!' She grips his arm with a trembling hand. 'I'm so glad you're here! How did you find out?'

Charley clasps her other hand in both of his. 'I'm sorry, I don't know what you mean. Has something happened?'

'It's Rosa,' says Mrs Bramble, her voice breaking. 'She's drownded.'

FIVE

C harley feels rather as though he, too, is drowning; he clutches Mrs Bramble's hand so hard that she cries out. He releases her at once and steadies himself against the door frame. He's dealt with dozens of deaths in his long career, yet none has ever hit him with such force, but for the pitiful passing of that six-year-old watch thief, so long ago. 'How did it happen?' he asks weakly. 'And where?'

'Hyde Park. She – she went off the bridge. The Rescue Society is calling it suicide, but I don't believe it for a minute.'

'Nor do I. It makes no sense. She was in fine spirits when I left her. Is there going to be a crowner's quest?'

'Tomorrow, at the Society's infirmary.'

'They're the ones that pulled her out?'

'Yes. She had nothing on her to identify her; no one would've even known who she was except that one of the Society fellows spoke up and admitted that he knew her.'

'He was a customer, you mean?' The detective in Charley is starting to push past the shock and pain, like a copper pushing aside the crowd at a crime scene and taking charge. 'Has he been here lately?'

'No. Not for months.'

'Rosa mentioned that she had a customer yesterday afternoon, one that frightened her. Did you know him?'

Mrs Bramble gives him a puzzled look. 'The stiff-necked fellow? He said he was a friend of *yours*. I wouldn't have let him in otherwise.'

'He's no friend of mine. Did he say what his name was?'

'I made him write it down, like I always do, so I have a record.' She consults the guest book on the hall table. 'Nick Necktie?' She makes a disgusted hissing sound. 'There's a made-up name if I ever heard one.'

'It doesn't matter; I know who he is. Did he put an address?'

'4 Whitehall Place.'

Charley shakes his head and sighs.

'Is that made up, too?'

'No. It's the address of Scotland Yard.' Charley rubs his hands over his face wearily. For the past year, he's been itching for a case to solve, and now that he's got one, he'd give anything to have it otherwise. 'Does her daughter know yet?'

Mrs Bramble nods sadly. 'I brought Audrey here; one of the girls is looking after her.'

'Well. I'll attend the inquest and see what I can find out. If this Nick fellow turns up again, you let me know right away.'

'Done. I'll make sure he sticks around till you come, too.'

'Don't put yourself or the girls in any danger.'

'If he's the one that did for Rosa, it's *him* that'll be in danger.'

Charley sleeps at the office again. He can't bear to face his wife and her mother. Not that they'd demand to know where he's been or what he's been up to, or anything of that nature. They long ago lost what little interest they may have had in his affairs, either the policing sort or the amorous sort. He just knows that, if he spends any length of time right now in their smug, sheltered, superior world, he's sure to say or do something he'll be sorry for.

Though they would have regarded Rosa with contempt, it should be the other way round. They have none of her admirable qualities – her warmth, her good humor, her talents. But they are the privileged; no one will ever have to fish one of them out of the cold waters of the Serpentine.

In the morning, he hangs a CLOSED sign on his office door; it's not likely that clients will be beating it down, anyway – at least not until his Inspector Bucket advertisement appears. Then he heads for the photography studio of his friend the Scarecrow. It lies in that section of the city Mr Dickens has dubbed Devil's Acre, not far from Parliament in terms of distance, but worlds away in terms of its surroundings. When the construction of Victoria Street 'improved' the area – that is to say, razed it – the building that houses the Scarecrow's studio somehow escaped improvement. Perhaps the engineers saw no point in demolishing it; it seems sure to collapse on its own before long.

So does the Scarecrow. As the name suggests, he doesn't really look like a man so much as a scrawny caricature of one, an effigy of a man. You might conclude from his appearance that he's suffering from consumption or some other wasting disease, but Charley suspects his precarious state of health is due to all the chemicals he's inhaled in the pursuit of his art – chloride of iodine and bromine, quicksilver, pyrogallic acid, ether, god knows what else.

Like so many of his acquaintances, the Scarecrow would have been dead or in prison long since if Charley hadn't taken him in hand. When they met, the photographer – whose actual name is Isam Jones – was pursuing a similar, but far more risky art: printing counterfeit banknotes, ones that were indistinguishable from those created by the Bank of England. Well, *almost* indistinguishable. One of the keys to judging a note's authenticity is the quality of the engraving. But with Isam Jones that didn't work; he was just too skillful. So Charley didn't bother much about the printing; he concentrated on the paper. He reasoned that a small-time counterfeiter wouldn't have access to paper as good as that used by the bank, and he was right. He tracked down the source of the Scarecrow's paper and then the culprit himself.

As usual, instead of summarily locking the man up, Charley

had a long talk with him and learned the circumstances of his crime. A few years earlier, after failures too numerous to count, Isam Jones – who trained as a chemist – had perfected a method of making what he called a 'stereotype plate,' or negative, that would enable him and other photographers to make as many prints of a picture as they desired. He spent the years that followed trying desperately to patent his invention, but the patenting process was so incredibly convoluted and expensive that it left him deep in debt, half insane, and more than half dead of starvation. In the meantime, another photographer – one with better connections and a bigger bank account – beat him to the punch. Desperate and bitter, he found other uses for his skills – ones that didn't require a patent.

Charley, who could see from the Scarecrow's legitimate photographs that he was no hack, proceeded to make use of his own connections. He saw to it that the man's debts were forgiven and he managed to drum up a few customers for him. Now, Dr Isam Jones Fine Photography is, if not a thriving business, at least a steady one; even better, it's legal.

At the moment, the Scarecrow has more customers than he can handle: a family of six have completely taken over his loft and are making themselves at home. The younger children, both boys, are playing hide-and-seek, wrapping themselves in the black velvet curtains that mask the doorway to the developing room, knocking over the folding screens that reflect rays from the skylight onto the photographer's subject. The two girls are trying on the Scarecrow's stock of hats, men's and women's alike, draping themselves in fake jewelry and equally fake furs, attempting to outdo each other in a game of Who Can Strike the Most Ridiculous Pose.

The parents – a corpulent fellow in garish clothing that looks a size too small, and his wife, whom Charley would not care to go up against in the ring – pay no attention to their offspring's antics; they're too busy haggling over the price of their portrait. When Charley enters, the Scarecrow greets him as a condemned man greets a reprieve. 'Inspector!' he cries. 'Come in, please! We're just finishing up here!' This fit of enthusiasm causes him to break into a bout of coughing that racks his skeletal frame.

The uttering of the simple term *Inspector* brings about a

radical change in the room. The children stop mugging and
cavorting and turn to stare at Charley as if he is some fabled
creature – an ogre, or a centaur. The father forces his face into
a semblance of a smile, the same strained expression Charley
has seen a thousand times, the one that says, 'Nuffing to worry
about from me, guv'nor; I'm as honest as the day is long.' Only
the mother is unimpressed; she eyes him the way she might a
mackerel at the fish market, mentally weighing it, deciding
whether it's worth bothering with.

Charley is doing some weighing of his own. He's encountered
the father before in the course of his duties; there was a time
when he would have recalled exactly where and when, and what
the man's transgression was, and probably his name as well,
but his memory isn't what it used to be – too many blows to
the head, no doubt. In any case, the bloke's not worth bothering
with now. Charley has bigger fish to fry.

He gives the stooped shoulders of the Scarecrow a comradely
pat and says to the customers, 'I hope my friend's work was
satisfactory. Many people say he's the best portrait photographer
in London.'

The woman still seems skeptical. 'Do they, indeed?'

'Oh, yes. In fact—' Charley leans in toward her and says, in
a confidential voice – 'Word has it he's one of the top contenders
for the position of Portraitist to the Royal Family.'

This breaks down the mother's defenses at last. 'You don't
say?' She elbows her husband vigorously. 'D'you hear that,
Rodney? We may be able to say we've had our portrait taken
by the Queen's personal photog'apher!' Rodney goes on smiling
stupidly. 'Well, don't just stand there!' she says. 'Pay the man!'

When the family has finally departed – Charley has to retrieve
a paste diamond necklace from one of the girls as she passes
– the Scarecrow collapses into a chair. 'My god!' he gasps.
'They've been here for *hours*! Each time I was about to expose
the film, one of the little blighters scratched himself, or stuck
out his tongue, or pulled his sister's hair. And we'd have been
another hour arguing about my fee, if you hadn't showed up.'
He counts the coins and chuckles. 'They gave me a shilling
more than I was asking. And I wouldn't be surprised if they
send more customers my way, to sit for the future royal

portraitist.' He chuckles again, so heartily that it turns into another coughing fit.

'Happy to be of help,' says Charley. 'And you'll be happy to know that you can do me a favor in return.'

It's a bit of a hike to Hyde Park from here, and Charley isn't at all sure the Scarecrow is up to it. They head east instead, toward the Houses of Parliament, hoping to find a cab – not such an easy task in the winter. When Parliament isn't in session, ladies and gentlemen of means retreat to their country houses, and many of the shops and businesses that cater to them close their doors or cut back seriously on their staff. Most of the licensed cabbies find greener pastures, so to speak; all that remain are the bucks, who have no fixed departure point but go mouching about from one likely spot to another, charging whatever the traffic will bear.

The street sellers, of course, are still easy enough to find. Charley and the Scarecrow pass the usual coffee stalls, match girls, and apple women, but also Christmassing costermongers with barrows full of holly, ivy, evergreen boughs, and mistletoe. Their young assistants fill the air with cries of 'Holly! Holly-oh!' their soprano voices now in harmony and now in wild dissonance, like some demented church choir.

By the time they locate a shabby growler driven by an even shabbier drunkard and then haggle over the fare, the morning is mostly gone. And by the time they reach the headquarters of the Royal Humane Society in Hyde Park, the coroner's inquest is over and done with. The jury and the spectators are filing from the building, already joking, trading insults, deciding where to go for drinks, casting off the gloomy atmosphere of the inquest like a threadbare cloak. One might think they were coming from a Christmas party or a dance, and not from passing judgment upon the poor soul for whose sake the inquest was held.

Charley has sat on his share of inquests, and it's always angered him to see how lightly his fellow jurors treated the matter, even though he understands the reason behind their jocular attitude – the profound sense of relief that it's someone else stretched out on that slab, and not them.

To his surprise, the last person to emerge from the building is none other than Constable Lochinvar Mull. 'Inspector!' says the young man. He holds out his hand, then withdraws it, perhaps recalling how painful their last handshake was. 'Whatever brings you here, sir?'

'I was wondering the same about you. Hyde Park is Division A.'

'You're right. But the woman resides – resided – in Westminster, so they sent me to see if there was any sign of foul play.'

Charley scowls. 'She has a name, you know. It's Rosa.'

'Of course. Sorry, sir. You knew her, then?'

Charley ignores the question. 'They couldn't even be bothered to send a detective,' he says. 'No offense, Constable, but I hardly think you're qualified to conduct an investigation.'

The young copper's face goes red. 'I know that. 'Twasn't my idea.'

'I suppose they ruled it a suicide.'

Constable Mull nods and shrugs. 'They found naught to indicate otherwise, sir.'

'I dare say they didn't try very hard. Come, 'Sam, let's have a look for ourselves.'

'Eh, do you mind if I go along, sir?' asks the constable. Charley hesitates, considering the request. 'It may be my only chance to see Inspector Field at work,' Mull adds earnestly.

Charley has to suppress a smile. 'I suppose it won't hurt – if you promise to do only what I tell you.'

'I will, sir. Cross my heart.'

As they make their way to the infirmary, the Scarecrow mutters, 'You sure you want him here? I don't care to be arrested for this.'

'You won't be,' says Charley.

He knows his way around the Royal Humane Society – much better than he'd like to, actually. In his early days as detective, he didn't get on well with his chief, and for a year or so he drew all the least desirable assignments, including the suicides. In most cases, there was nothing for him to discover, except perhaps the identity of the victim. Even though *felos de se* are officially considered criminals, Charley has always thought of them as victims.

He was hoping he might find a familiar face in charge of the
infirmary, but luck isn't with him. The orderly is a tall fellow
who can't be much older than the baby-faced Constable Mull.
Sometimes it seems as if the whole world is being run by
children. 'Forget something, Constable?' says the orderly.

Mull looks uncertainly at Charley, who whispers, 'Tell him
we're here to identify the body.'

'Eh,' says the constable, 'these are, um, friends of the
deceased. I've asked them to make a positive identification.'

'But I've already identified her,' says the orderly. 'That is—'

'So you're the one.' Charley moves in close to the fellow and
says quietly, 'No need to look so sheepish, son. If keeping company
with a prostitute is a sin, then Hell must be overflowing.'

He approaches the table where the body is laid out, still
clothed. Part of him has been hoping all along that there was
some mistake, that it was some other unfortunate girl. But
there's no mistaking the red hair that flows like blood across
the table, or the mole on her cheek, which she tried to conceal
with white wax, though Charley insisted that, not so long ago,
such 'beauty spots' were much coveted. 'Did you have a hand
in pulling her out?' Charley asks the orderly.

'Yes, sir. We tried to resuscitate her—'

'How?'

'Well, the usual. We turned her on her stomach and pushed
the water from her lungs and—'

'How much water came up?'

'Uh, well, not a lot. A pint or two, I suppose. Why do you—'

'Thank you. Constable Mull, would you take this gentleman
into the next room, please, and see what more he can tell you?'

Though Mull looks a bit baffled, he lives up to his promise.
He ushers the orderly from the room, while the man protests,
'But I – but I already testified at the inquest—'

'Now, get the blood,' Charley whispers to his companion.
'And be quick about it.'

From inside his greatcoat, the Scarecrow draws a scalpel and
a brass syringe. Despite his decrepit appearance, when the occasion warrants it he can move with surprising speed. He pushes
up the sleeve of the dress and makes a deft cut in the brachial
artery. With a shiver, Charley recalls Rosa's words of the night

before: 'I hope they make sure I'm good and dead before they cut *me* up!'

The Scarecrow inserts the needle of the syringe into the cut. Slowly he pulls on the plunger; with a faint sucking sound, Rosa's blood is drawn into the device. 'It's thick, and doesn't flow well,' murmurs the man. 'I hope this'll be enough.'

'It'll have to be.' There's barely time to pull down the sleeve of the dress before the orderly returns. Charley steps forward and, putting an arm around the young man's shoulders, guides him toward the hallway, buying time for the Scarecrow to conceal his tools. 'What arrangements have been made for her burial?'

'Her employer's taken care of it. She asked us to tell the undertakers that the girl's death was accidental, so she may be buried in consecrated ground.'

'And will you?'

'It would be a lie.'

'That may be. But—' Charley lowers his voice and speaks directly into the young man's ear. 'What if it was neither accidental nor a suicide?'

'What else could it—?' The orderly turns to stare at him. 'You don't think—?'

'What I think is that you can truthfully tell the undertakers the girl was murdered.'

SIX

There's no shortage of transportation in the vicinity of Hyde Park. As Charley and his accomplice are about to climb aboard a weathered Uxbridge Road omnibus called, paradoxically, *The Paragon*, Constable Mull catches up with them. 'Inspector! Do you not want to hear what I found out?'

Sighing, Charley waves the Scarecrow onto the bus. 'You go on ahead, 'Sam. I'll meet you at the studio.' He turns to the young constable. 'Come on. I'll buy you a coffee.'

As they're heading up Stanhope Street, Mull says, 'Could we find a place that also serves tea? I've never had much of a taste for coffee.'

'Just as well. It's not what it used to be.' The Worker's Rest has long been one of Charley's favorite haunts; not only is he partial to their dark-roasted coffee and crusty rolls and the casual but clean surroundings, it's always proven a valuable source of scuttlebutt. In the years between the Chartist riots and the Great Exhibition, it was a meeting place for radicals of all stripes, and Charley spent a good deal of time there, disguised as an out-of-work bricklayer, his eyes perusing copies of *The Leader* and *The Northern Star* while his ears took in the conversations around him, alert to any conspiratorial tendencies.

As it turns out, the Worker's Rest is not what it used to be, either. For one thing, it's now called the Sussex Square Coffee-House. For another, there are no newspapers or magazines and no chess tables or comfortable chairs or ottomans, only boxes and tables and stools, all made of wood so dark that it seems to suck up all the light in the place.

There's no sign of the cordially argumentative owner, either. Instead they're waited on by a pimply faced youth whose ginger hair looks as though it's been combed with a hay rake. 'What's become of Mr Puffnell, then?' asks Charley, fearing that the old fellow's outspoken radicalism might have been his undoing.

'Went bankrupt, 'e did. They say that, 'owever 'igh the price of coffee and tea got, 'e refused to charge more'n a penny a cup.'

'And how much do you charge now?'

'Well . . . a penny a cup.' The boy scratches his spiky mop. 'I s'pose the price of coffee and tea must've went down.'

'That's because it's not coffee and tea,' says Charley.

''Course it is. What else would it be?'

Charley waves a dismissive hand. 'Never mind. We'll have a so-called tea and a so-called coffee. And some bread and butter – provided the bread isn't half alum and plaster.' When the lad slouches off, Charley says to Constable Mull, 'You didn't go pale back there, or avoid looking at her, as most young constables would do. You've seen dead bodies before.'

'Yes, sir. More than I cared to. When I was about eight, my

father went to sit with a dying man; on the way back he fell
asleep and tumbled out of the pony chaise, nearly broke his
neck. After that, my mother made me go along, to drive him
home. If you dunnot mind my saying, sir, *you* looked a bit pale.
You wunnot just making up that bit about being a friend, were
you?'

'No. I've known her for several years.' He could lie, say that
Rosa was Jane's friend, or a relative, or something of the sort,
but that seems unfair, somehow, as if he's ashamed of her, which
he's not. 'She worked at Madame M'Alpine's Seminary.'

'She was like a schoolteacher, then?'

'Not exactly.' Charley smiles wryly. 'Although she did teach
me a few things, I admit.'

Constable Mull may be naïve, but he's not stupid. 'Oh. The
seminary isn't actually a seminary, is it?'

'No.' Charley glances at the young man's face, which shows
definite signs of disapproval. 'Oh, don't go getting all righteous
on me.'

'I'm sorry. 'Tis just that I was taught—'

'I know what you were taught, lad. I've heard it all, and most
of it, however well-meaning, is bollocks.'

The pimply boy interrupts to set their food and drink before
them. Charley takes a sip of the coffee; it's no worse than he
expected, but no better, either. He butters a slice of the bread
and waves it in the constable's still-skeptical baby face. 'You'll
meet a lot of prostitutes in the policing business, Mr Mull, and
you'll hear two prevailing opinions about them: One, that they're
disgraceful and depraved; the other, that they're "poor
unfort'n'ts." If you treat them like either one, they'll never trust
you. Just treat them like people, and you'll find that they're not
some separate species, any more than criminals are. They're
like – like a big basket of fruit.'

Constable Mull can't help laughing. 'How's that?'

Charley shrugs and says, around a bite of bread, 'Some of
them are sweet, some are sour; some are hard, some soft; some
are green, some – I won't say rotten, but overripe. This bread
isn't so bad. Or it could be I'm just too starved to care.' Despite
all the cadavers he's encountered over the years, seeing Rosa's
body was like being punched in the gut by Bendigo Thompson.

But his appetite has never deserted him for long. Maybe his sudden hunger springs from the same source as the jury members' mirth: Relief that – for the moment, anyway – he's not the one lying stiff and cold on a tabletop.

He wishes he'd done more for Rosa while she was alive – found her and Audrey a better flat, found a buyer for her paintings, something. All he can do now is find out who killed her and why. 'Did you pry anything more out of the orderly?'

Mull pulls out his nearly pristine notebook and examines it earnestly, as if it contains a wealth of damning evidence, then admits, 'Eh, not much. He mostly wanted to know who you were, and why you were asking so many questions. You think he has summat to do with her death?'

'I never rule anyone out, but I doubt it. Those fellows are in the business of saving lives, not taking them.'

'So you dunnot believe it was suicide, either?'

'Either?'

'I'm no detective, sir, I know that. But I've been thinking about what the other constable told me.'

'The other constable?'

'Before the inquest, I dropped in at the Hyde Park station and talked to the men as were on duty night before last. The station house is right nigh the bridge, so I thought they might have heard or seen summat.'

'And?'

Mull blushes a bit. 'Eh, most of them just told me to run along like a good boy and stop bothering them and that. But one fellow – Spills, his name was – said that, around one or two in the morning, he went outside to . . . you know, relieve himself, and he thought he heard somebody cry out – a woman's voice, he thought, but he couldn't say for sure, because it was very quick-like. Then he heard a splash.'

'Just a single splash?'

''Tis what he said. I specifically asked him, because I thought that a person who jumped in of their own accord would likely do a bit of thrashing around before they . . . um, went under.'

'You're right. Good thinking.'

'Thank 'ee, sir. Anyway, whenever he headed for the bridge to investigate, he saw two fellows approaching from the other

end. They said they'd heard the splash, too, and were afraid
someone had jumped off. The constable told them they mun go
alert the Rescue Society, meanwhile he would see if he could
spot a body. He said that, if it's a woman, oftentimes the air in
their clothing will keep them afloat for a while.'

'Yes, I know,' says Charley impatiently. 'Go on.'

'Sorry. He couldn't see naught, so he waited for the Rescuers,
only they didn't come; he had to go roust them out himself.
The fellows he'd sent to do it had never showed up.'

'Did he give a description of the men?'

'I guess it was too dark. He did say one of them was tall
and thin and the other one shorter and stouter.'

'That's all?'

Mull glances at the notebook. 'Eh, wait, now. He said one had
a sort of a high-pitched voice – he thought it might have been
him that cried out. The other one sounded kind of hoarse, like
he had a bad case of the ague.'

'Neck,' murmurs Charley. 'And Neckless.'

'Necklace?' echoes the constable.

'Neck-*less*. It's what the coppers call this burly bloke whose
real name is—' Charley consults his list of Wrongdoers Who
Got Away. 'Hoggles. He's got a head like pumpkin and it sits
right on his shoulders. I arrested him half a dozen times, but
never could get anything to stick. He's been seen keeping
company with a thief and arsonist known as Neck. I'd bet a
crown they were the coves your Mr Spills saw on the bridge.
And I'd bet a week's wages – which at this point isn't much
more than a crown – that they weren't there to save anybody.'
Charley downs the rest of his bread and coffee and gets to his
feet. 'You've been a great help, Constable. If I can ever return
the favor, don't hesitate to get in touch.'

Now Mull's face truly turns red. 'You mean it?'

'If I didn't, I wouldn't say it.' He tosses a shilling on the
table. 'Get yourself some bags o'mystery or something, will
you? You're a growing boy.'

'Bags o'*mystery*?'

'Sausages, in the Queen's English. Now, if you see or hear
anything of our Mr Neck or Mr Neckless, you'll let me know?'

'That I will, Inspector.' As Charley is leaving, Mull calls

after him, 'Just one more thing, sir, if you dunnot mind. You asked the orderly how much water came up when they tried to resuscitate her, and he said there wasn't much. Is that a clue?'

'It could be. If Rosa was conscious when she went in the river, her lungs should have been full.'

'Aha. It didn't look as if she'd been struck or aught. You think she might've been drugged?'

'Well,' says Charley, 'with any luck, we're about to find that out.'

His friend's training as a chemist has proven valuable more than once. When Charley wanted the bottles of Dr Benjamin's Panacea tested for poison, he took them to the Scarecrow. The former counterfeiter also concocted a chemical compound for testing the ink on suspect banknotes. And he once helped Charley nab a kidnapper, by booby-trapping the ransom money: He filled a flask with red ink, sugar, and German yeast and concealed it inside the satchel; when the bag was opened, a clamp was released and the foaming brew drenched the kidnapper, who was caught not only red-handed but red-faced.

The procedure the Scarecrow is undertaking today – testing a sample of Rosa's blood for the presence of chloroform – is considerably more complicated. Though the compound has been in use for less than a decade, it's become the anesthetic of choice for dozens of prominent physicians. Earlier this year, the Queen herself partook of it, to ease the pain of giving birth to her eighth child, little Prince Leopold.

It's also become the drug of choice for thieves, abductors, and killers to subdue their victims. If Rosa was dumped unconscious into the river, chances are she was chloroformed – perhaps twice, if she recovered from the first dose enough to cry out.

Though Charley is a clever fellow, he can't begin to grasp the intricacies of chemistry, even when the Scarecrow explains each step in detail, and what it's meant to accomplish. Several times, Charley has watched him prepare his photographic plates and develop the resulting portraits, and each time it flabbergasts him; the man might as well be performing magic.

The same applies to the task at hand. The Scarecrow squirts the blood into a glass flask and heats it over a gas flame, creating a vapor that he catches in a second flask, which is coated with nitrate of silver. The chloroform is magically transformed into chloride of carbon, carbonic acid, chlorine, and hydrochloric gas, which magically combines with the silver nitrate to form a white powder – silver chloride. The amount of silver chloride powder gives a rough measure of how much chloroform was in the victim's blood. 'A lot,' says the Scarecrow. 'She must have given them quite a struggle.'

'She would,' Charley says softly. 'She was a strong woman.'

The meticulous photographer sets about testing the residue with ammonia and nitric acid, to make sure it is indeed silver chloride. 'The thing I can't understand,' he says, 'is *why*. Surely what little money she had on her wouldn't be worth killing for.'

'I have a theory about that,' says Charley. 'I'd spent some time with Rosa earlier that evening. So, apparently, had our old acquaintance Mr Neck. She said he'd been boasting about some scheme that he was involved in and that promised to be very lucrative. She wouldn't go into detail, but I have no doubt it was also very illegal. If so, he may well have regretted his rashness and decided to shut her up.' Without warning, the analytical part of him, which so far has had the upper hand, is shoved aside by the emotional part. He slams a fist on the photographer's worktable, making the glassware rattle. 'Damn! If only I'd questioned her more closely when I had the chance! If I'd stayed with her, if I'd walked her home—' His voice breaks, and he smacks the table again.

The Scarecrow lays a bony hand on his arm. 'Don't be blaming yourself, Charley. You couldn't know. Any idea where to look for this Neck fellow?'

Charley shakes his head. 'But I expect he won't be hard to find. Though he may lie low for a little while, criminals are like corpses – eventually they always float to the surface. If he's making money hand over fist, he's not prudent enough to put it in the bank; he'll go out and spend it. All I have to do is wait until he turns up.'

Normally, Charley is a patient man. To his fellow coppers, he was known – among other things – as the Ferret, not only for his ability to ferret out the truth but because, once he's sunk his teeth into something, he won't let go. Some of his cases have required him to hang on for years; he's determined that this won't be one of them. He doesn't want to just hang on, he wants to seize the villain by his stiff, stretched-out neck. He wants to be a lion, not a ferret.

Luckily, another case turns up to keep him occupied, so he doesn't spend all his time seething and stewing. Late that afternoon, as he sits drumming his thick fingers on his desk and trying to decide where to have his supper, there's a soft rapping at the door. 'Please come in!' he calls.

From the delicate nature of the knock, he's expecting a woman. But the visitor is in fact a rather robust fellow of thirty or so, with a distinctly Bohemian look about him, from his unfashionably long locks and sparse beard to his colorful frock coat – the fabric of which would make a fine carpetbag if it weren't so worn – to his trousers, which are tight enough to reveal the outline of the few coins in his pocket, not to mention his family jewels.

He also has that distinctly melancholy look so prevalent among poets and dramatists and painters, which may be attributed to despair and slow starvation, but just as often to the notion that struggling artists are expected to look melancholy. Since this fellow's fingers are flecked with ink and not paint, and since no dramatist he's ever met would deign to sport a beard, Charley pegs him as a poet, and a poor one at that – in terms of income, that is; he wouldn't presume to judge the fellow's work solely from his appearance.

Well, the poverty part goes without saying; all poets are poor, with the exception of Mr Tennyson. But this one is likely worse off than most, since his lodgings are somewhere near the glue and bone works, judging from the bone dust that clings to his boots – boots that are in much better condition and of far better quality than you'd expect on a Bohemian – and the sickly smell of boiling horse carcasses that lingers on his clothing even after the long hike here. There's no question that he walked all the way; he clearly can't afford a cab. Not a good sign, for how will he afford a private enquiry agent's fee?

Still, Charley can't afford to turn anyone away. 'May I help you, sir?' he says, as brightly as possible given the air of gloom that the young man spreads about him, like the scent of the glue works.

'I doubt it,' moans the poor poet. He slumps down in the client's chair and sinks his head in his ink-stained hands. 'I think I'm going mad.'

SEVEN

'I'm afraid,' says Charley, 'that insanity is a little outside my area of expertise.' He could suggest consulting a mad-doctor, but he has a feeling the fellow is exaggerating just a bit. Maybe all he really needs is a good cup of tea. As Charley fills the teakettle from his ewer and puts the kettle on the hob, he says, 'Why bother to come all the way from Bermondsey if you don't think I can help you?'

'I didn't know who else to turn to, and Mr Dickens says that, when it comes to solving mysteries, you're the best. But—' He raises his head and stares at Charley, blinking in puzzlement. 'But how on earth do you know where I live?'

'I'll explain it sometime. Right now, it's you who needs to do the explaining, Mr—?'

'Mumchance. Geoffrey Mumchance.'

'And you're a friend of Mr Dickens?'

'Not a friend, no. I've submitted a few poems to his magazine, that's all.' Aha, just as he guessed – a poet; Charley mentally chalks up another point in his own favor. 'Well,' says Mr Mumchance, 'more than a few. He's turned them all down.'

As the man seems about to break into tears, Charley quickly diverts his attention. 'I can't promise anything, except that I'll do my best.' He knows what the fellow will say next, and he heads him off. 'We won't worry about fees and such things yet. For now, why don't you just tell me the nature of this mystery you mentioned?'

Mumchance gives a melancholy sigh. 'It involves a betting shop.'

'Hmm,' says Charley. Stories involving betting shops seldom

turn out well. They also tend to be quite long, full of excuses and rationalizations. Taking out his meerschaum, he fills it and lights it from the fireplace.

'At least,' continues the poet, 'I *think* there was a betting shop. There are times when I'm convinced that I imagined the whole thing.'

'May I suggest, Mr Mumchance, that you begin at the beginning, and go straight through to the end? Stories generally make more sense that way.'

'All right,' says the young man dubiously, as if poets are not normally required to make sense. 'I'll try. It started with this idea I had, of buying a really special gift for Emmeline.'

'Your wife?'

'No. Well, that is, not yet. Someday, I hope. This idea of the present was part of my plan – to win her over, you see. Well, it's more her parents that need winning over, actually.'

Charley almost says, 'Have you considered a snuffbox?' but he doesn't want to distract the fellow just as he's getting started, so he simply nods.

Emmeline, at least according to Mr Mumchance, is the sweetest and loveliest creature ever to walk the earth. Unfortunately, her parents are determined to marry her off to the wealthiest prospect they can find – another familiar tale that seldom ends well, except in novels of a certain sort. As far as the parents are concerned, Mr Mumchance would more aptly be called Mr No Chance.

As poets will do, he supposed that he could change their minds, or at least get their attention, with some grand, romantic gesture that would reveal what a splendid chap he really is. Seeing how envious they were of the fashionable ladies and gentlemen who ride in carriages and on horseback through Hyde Park each Sunday, he settled on the very thing that would impress them the most: He would buy Emmeline a horse. The problem being, of course, that he had scarcely enough funds to buy a *picture* of a horse.

But then he came upon the betting shop. Curiously enough, though the shop lay on the route he often took to the newspaper offices in Fleet Street, he couldn't recall ever seeing it before. And yet there was nothing temporary or fly-by-night in its appearance; in fact, there was quite a large, expertly painted sign above the door that read *THE ARISTOCRATIC CLUB. Wagers accepted all races.*

'At first,' says Geoffrey, with an embarrassed laugh, 'I couldn't make out the meaning of that. I thought it meant that anyone was welcome there – Chinese, Ethiopians, Aborigines . . .'

'Irish,' suggests Charley, which draws another laugh from his client. He hands the fellow a cup of freshly brewed tea. 'Go on, please.' He takes out his notebook and lead pencil and reluctantly dons his spectacles.

The races referred to were, of course, the kind involving a track and horses. Geoffrey wouldn't have given the place a second thought except that, a few days earlier, one of his literary friends was boasting that he had won several pounds betting on the ponies. Of course, the friend had an advantage Geoffrey did not – a modicum of money to make a wager with. Still, the poet was intrigued enough to press his face to the window and peer inside.

The walls were hung with half a dozen large portraits. They were not the likenesses of famous politicians and military figures that are so common in public houses, but portraits of horses – presumably famous ones. There were also several even larger chalkboards with the names of racetracks at the top – Aintree, Ascot, Epsom Downs, Beverley – and beneath that a list of other names: the ponies entered in each race, Geoffrey assumed.

At the rear of the room was a fancy divider made of wood and wrought iron, with two openings in it, like the tellers' windows in banks. Half a dozen people – working men, mostly – were lined up at each window, putting down their money. A voice spoke almost in Geoffrey's ear, startling him. 'Ever bet on the nags, lad?' The speaker was a slight, respectable-looking fellow with a knowing smile. 'It's tempting, ain't it? But let me tell you, it's a fool's game. Don't try it.'

Geoffrey thanked him for the advice and was about to move on when the man caught him by the sleeve. '*Unless*,' he said. 'Unless you happen to have inside information. Now my problem is, I've *got* the information, I just can't do nothing with it.' To illustrate his point, he turned his pockets inside out. He moved closer and said quietly, confidentially, 'I was a horse trainer, you know, up until a few weeks ago, when one of our nags went lame. It wasn't my fault, but of course I got blamed for it, and sacked. I haven't had a day's work since. But—' He tapped his head with a forefinger—'I still have my knowledge of horses. I know which ones just *look* good, and which ones have what it takes to win.'

If Geoffrey provided the money, the man said, he himself would provide that inside information, in return for a small share of the winnings. The offer was too good to pass up. Though Geoffrey had no more than two shillings to his name, he did have something worth a lot more – his father's watch, which, the trainer assured him, was as good as cash. And when he won big, as he was certain to do, they would return the watch to him as part of the payoff.

He was instructed to bet on a horse called Virago in the third race at Shrewsbury. The man at the teller's window took his watch, scribbled the details of the wager on a slip of pasteboard, and handed it to Geoffrey. 'Come back tomorrow afternoon. We won't have the results until then.'

'And did you go back?' asks Charley.

'Of course I did. Only . . .' The poet shakes his head in bewilderment. 'Only the betting shop was gone.'

'*Gone*? The whole building, you mean?'

'Well, the shops there all look about the same. I would have sworn I had the right place, though. Except it wasn't a betting shop any longer. It was a tobacconist.'

Charley looks up from his notebook and removes his spectacles. 'And have you been back there since?'

'Many times. I thought perhaps I was mistaken, so I searched the street in both directions.'

'Many times?' echoes Charley. 'How long ago did this happen?'

'Around the middle of November.'

'A *month* ago? Why the devil did you wait this long to report it?'

Geoffrey stares at his well-made boots and shrugs. 'I was ashamed. I thought surely I'd find the place and get it sorted out.'

'Of course. Sorry.' Making the client feel stupid is probably not a good business tactic. 'I didn't mean to chide you; I was just surprised, that's all.'

'I don't even know whether or not I won.'

Charley pours them each another cup of tea. He takes a flask of brandy from his desk, pours a dram into his drink, and offers the same to Geoffrey, who nods gratefully. 'I think,' says Charley, 'we can safely conclude that there *were* no winners, except for the cove running the betting shop. And the prophet who gave you the tip, no doubt.'

'You really think so? He seemed so . . .'

'Sincere? Most gammoners do.' Charley slips on his spectacles and glances at his notes. 'You said he was slight and respectable-looking. Anything else you recall about him?'

Geoffrey ponders this. 'He had on a flat cap, I think, and a waistcoat.'

Like half the working men in London, Charley thinks but doesn't say. 'And what about the fellow at the ticket window?'

'He was decked out more smartly – frock coat, bob hat, cravat. Tall sort of chap – taller than me, anyway – well built, good looking.'

Charley puts down his pencil and glances out the window. 'It's getting late. There's not much point in pursuing this today.'

'But you'll take the case?' the poet says eagerly.

'Well, I have to say, you've piqued my interest. The Vanishing Shop. Perhaps you can write a poem about it. Why don't we meet tomorrow around noon at the spot where you think – where you *saw* the betting shop, and we'll go from there?'

Charley can't put off any longer the ordeal he's been dreading – spending the evening in the company of Jane and her mother. It will undoubtedly go much better if he comes bearing gifts. At the grocer's in Denbigh Street, he has the boy fill a basket – a small one – with assorted fruit, nuts, and sweets. From a costermonger, he purchases a fir tree – also small – wrapped in jute cloth.

In an effort to raise his spirits, as he walks he belts out several verses of 'Thou Art Lovely, Queen of the Valley.' He used to sing it for Jane, when they were courting, but those days are long gone. When he nears Holywell Street, he switches to a

Yuletide carol, 'I Saw Three Ships.' There's not much notice taken of the holiday season here; Millbank is not, for the most part, a place where people live or where they buy things; it's a place where things are made: lumber, pianos, gin, pottery. Still, there are a few shops and residences scattered here and there.

Charley pauses before a stationer's whose outdoor table is piled high with books. He glances through them, hoping to find something that will appeal to his wife's tastes. It shouldn't be difficult; she generally reads whatever everyone else is reading. Charley himself rarely reads solely for amusement; the volumes in his personal library are mostly the sort that convey interesting and useful information – which is a sort of amusement, as far as that goes: *Manual of Electricity, Magnetism and Meteorology*; *Habits and Instincts of Animals*; *The History of Rome*; *Essay on Probabilities*, and so on.

The name Shirley Brontë on a book's spine attracts his attention. He's heard of Charlotte and Emily, but Shirley? When he opens the cover, the mystery is solved: *Shirley* is, in fact, the title, and Charlotte Brontë the author. He pays for the book, tucks it under his arm, and proceeds to his wife's house – he never has come to think of it as his house, too, or as home.

Jane and her mother are finishing up an early supper; the Irish house girl, Hanora, is clearing the dining table, but when she spots Charley she smiles apologetically and brings back the platter containing the beefsteak pudding.

Charley manages an apologetic smile of his own, mainly to Jane. 'Sorry to be so late. I had a client.'

If this bit of news pleases her, or even interests her, she doesn't show it. Her mouth does turn up at the corners, but that's about all. 'Well, it scarcely matters, does it, since we so seldom know whether you'll appear at all.'

They must have expected him to appear, though, judging from the number and variety of dishes on the table. Neither woman has much of an appetite – for food, or for much else, really, aside from books and gossip. The mother suffers, quite volubly, from a chronic stomach complaint that, for unknown reasons, can't abide anything but white food – a provision that doesn't seem to apply to wine, however.

Charley suspects that Jane's dainty eating habits spring more from a desire to keep her figure. It's worked, for the most part; she's remained far more trim and attractive than most women her age, which Charley puts at around sixty – like her financial assets, it's hard to determine exactly.

Though Charley has always had a keen appreciation for a pretty face and figure, he's come to value other qualities much more, qualities such as kindness, good humor, intelligence – and, for want of a better word, sweetness. It's odd, when you come to think of it: Where food is concerned, sweetness doesn't hold much appeal for him. With women, it's a different matter altogether.

Considering the ladies' indifference toward food, it hardly makes sense to bring them a basket of it. Of course it's not for eating; it's for decorating the tree – which makes even less sense, but there you are. When he plunks the basket down in the center of the table, Hanora's eyes light up at the sight of all that bounty; by Christmas Day, she'll have made serious inroads into the tree decorations, no doubt. Jane looks rather surprised that her husband would think of such a thing. The mother eyes it like a pawnbroker assessing the worth of some arcane object.

Charley places his peace offering, the Brontë book, in front of his wife, who actually appears pleased with it, or as nearly as he can tell. 'What is it?' asks the mother, rather suspiciously, as if she wouldn't put it past Charley to present her daughter with a hedgehog or a boa constrictor.

'A book,' says Jane.

'I can *see* that. What book?'

'*Shirley*, by Charlotte Brontë.'

The mother – she has a name, of course: Dimity, but Charley never thinks of her as anything but 'the mother' – the mother reacts with something resembling incredulity or disgust; again, it's hard to be sure. 'You've *read* that. Several times.'

'Well, yes. But it's the thought that counts, isn't it?'

'Is it? Then perhaps he should have given it more thought before buying it.'

Charley is accustomed to being spoken of as if he's not there. He's barely listening anyway; he's looking around for some-where to put the tree. 'Where would you like this, my dear?'

Though he no longer finds her very dear – except perhaps in
the sense of costly – he goes on using the term out of habit, as
people go on calling him Inspector.

'Hanora, would you please set up the tree up in the front
room?' calls Jane.

'Just don't put it near the window,' adds the mother. 'It's so
small; we don't want folks thinking we can't afford any better.'

As Charley hands over the tree, Hanora – who is quite petite
– murmurs, ''Tis the very thing she's after sayin' about me.'
They both chuckle, drawing a disapproving look from Jane,
who now has more evidence to support her long-standing and
completely unfounded theory that the two of them are carrying
on behind her back.

Though Charley is restless, he forces himself to join the
women in what his wife likes to call 'the lounge,' a less formal
room than the parlor in which they entertain the occasional
visitor – mainly the ladies from Jane's reading circle. Charley
lays first claim to the *Daily News* that lies on the tea table, but
just as he is about to find out what Russia and Turkey are up
to, a peevish voice says, 'Do you mean to hog the entire
newspaper?'

'Oh, I'm sorry,' says Charley, civilly enough, and hands the
mother the section containing the obituaries, which she seems
to delight in reading – another instance of the 'glad it's them
and not me' syndrome, no doubt.

'Oh, I'm tired of people dying,' she says. 'Give me the front
section.'

'It's full of people dying, too,' says Charley. 'There's a war
going on, you know.'

'Well, at least they're dying *for* something.'

'Oh, really?' says Charley. 'And what would that be?'

'Well . . . for their country, I suppose.'

'If by *their country*, you mean the politicians and men of
business whose wealth comes from trading with the Turks, I
would agree.'

'Now, Charles,' says Jane, quietly but firmly. 'Don't start an
argument, please. Arguments are so vulgar.'

Charley takes several deep breaths and returns to his paper,
trying to lose himself in a piece about Cuba and the slave trade,

but he can't escape the mother's querulous voice. 'Oh, for goodness' sake. Another young woman has thrown herself into the river. Well, not so young, actually. Thirty-four, it says here.' She makes a tsking sound, which causes her artificial teeth to click together in a fashion that Charley finds unreasonably irritating. 'You'd think she'd know better.'

'Does it give a name?' asks Jane.

'Why? You're not likely to know her, are you?'

'I suppose not. It's just that it's even sadder, somehow, if they're nameless.'

'I don't see why. Anyway, it does give her name: Rosa MacKinnon.'

Charley stifles a curse, but not completely enough to avoid his wife's notice. 'Is something wrong, Charles?'

'No. No. As you said, it's just . . . just sad.'

'Personally,' says the mother, 'I find it hard to have much sympathy for a person who takes her own life.'

Charley can contain himself no longer. He jumps to his feet and flings down the paper. 'Well, that's hardly news, is it? As far as I can see, you have precious little sympathy for *anyone*, alive or dead!' He reaches the hallway in six strides. As he's donning his greatcoat and hat, Jane catches up with him.

'Charles! You've hurt my mother's feelings; I must ask you to apologize to her at once.'

'All right,' says Charley.

She seems taken aback. 'You agree?'

'No. You said you must ask; all right, you've asked. And I must decline. So, now we know where we stand.' He opens the door and gazes out into the street. It's another fog-swathed night, the kind that makes you question whether you're not better just staying home. But of course, he isn't really at home.

'Where are you going?' asks Jane.

'Somewhere I can have a smoke and a drink, and a think, as well.'

'Do you have to? I was hoping we could have a nice evening together for a change.'

That would *be a change*, Charley says silently. 'So was I. I'm not sure that's possible, though, at least not now.'

'If not now, when? It's nearly Christmas, Charley. It's

supposed to be a time for families to come together, to celebrate.'

'Only for the lucky ones, my dear. Some aren't quite so fortunate. They're dying on some battlefield in Crimea. They're being chloroformed and dumped into an icy river.' He steps out into the fog. 'Goodnight, Jane.'

Wishing for a good night doesn't make it so. This is one of those evenings when the air is so thick and damp that it closes in on you, half blinds you, nearly suffocates you. But in a strange way, it's comforting, too. Like new-fallen snow, it softens everything; he can barely hear the ever-present rumble of wagons or the clatter of the machinery at the marble works. Best of all, he can no longer hear anyone complaining or criticizing or voicing opinions about things of which they have no knowledge.

EIGHT

C harley spends the rest of the evening at the Cider Cellar, where he can read the paper and puff his pipe in peace, over a pint of perry. There's no shortage of uninformed opinions being voiced here, either, but they're so many and so varied that they cancel each other out.

He doesn't return to the house until he's certain the ladies will be in bed. Luckily, despite the fact that they rise so late in the morning, they also retire early. It's been years since he and Jane slept in the same bed or even the same room; he has his own small sitting/sleeping room, and Hanora has been thoughtful enough to build him a fire.

In the morning, Charley is up and out of the house before Jane and the mother are even aware he was there. Though the fog is gone, the air is still damp and chilly and feels like snow. Charley wraps his wool scarf snugly around his neck and pulls it up over his ears. When he was a copper on the beat, he never would have deigned to do such a thing, for fear of seeming soft, but he's since concluded that a little softness is not a bad thing – though he's still not happy about the padding around his middle.

When he reaches the area near Blackfriars Road where Mr Mumchance last saw his vanishing betting shop, it's still early. Several of the shops are just removing the boards from their windows. He strolls past the supposed location of the betting shop. As Mumchance indicated, it's now occupied by a tobacconist. At least it *could* be a tobacconist; the sign above the doorway is so weathered and soot-stained – like the building itself – that it might say nearly anything. There are a few pipes and tobacco tins displayed in the grimy window, but there are also books, writing implements, wooden toys, and an eerily lifelike porcelain doll.

Charley doesn't want to arouse suspicion by going inside. Instead he casually questions several nearby shopkeepers. The baker remembers that one day, a month or so ago, the tobacconist had a sudden flurry of business, which was puzzling, since normally it doesn't attract more than three or four customers in the course of a day, if that, and why would it? It's such an unremarkable establishment that, prior to renting these premises, the baker says, he passed by a hundred times without giving it a second look. He has no idea who the owner is, but the fellow mustn't be much of a businessman, for he sometimes closes the place for days at a time.

When Charley exits the bakery, the uniform army of clerks have begun their daily forced march from Newington and Lambeth to the firm of Bosh, Hogwash, and Flammery or the Bureau of This, That, and the Other. He questions some of them, too; their replies are as interchangeable as the men themselves: They weren't at all aware of the tobacconist, nor did they ever notice a betting shop.

Then Charley spies one of the clerks surveying the place intently, like a thief contemplating a break-in, only this fellow doesn't look cunning or clever; he just looks baffled. 'Good morning, sir. I'm Detective Field.' No harm in using that title; the coppers have no monopoly on it. 'Can I be of any assistance?'

'I doubt it,' says the man. 'I think I'm going mad.'

Well, that sounds familiar. 'Don't tell me; you're seeing things that aren't there. A betting shop, for example.'

The clerk gapes at him. 'How did you know?'

'I told you – I'm a detective. It's my business to know things.'

'Well, then, do you know what became of the betting shop?'

'Not yet. But I will.' He takes out his notebook. 'If you'll give me your name and address, I'll keep you informed. I'd also like you to tell me everything you recall about the vanishing shop. I'm assuming you placed a wager there?'

'Yes. At least I thought I did.' His account is almost identical to that of Geoffrey Mumchance – with one notable exception. Since he's employed by a jewelry broker, he tends to notice what sort of ornaments people are wearing, and the chap at the betting window had an impressive ring on his right hand. 'It was silver – not sterling, I'll wager; at least half pewter – and it had a curious design with a skull and a compass and the letter B.'

Charley takes all this down and gives a satisfied nod. 'You've been very helpful, sir. I won't keep you any longer.'

Though Bohemian types are not known for being either punctual or reliable, Mr Mumchance appears at the appointed time and looks the place over with the same bewilderment displayed by the clerk. Charley approaches him. 'Shall we go in?'

The poet turns, startled; Charley hasn't lost the habit he acquired as a constable, of creeping up on people unnoticed. 'Oh, good day, Inspector. I suppose we should. But what do we say?'

'Say you'd like to buy some tobacco or a pipe. Just don't mention the betting shop, all right? Speaking of which, do you still have the ticket they gave you?'

Geoffrey pulls the crumpled pasteboard from his pocket. It certainly looks legitimate. At the top are the words *ARISTOCRATIC CLUB Gentlemen's Betting Parlour All Racecourses*. The date, the track, the number of the race, the horse, and the amount of the wager are entered by hand, in an elegant, almost artistic script.

There's nothing elegant or artistic about the interior of the shop, or its proprietor. Both are drab, homely, dusty-looking, and seem to have very little to offer a potential customer. Charley strides up to the sallow, sad little fellow behind the chipped counter – which shows no sign of ever having had teller's windows – and thrusts out a hand. 'Good afternoon, sir! Mr Milford, isn't it?' He has no notion of the man's actual name, of course; this is his way of finding out.

'No, sir, it's Blimely. Grodon Peter Blimely, to be exact.'

'Mr Blimely, of course! How could I forget? It's just like "Blimey."' Charley laughs heartily. 'But I'm sure you've heard that one a thousand times.'

The man just gives a weary smile and a shrug.

'Well,' says Charley, 'I've just been telling my friend here about your shop, and how you carry only the best pipes and the finest mixtures.'

'Really?'

'Yes, indeed. If you don't mind, I'll just look around while you see to his smoking needs.' To Mumchance, he mutters, 'I'll need five minutes. Keep him busy.'

Charley studies the dingy plaster and worn wainscoting on the walls as if, like Daniel in Belshazzar's castle, he can decipher some message written there. He bends and, slipping on his spectacles, examines the edge of the floor until he finds what he's looking for. Then he returns to the counter. While Mr Blimely searches his sparse stock for a pipe to suit Mumchance, Charley crouches and runs his fingers over the floorboards. 'Hmm,' he murmurs. Rising, he puts a hand on Mumchance's shoulder. 'Let me pay for that,' he says, indicating the unexpectedly fine cherrywood pipe in the poet's hands. To the proprietor, he says, 'These poets; they never have one penny to rub against another.'

'I can sympathize. Not that I'm a poet, mind you, just that I know what it's like to be poor.'

'Perhaps you should consider some other line of business. A coffeehouse, for example. Or, I don't know, a betting parlor.'

Mr Blimely's face registers astonishment. 'How odd that you should say such a thing! In the past month, a dozen fellows have come in asking what became of the betting shop!' So preposterous is the notion that the man bursts into laughter.

Charley laughs along with him. 'And what did you tell them?'

'Well, that I've been renting this space for twenty years, and there's never been a betting shop anywhere near here. Most of them just went away, shaking their heads, but one threatened to have the law on me if I didn't pay him his winnings.'

'That is curious, indeed. Something else struck me as odd: When we were here a few weeks ago, the place was closed up tight.'

'Really? Perhaps it was a Sunday.'

'I remember the date,' says Charley – from the pasteboard ticket, of course. 'It was November 18th.'

The man consults a calendar on the wall. 'That was a Friday. What was I—? Oh, yes. I was in Bath, visiting my sister, the poor old thing; she's not well, you know.'

'I'm sorry to hear that. So you were gone for several days, then?'

'Three and a half days, more or less.'

'Did you tell anyone you were going?'

The man scratches his scabby, balding head. 'I may have mentioned it to one of my customers. Business is a little slow sometimes, so when a customer does come in, I'm afraid I tend to go on a bit too much. Am I going on too much?'

'No, no. Thank you for taking such good care of my friend, here. A poet must have a proper pipe, of course – inspiration and all that.' Before Mr Blimely can reply, Charley hustles Mumchance out the door.

'Actually,' says the poet, once they're well away, 'I have no use for a pipe; I smoke only cigarettes. When I can afford them.'

'I'll be glad to take it off your hands.' Charley glances at the fellow's expensive boots. 'Why don't you ask your parents for money? I'm sure they have plenty.'

Geoffrey gapes at him for a moment, then nods, a bit sheepishly. 'You're right once again. My old man owns a woolen mill in Gloucestershire. He's rich as Croesus, but he pays his workers a pittance and treats them like slaves. I didn't want to be a part of that, and I don't want to profit from it.'

'Good for you. I like a man with principles.'

'Yes, well, I wouldn't mind also being a man with money.'

'Hmm. Let's start by getting back your father's watch.'

Over cups of coffee at a chop house, Charley reveals his

findings. 'First off, you weren't imagining things; there *was* a betting shop in that location. For approximately three days.'

'Three days—? Oh, I see. While Mr Blimey was away, visiting his sister.'

'Exactly. When our culprits learned he'd be gone, they moved in – under cover of night, no doubt – installed the betting windows, hung up some pictures and chalkboards, and stuck a pre-painted sign above the door.'

'The devil take me! How did you deduce all that?'

'There were crumbs of chalk on the floor, some freshly hammered nails in the wall, and screw holes in the floorboards next to the counter. My guess is, they built the dividers some-where else, in sections, and just stuck them up there, like the flats in a stage set. Which brings us to the matter of who these coves are. You didn't happen to notice the ring worn by the man at the teller's window?'

'If I did, I've forgot it.'

'Apparently it was made of silver and pewter, and had images of a compass and a skull.'

'Masonic symbols,' says Mumchance. 'But there are dozens of lodges in London; how on earth—'

Charley holds up a hand, cutting him off. 'There was another image as well. A large letter *B*.'

'But even so—'

'*And* I happen to know who is likely to sport such a ring.'

The early afternoon air is, in the words of Horatio, nipping and eager, but the coffee – though it tastes of beans that never saw a coffee plant – warms them well, and it's an easy walk to the Haymarket Theatre. Charley once performed there, in the coppers' Christmas pantomime, but that was so long ago that no one is likely to recognize him. Just to make sure, he stops in a pawnshop and purchases a silk hat, a pair of pince-nez glasses, and a fur-trimmed coat that makes him appear quite the swell – as long as you don't look closely enough to see the moth holes.

In the alley beside the Haymarket, Charley says, 'Follow my lead,' and strides through the stage door as if he owns the place.

Ignoring the fact that there's a rehearsal in progress, he approaches the harried-looking stage manager and speaks in a voice as booming as that of Mr Dickens and an accent as posh as that of Lord Chumley. 'My fwiend Chahley Dickens sent meh. Heh's wented your theataw in the pahst, and tells me it's an excellent venue.'

'Please keep your voice down, sir! Come with me!' The stage manager leads them down a set of stairs to the lower level, where the scene shops and dressing rooms are found. 'If you're interested in renting the theatre, sir, you'll have to talk to Mr Webster.'

'Oh, deeah. I was so hoping we could at least look awound a bit, see whethew the place is seeootable?'

'Well . . . I suppose it wouldn't hurt, if you pwomise – *promise* to do so quietly.'

'Upon my honnah, sah, we shall be as silent as church mice. Or is it church mice that are pooah? I can nevah wemembah.'

When the man is well out of hearing, Geoffrey gives in to the laughter he's been suppressing. 'That,' he chokes, 'was quite a performance!'

'My deeah Mistah Mumchawnce,' says Charley, 'will you pleeahs contwol yooahself?' As they explore the rooms on either side of the long hallway, Charley whispers, 'Did you see his ring?'

'No. Is it the same one?'

The detective nods. 'It's worn by the members of the Bedford Lodge, most of whom are theatre professionals – actors, stage-hands, carpenters, and . . . set designers.' He opens a door labeled SCENE SHOP, slips inside, and turns up the gas lamp, revealing what looks like a combination of a Roman ruin and a village that's been razed by a cyclone. 'This is where they store the sets from previous productions. And look there.' Leaning against the wall are several panels made of wood and wrought iron; one of them has an opening similar to a teller's window. Next to it is a large chalkboard with the word *Ascot* painted at the top in white letters. Behind it, half concealed, is something that looks very much like a painting of a racehorse.

'Well, I'm damned!' breathes Geoffrey. 'How did those end up *here*?'

'No doubt they were constructed here – perhaps for a play, perhaps specifically for the purpose they were put to.'

'Constructed by whom?'

Charley lifts his crooked index finger to his lips and whispers, 'I think we're about to find out.' He turns down the gas and flattens himself against the wall. The footsteps he heard in the hallway grow louder, then stop. The door hinges squeak; a dark form enters the room and turns up the gas.

Charley slams the door shut and leans casually against it. 'Good afternoon, sir,' he says, shedding both the pince-nez and the Lord Chumley accent.

The man is the way Mumchance described him: tall, good-looking, and well built. But now he's wearing a carpenter's outfit – corduroy trousers and waistcoat, a leather apron, a hat made of folded paper. He glares at them. 'What are you doing in my workshop?'

'Looking for a particular stage set.'

'Who are you?'

'I'm Detective Field. This is Mr Mumchance. And you . . .' Charley produces the play program he discovered in one of the dressing rooms and reads from it. 'You are "Matthew Turple, Scenic Designer," I believe. An impressive job title, but I'm guessing it doesn't pay accordingly, or you wouldn't be obliged to put on your own little productions in your leisure time.'

'I have no idea what you mean.'

'Mr Mumchance here attended one of your performances a month ago and found the ticket price far too steep. We've come to ask for a refund.'

'You're talking a lot of nonsense,' growls the man. 'And even if it's true, you can't pin anything on me.'

'If I were you,' says Charley, 'I wouldn't bet on it.'

NINE

When Charley mentions the possibility of prison, the man's defiant facade quickly crumbles. He confesses that he and his confederates have pulled the vanishing betting shop stunt half a dozen times and have made a pretty profit, both in cash and in valuables, which they sell to flash houses – receivers of stolen goods.

'Then you no longer have my watch?' asks the poet.

'No, I'm sorry,' says Turple. 'I'm more than happy to give you what it was worth, if you don't report me. Will two pounds cover it?'

Mr Mumchance nods.

'But,' says Charley, 'there's also the matter of my fee.'

'He hired you; let him pay you.'

'I prefer to collect from you. Thirty shillings, plus expenses. Let's say another two pounds.'

The carpenter grudgingly surrenders the money. 'Now we're square, right?'

Charley smiles and says, 'Not quite.'

Three days later, on Christmas Eve, Charley and Geoffrey are again standing before the tobacconist's – though it hardly looks like the same shop at all. The window frames are freshly painted, the sooty bricks have been washed and whitewashed. A large sign above the door reads *MR BLIMEY's Smoke Shop Fine Tobaccos and Related Items*.

'Turple and his men did an admirable job,' says Charley.

'There's just one small problem,' the poet points out. 'They misspelled Mr Blimely's name.'

The interior of the shop has undergone a similar transformation. The plaster is patched and painted, the wainscoting scrubbed and varnished, the countertop replaced. 'I've ordered in some new stock, as well,' says Mr Blimely. 'I expect I'll have more customers now.'

'I'll have Mr Turple correct the spelling of your name,' says Charley. 'I'm sure it wasn't deliberate.'

'Oh, but it *was*, sir! I told you I was thinking of changing my name, and now I've done it! Well, why not? Everyone calls me Blimey, anyway. Besides, it's more eye-catching, more . . . more *memorable*. A businessman has to think about such things, you know.'

The display in the window has been completely redone, too; an attractive array of pipes, tobaccos, cigar boxes, and humidors rests on a bed of cotton wool surrounded by evergreen boughs and ornaments. 'When we were here before,' says Charley, 'I noticed a doll in your front window. Do you still have it?'

The grateful Mr Mumchance treats him to dinner at an oyster house where the food is, if not topping, at least cheap and plentiful. By the time Charley reaches his office, it's nearly dark, and snow has begun to fall. The postman has been by, and for the first time has left something besides advertising circulars. There are no fewer than three envelopes addressed to Inspector Bucket's Private Enquiry Agency. The notices he planted in the papers are bearing fruit.

Unfortunately, none of the appeals is worth bothering with. The first is from a sorry-sounding chap who wants help finding a suitable wife. The second is from a fellow enquiry agent, offering to take on some of Inspector Bucket's 'no doubt enormous load of cases.' There's also a plea from a man whose wallet has been stolen. Charley sighs; he'd been hoping for an excuse not to go home, but it appears that he's doomed to spend Christmas Eve with the wife and the mother.

He locks up the office and descends the stairs. Just as he steps onto the snow-dusted pavement, a cab pulls up, strewing slush with its wheels, and a pretty face is thrust around the front edge of the passenger enclosure. The woman's mouth and jaw are concealed by a scarf; above it, her dark eyes are wide with anxiety and alarm. 'Mary!' says Charley. 'What is it?'

'I went to your house first; they said I might find you here! Come with me, quickly!'

The driver releases the side doors and Charley clambers into the cab. 'He's back, isn't he? The man with the stiff neck?'

Mary nods. 'I only hope we're not too late.' Her words are indistinct, thanks to the phossy jaw, but Charley is used to deciphering all sorts of strange dialects and accents.

'Is he with a girl?'

'He was when I left. Mrs Bramble put a dose of something in his drink, to knock him out, but she didn't know how long it might last.'

Though Mary is clearly distraught, Charley learned long ago the importance of staying calm and clear-headed, however dire the situation might seem. He raps on the roof with his walking stick and the driver opens the little hatch. 'If you get us there in ten minutes,' calls Charley, 'there's an extra shilling in it for you.'

'I'll do me best, sir,' says the cabbie. 'And so will Petunia. That's me 'orse.'

'I guessed as much.' Charley leans forward and speaks to the horse. 'Put on some speed, Petunia, and I'll see that you get an extra ration of oats.' She cocks an ear and picks up the pace. Settling back in the seat, he says to Mary, 'Do you prefer the shilling, or the ration of oats?' and she gives a startled laugh. Surreptitiously, Charley feels the inside pocket of his greatcoat, making sure the cast-iron cuffs are where they're supposed to be.

When they near Madame M'Alpine's Seminary, Charley raps on the roof again and hands the fare and the bonus to the driver. 'Release the doors now, please; we can't afford to waste even a second.' Before the cab has quite come to a halt, his feet are on the pavement and he's sprinting for the front entrance. Mrs Bramble is at the door, waiting for him. 'He's upstairs!' she whispers. 'In Rosa's room!'

It would be foolish to go thundering up the stairs. He takes them swiftly but quietly, stepping on the outsides of the treads to avoid any squeaking; there's no telling whether Neck might be dead to the world or fully alert. He doesn't dare try the door on Rosa's old room, either, to determine whether it's locked. He's had plenty of experience at knocking things down and, though he's not as fit as he once was, when he throws himself into it shoulder-first, the door gives way with a satisfying splintering sound.

To his relief, the girl who was entertaining Neck has slipped out at some point. The stiff-necked cove is in the room alone, stretched out on the rumpled bed, naked except for his shirt, snoring in the same gravelly, grating way that he speaks. Charley is sorely tempted to brain the bastard with the heavy head of his walking stick, and if he were a hundred percent certain that Neck is to blame for Rosa's death, he might do it. But he's been wrong before – not often, but occasionally. Instead, he fishes the bracelets from his greatcoat pocket, leans across the bed, and deftly clamps one of the cuffs onto the man's right wrist.

Before Charley can fasten the other end to the bedstead, Neck abruptly sits up and looks around, the way he must have done when he came back from the dead. But this time he doesn't say, 'This don't look like Hell to me.' In fact, he doesn't utter a word. He springs from the bed, yanking the cuffs from Charley's grasp, and stumbles toward the wooden valet where his overcoat is hanging. Thrusting a hand into the side pocket, he comes up with a revolver – the same sort he previously pulled on Charley.

Once again Charley is too quick for him. He brings his walking stick down on the man's wrist so hard that you can hear bones crack. Neck lets out a hoarse roar of pain. But instead of clutching the wounded wrist as any normal person would do, he does something totally unexpected: He snatches up the woolen bedspread, flings it around his shoulders like a cape, and lunges across the room – not toward Charley, but toward the window. He hits it full force, the way Charley hit the door; the mullions splinter, the glass explodes outwards, and the man tumbles out of sight.

Snatching up the revolver, Charley flies to the window and thrusts his head through the opening. He knows the Seminary's surroundings well enough to know that, unfortunately, his prey hasn't gone plummeting to the street. There's a building adjacent to this one, a harness shop that's only two stories high. Neck has somehow managed to land atop it without breaking any bones and is teetering along the peak of the roof, his bare feet slipping on the snow; he loses his footing and slides on his arse down the slope, but is brought up short by the brick parapet. He flings aside the bedspread and scuttles onward.

Back when Charley was a callow constable, he would have leapt from the window, too, without thinking – and would most likely have snapped an ankle or even a leg and lost the suspect to boot. For better or worse, he's more calculating and cautious now. Though he's no crack shot, the revolver is his best bet. He has no qualms about plugging the man; whether he killed Rosa or not, he's committed more than enough crimes to deserve shooting. Charley rests the gun butt on the window sill, wraps his finger – the middle one, not the crooked index finger – around the trigger, takes careful aim, fires.

The bullet finds its target; Neck falls to his knees, clawing at his shattered shoulder blade. Charley is sure he's done for. But that's what the hangman thought, too. It seems the damned villain is indestructible. He's down for only a moment before he staggers to his feet and stumbles forward. When he reaches the far end of the roof, he swings himself over the edge and disappears.

Charley wastes no time berating himself or cursing the culprit; he bursts from the room, scrambles down the stairs and out the front door, heading for the alley at the other side of the harness shop. It's empty. So is the courtyard at the end of the alley. He checks the doors that open onto the courtyard. They're all locked.

The detective scans the pavement for drops of blood or foot-prints that might lead him in the right direction, but it's hopeless; there's too little light and too much slush. Among the many valuable things Charley learned during his policing career is his vast vocabulary of curse words. Normally he makes sparing use of them, but now he avails himself of all his favorites.

Returning to the alley, he surveys the side of the harness shop. He's always despised drainpipes; they provide much too convenient a ladder for lead-stealers and attic thieves. Now he has even more reason to hate them; it's obvious from the way the pipe is pulled away from the brick wall that, despite his grievous wound, Neck somehow managed to clamber down it.

Charley wouldn't be surprised to learn that the rooftop escape route was more than just an expedient, a desperate resort of the moment; Neck may well have made a mental note of it, in case he ever found himself trapped. You have to hand it to the blighter; though he's a nasty piece of work, he's also resourceful and fearless. Maybe once a man has cheated death, it no longer holds any terror for him.

The trouble with having no fear is that you often don't have much sense, either. Charley once spent weeks tracking down a daring cracksman who didn't bother with the fine points of opening safes; he simply blew the doors off with an explosive known as pyroglycerine. When Charley finally caught up with the fellow, there wasn't enough left of him to arrest; he'd had a fatal attack of hubris and had blown himself into the next world.

When he brushes the snow from his coat and reenters the Seminary, all the unoccupied girls are gathered in the front hall, awaiting word of Neck's fate. Rosa's daughter, Audrey, is with them, a sturdy lass of seven or eight, with wine-colored hair like her mother's. 'Did you get him?' she asks, wide-eyed and hopeful.

Charley shakes his head ruefully. 'He's harder to hang onto than an eel. He can't have gone far, though, with a bullet in him.' He takes Mrs Bramble aside. 'You did well, drugging him that way. I only wish I'd got here sooner. If I'd been home, where a man should be on Christmas Eve—'

'Don't be blaming yourself, now, do you hear? You can't be everywhere at once. Do you have any idea where he'll go next?'

'To Hell, I hope. But I won't count on it. Still, he's wounded badly enough to need a doctor. Do you know of any close by?'

'No legitimate ones. But there's Dr Smoot, who has a sort of an office in Wilton Street. Sweeney Smoot, they call him, after Sweeney Todd.'

'Oh, yes, because he supposedly slit the throats of his patients and sold their bodies to the medical school.'

'I expect that's just a myth. He may not be much of a doctor, but as far as I can tell he's harmless, just a bit too fond of his liquor. People go to him who can't afford any better.'

'Or who have something to hide?' Charley turns back to the group of anxious girls. 'There's no need to worry, ladies. Now that he knows I'm onto him, he won't be coming back here. Please be very careful, though, in going to and from the Seminary. It's best if you travel in pairs. I'll let you all know as soon as I've caught the wretch.' He bends down to tousle

Audrey's already tousled hair. 'And I will catch him, my dear, I promise you.'

As Charley is stepping out into the snow, the fat flakes fluttering like moths, Mrs Bramble calls after him, 'Whatever happens, you may as well come back here. You'll be tired and hungry. I'll leave a light and the kettle on.'

Charley gives her a salute and a smile that's grateful but at the same time slightly sad. How curious it is that he feels more welcome and more at ease in a molly house than in his supposed home. He can't help wondering how many other men – and women, for that matter – feel the same way. Perhaps that's why the city boasts such a wealth of public houses and introducing houses, not to mention supper clubs and sporting clubs and every other sort of club and association. People need that sense of belonging, and they'll take it where they can find it.

Of course, not everyone is lucky enough. Charley has known far too many lads like Wink – and men like Neck – who grew up on the streets, or in a hovel furnished mainly with neglect and abuse, and never do manage to find themselves a warm and welcoming place, but always find themselves on the outside looking in.

Charley has one other memento of his policing days – a smashing pair of thick-soled leather boots, issued to him only a few months before he retired – and he's thankful for them now, as he goes slogging through the slush. Though he prides himself on his knowledge of London streets long and short, large and small, he might never have found Wilton Street if Mrs Bramble hadn't pointed him in the right direction. It's only a few blocks long, and scarcely wide enough for a wagon.

There's nothing to indicate that the building housing Dr Smoot's office is anything other than a tenement. If the medico ever did hang out a shingle, it's disappeared. Perhaps he's not very interested in attracting business – or unwanted attention. There's no bell pull on the door; Charley doesn't want to announce his presence, in any case. It is equipped with a lock, but it's no Chubb; he fishes out his ring of picks and rakes and swiftly, silently coaxes it open. Beyond is a dark, damp, dirty entryway and a second door with a border of yellow light all around it; it has no lock, not even a doorknob. Charley takes a deep breath and eases it open, just enough to allow him a view of the room, which is lighted by a smoky oil lamp.

At a battered deal table sits a figure with its back to him. Though the man's face isn't visible, it's easy enough to tell, from the way his head is drooping, resting on his folded arms, that it's not Neck. Neck has been here, though, judging from the bloody linen shirt that lies bunched up on the floor. Charley slips through the doorway and approaches the man.

A rustling sound from close at hand startles him; he pivots in that direction, his stick raised, but there's no threat, only a mouse scampering away, abandoning the chunk of stale bread he'd been chewing on. Charley turns back to the man at the table, who hasn't stirred. 'Dr Smoot?' he says softly, then again, more loudly. There's no reply. Oh, lord; it looks as though Neck has done for him, too.

TEN

Charley strides forward and, taking hold of the doctor's greasy hair, gently lifts his head. Something wet is oozing from his mouth, but it's not blood, it's only drool. The detective almost laughs with relief. The man isn't dead at all, just dead drunk and reeking of gin. There's no time to sober him up in some civilized way. Charley shakes him roughly, delivers a couple of slaps to his face, then wipes the drool and hair oil from his palm, using the man's sleeve. The fabric of his frock coat is nearly as greasy as his hair.

'Doctor! Dr Smoot! I need to ask you some questions!'

The doctor pries open his eyelids, revealing orbs so bloodshot they look like cut persimmons. 'I don' know . . . I don' know an'thing . . . about an'thing.'

'Really?' says Charley. 'I suppose you've no idea how *this* got here, then?' He picks up the bloody linen shirt and dangles it in front of Smoot's face.

'Never seen it b'fore. C'n barely see it now.'

'That's a shame. I was hoping you could help me.'

'You sick?'

'Only with remorse. You see, I had a run-in with a fellow earlier in the evening – over a woman, you know. Silly business.' He shakes Smoot again. 'Are you listening?'

'I'm listing-ing,' says the doctor, though he seems more intent on the task of jamming his grimy bare feet into a surprisingly colorful pair of Berlin wool slippers.

'He challenged me to a duel, but then he got cold feet at the last moment and turned tail – just as I was firing my pistol. I think I may have hit him. If so, he'll need medical help, but he doesn't dare go to just any doctor; as you know, dueling is illegal.'

'I don' know an'thing about—'

'Of course, it's also illegal to treat a gunshot wound and not report it.'

'Is it, now?'

'It is.' Well, it *should* be, at any rate. 'But what else can you do, right? You're a doctor; you're sworn to help anyone who needs it. If a man with such a wound comes in, you're obliged to treat him. There's nothing wrong in that; you're just doing your duty.'

'Tha's right. My du'y.'

'I'm sure you did a fine job, too. Were you able to remove the bullet?'

'Oh, my, yes. 'M a capital surgeon, y'know – once I've had a d'ink or two to steady my hands. It broke the scrap – the *scap*ula, but din' go in deep. A .31 caliber never does, 'less it's fired from close up. 'F he keeps his arm in the sling, it'll – *hic* – heal up in no time.'

'I suppose you cut off the handcuffs as well.'

'Yes, I did.' The doctor shakes his head. 'Just a min't. 'F you were dueling, why would he—'

'Never mind that. I hope he paid you well for your services.'

'He din' have his wallet. Or his trousers, for that ma'er. I – *hic* – had to lend him some, and a coat 's well. Not the sor' of fellow you say "no" to. Tol' me he'd be back in a day or two.'

'I don't suppose he gave you his address?'

'I din' ask.'

'I'll tell you what. I'll pay his bill for him. It's the least I can do.' Charley tosses half a crown onto the table. 'There'll be more, if you find out where he lives. Tell him you like to look in on all your patients, see how they're getting along.'

Dr Smoot snickers. 'Can't remem'er the last time I did *that*.'

'And there's no need to now; I'll pay him a visit myself. If I can see that he's all right, it'll soothe my conscience no end.'

Charley's conscience actually does bother him a bit – not because of Neck, of course, but because of Jane, who will be wondering why he can't at least make it home for Christmas Eve. She seems to still imagine that they're a happy family, or at least a contented one; no doubt she went on believing in Father Christmas, too, long after she was old enough to know better.

Well, she'll be asleep by now, in any case, and in the morning he can make it a point to be there before she wakes up. Though Mrs Bramble has prepared another room for him, he insists on staying in Rosa's old room – after nailing boards over the broken window. She brings him a sandwich and a glass of eggnog made with liberal amounts of brandy and rum.

As he's going through the pockets of Neck's overcoat, the door swings open a foot or so – though it's a little askew, it's still on its hinges – and a face wreathed by red hair appears. 'May I come in, Inspector?'

'Please do, Audrey. I was just looking for clues.'

'Did you find any?'

'No. For a thief, he has very empty pockets.'

Audrey nods at the Colt's revolver lying on the bed. 'Is that his gun?'

'It was. Now it's mine.'

'I thought you didn't like guns.'

'I don't. I'll lock it up somewhere safe.'

'Did you shoot him with it?'

'You ask a lot of questions.'

'I'm a child; it's what we do.'

'It's what detectives do, too. Perhaps you'll be one someday.'

She laughs. 'Oh, there are no women detectives. Are there?'

'Not yet. You could be the first.'

Audrey holds up her arms, and he lifts her effortlessly onto the bed. She eyes the overcoat suspiciously. 'Did *he* kill my mother?'

'I'm not sure.'

'She didn't kill herself, I know that much.'

'No. Perhaps we shouldn't be talking about this. Why don't we sing some carols, instead? It is Christmas Eve, you know.'

'It don't feel like it.'

'Well, maybe it'll feel more like it if we sing.' He launches into 'The First Noel'; after a few moments, Audrey chimes in, her voice high and soft and sad. By the time they segue into 'Tomorrow Shall Be My Dancing Day,' her voice is stronger and she's smiling just a little. Charley hears another voice pick up the tune, and another, and he looks up to see half a dozen of the girls clustered outside the doorway, singing along. Despite her handicap, even Mary joins in.

They proceed to 'God Rest Ye Merry, Gentlemen' and 'While Shepherds Watched.' At some point, Charley feels Audrey's head come to rest against his shoulder. 'Is she asleep?' he whispers to Mary.

She nods and, moving stealthily into the room, lifts the young girl in her arms. 'It's long past her bedtime.'

As she turns to leave, Charley calls softly, 'Wait!' He reaches into the spacious inside pocket of his greatcoat and pulls out the porcelain doll given him by the tobacconist; though he tried to pay, Mr Blimely wouldn't hear of it. 'Give her this, will you? It's a Christmas present.'

Charley has never had the least trouble falling asleep, especially with a little rum and brandy in him; once the familiar keyed-up feeling that always accompanies a case has subsided, he turns down the gas and stretches out on the bed, still fully clothed, the Colt's revolver tucked beneath his pillow. Though there's not a chance in the world that Neck will return for his gun and his clothing, he could conceivably send someone else, and Charley likes to be prepared.

Just as he's drifting off, he hears the mangled door creak, and the bottom of it scrapes along the carpet. Charley carefully slides the pistol from beneath the pillow. Then, just as carefully, he slides it back, confident that he has little to fear

from an intruder who is wearing such fragrant Florida water.
'Mary?'

She lies down next to him and drapes an arm across his chest.
'Audrey woke up long enough to see her dolly. She loves it.
She's already named it Charlene. *Inspector* Charlene, in fact.'

Charley laughs softly. 'Inspector Charlene, eh? Well, who
knows, we may have women on the force one day. They'd make
quite good inspectors, actually. At least my wife and mother
would. They never let me get away with anything.' They're both
silent for a time, then Charley says, 'What will become of her,
do you think?'

'Audrey? Well, Mrs Bramble don't feel it'd be good for her
to stay on here. She's found a place for her at the Priestley
Orphans' Asylum. Several of the girls have placed children
there – you know, when they couldn't care for them any longer
– and I guess they're treated pretty well; of course the more
money you donate the better they're treated. We've all chipped
in a little.'

'You can count on me for some, as well.'

'I know.' Mary's delicate fingers toy with the buttons on his
waistcoat, begin undoing them one by one, then move on to
the buttons of his braces.

Though Charley has seldom said no to an amorous opportunity, this seems not quite right, somehow, so soon after Rosa's
death. 'You don't need to do this, Mary.'

'I want to. And I think Rosa would want me to.' She runs a
fingernail lightly down his knuckle-beaten nose and along the
day-old bristles on his jaw. 'Consider it a Christmas present.'

The presents Charley receives from Jane and the mother are
well meant, he supposes, but only serve to demonstrate how
little they actually know him. He's never worn a smoking jacket
in his life – though of course he'll have to now, at least within
the confines of this house – nor has he ever shown the least
fondness for monogrammed linen handkerchiefs; a bandana
serves the purpose much better, and may also be used to bind
a wound or wipe sweat and smuts from your face. And, come
to think of it, if they object so strenuously to his tobacco habit,
why buy him a smoking jacket?

Of course, the snuffboxes – which Hanora wrapped for him – don't exactly create a sensation, either. Jane at least makes a show of being pleased with hers, but she can't quite hide a look that says, 'What on earth am I to do with this?' The mother doesn't even try; in fact, she comes right out and says it.

Charley feigns an expression of surprise. 'I thought you'd be sure to know, Mother. My sources assure me that they're all the fashion among society ladies.'

'Oh. Well, yes, of course,' replies the mother, scrambling to save face. 'But they're usually much more . . . fancier.'

Somehow he manages to make it through the day without insulting anyone very grievously or doing anything more ill-mannered than putting his elbows on the table during dinner. The courses are unaccountably numerous and huge, which is not such a bad thing; Hanora and her family will feast well on the leftovers. What's more, Charley can overeat and then use it as an excuse to retire to his little study for a long winter's nap.

The following day, he has the house to himself while the wife and the mother attend Sunday services; it's continued to snow on and off, so he makes himself useful by shoveling the walk. By Monday morning, he's had all the domesticity he can stand. Luckily, like Neck, he has an escape plan. This is the day Mr Dickens is scheduled to present his reading of *A Christmas Carol* in Birmingham, and it's Charley's duty to see that there are no disruptions.

Preventing disruptions is a lot easier when you're wearing a copper's uniform, or when the locals recognize you as a figure of authority, even if you're in plain clothing. That is, in fact, the whole idea behind the New Police – not to capture wrong-doers so much as to deter them. Charley's been to Birmingham a few times, first as a boxer, then on police business, but he's not widely known there, so his presence won't be much of a deterrent. He's going to have to use his well-trained eye to spot trouble before it starts. If the enchanting Miss Fairweather herself shows up, he's sure to notice her, but she may well send in someone with a bit more muscle to do the job for her.

It's an hour's walk to Euston Station and, as sloppy as the streets are with melting snow, he probably should take a cab.

But he needs the open air, especially with a long train ride ahead of him, and who knows how long he'll be cooped up in the Town Hall with the other theatregoers, or how tightly packed they'll be. Mr Dickens never fails to draw a crowd, and he's not known for being short-winded; he likes the sound of his own voice. Luckily for him, so does his audience.

By the time Charley reaches the station, he's been splattered three times by the wheels of passing hackneys; his trouser legs cling clammily to him, and his greatcoat has doubled in weight from all the water. He'll need the five hours on the train just to dry out.

If people are flocking to Mr Dickens' reading, they're not coming from London. The second-class cars on the London and North Western are half empty. Charley settles into an unoccupied compartment, but just as the train begins to move, the door to the compartment flies open; a latecomer springs aboard and collapses breathlessly on the seat opposite him. 'Whew!' exclaims the man. 'I was verra nearly left behind!' Once he's regained his composure, he seems a well-mannered sort, very distinguished-looking, with a Van Dyck beard and pomaded hair going gray at the temples. Out of old habit, Charley peruses the man's face. Though the eyes are heavy-lidded, as if he's about to doze off, there's something unsettling about them. Whereas most folk won't engage a stranger's gaze for more than a moment, when the man feels Charley's eyes on him, he readily meets and holds them. Here's a man who's used to being scrutinized – a politician, perhaps? An entertainer?

They nod amiably to each other. 'I apologize for the smell of wet wool,' says Charley. 'I should have taken a cab here.'

The fellow waves a hand dismissively. ''Tis easily overcome by the smell of a good cheroot.' Charley notes the slight Scots burr. 'If you dinna mind, of course.'

'No, no, I don't mind. I was considering lighting up my pipe, in fact.'

The bearded man produces a cigar case decorated with, of all things, an illustration showing Mr Scrooge being confronted by Marley's ghost. Frowning, he shakes it. 'Blast! I meant to stock up at Euston Station.'

'I spotted a basket girl boarding the train,' says Charley. 'They often have cigars.'

'Trichonopolies, no doubt. But beggars canna be choosers. I'll see if canna catch her at the next station.' Sure enough, when they stop at Watford Junction, the basket lady comes down the platform, calling in tones only a little less piercing than those of the steam whistle, 'Apples! Orrrranges! Cigarrrs! Cigarettes!' Just as the bearded fellow is rising from his seat, the basket girl's face appears at the window – though the term *girl* is ill-advised. She is, in fact, a singularly unattractive woman with tangled gray hair, a single unbroken eyebrow, erratic teeth, and a wen on her cheek the size and texture of a walnut. To her credit, she's done her best to hide her features with a headscarf, but it's no use.

Homeliness that profound leaves you with only two options: either you stare in stupefaction, or you avoid looking at her altogether. Charley chooses the latter, busying himself with his pipe. Only when the woman is gone does Charley realize that he should have asked whether she carried matches. But his companion is well equipped with them, and comes to his aid. The fellow was right about the quality of the cigars; the cheroot fills the car with an odor like that of singed hair. Fortunately, Charley's pipeful of Rainbow tobacco – which advertises itself as being 'sweet-scented' – creates a pleasant aura all its own.

'You're on your way to Mr Dickens' reading?'

'I am. How did you – Oh, aye. The cigar case.' The man leans forward and says confidentially, 'Do you know, 'twas actually given me by the Great Man himself?'

'You don't say.'

The stranger shrugs modestly. 'I provided him with some small assistance regarding apparitions.'

'Ghosts, you mean?'

'I prefer the term *spirits*.'

'I'm quite fond of spirits, myself,' says Charley, drawing an appreciative laugh from the man.

'I suppose we should be civilized and introduce ourselves, eh?' The Scotsman extends a graceful, well-manicured hand. 'Malcolm Sledge, sir.'

Charley, whose grasp often errs on the side of firmness, gives the hand a careful shake. 'Charles Field.'

'Not *the* Charles Field, surely? The inspiration for Inspector Bucket?'

'I can't deny it.'

'Well, sir, what a privilege this is! And how odd, that two of Mr Dickens' resources should come face to face this way. 'Tis a coincidence worthy of a Dickens novel.'

'Hardly surprising, though, considering we're both bound for the same place.'

'If I may ask, are you going in some official capacity?'

'No, no. I'm no longer on the force. It's just for my own amusement.' No point in showing his hand; for all he knows, this fellow may be an agent of Miss Fairweather, charged with wreaking her vengeance. 'And if I may ask, how is it that Mr Dickens would consult you about ghosts–sorry, *spirits*? No, wait; I have it. You're a medium.'

Sledge gives an appreciative smile. 'Verra perceptive, Inspector. People seldom guess my occupation, since so many of those who pursue it are women.'

Charley notes that he calls it an occupation, not a skill or gift. That would seem to indicate that he makes an income from it – which in turn suggests that, like Charley's mother, he's more in touch with the living than with the dead. Over the years, Charley has investigated half a dozen people – all women – who claimed to commune with the spirit world; the few who actually showed some evidence of psychic ability refused to accept money for their efforts.

'I know that look, Inspector. 'Tis the look of a skeptic.'

Charley holds up his hands defensively. 'I'm neither a believer nor a skeptic. A good copper learns not to judge anyone or anything until he's examined the evidence.'

'And Mr Dickens clearly considers you a good copper.'

'I like to think so.'

'Well, sir, as it happens, I have need of someone like you, who trusts only the evidence of his own senses. As you may know, there are far too many mediums out there who resort to trickery and trumpery – most notably the Fox sisters, of course – and they've given us all a bad name. The public has grown quite suspicious of the whole concept of spiritualism. If you were to sit at one of my séances, you would see for yourself that there's no deception involved; I'm simply a conduit, conveying messages from the other side.' Sledge takes a card from his wallet and hands it to Charley. It reads:

PROF. MALCOLM SLEDGE
Spiritual Consultant
Séances each Tues. 6 p.m.
or by special arrangement
18 Oat Lane, Aldersgate

'I'd be happy to pay your usual fee; 'twould be worth it, to have my legitimacy established by an objective observer.'

'And what if I establish that you're *not* legitimate?'

Sledge smiles tolerantly. 'I'm confident that willna happen. But in any case, you'll receive your fee.'

'Well, then, I can hardly refuse, can I?'

'Excellent. Shall we say a week from Tuesday, then? You'd be welcome to drop in any time, of course, but I'd like to make sure we save a place for you; otherwise, it may be a bit crowded. In all modesty, I have quite a following.'

'Hmm.' In Charley's experience, the popularity of mediums has little to do with how genuine their séances seem and much to do with how theatrical they are. People want to be astounded by tipping tables, disembodied voices, incorporeal forms, floating violins played by invisible hands.

The walk from the Birmingham railway station to the Town Hall is more in the nature of an Arctic expedition. The sleet stings their faces like a swarm of bees driven mad by the wind, which is itself insane; even indoors Charley can hear it moaning and crying like a chorus of damned souls. But despite the awful weather, the hall promises to be filled to capacity – and by Charley's estimate it must seat about two thousand. Too many for him to keep proper track of, that's for certain.

Before the performance begins, he takes up a post by the entrance door, so he can scan the audience members as they file in; he's looking for familiar faces, particularly the lovely countenance of Julia Fairweather, which he can picture perfectly, even though it's been over a year since he saw her on stage.

He has a knack for remembering faces in general, of course, but he recalls hers better than most. In fact, it's appeared to him more than once in his dreams, attached to a body that he's forced to imagine, never having seen it in its natural state.

When the audience is seated, Charley takes up a station at the top of the stairs leading to the balcony. From here, he has a view of both the main floor and the upper level. He sees no sign of Miss Fairweather, nor anyone else he recognizes, except for Mr Sledge and the enterprising basket woman from the train, who is doing a brisk business in spite of her grotesque appearance – or perhaps because of it; some are likely buying her fruit and cigars more out of pity than need.

The ushers turn down the lamps that line the walls and turn up the ones that light the dais at one end of the hall. After a halting introduction delivered by a nervous young woman, Mr Dickens strides onstage to a generous round of applause, which he acknowledges with a smile and a little bow. He waits for the audience to settle itself, then steps to the lectern, opens a beautifully bound book, and begins to read – or rather recite, since he's clearly committed most of the story to memory:

> *Marley's Ghost. Marley was dead: to begin with. There is no doubt whatever about that. The register of his burial was signed by the clergyman, the clerk, the undertaker, and the chief mourner. Scrooge signed it: and Scrooge's name was good upon 'Change, for anything he chose to put his hand to. Old Marley was as dead as a door-nail.*

The man would have made an excellent medium, and an even better mesmerist. In fact, you could say that he is a bit of both, hypnotizing his audience with words, conjuring up the ghostly images and disembodied voices of a dozen different men and women – not dead ones, but ones who never existed at all. He has no need of tricks or illusions; he holds his audience spellbound solely by the magic of his voice and the expressiveness of his face, augmented by a few telling gestures.

Even Charley finds himself being drawn into Mr Dickens' world, and he shakes his head like a punch-addled fighter. He needs to stay alert and aware so that, if trouble is afoot, he can trip it up. He spots a big, beefy cove leaning over the railing of the balcony; it could be that he's only trying to hear better, but he could just as easily be getting himself in position to throw something at the stage.

As Charley is edging in that direction, keeping to the shadows at the rear of balcony, the room below erupts with sound – a rapid series of pops and bangs, almost like gunfire, accompanied by startled cries and shrieks from the audience. Charley rushes back to the head of the stairs. The men and women who were seated on the aisle are now trampling their neighbors' feet and stumbling into their laps in an effort to escape the barrage of flashes and explosions happening in the center of the hall.

'Firecrackers!' mutters Charley under his breath. They weren't thrown by the beefy fellow in the balcony, though; no, Charley has spotted the culprit, who is in the process of lighting up another string of jacky-jumpers. He scrambles down the stairs, tackles the basket woman from the train, and half drags, half carries her into the foyer and out through the front door. En route, the fireworks fall from the woman's grasp and crackle around their feet; Charley kicks them out into the wet snow, where they fizzle and smoke helplessly.

'Let me go!' cries the woman, and swings her basket at his head. Charley blocks the blow, which is surprisingly fierce, wrenches the basket from her hands, and flings it, too, into the snow. He's tempted to send the woman tumbling after it, but restrains himself; he attempts to restrain her as well, but he can't seem to locate his cuffs. And then he remembers: When that infernal miscreant Neck made his escape, he took Charley's bracelets with him.

The woman kicks him in the shins, now; out of patience, Charley seizes both her wrists, yanks them behind her back, and secures them with a grip as steely as that of the missing cuffs. In the process, he can't help noticing that her hands are not the worn, chapped hands of a basket woman, but those of a pampered lady.

Charley shakes his head in wonder. 'Well, Miss Fairweather,' he says, 'that was quite a performance.'

ELEVEN

J ust as Charley seldom forgets a face, he has an astounding ability to remember every coffeehouse he's ever been to, and whether or not it's worth revisiting. On his way here from the station, even half blinded by sleet, he spotted the cozy establishment called Crumpet's, which he'd discovered on a previous trip to Birmingham. He steers Miss Fairweather in that direction now. It wouldn't do, after all, for them to be outside the Town Hall when the audience emerges; there would be far too much explaining required.

He keeps a firm hold on one of Miss Fairweather's slender arms, which is trembling a little – perhaps because she's angry at being foiled, but just as likely because she's freezing. Her attire is well suited to her name; it's unfit for such foul weather. She has no gloves, and no coat or cloak, only a dingy woolen shawl draped over her shoulders. Charley sheds his greatcoat and wraps it around her. He doesn't expect her to react with gratitude, but neither does he expect the look of contempt it earns him, which is made even more unpleasant by the crooked dentures she's wearing as part of her disguise.

By the time they reach Crumpet's Coffee-house, he's freezing, too. Luckily, both the establishment and its owner are still as warm and welcoming as he remembers them. Mrs Crumpet is also very perceptive and tactful; she shows them to a secluded box in a back corner of the room, away from the prying eyes of the other customers.

Miss Fairweather has remained sulkily silent all this time; no one – except Charley, of course – would guess she's the same woman who regularly delights audiences with her élan and allure. Charley sees no point in badgering her; that'll only make her more resentful. Better to give her some time to pull herself together. He orders two coffees, glancing at Miss Fairweather to see whether she'll object; she doesn't.

Once they're alone, she rummages through her shabby reticule and comes up with a compact mirror, a jar of Crème Céleste, and a couple of soft cotton cloths. She pulls the gray wig from her head and unpins her real hair – a curly mass of lustrous black locks that tumble about her shoulders like ebony shavings from a carpenter's plane. She removes the crooked prosthetic teeth, the eyebrow addition, and the nutlike wen and wraps them in one of the cloths, then proceeds to clean off the pearl powder that gave her such an unhealthy pallor. Charley is a bit taken aback to see that, without stage cosmetics, her skin bears little resemblance to alabaster, as is the fashion; instead, it's an appetizing golden brown, like a toasted muffin or a good ale.

It shouldn't come as a surprise, really. He's well aware, thanks to his theatre acquaintances, of the rumors about Miss Fairweather's origins. They say she's the illegitimate daughter of Ira Aldridge, the American actor of African descent who toured the provinces two decades ago before performing Othello at Covent Garden, to great acclaim. As far as Charley knows, she's never denied these rumors. Why would she, when they've brought her such notoriety? Notoriety is an even greater asset than beauty or talent.

What really fascinates him is how, as she divests herself of her disguise bit by bit, her character undergoes a subtle change as well, from sullen to civil to, ultimately, charming. The charm takes a while to surface; first she has to express her exasperation. 'There was no need to wrestle me into submission, you know. I had no intention of hurting anyone.'

'I didn't suppose you had,' says Charley. 'But after all the theatre fires these past few years, it doesn't take much to send a crowd into a panic.'

'Well, then they're foolish,' she grumbles.

'Oh, I grant you that. If they weren't, would they brave this weather just to hear Mr Dickens recite a story they've read a dozen times already?'

He draws a reluctant smile from her. 'Or seen acted upon the stage.'

Mrs Crumpet sets their coffees before them and retreats without showing the least surprise at Miss Fairweather's startling transformation. Charley blows and sips and licks his lips. 'How on earth does she do it, I wonder?'

'How does who do what?'

'How does Mrs Crumpet manage to serve real coffee? In London, it's all been adulterated with every conceivable sort of stuff.'

Miss Fairweather raises her now-perfect eyebrows. 'Adultery, sir? My, my. I'm blushing.' She isn't, of course, but Charley can sense his own face going red. She seems not to notice; she's busy packing all her paraphernalia into the reticule. 'Tell me, Inspector; at what point did you "make" me? That's the term you coppers use, isn't it?'

'Yes.' Of course, the term – as she no doubt knows – also has a sexual connotation. Charley feels his blush grow deeper. 'Though it injures my pride,' he says, 'I have to admit that you had me fooled right up until the moment I took hold of your hands . . . that is . . .'

She's clearly enjoying his discomfiture. 'When you manhandled me, you mean.'

'Yes. I'm sorry if I hurt you.'

'Well, I'm sorry I hit and kicked you.'

He shrugs. 'If I had a penny for each time a perpetrator hit me, I'd—'

'Be rich?'

'Well, no, but I'd have an extra pound or two.'

She rubs her wrists, where his grip chafed them. 'A perpetrator. Is that what I am, Inspector Bucket?'

'You know me?'

'Not exactly. I eavesdropped outside your compartment on the train. So, what now? Is it your duty,' she says, archly, quoting from *Bleak House*, 'to take me and keep me under remand?' Somehow she makes the process sound not like an arrest so much as an assignation.

'I'm not an officer of the law any longer, Miss Fairweather. My only duty was to Mr Dickens, and I failed in that.'

'So I'm free to go?'

'Of course,' says Charley. She starts to rise, smiling rather smugly – until one of his hands captures one of hers, like a battle-scarred cat pouncing on a sleek brown mouse. 'Just as soon as you've made up for the money you cost me.'

'I *beg* your pardon?' The mouse struggles, but the cat tightens its grip.

'Mr Dickens promised me a bonus if I prevented you disrupting his performance.'

Her lovely brown eyes fix him with an unlovely glare. 'It's not my fault you couldn't handle the job.'

'But I *am* handling it, Miss Fairweather. Or manhandling it, at any rate.' Only when she plunks herself down in the box again does he release her hand – a bit reluctantly, to be sure.

'How much?' she says with a growl and a scowl. It's astonishing what a range of tones and expressions the woman commands, and how effortlessly she glides from one to another. Most well-bred ladies would consider it shameful to display so much untoward emotion. But of course no one would accuse an actress of being well-bred; on the ladder of respectability, women of the theatre are considered only one rung above women of the street, and for the most part they make little effort to dispel that image.

'A pound should do it,' says Charley.

'I'm not a *count*ess, Mr Field, I'm an *act*ress.'

'And a very good one. You might almost convince me that you haven't a shilling to your name.'

'Almost?'

'If I hadn't spotted you after a performance of *The Willow Copse*, climbing into quite an impressive carriage.'

'It certainly wasn't mine.'

'I didn't imagine it was. But you clearly have a wealthy admirer.'

'More than one, as a matter of fact,' she says haughtily, then does one of her quick changes and turns coy on him. 'You know, Mr Field, a real gentleman would never ask a lady for money.'

'It's lucky, then, that I'm no gentleman, isn't it?'

'You may as well say it: And I'm no lady.'

'I wasn't even thinking it. However, you do make a very convincing basket woman.'

'Thank you. Speaking of which, I invested several shillings in that basket and its contents. I assume you'll deduct that from the amount I must pay to gain my freedom.'

'Fair enough.'

She digs in her reticule again and comes up with a sovereign purse; retrieving several coins from it, she flips them onto the table. 'Satisfied?'

Charley nods. 'Only . . .'

'What?'

'Well, I hope I've left you enough for your return fare.'

She rises and, slipping out of his greatcoat, drapes it over his head as if he's a coat rack. 'Oh, don't worry about me,' she says airily, but with a touch of sarcasm. 'If I need help, I'll just ask one of my wealthy admirers.'

As she heads for the door, the eyes of every man in the coffeehouse follow her – including Charley's. She takes her time about it, clearly relishing her ability to turn heads even in the attire of a basket woman. When she opens the door, the wind tosses her black curls about, making her look like Catherine Earnshaw upon the wild moor; she assumes an appropriately tragic mien, as if she's going to meet her fate and not merely a train. The woman knows how to make an exit; Charley is tempted to applaud.

He probably should start for the station soon, as well. But first he needs to question Mrs Crumpet about her coffee. Her secret, it turns out, is that she roasts and grinds it herself, rather than relying on a commercial roaster as most coffeehouses do these days. 'You know, you could do the same, sir. All that's required is a roasting pan and a small grinder.'

Charley laughs at the suggestion. 'I'm afraid that's beyond my capabilities. I can barely brew tea properly. Or so my wife keeps telling me.'

'You never know what you're capable of, sir, until you try.'

There's one thing he knows he's incapable of, because he's tried, and that is getting Miss Fairweather out of his head. Not that she's displaced Rosa, by any means. His red-haired friend is likely to haunt him for a long while yet; unfortunately, instead of picturing her lively and laughing, as she was in life, he keeps seeing her stretched out on that table, pale and silent and still.

For some reason, the actress seems determined to haunt him, too. On the train to London, Charley once again finds an unoccupied compartment, and once again ends up sharing it – not with Mr Sledge this time, but with Miss Fairweather herself.

What's more, she takes a seat not across from him but right next to him. 'I hope you don't mind, Inspector. You see, when I travel alone, I seem to attract men. Being admired is one thing; being approached is another.'

'You might try putting on your disguise again. I'll wager that would keep them at bay.'

She smiles wryly. 'Probably so. But after an hour or so, it begins to itch.'

'Well, I don't mind people thinking I'm your traveling companion, if you don't.' He fishes his new cherrywood pipe from his pocket. 'Since we're being so civil, I suppose I should ask how you feel about pipe smoking.'

'I don't much care for it,' she says. Charley is about to put the pipe away, when she adds mischievously, 'I prefer cigarettes. But you're welcome to light up.'

'Thank you. I've been a bit deprived of late; my wife won't allow smoking of any sort in her house.'

'In *her* house? That's an odd way of putting it. Isn't it your house, too?'

'Not really.'

'Oh. Well, thank goodness I have a place of my own. I don't like others telling me what I can and can't do.'

If she were a man, Charley would already have deduced the fact that she lived alone, plus half a dozen other things about her. But he's always found women harder to read than men. Is it because they're more complicated? More deceitful? More careful about their appearance? Or maybe it's due to some defect in him; maybe he tends to look at them more as a man than as a detective.

Certainly when he looks at Julia Fairweather, it's difficult to stay detached and objective. Objective, defective, detective. It has the makings of a good music hall song – perhaps to the tune of 'You Gentlemen of England.' Mentally, he creates a new set of lyrics: *You coppers and detectives, heed what I have to say/You need stay objective if you want to earn your pay/Just you follow this directive and you'll always be effective* . . . Chuckling, he abandons the effort but continues softly humming – though apparently not as softly as he thought, for now Miss Fairweather takes up the tune. At first she only

hums, too, but then supplies the rightful words in a sweet alto
voice:

> You gentlemen of England who lives at home at ease,
> Oh, how little do you dream of all the dangers of the seas.
> So give ear to us sailors, sir, and we will plainly show
> All our fears and all our cares when stormy winds do blow.

Charley joins in, and between the two of them they recall all
the verses. In spots, he even provides a little harmony. They
finish up with a grand flourish – 'All the day we drink awaaaay
. . . though stor-hormy winds do blow!' – and a good laugh.

'You surprise me, Miss Fairweather. How does such a serious
actress come to know such a frivolous song?'

'Oh, I'm full of surprises, Inspector.'

'I believe it.'

For a time, she sits staring out the window, as if at something
in the distance. Finally she says, 'My father taught me that one,
actually. Each time he came home, he had a new ditty, which
I learned and performed for him.'

'Was he in the theatre himself, then?'

Miss Fairweather turns her dark eyes on him. 'Are you trying
to interrogate me, Inspector?' She even manages to make the
word *interrogate* sound suggestive.

Though he finds her cool gaze unsettling, he doesn't let it
show. In his profession, one has to develop a certain amount
of acting skill as well. 'Not at all. Just making conversation.
It's what traveling companions do, you know.'

'I know. The trouble with conversation is, to do it properly
you have to be yourself. I'm much better at being someone
else.'

'Well, as Mrs Crumpet says, you never know what you're
capable of until you try.'

The actress lets out a lilting laugh. 'Mrs Crumpet of the
coffee shop?'

'The same. She says that, if I want a good cup of coffee, I
should roast and grind the beans myself. I think I may give it
a go.'

'With your wife's approval, of course.'

'Oh, she'd never stand for it, and it would send her mother's refined senses into some sort of shock. I'll have to do the deed in my office.'

'Once you've mastered the process, you must invite me over for a cup.'

'Hmm. I don't know if that's a good idea.'

'Why? I won't report you to your wife, I promise.'

'It's just that ordinarily when people have coffee together, there's also conversation involved.'

'Oh. Well, if you can try making coffee, I suppose I could try to make conversation.'

'You're doing pretty well just now.'

'Thank you. Normally, my companions don't much want me to talk; I'm just expected to look good, and to laugh at their ravishing wit.'

'You're doing pretty well with that, too – looking good, I mean.'

'And you,' she says, 'are doing a fair job of blushing.'

She seems to lose all interest in conversing, then; after trading seats with him, she spends most of the remaining miles gazing out at the snow-swaddled landscape. Charley, meanwhile, amuses himself by composing more lyrics for the Defective Detective song; perhaps the boys in B Division can use it in their next pantomime. At one point, Miss Fairweather stirs from her reverie enough to say, 'Do you suppose Mr Dickens will forgive me for ruining his show?'

'I'm sorry to disappoint you, but I hardly think it was ruined. I'm sure he recovered admirably; he always does. The question is, will *you* forgive him for ruining yours?'

'Probably not. But the theatre is a small world; one can't afford to make too many enemies.'

Charley wonders whether that small world includes other types of performers – mediums, for instance. He pulls Sledge's card from pocket and hands it to Miss Fairweather. 'Do you know this fellow, by any chance?'

'Only by reputation. Several of the other girls have been to see him. I don't think they enjoyed the experience very much. They thought it was going to be a lark – something like a magic show with spirits – and found it quite different; I think it threw a scare into them, actually. Are you planning to consult him?'

'Not exactly. He's asked me to attend one of his séances, to see what I make of it.'

'And will you?'

'Well, as I told Professor Sledge, I *am* fond of spirits.' He glances at her expectantly. 'That's my attempt at ravishing wit.'

Miss Fairweather obliges him with a charming laugh. Whether it's genuine or the result of much practice, Charley can't quite tell.

TWELVE

The streets outside Euston Station are ankle-deep in slush. 'Where do you live?' asks Charley. 'I'm not interrogating, just wondering how far you have to go.'

'Covent Garden.'

'You'll want a cab, then. Don't worry, I'll pay the fare. In fact, I'll ride along, if it's all the same to you. We don't have to converse.'

But she's changed moods yet again; in the close confines of the cab she becomes almost chatty. 'And where is "your wife's house", as you insist on calling it?'

'Millbank. I think I'll spend the night in my office, though.'

'Oh? Does this mean you've been a bad boy, and she's banished you? Or is it some clever ploy, designed to make me feel sorry for you and offer you a place to stay?'

This tantalizing prospect gets Charley blushing again; luckily, the lamp at the front of the cab doesn't cast enough light to betray him. 'Neither. I have other cases to investigate, that's all. I want to get an early start.'

'Oooh, *other cases*! Something mysterious and exciting, I hope? I'm sorry I wasn't able to provide more in the way of mystery and excitement.'

In truth, she provides quite enough of both, but it doesn't seem proper to say so. 'I've had plenty of those in my policing career. Now I'm content with tracking down missing dogs and wayward husbands.' And murderers, he might add, but he doesn't care to open that box. Bad enough to have the papers trumpeting all the details of Rosa's demise, for the public to gasp and shiver over. The dead deserve a little dignity.

When they reach the Theatre Royal, Miss Fairweather raps on the roof and the cab comes to a halt. 'I'll just get out here.'

'Are you appearing at the theatre?' asks Charley. 'Again, not interrogating, just asking.'

He detects a trace of bitterness in her laugh. 'I wish I were. No, my lodgings are nearby, but I make it a habit never to reveal exactly where. I can't have all those admirers flocking to my door, you know.'

'No. Of course not.' Charley climbs from the cab and helps her down. He nods at the building across the street – two adjoining stucco houses with an officer in an oilskin cape out front, standing smartly in the glow of the gas lamp like a costumed actor posing in the limelight. All the other station houses boast blue lamps, but not this one; the Queen, who frequently attends the theatre, found it somehow offensive and ordered it replaced. 'That's where I got started on my policing career. Bow Street Station.'

'You weren't a Runner, surely?'

Charley gives an embarrassed grin. 'I was, in fact.' It hurts to admit it, for it was so long ago – nearly thirty years, now – that it makes him seem ancient.

'You must have lied to them about your age.'

'Well, I had to; they don't normally take ten-year-olds, you know.'

This time her laugh is clearly genuine, though a little shaky from the cold. She wraps her shawl about her more tightly. 'I should go.'

'Would you like my coat?'

'No, thank you. I'll be fine. Good luck with your cases, Inspector.'

She moves off, but he stays put, watching to see which direction she'll take. She catches him at it and angrily waves him off. With an apologetic shrug, he reenters the cab and signals the driver to go on. When he glances back, she's standing in the same spot, waiting for him to pull out of sight.

While it may be true that she doesn't want her admirers to

know where she lives, Charley senses there's more to it than
that. Despite the fact that it boasts the city's most prestigious
playhouse, Covent Garden is hardly a high-class neighborhood.
To be sure, the Lowther Arcade, with its elegant shops, is close
by. But Her Majesty's Theatre – also known as the Royal Italian
Opera – is flanked on one side by the sprawling, chaotic produce
market, which threatens to overwhelm it, and on the other side
by the gin palaces and teeming tenements of Drury Lane and
Great Wild Street.

If Miss Fairweather's lodgings are in one of those blighted
byways, it's easy to understand why she would want to
discourage visitors. And if Mr Dickens was responsible, even
in part, for putting her in such straitened circumstances, it's no
wonder she holds a grudge against him. No wonder, too, that
she was so reluctant to pay Charley that extra pound; he wishes
now that he could return it.

When he enters his chilly office, he finds no flood of letters
requesting his services, only a second appeal from the swell
who lost his wallet; this time, it's his watch that's missing. With
a sigh, Charley sets about building a fire in the grate. He wishes
he'd had the cab stop at a coffee stall. But perhaps it's just as
well; chances are, the stuff wouldn't have been worth drinking,
anyway. If only Jane had bought him a coffee mill and a roasting
pan for Christmas, instead of that pathetic smoking jacket.

It's probably just as well, too, that he has no new cases; this
way, he's free to pursue the only investigation he really cares
about at this point. In the morning, Charley makes his way back
to Sweeney Smoot's so-called surgery. He carries, bundled under
one arm, the coat and trousers that Neck left behind when he
fled the Seminary. Charley is fairly certain that the villain will
neither return Dr Smoot's clothing nor pay him for his services.
It's only fair, then, to give him Neck's coat and trousers, which
are of good quality – certainly far better than anything the
doctor could afford. Perhaps when Neck claimed that he was
involved in a lucrative scheme, it wasn't just an idle boast.

To his surprise, halfway there he crosses paths once again
with young Constable Mull. 'Well, lad! You're coming up in
the world; they've put you on day patrol already?'

Mull gives a sheepish grin. 'Only because 'tis the holidays, and all the married men are out sick.'

'Hmm, yes. I've pulled that one myself a time or two.'

The constable eyes the bundle of clothing. 'Still no clients to speak of, then?'

'Why do you say that?'

'Eh, no offense, sir, but if you're reduced to pawning your clothes . . .'

Charley laughs. 'A sharp observation, Mr Mull, but unfortunately quite wrong. These were left at Madame M'Alpine's by the notorious Mr Neck, who fled the scene wearing nothing but a shirt. Well, actually, he also had my handcuffs. And a bullet in his back.'

'You shot him?'

'Not fatally, I'm afraid.'

'Where is he now?'

'Good question. I'm hoping Dr Smoot will have the answer.'

'Do you need any help, Inspector? I've naught else in particular to see to.'

Though Charley would, of course, be fine on his own, he can see how eager the boy is to do some real policing, to get his hands dirty, to make a difference. He remembers that feeling, as vividly as if it were yesterday, and he misses it. 'It wouldn't hurt,' he says. 'You never know what we might find.'

What they find is, indeed, something they never counted on.

At first, there's no indication that anything is amiss. The entrance door is locked, just as before, and Charley deals with it in the same fashion. Constable Mull watches, fascinated, as Charley plies his picks. Wistfully, he says, 'Could I learn how to do that, do you suppose?'

'I don't see why not,' says Charley. 'There's just one problem.'

'What's that?'

'Well, if you get good at it, you'll have to change your name.'

'Change my name?'

'Coppers are fond of nicknames, you know – particularly ones involving bad puns. I can almost guarantee they'll dub you *Un*lockin'var.' Charley begins singing softly, so as not to alert anyone within, 'Oh, Unlockinvar is come out of the west/Throughout all the city, his skills were the best/And save his good lock picks, he weapons had none—'

Lochinvar has to cover his mouth with one hand to stifle the snickers. Grinning himself, Charley slips through the door and into the entryway, where he pauses, sniffing the air. Someone's been burning something – a roast, it smells like. A pity; the sort of folk who live here can scarcely afford to ruin a good chunk of meat. But when he eases open the door to the doctor's office, he discovers the source of the smell. It's not a cut of beef or lamb that was left on the fire too long. It's a human body, burned to a crisp.

Charley is aware of Constable Mull bursting out through the entrance door and vomiting violently in the street, but he pays little attention. He's focused on the room, watching and listening for any sign of another presence. As before, the only thing moving is a mouse, heading for some sanctuary within the walls; it strikes Charley that there's something odd about the creature's appearance, but before he can decide what it is, the mouse disappears beneath the baseboard.

The charred corpse is sitting upright in a chair. Though it's burned beyond recognition from the waist up, from the knees down it's unscathed, and there's no mistaking the colorful but soiled Berlin wool slippers on the man's feet.

Constable Mull moves hesitantly up behind Charley. 'Who–who is it, Inspector?'

'Dr Smoot, I'm afraid. He's the one Neck came to, to have his wound treated.'

'Could Neck have done this to him, then, to shut him up?'

'I wouldn't put it past him, I know that. But it doesn't look like murder to me.'

'Eh, sorry, sir, but – I mean – what else could it be? Surely no one commits suicide by burning himself to death?' Mull moves closer to the blackened body and, though he looks ready to upchuck again at any moment, forces himself to examine it. He turns to Charley, his eyes wide with astonishment. 'You dunnot think – it couldn't be—'

'What?'

'Well, sir, you recall what became of Mr Krook in *Bleak House*.'

'You think it was spontaneous combustion, do you?'

'I dunnot know. 'Tis possible, isn't it?'

'Hmm. You said you'd seen quite a number of dead bodies, Mr Mull. Were any of them victims of spontaneous combustion?'

'No, sir.'

'I thought not. Why don't we see if we can't find some more . . . ordinary explanation? Now, if someone else committed the deed, he'd have doused the doctor with something flammable – say, lamp oil – and the whole thing would have gone up at once, right?' Clearly determined not to jump to any more conclusions, Mull considers this a moment, then cautiously nods.

One of the many useful items Charley carries in the generous pockets of his greatcoat is a folding knife. Crouching down next to the body, he picks with the point of the knife at the fragile, blackened remains of the doctor's coat pocket. 'But it looks to me as if the flames started here, and spread upward. Would you agree?'

'That would seem to be the case, yes, sir.'

'So, the question is, what was in that pocket?' He stands and surveys the room. On the deal table is a tobacco pouch and, next to it, several ill-made cigarettes. The floor is littered with blackened Congreve matches. Lying among them is a silver hip flask, which Charley retrieves and gives a shake – empty. 'Now, if Neck was here, he wouldn't have passed this up. It's worth at least a crown. I don't think he'd be likely, either, to lock the door behind him when he left.'

Charley hands the knife to Mull. 'Make a cut in the lining of his coat, near the hem, will you? I dare say that, like most of us, the doctor had at least one hole in his pocket; let's see whether anything fell through.' While the constable is busy with this, Charley dons his eyeglasses and inspects the area of the baseboard where the mouse disappeared.

A few minutes later, Mull says, 'Mr Field? Take a look.' He approaches, holding out one hand; in the palm are two unburnt matches, a shred of thin paper, some bread crumbs, and several dark objects the size of rice grains.

'Very thorough, Mr Mull; thank you.' Slightly embarrassed by the spectacles, he tucks them back in his pocket. 'Well, it's pretty clear now what happened here.'

'It is?'

'I'm willing to bet that it's neither homicide nor suicide. I think Dr Smoot was the victim of an unfortunate accident – an unlikely one, I admit, but perhaps not as unlikely as spontaneous combustion. You're not a smoker, are you, Mr Mull?'

'No, sir.'

'But you are familiar with phosphorus matches and how little it takes, sometimes, to get them going?'

'Yes, sir.'

'You think they could be set off by, say, a mouse chewing on them?'

'I suppose so.' Mull examines the evidence he holds in his hand. 'Eh, I see. Those are mouse droppings. The creature mun have been after a crust of bread or something, and while he was in there, he gave the matches a try. But would that be enough to start a fire?'

'It would if the pocket was full of cigarette papers. And if the fabric of the coat was greasy enough. And especially—' He holds up the flask. – 'if the doctor happened to spill some gin on himself. The poor blighter. He was probably too drunk to notice what was going on until it was too late. Apparently the mouse was luckier – though I'd say he got his fur singed a bit, judging from how much scraped off during his escape.' Charley gestures toward the mousehole and shakes his head ruefully. 'He and Neck are two of a kind – they wreak havoc, and then just scamper off to their hidey-holes.'

'At least you singed the villain's fur a little,' says Mull.

'Yes. Maybe if he's laid up for a while, it'll give me a chance to track him down. Well. I suppose you'll have to write up a report on all this. You want me to come with you?'

'If you dunnot mind, sir. I've never made a report on anything so drastic.'

'Well, a word of advice, for this case or any other: The less drastic you make it sound the better they'll like it. I would include the word *accidental* as often as possible.' Constable Mull says something in reply, but Charley doesn't catch it. He's thinking of Rosa's death, and how ready the coroner and his jury were to rule it suicide. He's thinking, too, about the power of words, about the profound effect one person can have on the life – or death – of another just by uttering the word *suicide* or *accident* rather than *murder*, *guilty* rather than *not guilty*. It's so much more simple and satisfying. Call an incident murder or suggest that a suspect may be innocent, and suddenly it requires a lengthy investigation, a trial, and considerable amounts of time and money. And if, in the end, a perfectly good suspect is found not guilty, it means that it's all been wasted effort; it means that the coppers failed to get their man.

'Inspector?' Lochinvar Mull is saying.

'Sorry. What?'

'I was just wondering – you said that the less drastic a case is the more they like it. But Inspector Barkley is always keen to have us put the cuffs on someone. He says that the more arrests we make the better it makes our division look.'

'That's so – as long as the case is cut and dried; they just don't want anything complicated. By the way, there's no need to mention my name in your report. We'll let them think you cracked the case alone; it'll earn you points, maybe even a little respect.'

'Thank'ee, sir. I could use some.'

'I believe it. It was easier, joining the force when I did, just as it was getting started. We were all fresh fish back then, floundering in the bottom of the same boat.'

'I suppose your old mates at the station house will be glad to see you.'

Charley laughs. 'I wouldn't count on it, my lad.'

The constables who are lounging about the Chelsea Division Headquarters greet him cordially enough, but the reception he gets from the burly, crook-nosed sergeant clerk is as frosty as the weather. As they're heading back out to Mull's beat, the boy says, 'Whatever has he got against you, sir, if you dunnot mind me asking?'

Charley gives a weary sigh. 'It's a long story, Mr Mull.'

'Those are always the best ones.'

'I'm surprised the other coppers haven't told you already. But it has been a year and, as Mr Dickens says, people have short memories.'

'Not the sergeant, apparently.'

'No. No, he's still nursing a grudge.' Charley heaves another sigh. 'Well, things do look pretty quiet out here; maybe I can relieve the tedium a little.'

If he served up just the meat of the matter, without all the trimmings, he could cover it with very few words: In his usual ferrety way, he had refused to let go of a case, and because of it, he was forced to resign, with ill feelings all around. But he knows the inquisitive Lochinvar won't be satisfied with that, so he begins his story with the incident that started it all – the poisoning of Mrs Bramble's husband.

Naturally, he has to recount in minute detail how he and the Scarecrow went about cracking the case, and naturally, Constable Mull is all ears. But the story doesn't get really interesting until the point at which Charley discovered the reason why Dr Benjamin's Panacea was so ubiquitous: It had been publicly endorsed by no less a personage than Lord Starkey, whose patrician profile actually appeared on advertising bills for the Panacea. *Well,* thought the hoi polloi, *if it's good enough for the likes of him, it's good enough for me.*

Of course, Starkey – who had lost nearly all his fortune through bad investments – was paid handsomely for his endorsement. The thing was, the baron's stern and mustachioed mouth had never actually touched a bottle of Dr Benjamin's. If it had, he would have suffered the same fate as those he had conned into buying the stuff – at best, severe stomach cramps; at worst, a slow and agonizing death.

Though Charley did his utmost to bring the man to justice, the long arm of the law couldn't quite manage to reach that high. No matter how strapped a baron may be, he's still a baron, and his peers will do everything in their considerable power to keep his name out of the courts or the crime columns.

Commissioner Mayne, who was becoming less concerned with crime than with his status in society, instructed Charley's superiors to muzzle him – which of course was like trying to muzzle a mad dog. When a verbal warning had no effect, the sergeant clerk and two of his cronies cornered Charley in a dark alley. Though they had meant to remain anonymous, it was easy enough to identify them the following day; one was missing a couple of teeth, one's eye was swollen shut, and the sergeant's Roman nose now looked more Egyptian – like the Sphinx's, to be precise.

'A week later, I was summoned by Commissioner Mayne himself and asked to resign. Well, I say *asked*, but it was more in the nature of an order. And there you have it. End of story.'

'But what about Starkey? He got away scot-free?'

Charley gives a sly grin. 'Not exactly. Like the mouse, he got his fur singed a little. I don't suppose you've been in London long enough to have seen the bills posted all about the city, advertising Dr Death's Panacea. They featured a remarkable likeness of Lord Starkey in a hooded cloak, with a scythe over his shoulder. We never did find out where those came from.'

'Eh, I cannot imagine,' says Constable Mull. 'But you know, that makes me think – what if we were to post bills like that with Neck's picture on them, offering a reward for information?'

'The coppers try that now and again; usually it's a waste of time. They're all torn down within a few hours. I'll probably have better luck talking to my old informants. In fact, if you'll excuse me, I'll start right now.' As Charley heads off down the street, a thought occurs to him, and he turns back. 'Being fresh fish, I don't suppose you'll manage to get home to Derbyshire at all during the holidays?'

'That I won't. I'm on duty nearly every night.'

'Any chance you could raise a glass with me and my wife on New Year's Day? Something without ardent spirits, of course.'

'I'd be honored. Only . . .'

'What?'

'Eh, aside from the uniform, I dunnot have much in the way of decent clothing.'

Charley hands over the coat and trousers that have been under his arm all this time. 'There,' he says. 'Now you do.'

THIRTEEN

hen Charley first joined the fledgling Detective Division – hard to believe it was over two decades ago – it seemed that nearly every week the names of Neck and his mates turned up in the route-papers that made the rounds from station house to station house. For a time, he and his pack of thieves – those who weren't incarcerated somewhere – worked out of the area of St Giles known as the Rookery. But then they were uprooted, along with several thousand other citizens – some law-abiding, some not – when half the lodging houses and night refuges were demolished to make way for the construction of New Oxford Street.

As far as the coppers are concerned, 'improving' an area in this way is like scratching at a nasty skin eruption; it only serves to spread the infection to other parts of the body. Neck's tribe became more nomadic, plying their trade in a new neighborhood every few months. As the likelihood of their being caught decreased, the scale of their crimes increased. When things grew too hot, they hooked it to some other town for a while. But, like swallows and spawning salmon, sooner or later they always returned to their breeding grounds.

Though the new thoroughfare cut out a good deal of proud flesh and drained off some of the infection, there are plenty of plague-spots remaining. Two years ago, Charley took Mr Dickens on a tour of the Rookery; the report published by the Great Man in his magazine, *Household Words,* drew a shocked response from his readers. But, as both Charleys have recently pointed out, people have short memories. Despite the existence of a Metropolitan Association for Improving the Dwellings of the Industrious Classes and a Society for Improving the Condition of the Laboring Classes, not to mention a Public Health Act and a Common Lodging Houses Act, conditions here look much the same now as they did then. It seems that folk are better at making up lofty-sounding names than at making an actual difference.

The narrow streets and alleys are still strewn with garbage, and the pigs are still rooting through it; the same drunks doze in doorways, the same scrawny, ragged children play an impoverished version of kickball with a rotting cabbage. Well, it's unlikely that they're the identical ones he saw two years ago – most of those drunks and many of the children and all of the pigs are no doubt dead by now – but they may as well be; it's the same little tragedy with a different cast.

The buildings that glower down on them resemble more than ever a ring of death's heads, with their siding like bleached bones and their windows like sightless eyes or rows of broken and blackened teeth. Though Charley doesn't venture inside, he's certain they're still packed with bodies of both sexes and all ages, curled up on bare floors that sag under their weight and threaten to send them plummeting into a cellar full of seepage from overburdened cesspools.

He wouldn't be surprised to find that the steep flight of stone steps descending into Rat's Castle has tumbled to ruin; it's been on the verge of it for years. But, no, it's still there, too. Charley makes his way carefully down the stairwell, remembering to duck when he reaches the Castle's doorway; his head is well acquainted with the slab of stone that perches over the entrance – one of the hazards of being a big man.

Somehow, even though it's underground, Rat's Castle has been spared the tide of sewage that has inundated most of the cellars hereabouts; perhaps its walls are better built. If so, they're the only things about the place that's well made. The tables and benches are close to collapse, as are some of the clientele – from drink or malnutrition or chronic illness, or some combination of the three. The pewter mugs are dented, the earthenware ones yellowed and cracked and mostly without handles – again, by and large, a fair description of the men drinking from them.

Charley's eyes rove the dimly lighted room, searching for familiar faces; he finds some, but not the one he's looking for. There's no point at all, of course, in shouting out, 'Anyone here seen Neck?' It would be like asking whether anyone there has stolen anything lately; the only response he's likely to get is a little raucous laughter and a lot of furtive looks.

Instead, he lays a crown atop what passes for a bar – two planks laid across two barrels – and tells the proprietor, a jolly cove known only as the Earl of Warwick, 'A glass of Yuletide cheer, sir, for all these fine lads!' This elicits a chorus of tenors and baritones belting out 'Hear, hear!' and 'Hurrah!' plus a sole basso roaring 'A toast! A toast to Inspector Bucket!'

Charley waves his hands aloft to quiet them and, to his gratification, they actually heed him. Though they may flout the law at every opportunity, they also respect it, when it plays fair with them. 'No, gentlemen, you may no longer call me Inspector. In case you haven't heard, the buggers threw me out; I'm tending my own backyard now, and not Scotland Yard. I'm what's known as a private enquiry agent.'

'What's that, then?' calls one of the tenors. 'You inspect privies, do you?'

More good-natured laughter from all, including Charley himself. 'I've been known to,' he admits. 'There was this case, not long ago, where a cove slid down one of the holes in an attempt to recover his wallet, succumbed to the fumes, and drowned in his own shite.' A true story, though it happened when he was still on the force. He's rewarded with a satisfying swell of groans and gagging sounds. 'The case I'm on now is more pleasant, but also more challenging. I'm hoping you men might give me a hand with it.' The room goes silent, as he knew it would. Respecting the law is one thing; actually helping it solve crimes is another.

'Not to worry,' says Charley. 'I'm not looking to run anyone in. The thing is, I've been hired by a mill owner up Yorkshire way. The poor blighter is dying of cancer. He's going to leave a fortune behind, and his only heir is a son he hasn't seen in years. Apparently, the lad went off to London and fell in with a bad crowd – so naturally I thought of you lot.' This prompts a round of laughter, and another round of drinks. 'Now, if I can crack this case, I'll come in for a pretty handsome fee – which I'm prepared to share with anyone who can help me find the missing heir.'

'What's his name, then?' asks a man in a faded Royal Navy coat that's been stripped of its buttons. 'Not that he's likely to still be using it.'

Charley consults his little book, just as if this is an actual case about which he's taken notes, and not a total fabrication – well, almost total. 'The old man is Gabriel Tufts. *Sir* Gabriel, in fact. The son started out as Thomas – though, as you say, he could be calling himself most anything now.' There's an outbreak of murmuring at the rear of the room. 'Someone recognize that name?' calls Charley.

A lanky young man at the farthest table raises his hand. 'I do, sir. I hail from Yorkshire mysen, and though I dunt know a Sir Gabriel Tufts, I've heard the name Tommy Tufts many times. He's a sort of a legend, up our way.'

'Oh? How's that?'

'Well, years ago, afore I was born, they convicted this Tommy Tufts of murder, and they hanged him. The only thing was, it didn't take. He survived it somehow, and they let him go free.'

The murmuring starts up again, louder now, and more wide-spread, and Charley hears the word *Neck* being tossed about as if it's a chestnut too hot to hold. 'You must be joking, gentlemen,' he says. 'Surely you're not suggesting that the heir to Sir Gabriel's fortune and the man we know as Neck are one and the same?'

'Well, sir,' puts in a small, scraggly fellow, 'I do hear that he's been bragging about how he's coming into a good deal of money soon.'

'Oh, dear,' says Charley. 'You don't suppose he knows about the inheritance already? If he contacts the old man of his own accord, there goes my fee.' He sighs and drains his cup of ale. 'Well, it can't be helped. If tracking down our Mr Neck were a simple matter, I'd have done it long ago, when I was still a copper. Thank you, boys; I appreciate your assistance, even though it'll likely prove useless.'

Like an actor who's confident of his skills, he makes a swift and undramatic exit; instead of applause he's followed by shouts of 'Good luck, Inspector!' and 'Happy New Year, sir!'

He doesn't get far before he hears footsteps behind him, padding through the mud and slush. Will it be the youth from Yorkshire, or the scraggly sot, or the sailor without a ship? 'Mr Booket?' calls a voice. Ah, the lad from God's Own Country.

Charley turns to him, feigning surprise. 'It's Mr Field, actually.'

'Sorry. Only I thought . . .'

'Folk tend to confuse fact and fiction, that's all. Is there something I can help you with?'

'Nay, sir. I thought happen I could help you. You see, I know where to find this Thomas Tufts, or Neck, or whatever you may call him.'

'Oh? You've come across him, have you?' Charley retrieves his notebook and pencil.

'Aye, sir.' The young man moves in closer and lowers his

voice. 'You won't let on it was mysen as told you? I don't fancy him coming after me.'

'If I nab him, my lad, he won't be coming after anyone, ever again.'

'All right, then. I seed him only yesterday, at a coffeehouse in Mincing Lane.'

'Near the Customs House?'

'Aye.'

'How on earth did you know it was him?'

'The bloke next to me said so; he used to be part of Neck's gang, till he got sluffed wi' it.'

It's a likely enough story, and Charley would like to believe it – after all, he has no other leads – but there's something about the lad's manner, the way he avoids Charley's gaze, that sets off that tiny alarm. 'Was he still bandaged up, where I shot him?' Charley pats his leg.

The boy doesn't even skip a beat. 'Aye,' he says gleefully. 'He had to use a crutch and all.'

'That's curious,' says Charley, 'considering I hit him in the shoulder.'

The lad's face falls. 'Oh.'

'You didn't see him at all, did you? In Mincing Lane or anywhere else.'

'Nay, sir.'

'You were just hoping to cozen me out of a shilling or two.'

'Aye, sir. Seethee, I've put nowt in my belly for several days now.'

'Except for ale, that is.'

'Only the round you bought. I was in there to get out o' the weather, is all.'

He's still stretching the truth, no doubt, but Charley is weary of lecturing lads like him – strong and willing rustics who left their homes and came here to make a mark on the world and were marked by it instead. Besides, he's only doing what Charley himself does so often – feeding folks a bunch of blarney in order to get what he wants. 'Well, come along, then,' he says. 'We'll top off all that ale with some coffee and a nice bowl of bean soup.'

*   *   *

There's a certain sort of copper who likes to badger the staff at small shops and eating establishments, just to show them who's in charge. Charley has never been one of those; he figures that anyone who runs such a place has trouble enough just making ends meet, without having to put up with overbearing customers.

But the coffee he's served at the chop house is so undeserving of the name that he can't bear to let the owner get away with it. Charley's in a cranky mood already, from having failed to track down his prey, and this just adds fuel to the fire. Still, he doesn't barge right up to the owner and start berating him. No, he waits until the Yorkshire lad has eaten his fill and departed and the tide of customers is at an ebb; then he takes the portly proprietor aside and politely but firmly demands the name and location of the coffee roaster who supplies him.

Charley has done enough walking for one day; he takes a cab to the roastery, which occupies the top floor of a warehouse near the London Docks. Despite the chill outside, the roasting-room is . . . well, roasting, and the reason is obvious: In the middle of the floor stands a contraption consisting of a perforated copper drum, roughly three feet in diameter, and beneath it a stove of sorts, filled with glowing charcoal.

There's a hand crank that rotates the drum, and the muscular fellow turning it is stripped to the waist and sweating profusely. His hair is as black and curly as Miss Fairweather's and his skin even darker; if hers is the color of a good ale, his is more like a cup of strong Mocha with a dollop of cream. Without slacking his efforts, the man calls, over the hail-like rattle of the tumbling beans, 'How may I help you, *senhor*? Forgive me for not stopping; the beans will burn.' His accent, too, is reminiscent of the best coffee – rich and exotic. No doubt he's also a product of Brazil.

The accent Charley settles on is more like a cup of Grey's tea – brisk and a bit tart, very different from the 'one of the lads' tone he used back at Rat's Castle. He perfected this one years ago, doing his impression of Commander Mayne for the amusement of the other Detective Branch boys, and he pulls it out whenever he needs to sound especially businesslike and no-nonsense.

'I'm opening a dining house,' he practically shouts, 'near the Inns of Court. Naturally I want to serve teas and coffee of good quality, but at the same time, I don't want to spend a fortune. I was told you could accommodate me.'

The fellow holds up his index finger in a 'one moment' gesture. He stops the drum, opens a door in the end, and tilts it. The fragrant contents tumble down a chute and into a giant metal bin already half filled with roasted beans. Mopping his brow with a bandana, the coffee man says, in a normal voice, 'I am sure that we can, *senhor*. You know that we do only the roasting? You will need to grind the beans yourself.' He shows his perfect white teeth in a laugh. 'Well, perhaps not you personally; you know what I am saying.' Picking up a wooden paddle, he stirs the beans so they'll cool evenly.

Charley maintains a dour, businesslike expression. 'Of course.' When he peers into the bin, the aroma is so luscious and powerful it nearly makes him stagger. 'You sell these by the pound, do you?'

'Yes, *senhor*. One shilling for the lighter roast; one and six for the darker.'

'Oh.' Charley backs away from the bin. 'Don't you have anything a bit . . . well, cheaper? Perhaps a – a mixture of some sort?'

The man's smile quickly fades. 'No, *senhor*. We sell only pure coffee.'

'Indeed? Perhaps I was misinformed.' He starts toward the door. 'Oh, well, there are plenty of other roasters in the city.' He's assuming that, if he threatens to go elsewhere, the man will change his tune.

He is wrong. The Brazilian just shrugs. 'You may try them, of course, *senhor*, but their prices will be much the same. So will the quality of their product.'

'No chicory or acorns, then? No horse peas?'

'No, *senhor*!' he says indignantly. Then, unexpectedly, the smile returns, but this time it's more sly and knowing. 'Ah, I understand now. You are trying to trick me. You are an inspector, *não é*?'

'I beg your pardon?' Charley was trying so hard not to look like a detective. Maybe he's been at it too long; maybe it's seeped into his skin somehow, like the ink on Mr Mumchance's hands.

'From the government, eh?' says the Mocha Man. 'We have been hearing for some time that you would begin inspecting coffee and bread and tea and such things. If anyone is adding chicory or horse peas or anything else, it is not the roasters, I promise you.'

Though Charley hasn't met many Brazilians, he's encountered coves from a lot of cultures, especially during the Great Exhibition, and as far as he can tell, no matter what their native language, their faces and eyes say pretty much the same things. This fellow is clearly telling the truth.

Charley doesn't bother enlightening him. There has indeed been talk of passing a Food Adulteration Act, but it hasn't happened yet; the mills of Parliament grind exceedingly slow. Still, if the coffee roasters want to think he's a government inspector, so much the better. It'll keep them honest.

The Inspector buys two pounds of the dark roast, in a pasteboard box, and solicits advice on how best to grind and brew the beans. On the way back to his office, he visits Mr Popper's pawnshop and comes away with not only a sturdy coffee mill but also a sleek silver-plated biggin pot with a wire strainer.

He spends most of the evening attempting to master the two devices. It begins to look as if Jane was right: Brewing beverages of any sort is beyond his capabilities. In his initial effort, the hot water fails to penetrate the ground coffee that he's spooned into the strainer; instead it cascades down the sides of the biggin and soaks into some of the faux paperwork on his desk.

Trained detective that he is, he deduces that he's ground the beans too fine and they're clogging up the strainer. He adjusts the mill for a coarser grind and tries again. This time, the water escapes faster than farthings through your fingers. After only four more abortive attempts, he manages to get the size of the granules just right. The water drains through in a leisurely fashion, and comes out the other side transformed into a potion so bracing and so beneficial that Dr Benjamin could bottle and sell it as a cure-all.

FOURTEEN

I f Inspector Bucket's Panacea is such a savory success, why in the world does he drop in at the local coffeehouse the next day and order a cup of their ersatz Mocha? And why does he repeat his folly in three other coffeehouses before the morning is out?

Well, truth be told, he doesn't actually drink more than a sip of the insipid stuff, nor does he add his usual healthy dollop of cream. Instead, he pours each of the servings of so-called coffee into one of the small glass jars he's brought with him. He labels the samples to show where they came from, secretes them in his greatcoat pocket, and delivers them to the studio of his friend and esteemed colleague, the Scarecrow.

As usual, the photographer looks as though he could use something bracing and beneficial. 'How thoughtful of you,' he says, 'bringing me not just one cup of coffee, but four.'

'I'm sorry, 'Sam. These are not for drinking; they're for testing. I'm assuming you have some magical way of determining what's in these – aside from the small percentage of actual coffee?'

The Scarecrow scratches his sparsely thatched skull. 'Well, I'd have no trouble if I could examine the ground beans themselves. Analyzing the brew will be a bit trickier. Luckily, there's sediment at the bottom; I can put that under the microscope. And if I take a little of the liquid and add a drop or two of hydrochloric acid and some potassium ferrocyanide, and then boil it—'

'Good, good,' says Charley. 'You do that. In the meantime, I'll fetch my grinder and my biffin and make you a cup of the real thing.'

Over the next few days, he divides his time between two very different lines of enquiry, one disappointingly fruitless, the other distressingly successful. The fruitless one involves flushing out all his old informants from whatever hole they're hiding in and squeezing them for information about Neck. The tool he uses may be a threat or it may be a bribe, whichever seems likely to work best, and sometimes both. All that squeezing yields nothing really juicy, only vague hints and speculations and inventions.

As he wanders about from dead end to dead end, he stops at every coffeehouse and grocer he passes, to collect a cup of Mocha or a bag of ground beans. This is the successful part of the investigation – more so than Charley would like, actually. Whether the Scarecrow runs his tests on the brew or the beans, his findings are equally damning and dismaying: not a single sample proves to be pure Arabica, or even Robusta. Not surprisingly, chicory is the most common contaminant, but the chemist also finds traces of wheat, rye, acorns, and mangel-wurzel, not to mention gypsum, coal, clay, lead, iron, tin, petroleum jelly, indigo, and arsenic. With each set of results, Charley is more grateful to Mrs Crumpet for persuading him to brew his own.

Thinking of Crumpet's Coffee-House, of course, leads him to thoughts of Miss Fairweather. She did say that, once he mastered the art of coffee-concocting, he should invite her over for a cup. But did she actually mean it, or was she just making conversation? Well, it scarcely matters, since he has no idea where to find her. Perhaps he could track her down if he tried hard enough; he is a detective, after all. Or perhaps not; perhaps he'd fail as miserably as he has with Neck.

Besides, he can't afford to spend all his time pursuing his own personal agenda; that won't pay the rent – which, by the way, is due next week. He's set aside most of his pension for that purpose, but it's not enough. Jane would lend him the remainder, of course, most likely even give it to him outright. But he'd sooner throw over the enquiry business altogether, and set up a coffee stall in Lumber Court Market. His wares would, of course, be one hundred percent pure.

But he's not ready to give up his investigating career just yet. Perhaps it would help to have a business card, like Professor Sledge's. After leaving the Scarecrow's studio, he stops in at a stationer's and orders a hundred cards imprinted with a condensed version of his newspaper advertisement. Then he returns to his chilly office and builds a fire, using as kindling the circulars that make up the entirety of the day's post.

He hasn't spent much time at the Holywell Street house lately, but he'll have to put in an appearance tomorrow; it's New Year's Day. *Appearance* is the appropriate word, since he will only appear to be there. Though his body will be present, his spirit will be elsewhere – rather like a séance in reverse. But of course that's what matters most to Jane and the mother: appearances. His wife will have invited all her friends – who might be more accurately called acquaintances – to drop by, and they must go away believing, as Jane herself seems to, that everything in the Field household is as it should be.

No doubt she'll expect him this evening, as well, to help her usher in 1854 – not that it needs any ushering; the years keep on coming, whether you welcome them or not. Truth be told, Charley enjoyed New Year's Eve a lot more when he was a green constable, patrolling the streets, making the rounds of the public houses, accepting a small glass of cheer at each, helping the harmless drunks find their way home, locking up the unruly ones.

He does his best to relive those days, dropping in at every taproom and tavern between Ebury Square and Millbank. He doesn't lock up any of his fellow carousers, of course, but he does escort an old trouper to his lodgings, both of them warbling the whole way, 'Mid pleasures and palaces though we may roam/Be it ever so humble, there's no-oh place like home!' He also breaks up a brawl by the simple expedient of flattening both the participants. Though neither is exactly a Stunning Smithers, it's gratifying to know that he still packs a pretty decent punch. For once, he allows the publican to stand him a glass of grog; he's earned it, after all.

By the time he reaches Regent Street, he could use a bit of escorting himself, but he's walked this route so often, his feet find their own way with no help from his muddled head. He'd been rather hoping that Jane and the mother would tire of waiting for him and for the New Year, and just go to bed at their usual early hour, but no. They've obviously prepared for the ordeal by taking a nap, for they look preternaturally alert – rather the way a copper looks when he's about to collar some dangerous fugitive.

'There you are,' says Jane, collaring him. 'I wasn't sure you'd turn up.'

'Have I ever failed to?' says Charley.

'Yes,' says the mother. 'Twice, in fact.' Leave it to her to keep score. No doubt the transgressions are recorded in her little book of Charley's crimes.

'Well, I'm here now.' He glances at the mantel clock. 'And with fifteen minutes to spare.' He winks at Hanora, who is setting the table with champagne and glasses, and she hides a smile. Before meeting Jane, Charley had never tasted champagne, and he could easily have gone on living without it, but his wife considers the sparkly stuff a symbol of good breeding and worldliness, like carrying a fringed parasol, or referring to their neighborhood as the West End when it's really just Millbank. Well, he had his share of brandy and spiced ale on the way here; it won't hurt him to humor her.

When, like Falstaff, they have heard the chimes at midnight, they clink their glasses. Charley clinks the way he shakes hands – a bit too forcefully – and draws a reproving look from his wife, followed by an expectant one. Charley knows well enough that he's supposed to say a word or two to solemnize the occasion, but he's neglected to prepare, and his brain seems to have deserted him.

Hanora, who is refilling his glass, murmurs, 'May the saints protect ye;' he seizes the cue like a drowning man grasping at a life preserver. 'May the saints protect ye!' he booms. 'And sorrow neglect ye, and bad luck to the one who doesn't respect ye!' As this doesn't seem to be going down very well, he dredges up another of the innumerable Irish blessings he's learned in public houses: 'May you always have a clean shirt, a clean conscience, and a guinea in your pocket!'

The mother stares at him incredulously for a moment, then puts down her glass and shuffles off to her chambers without so much as a goodnight.

'That was very . . . colorful, Charley,' says Jane. Well, that's better than *vulgar*, which he sometimes thinks is her favorite word. 'I trust you'll be a little less colorful tomorrow, when we have company?'

'Not to worry, my dear. I shall be as drab as a sparrow.'

His choice of metaphor is an apt one, for the next day the house resembles nothing so much as an oversized bird-feeding table. To keep himself amused – god knows there's little else – Charley makes a game of identifying the various species as they come and go.

Reverend Grimstone is, of course, a crow – all clad in black, cawing with laughter at his own feeble jokes, his beady eyes scanning the delicacies spread upon the table, searching for the most desirable titbits. Mrs Snooks is a dead ringer for a partridge – the sort so often and so fancifully pictured in a pear tree – down to her russet bodice and the plumes projecting from her head. Judge Jellineck with his bristling side-whiskers bears an uncanny resemblance to a glum old owl. The buxom Miss Buffle can be nothing but a Pouter pigeon, and the gangly Mr Langley is so stork-like that Charley almost expects him to dip his long beak into his wine, instead of lifting the glass to his lips.

Of course the conceit can only divert him for so long; just as he's about to sneak out for a smoke, Hanora waylays him. 'Mr Field, there's a good-looking young fella at the door. Says you invited him to stop by.'

'Good lord, it's Lochinvar. I forgot about him.'

Hanora giggles. '*Lochinvar*?'

'Mr Mull to you. Show him in, will you? And no flirting, please; he's a mere babe.'

He had meant to let Jane know about Constable Mull in advance, but maybe it's better this way. If he'd broken the news last night or this morning, they would have had words, no doubt about it. She's always felt about Charley's friends the same way she does about tobacco and muddy boots: She can't stop him from having them, but she doesn't want him dragging them into the house. If Constable Mull is already here, however, she can hardly throw him out, nor is she likely to make a stink about it in front her own friends. Charley will catch it later, of course, but that's nothing new.

Constable Mull looks quite presentable in Neck's abandoned finery, though he's had to roll up the sleeves of the frock coat a bit. He peers anxiously at the flock of visitors flitting about the dining room. 'I didn't know there'd be so many people, sir. I'm not much of a mingler.'

He's also, as Charley recalls, not much of a drinker. But Hanora, overhearing the lad's comment, presents him with some wine and a fetching smile. 'They're easier to bear,' she whispers, 'once you've had a glass or two.'

Though the constable eyes the wine a bit dubiously, Charley is betting he'll have a few sips at least, not wanting to seem a mollycoddle or a poor sport, particularly in front of an attractive young woman. Sure enough, he gives it a try. ''Tis good,' he says, licking his lips.

'For what my wife spent on it,' says Charley, 'it had better be.' Though Young Lochinvar would no doubt be happier in the company of Hanora, Charley is obliged to pry the two apart; if Jane sees them together, the girl will be in for a royal dressing-down. Quelling his craving for a pipe of tobacco, Charley plays the role of host and introduces his protégé around the room.

Jane manages to be reasonably gracious. The other ladies chirp and twitter over Mr Mull as if he's eight years old, not eighteen. The Reverend Crow goes on at astonishing length about the week he once spent in Derbyshire and everything he saw and did there, as if trying to convince Mull that the place is well worth a visit, when the boy has lived there all his life until now.

Unable to get in a complete sentence of his own, Mr Mull sips persistently at his wine and doesn't object when Hanora gives him a refill – and another conspiratory smile. When Judge Owl learns that the lad is a constable, he launches into a lecture about the need to administer justice with a heavy hand, in order to discourage crime; Charley suspects it's aimed more at him than at educating the young constable. Mr Stork, who is in politics, recounts in painful detail the gripping events surrounding Lord Palmerston's resignation and subsequent reinstatement.

When Charley sees Lochinvar's eyes getting a glazed look, he steers him toward the buffet table. The lad's legs seem a bit wobbly; in fact, he collides with one corner of the table, rattling the glassware and sloshing the punch. Charley beckons to Hanora. 'You'd better take him into the kitchen,' he murmurs. 'Give him a cup of tea or something. I shouldn't have let him drink so much on an empty stomach.'

But Mr Mull seems transfixed, staring at the center of the table, which is occupied by an enormous joint of cold roast beef. Charley can guess, from the distressed look in the boy's eyes, what's going through his head. He's not seeing a roast at all; he's seeing the charred remains of Dr Smoot. Charley puts an arm around the constable's shoulders and hustles him toward the kitchen doorway, but it's too late. Mr Mull noisily deposits his share of the excellent wine on the edge of Jane's treasured oriental carpet.

Luckily, most of the others are too busy stuffing themselves and chattering to notice – except for Jane, of course, who has been keeping an eagle eye on the interloper ever since he arrived. Charley and Hanora exchange guilty grimaces. 'Why don't you be after making the tea, sir,' whispers the house girl, 'and I'll clean this up?'

Once they've gained the kitchen, Charley is tempted to just keep going, but he can't abandon Hanora to bear the brunt of Jane's wrath. In between groans, Mull stammers out an abject apology, while Charley swears that it's nothing at all and that in any case he himself is the one at fault. Then, leaving the boy in Hanora's capable hands, he returns to face the music.

You would think that, in a room full of guests, Jane could only do just so much chastising, but she somehow manages to accuse him of having lost his mind and of trying to utterly destroy her social life while simultaneously smiling and glancing about brightly, nodding at each of the guests in turn, assuring them that, no, she hasn't forgot them.

At least she's got it out of her system. Once the birds have flown off to other feeding grounds and Constable Mull has recovered enough to slip away, she is content to punish Charley with silence for the rest of the evening, and to pointedly ignore him – which is somehow different from the manner in which she normally ignores him. She does deign to interact with him briefly when she retrieves a small envelope from her pocket and hands it to him. 'This arrived yesterday, by messenger. I'd have given it to you sooner, but I didn't want you using it as an excuse to rush off somewhere.'

Charley sighs. The fact that it required a messenger suggests that it might be urgent, but there's little point in saying so. Even before he reads the note, he knows who it's from; he recognizes the careful, stiff lettering and the tasteful, cream-colored stationery. It's from the same gent who begged Inspector Bucket to solve the mysterious case of the misplaced wallet and the wayward watch. Only this time, it's not mere money that's missing, or some personal possession. It's his son.

FIFTEEN

I f he had suspected that Eustace Pillbeam, the author of the note, was such a wealthy man, Charley would have answered the very first summons. Pillbeam's residence in St James's is the grandest in a row of grand houses that, if they had noses, would look down them and sniff disdainfully at the little people scurrying about in the street below – most of whom are fulfilling the practical needs of the very houses that lord it over them so.

Charley assumes that, with all Pillbeam's money and pretensions, he'll have a full complement of servants, from scullery maids to a valet. To his surprise, the door is answered not by a butler or a footman but by a frazzled-looking housekeeper. 'Inspector Bucket,' says Charley, 'to see Mr Pillbeam.'

The woman's mouth falls open. Clearly she's a devoted Dickens reader. 'Inspector Bucket! Such a pleasure to meet you!'

'Well, technically it's Detective Field, but your master will likely know me by my professional name.'

'Oh. I see. And is he . . . will he be expecting you, sir?'

'Well, I don't have an appointment as such, but I did receive this.' Charley holds up the envelope.

She takes it gingerly, reads the addressee's name, and gives him another awestruck look. 'Inspector Bucket. My goodness. Will you please wait here, sir? I'll see if he's available.'

Charley barely has time to take in the lavishly decorated and furnished entrance hall before the woman is back. 'I'm so sorry, Inspector. Mr Pillbeam says . . . he says that he never contacted you, and that he knows nothing about it.'

He senses something suspicious in the woman's apologetic manner. 'Nothing about what?'

'Well, about . . . about whatever it might be that you're investigating.'

Baffled, Charley backs out the door and slowly descends the steps. He's almost to the street when the woman comes after him, calling, 'Oh, Inspector. Don't forget your note!' As she hands it to him, she gives him a look that is clearly meant to be meaningful, but precisely what the meaning is, he can't quite determine. 'Perhaps you should read it again,' she says softly, then scurries back into the house.

When Charley is well out of sight, he takes the note from the envelope. The original message is just as he remembered it: *Sir: Please see me at your earliest convenience regarding the disappearance of my son.* A sentence has been added, however – hastily, from the looks of it, but in the same hand: *Meet me in the Square in a hour.*

What better way to occupy an hour than to purchase a couple of buttered muffins from a vendor – no coffee, thank you, not now that he knows what's likely to be in it – and share them with the pigeons in St James's Square? He keeps an eye out in the direction of Pillbeam's place. Though he still hasn't met the man, Charley expects to pick him out easily enough. These tycoons, as the Yankees call them, are all cut from the same cloth; the only thing that varies is the size.

But it's not Pillbeam who shows up; it's the Dickens-fancying housekeeper. She glances about furtively before approaching him. 'I can't stay long, sir. I'll be missed.'

'We will make it quick, then. I presume it was you who wrote the note, Miss—?'

'Mrs Worthing. Yes, sir. All three notes, in fact. I didn't think you weren't likely to come if summoned by a housekeeper, and Mr Pillbeam would never hire you himself.'

'And why is that?'

'Well, sir, it's hard to explain.' It's clear from the way she wrings her hands that she's not one of those servants who relish sharing their employers' secrets. 'You see . . . well, in his eyes, Master Davy – that's his son – can do no wrong. *David*, he insists on being called now. He says he's not a child any longer. But he still behaves like one much of the time.'

'You think Davy stole the wallet and the watch, then.'

'I don't like to say so, sir. Mr Pillbeam would never consider that possibility, of course; he was sure one of us was to blame, and he starting letting us go, one by one – first the butler, then the valet, then the maid of all work. I thought maybe if you investigated—'

'I'd prove that Davy was the culprit?'

Mrs Worthing lowers her eyes and nods faintly. 'Yes, sir.'

'And now the boy himself is missing?' Charley pulls out his notebook. 'When was the last time you saw Master Davy?'

'Three days ago, sir. He was acting a bit odd, but I didn't think much of it. He's been like that a lot lately.'

'Odd? In what way?'

'Sort of . . . twitchy, you might say.'

'Twitchy.'

'Yes, sir. Are you a coffee drinker?'

'I am, in fact, but—'

'You know how you get when you've had one cup too many?'

Oh, yes, Charley knows very well how he gets: Edgy. Irritable. Twitchy. 'Did he seem worried, or fearful at all?'

'Maybe a little.' She glances about again, then lays a hand gingerly on his arm. 'You won't let on that I've told you any of this, will you, sir?'

'I promise. Just a few more questions. Are you in charge of the post?'

'Yes, sir; I see all the letters that come and go.'

'Has he received anything lately from an unknown source?'

'You mean . . . you mean a ransom note, don't you? That's what Mr Pillbeam thinks, too – that Davy's been abducted. He's talked to the police; they say there's nothing they can do until the kidnappers contact him.'

'And no one has.'

'No, sir.'

'Well, people are abducted for reasons other than ransom. Down at the docks, able-bodied men are shanghaied every day.'

Mrs Worthing gives a thin smile. 'With all respect sir, I doubt anyone would want Master Davy on their crew. He's not much of a one for work.'

'Hmm. Perhaps he's fallen in with bad company, then. Have you seen him with anyone unfamiliar or disreputable-looking?'

'Well, his friends are a lot of roisterers and layabouts, but I don't know that you'd call them disreputable; they are from good families.'

'Can you give me names?'

'You're not going to interrogate them, are you, sir? If you do, word will get back to Mr Pillbeam, and I'll be out of a job.'

'I'm afraid I may need to, Mrs Worthing. You haven't given me much to go on.'

'Maybe this will help.' She pulls from her apron pocket a small photographic portrait of the boy, in an oval metal frame. 'I borrowed it from Mrs Pillbeam's room; please be sure to return it.'

Mrs Worthing is right; a press gang would have to be pretty desperate to want Master Davy. The lad is scrawny as an alley cat and his face is so pitted as to resemble the surface of the moon – from smallpox, no doubt. Though vaccination is commonplace now – compulsory, in fact – a decade ago it was regarded with suspicion. Well, at least he'll be easy to recognize. 'Thank you. But I still need some indication of where to start looking.'

'I don't know whether this will tell you anything.' She dips into the pocket again and comes up with something wrapped in a handkerchief. 'When I was cleaning one of Master Davy's frock coats, I found it in the pocket.' She unfolds the cloth to reveal a handful of what look like tea leaves.

'Hmmm.' Charley examines the leaves, feels them, smells them, even tastes them, then gives a satisfied nod. 'Now we're getting somewhere.'

Now, if what Mrs Worthing discovered actually were tea leaves, that would tell Charley very little. But if his nose and tongue can be trusted, and they usually can, the substance in the handkerchief is in fact shredded opium – or what remains of it after the good stuff is cooked out.

Charley is no stranger to the smoky, shadowy world inhabited by opium smokers – Lotos-eaters, he calls them, after Mr Tennyson's poem. In his policing days, he was always sure of finding at least one notorious thief there, watching his ill-gotten gains go up in smoke. When such fellows are collared, they're generally quite agreeable and docile – at least until the effects of the drug wear off. Charley tried a pipe once, just to see what the attraction was; it was pleasant enough, but he didn't much like the prospect of the tables being turned, of one of those thieves finding *him* there, with his brain befuddled and his defenses down.

As they have done with fogs and slums and crazed murderers, the penny bloods greatly exaggerate the presence of opium dens and the threat posed by them. Charley has encountered fewer than a dozen in his long career; most were small and innocuous, tucked away in one room of a Chinese boarding house or in the rear of some shop that sells oriental foods and fabrics. The most-frequented puffer's paradises are in the Isle of Dogs, but those draw mainly Malays and Lascars from the East India Docks. Bohemians and theatre folk and upper-crust gents who are slumming tend to prefer the slightly less gritty surroundings of Bluegate Fields – also known as Tiger Bay, after the tigress-like tarts who lurk there, waiting for prey.

The Fields was once quite a prosperous neighborhood, but the docks have had a bad influence here, too. Though you're not quite as likely to be bludgeoned and stripped of your clothes and possessions as in the Isle of Dogs, it's not out of the question. In fact, the area boasts one of the most dangerous dens of vice in the city: Ah Choy's, a chaotic combination of gambling hall, smoking saloon, and molly house.

In a way, your typical pleasure palace is no different than, say, a department store; it caters to a core of 'regulars' who provide most of its business. Ah Choy's, however, is more like a shearing shed, or perhaps an abbatoir; the poor lambs who are lured there by gay ladies always emerge many pounds lighter – if they emerge at all. Its reputation is such that coppers do their best to avoid it; certainly they wouldn't think of going in there alone. But Charley is no longer a copper, and has no fellow constables to call upon.

If Davy Pillbeam has indeed disappeared, and if opium is

involved, this is a likely place to start looking. It won't do, of
course, to just go barging in; he'd never get past the Chinese
Colossus who guards the door. This seven-and-a-half foot giant
was once a star attraction on the stages of England and Europe;
when the novelty wore off, Ah Choy hired him as both a means
of drawing people in and of chucking them out when
necessary.

Charley strolls over to the tavern called the Coal Whipper's
Arms and strikes up an acquaintance with the most pitiful-
looking of the painted ladies who loiter there; he figures she
needs the business. With the girl – whose name is Anna – on
his arm, he saunters into Ah Choy's unchallenged. Once they're
ensconced in a private room Charley pays her off, then excuses
himself and goes poking about the premises until the scent of
burning opium leads him to the lair of the Lotos-eaters.

With all the money Mr Choy rakes in, you'd think he could
provide more pleasant surroundings. There's only one bed as
such, occupied by four slack-jawed smokers. The rest are
sprawled on filthy mats or on the bare floor. The room is perme-
ated by a bluish mist and the walls and ceiling are gray-washed
with the residue from a thousand pipes. But of course the coves
who come here don't care much about atmosphere. The moment
they begin to play the bamboo flute, they're no longer at Ah
Choy's, or even in England; they're transported to Lotos Land.

A haggard woman kneels in front of the fireplace, cooking
the shredded opium, which is spread on a square of canvas
stretched over the top of an ordinary saucepan. Though her skin
has a yellowish cast, Charley suspects it's not a racial trait but
a sign of illness, for her features are those of an Englishwoman.
At a dilapidated table sits a small Asian man with a queue and
a grimy embroidered jacket; he's preparing the cooked opium
for smoking.

It's a surprisingly delicate, elaborate process. First he heats
the tip of a thin-bladed dagger over a spirit lamp; then he dips
the blade into a porcelain cup and lifts out a small blob of what
looks very much like treacle. He holds it over the lamp until it
hardens, then dips out another layer and does the same. When
he's accumulated a ball the size and shade of a roasted coffee
bean, he deposits it in the clay bowl of a pipe with a bamboo

stem, lights it with a sliver of wood and, like a priest adminis-
tering the Eucharist, places the holy object in the trembling
hands of an eager communicant.

As Charley weaves his way among the limp forms of the
Lotos-eaters, he gives each a glance; one is all it takes, in most
cases. He rules out two of them right away, since they're women.
And, unless Master Davy has donned the tarry canvas clothes
of a sailor, half a dozen others aren't worth a second look.

But several of the men wear more genteel attire: flannel
trousers, linen shirts, checked waistcoats. Charley lingers a bit
longer over these, scanning their faces. There's no need to
compare them to the photograph provided by Mrs Worthing;
even allowing for the changes that a drug-induced stupor may
produce, not one of them remotely resembles Davy.

To his surprise, though, Charley finds two of the faces quite
familiar. One belongs to a celebrated stage actor whose name
you would surely recognize if I revealed it, though I won't; for
all we know, this may be his first and only visit to an opium
den. Everyone is entitled to one mistake. The other face might
be drawn from the pages of Mr Lavater's *Science of Physiognomy*,
for it strongly supports the theory that a criminal *looks* like a
criminal.

Though Charley's last encounter with Bad Hat Henry was
five years ago or more, there's no forgetting the fellow's face
– it would not look out of place on an orangutan – or his
despicable deeds, which run the gamut from beating helpless
animals to slitting throats. In fact, Charley had no intention of
forgetting him; Henry occupies a prominent place in his list of
Wrongdoers Who Got Away, lagging behind only Neck and
Neckless. And if that's not enough of a reminder, there's always
the six-inch scar that decorates one of Charley's forearms.
Seizing a fistful of shirt and waistcoat, he pulls the muzzy
miscreant to his feet.

'Is it time?' murmurs Bad Hat Henry.

'Yes,' says Charley. 'It's time.' Time the man was locked up,
or maybe hanged. Though the inspector has always been willing
to go easy on those who show some remorse and some promise
of improvement, Henry used up all his chances long ago.

Charley wishes now that he'd got himself another pair of

handcuffs. But he may not need them; the prisoner seems quite content to follow wherever he's led. The man with the queue makes no objection, either; he barely registers their passing. It looks as if Charley may manage to get out of the place as effortlessly as he got in.

It doesn't look that way for long. Just as he's about to open the door, it flies inward, nearly knocking him off his feet. Apparently his new friend Anna has sensed something amiss and summoned help, for standing in the doorway – filling it completely, in fact – is the Chinese Colossus.

SIXTEEN

The Colossus has to duck his head quite low in order to enter the room. It's the perfect opportunity for Charley to ram his walking stick into the giant's midsection and then make a run for it. But after five years of hunting Bad Hat Henry, he's not about to leave the bloke behind. 'This man is a notorious criminal!' he announces to the room at large. 'I'm turning him over to the police!'

The Colossus is not inclined to discuss the matter. He yanks Charley's stick from his hand and tosses it aside, then wraps his massive arms around the detective as if greeting a long-lost friend – though he must have a serious shortage of friends if he's accustomed to squeeze them this tightly. Charley is lifted off his feet as easily as he himself lifted Rosa's daughter. Unable to move or protest or even breathe, he's carried like a sack of grain into the hallway and down the stairs to the rear exit, where he's flung into the soot-sprinkled, piss-laden snow that fills the alley.

He's had the wind knocked out of him in the ring more times than he can count, but that was thirty years ago. Now, it takes him a while to recover, and even then it hurts to breathe; the outsized oaf must have sprung one or more of his ribs. Well, that's nothing new, either. Groaning, he gets to his feet. There's probably no point in going back in there; Bad Hat Henry will be long gone, and in any case the Colossus would only throw him out again – or perhaps do him in.

Charley is no coward, but neither is he a fool. He and Henry will surely cross paths again, when the odds are more in his favor. Besides, he's learned what he needs to know – that he'll have to look elsewhere for Davy Pillbeam. When Charley does find him, the little blighter and his doting da had better be very grateful. For one thing, they're going to buy him a new walking stick.

In terms of both atmosphere and clientele, the place known as Poppy's is several steps up from Ah Choy's. The entryway and the smoking saloon are decorated with ornate mirrors, cloisonné vases, stylized statuary, silk hangings painted with Chinese characters. Poppy himself is a cordial chap of indeterminate age who speaks perfectly acceptable English, not the pidgin variety. Though he dresses in the traditional robe and baggy trousers – after all, what self-respecting smoker would trust an opium master who looks like a bank clerk? – he forgoes the queue, preferring to shave his entire head.

Poppy has proven helpful to the police more than once, and Charley and his colleagues have always treated him with a certain amount of respect – the sort of respect that doesn't depend on being seven-and-a-half feet tall. 'I apologize for my appearance,' says Charley. 'I had a bit of an altercation with the Chinese Colossus.'

'Altercation?' says Poppy. 'Do you mean a fight?'

'No, no, I've been in many fights, and this wasn't one, I assure you.'

'You went into Ah Choy's alone? Why would you do such a thing?'

'I'm trying to find this boy.' Charley shows him the daguerreotype.

Though Celestials are known for being inscrutable, it's clear that Poppy recognizes the face. 'Is he wanted for a crime?'

'Only if you consider being stupid and lazy a crime. When was he here?'

'He came two days ago,' says Poppy. 'He gave me a sovereign and said to keep filling the pipe until the money ran out.'

'And you obliged? Do you realize the boy is only seventeen?'

Poppy grimaces; so much for inscrutability. 'If I had, I would have thrown him out.'

'Even worse, his father is a real big shot. That is to say—'

'I know the meaning of the phrase. Do you think the father will make trouble for us?'

'He might. No doubt he has some very influential friends. But maybe I can avoid telling him where I found his son.'

'I would be grateful, Inspector. And I can be very generous in showing my gratitude.'

'So I've heard. Well. The first order of business is to get him out of here.'

For a novice like Davy, the effects of a pipe can last several hours. Unfortunately, he's starting to stir and, when Charley and Poppy lift him to his feet, he protests. 'What're you doing?' he mumbles. 'Where're you taking me?'

Charley knows better than to say *To your father*. 'To the privy.'

'Oh,' says Davy, and smiles dreamily. 'Thank you.'

Though even the most shabby hackney coach bears only a superficial resemblance to a privy, Davy seems unable to make the distinction. As soon as the cab door closes, he starts unbuttoning his trousers. 'No, no,' says Charley. 'Not yet.'

The rocking of the cab makes his injured ribs feel like knives stabbing him. It also throws Davy off balance and onto the seat. Puzzled, the boy pats the upholstery. 'There's no hole in this privy.'

'I lied,' says Charley. 'It's a coach. We're going to visit the Queen.'

'Oh, good. I was just dreaming about her, you know. She's very pretty.' Davy curls up in the corner of the seat and closes his eyes. 'Let me know when we get to Buckingham Palace, will you?'

With any luck, he'll sleep all the way to St James's. If necessary, Charley can administer a dose of the opium tincture provided by Poppy, who also turned over a wallet that Davy gave him for safekeeping – Mr Pillbeam's, no doubt.

The boy is not asleep after all. He murmurs, 'My father won't be there, will he? I get nervous when he's around. I feel as if I can never do anything right.'

Charley knows the feeling well, thanks to Jane and the mother. 'Indeed? From what I hear, your father thinks you can do no wrong.'

'Well, but, that's the thing, isn't it? How am I supposed to live up to that?'

'So, you're doing your best to show him that he's mistaken.'

Davy gives a wry grin. 'Yes. Yes, I suppose I am.'

When the cab lets them out at Pillbeam's place, Davy still needs a bit of support, and Charley provides it, ignoring the complaints from his poor ribs. Mrs Worthing greets them at the door. 'Oh, Master Davy! You had us so worried!'

For the moment, young Mr Pillbeam forgets his insistence on being called *David*; he seems content to be treated like a naughty boy who has run away from home or eaten too much marzipan. Charley passes him off to a maid, who helps him upstairs.

'How did you manage to find him, Inspector?' asks the housekeeper softly.

'Oh, I never divulge my methods, Mrs Worthing.' He hands her the daguerreotype and the bottle of laudanum. 'He's going to be sick for a while, almost as if he had the ague. Give him a spoonful of this, and decrease the dosage each day, until he's better.'

'Yes, sir. If you'll wait here, I'll fetch Mr Pillbeam.'

Though Charley dodged the housekeeper's questions deftly enough, her master is not so easily put off. Pillbeam wants a detailed account of all that transpired, as if he suspects the detective of inventing the whole episode and means to trip him up. Charley obliges, but omits the part about the Chinese Colossus; he has his pride, after all. Nor does he mention the name or the whereabouts of Poppy's establishment.

That's not good enough for Pillbeam. 'Inspector, I am a man of business. Now, I suppose you expect to be rewarded for your services – even though I didn't actually engage you and so, strictly speaking, I'm under no obligation to pay you.'

'What I expected, sir, was that you would be grateful to have your son back.'

'Oh, I am, Inspector, I am. And I have every intention of showing my gratitude. *But*—' The man raises his voice and an admonishing finger, as if delivering a speech in Hyde Park or on the floor of Parliament. 'I also intend to see that the black-guards who prey upon young men like my son are not permitted to get away with it. If they want to cater to the vices of sailors and other riffraff, let them. But when they begin luring innocent lads of good families into their clutches, it's time for law-abiding citizens to say, "Enough!" No, if you want anything from me, Inspector, you must first give me what *I* want – the exact location of this den of depravity.'

Charley suspects that the man means what he says. But he also suspects that, as a businessman, Pillbeam is used to bargaining. 'I'll consider it, under one condition.'

'What's that?'

'You hire back the servants you let go.' He digs out the wallet and places it in the man's hand.

Pillbeam's face falls. 'Oh. You . . . um . . . you didn't find a watch, by any chance?'

'No. I imagine it was sold.'

'I see.' Pillbeam takes a moment to regain his composure. 'Very well, I agree to your condition. Now. The location of that opium den.'

With a sigh of defeat, Charley takes out his notebook and sets about sketching a crude map of Blue Gate Fields.

That very night, there's a spectacular fire in Tiger Bay that sends the tigresses and the gamblers and the Lotos-eaters scattering like sewer rats. Though the district fire brigade is on the scene within ten minutes, the Leather-Breeches make no attempt to save the building that houses the opium den. One might almost think that they had been instructed by Superintendent Braidwood – who is, no doubt, a friend of Mr Pillbeam – to let it burn. With the help of a dozen bystanders who man the pumps, the brigadiers wet down the adjacent buildings, though, to prevent the flames from spreading.

Within half an hour, all that remains of Ah Choy's is a mound of charred timbers and smoking ash; at least one of the Lotos-eaters is observed inhaling the smoke, determined to get his money's worth. The other clients and the displaced employees view the ruins with resignation, confident that Mr Choy will quickly establish a new base of operations. That's one thing you can count on: Vice will always find a place to flourish.

Like all conflagrations, this one has attracted most of the local populace, including Mr Poppy. Needless to say, the opium master is not sorry to see his competitor's place destroyed – though it wasn't the competition that bothered him so much as the fact that Ah Choy's was giving the whole neighborhood a bad name. He's a smart fellow, is Poppy, and he surely knows how the fire got started; hiring an arsonist is a simple enough matter, and not even very costly. No doubt he also knows why Ah Choy's establishment, rather than his own, ended up as the target of Mr Pillbeam's wrath. A few days from now, Charley will be receiving a package from Poppy, containing a very unusual and quite extravagant token of his gratitude.

Mr Pillbeam, who is not ordinarily known for his generosity, has already displayed his gratitude in the only way he knows – with money, and far more of it than Charley expected. He also took a small stack of Charley's new business cards and will hand them out to his wealthy friends, along with a glowing recommendation. It begins to look as if Charley will be able to pay his rent after all.

He's on hand to watch the opium den burn, too, but he remains well in the background; he doesn't want the Chinese Colossus or Mr Choy himself thinking that he had anything to do with the fire. When the flames have died down, he turns away and heads – where? His office is nearer and in many ways more inviting than his wife's house, but he really ought to bathe and change clothing and see whether Hanora can do anything with his soiled, smelly greatcoat. He's going to have to bite the cartridge and endure an evening with Jane and the mother.

It's a pity, really, that neither woman has acquired a taste for opium or laudanum; it would do them good to have a few vices. At least he can always count on them to retire early. Once they're out of the way, he fixes himself a beef sandwich with plenty of mustard plus a cup of Assam tea so strong as to almost qualify as coffee and sits in the kitchen watching Hanora work her magic on the coat.

The house girl is a cheerful and pleasant sort, and Charley can almost see how his wife might suspect him of carrying on with her. He'd never consider it, of course; if Jane had any real evidence of hanky-panky, she'd let the girl go, and he knows how badly Hanora needs the work. Besides, it would be devilish hard to find a replacement who's anywhere near as capable or clever. How many maids, after all, would know to use the heel from a loaf of bread to get the stains out of his coat, or to banish the smell with, of all things, a mixture of black tea and rum? She's even frugal; she makes sure the rum-laced tea that's left over doesn't go to waste.

Well, in any case, Hanora would scarcely welcome any advances from him; it's clear that she has her cap set at Young Lochinvar. In the course of half an hour, she asks a dozen questions about the lad, most of which Charley can't begin to answer. She seems to have totally forgotten the embarrassing New Year's Day incident. Or perhaps it actually makes Mull more endearing somehow. Strange as it may seem, some women are drawn to fellows who need a bit of looking after. Maybe things would have worked out better for him and Jane if Charley had required more mothering, if it didn't seem to him so much like smothering.

Hanora hands him a crumpled business card that she's rescued from the pocket of his greatcoat. Charley assumes it's one of his, but no, it's the card given him by Mr Sledge, the medium. He'd almost forgotten he agreed to attend the man's next séance, which takes place – he glances at the card – tomorrow evening. 'Tell me, Hanora,' says Charley, 'do you believe that the spirits of the dead can communicate with us?'

She gives him a wide-eyed look. 'Sure, and doesn't everyone? Don't you, sir?'

'No. But I don't disbelieve it, either.'

'Hmph. If your ould grandmammy turned up at the foot of your bed a few moments after she died, as mine did, there'd be niver a doubt in your mind.'

'Wouldn't it be handy,' muses Charley, 'if murder victims could manage that? It'd certainly make my job easier.'

'How d'you know they can't? Have you iver tried?'

'Well . . . no. If I had, they'd have thrown me off the force.'

'That's as may be,' says Hanora. 'But you're not on the force now, are you, sir?'

SEVENTEEN

Like Mr Pillbeam's residence, Malcolm Sledge's lodgings in Aldersgate are somewhat grander than Charley expected. Apparently séancing pays a bit better than private enquiring. Though the neighborhood itself is not much to look at, the brick building that houses the spiritual consultant's headquarters is. It has the feel of an earlier, more elegant era, with its arched entrance and its tall windows separated by stone pilasters. It wouldn't seem at all surprising to see a man in a periwig or a lady in a farthingale emerging from it – or, for that matter, to glimpse their ghosts peering from one of those upstairs windows.

There's nothing Georgian about the interior, though, or even William-ian. The other séances Charley has attended were held in rooms that resembled the inside of a coffin, all dark velvet curtains and plush carpets. You might think that being dead would be depressing enough, and that spirits would welcome a spell in somewhere a bit more cheerful. Professor Sledge certainly seems to think so. His parlor is more like a greenhouse – bright and open, with lots of potted plants and even what appears to be a bamboo tree.

Nor do Charley's fellow spirit-summoners – four females – seem at all gloomy or fusty; though they range in age from perhaps twenty-five to something like sixty, they seem more than anything like a group of rather giggly schoolchildren about to embark on an outing.

Charley imagined that Sledge would appear in formal evening wear, like a stage magician or a mesmerist, but no; he's clad quite casually in a loose, fawn-colored frock coat – a bit too loose, perhaps? Charley eyes the clothing carefully, looking for telltale bulges that might indicate a concealed wad of ectoplasm or a galvanic battery. No point in being subtle about it; Sledge is paying him to be critical, not gullible.

After the necessary introductions, the housekeeper brings in the tea cart. While the others chat and sip and nibble, Charley gravitates toward the round, claw-footed table that occupies a spot near the windows. In the center of it sits a curious apparatus very much like the dial telegraph devised by Mr Cooke and Mr Wheatstone. Charley catches the Professor's attention. 'Do you mind if I examine this?'

'By all means. I'd prefer that you not handle it, though. 'Tis verra sensitive.'

'Of course,' says Charley. 'I'm quite sensitive myself.'

Sledge smiles appreciatively. 'I hope you dinna object to being touched; we'll be holding hands, you ken.'

'Oh, that's fine; just be sure to seat me next to Miss Treville, will you?' he says, referring to the pert young woman with the blonde ringlets.

Left to his own devices – or rather to Mr Sledge's device – Charley surreptitiously dons his spectacles and examines the face of the dial, which is perhaps six inches across. It has a pointer, like a clock's minute hand, and, as with the Wheatstone telegraph, the letters of the alphabet are inscribed around the edges like the numbers on a clock. But mixed in with the letters are several words and phrases: *Hello. Yes. No. Don't know. Mistake. Spell out. I must leave. Goodbye.*

The reverse side has an identical dial. Attached to the top of the apparatus and hanging down the sides of it are two thin wires that disappear through tiny holes drilled in the tabletop. Charley crouches, grunting softly as pain lances his bruised ribs, and surveys the underside of the table. At the end of each wire is a lead weight suspended several inches from the floor, which is covered by a small oriental carpet.

While he's down there, Charley glances about for any sign of a mechanical contrivance that might be used to tip the table. Table-tipping has been a common feature of the previous séances he's attended; though the other sitters were clearly awed by this phenomenon, it seemed obvious to Charley that the medium was performing some maneuver involving her knees.

'I suppose,' says the Professor in a strong stage voice, 'we should begin. We dinna want to keep the spirits waiting.' This elicits a nervous titter from the two younger ladies, Miss Treville and Miss Randolph. The middle-aged Mrs Morley appears to actually relish the prospect, while Mrs Joliffe, a sweet-faced, grandmotherly sort, looks rather alarmed, perhaps with good reason; after all, who knows what the spirits might do if they get impatient?

The housekeeper turns down the gas – 'Oh, my!' says Mrs Joliffe – and, even though it's quite dark outside, pulls the draperies closed. 'We don't want any peeping Toms,' says Sledge. He places a single lighted candle on the table, next to the dial device. 'For those who dinna ken already, this is called a spiritual telegraph. If we're fortunate tonight, we may receive a message on it, from the other side. The wires you see there are attached to weights beneath the table; they hold the pointer steady. Try not brush against them, if you can help it.'

'Will we actually see any spirits?' asks Mrs Morley eagerly.

'Probably not,' says Sledge. The woman gives him an indignant look, like a person who has been promised roast duck and is served beans on toast. 'I'm sorry to disappoint you, Madam, but the fact is, most so-called spirit manifestations are nae more than an illusion created by the medium or an assistant. Normally, spirits may be seen only by those with strong psychic powers. However, thanks to the spiritual telegraph, they can make their presence known to all of us. Shall we sit?' He indicates each person's place, and Charley does indeed end up comfortably close to the charming Miss Treville, with the rather silly seeming but also attractive Miss Randolph on his other side. When the Professor says, 'Join hands, please,' he's happy to oblige.

'Let's be silent for a moment, now,' Sledge murmurs. 'Eyes closed. If there's someone you wish to contact, please concentrate on that person's name, and visualize his or her face.'

Without even meaning to, Charley finds himself picturing Rosa – but, as always, it's her pale, lifeless face he sees, and he'd rather not. He's not here to commune with the dead, anyway; he needs to keep his eyes on the living, particularly on Professor Sledge. With the candle between them, it's difficult to make out small details, but the man doesn't appear to be up to anything; he's just sitting there with his head bowed and his eyes closed, like everyone else.

Charley hears a slight jiggling sound, then, and he glances

at the spiritual telegraph. The pointer is twitching, like a person with a nervous tic. Beside him, Miss Randolph gives a slight gasp. Miss Treville's slender fingers tighten their grip on Charley's large-knuckled ones.

'We are listening, spirits,' intones the Professor. 'Speak to us.'

The pointer jerks counterclockwise to the words *Spell out*, then springs back. 'Oh, my!' utters a startled Mrs Joliffe.

'Sshhh,' says the medium softly, then: 'Go ahead.' The pointer makes a small movement clockwise. 'The letter A.' A much larger movement. 'The letter L. It may be spelling out a name. The letter M.'

A sound issues from Mrs Morley's lips, like the cry of someone wounded. 'It's *my* name! It's spelling *Alma!*'

The pointer flies to the word YES. 'Can you tell me who is speaking, spirit?' whispers the Professor. 'The letter J. The letter A. The letter M—'

'James! It's my husband!' Mrs Morley glances about the table, almost frantically, as if it's important that they all understand. 'He passed away two years ago today! We agreed that I would try to contact him each year, on the anniversary of his death! I tried last year, but—' The pointer flips vigorously back and forth.

'He hears you, Mrs Morley. You may speak to him.'

'Just – out loud, you mean?'

'That's right.'

'I – I miss you, James. But don't be sad. I'm doing all right. You're not sad, are you?'

N-O S-O-R-R-O-W O-R J-O-Y H-E-R-E J-U-S-T. A long pause.

'Just what, James?'

M-E-M-O-R-Y

'Then try to remember the happy times, will you?'

YES L-O-V-E

Even in the dim light, Charley can see the tears welling in Mrs Morley's eyes. 'I love you, too. I always will.'

F-R-A-N-K

'Frank is doing fine. He's working for the railroad now. He's so big, you'd barely recognize him.'

L-O-V-E

'Yes, yes, I'll tell him.'

I MUST LEAVE

'No, no, not yet, please! Just a few more moments—'

GOODBYE

There's a sort of collective sigh, as if everyone around the table has been holding his or her breath. 'You may let go hands,' says the Professor, 'and take some time to collect yourselves. These experiences can be quite intense.'

'Oh, my!' says Mrs Joliffe yet again. 'I'm all a-tremble!'

Miss Treville produces a handkerchief and dabs at her eyes, then pats the perspiration from her palms. 'I'm so glad you were able to contact your husband, Mrs Morley.'

'Thank you, dear. And thank *you*, Professor. Last year, I tried a different medium – the same one who holds séances at the palace, in fact – but she was unsuccessful.'

'Well, with due respect to Their Majesties,' says Sledge, 'I suspect they're looking more for entertainment than enlightenment. Before we continue, Mr Field, do you have any questions about the proceedings?'

'Just one, Professor. If you don't mind, I'd rather we discussed it privately.'

'Of course. If you ladies will excuse us for a few moments?' Sledge leads the way to the tea cart, turns up the gas lamp a little, and offers Charley a biscuit. 'Having doubts, Inspector?'

'Not exactly. It's just that I noticed something odd.' Charley is a great believer in giving suspects enough rope to hang themselves. He takes a leisurely bite of the biscuit and watches the medium's reaction.

To his surprise, Sledge shows no alarm, but a good deal of amusement. 'Well, if you think about it, the whole business is a wee bit odd, isn't it? Talking to the dead? Was there something in particular that bothered you?'

'I didn't want to bring it up in front of Mrs Morley; she's clearly convinced that she was speaking with her husband, and no doubt it did her good, so I don't care to disillusion her. But I couldn't help noticing your hands.'

'My hands?' The Professor glances at them as if expecting

to find one missing. And, in fact, a missing hand is exactly the problem.

'It was difficult to see,' says Charley, 'what with all the shadows, but I'd swear that only your left hand was on the table. Miss Treville was grasping the fingers, and Mrs Joliffe had hold of the wrist.'

The medium gives an embarrassed laugh. 'Well, you've got me dead to rights, Inspector. So you're wondering what my other hand was up to?' He glances toward the table to make sure the ladies aren't looking their way. Then he hikes one leg of his trousers to reveal an angry red patch of skin behind the knee. 'Eczema. It itches like the devil. I thought it wise to leave one hand free to scratch, so I wouldna be squirming about during the séance.'

Charley gives the leg only the briefest glance; he's watching the Professor's eyes. Though he sees no sign that the eczema story is a lie, it just seems a little too convenient. Before he can ask any more questions, Miss Randolph lets out a squeal. 'Professor! It's moving again!'

Sledge scurries back to his seat. 'What letter? What letter?'

'C! I think.'

'All right. There's an H. And an A. An R. An L. E. Y.' The Professor glances at Charley, who hasn't moved from the tea cart. 'Did you call upon someone, Inspector?'

'Uh – no. At least – at least, not deliberately.' Rosa's name and her bloodless face were in his head, of course, but only for a moment.

'That's curious. Perhaps you should answer.'

'Answer? But I don't know—' He was about to say *I don't know who it is*, but that sounds as if he's convinced that, in fact, some spirit is speaking to him, and he's *not* convinced, not entirely. All he knows is that it's not Sledge who's creating the messages, unless he's moving the pointer with his mind.

Softly, the Professor says, 'The spirit will make its identity known. Give it a chance.'

'Should I – should I sit, or—'

'It's not necessary.'

That's good; it seems easier to stay objective if he remains outside the circle. He clears his throat and says, so loudly that it startles everyone, 'I'm here!'

'There's no need to shout, either,' whispers the medium.

The pointer dips counterclockwise, to the R, then the O, then the S, then a little clockwise tick, to the A. Charley has that punched-in-the-gut feeling again, the one he had when he viewed her corpse at the Rescue Society.

'Rosa?' he says weakly.

HELLO

Though he's spent twenty years questioning people, he's never interviewed a dead one before. If he wants to be sure it's her, he should ask something only he and Rosa would know the answer to, but nothing comes to mind. Besides, there's something more important he wants to say, just in case it is Rosa. 'I'm sorry. I shouldn't have left you. If I'd stayed, or walked you home, you'd still be alive.'

N-O-T Y-O-U-R F-A-U-L-T

Just what Rosa would say. Charley's throat feels so tight, he can't get any words out. But it doesn't matter; the spiritual telegraph spells out another message.

A-U-D-R-E-Y

'Uh – she's – she's fine. I mean, she misses you, of course. But Mrs Bramble found her a place at an orphan asylum, a fairly pleasant one, I understand.'

V-I-S-I-T

'Not yet. But I will soon, I promise.'

G-I-V-E C-A-M-E-O

'What do you—?' Charley starts to say, but then he under-stands: Rosa had a delicate cameo, decorated with roses, that she prized but seldom wore. She wants him to give it to Audrey. 'Yes,' he says. 'All right. I will.' Recalling how brief Mrs Morley's conversation was, he hastens to add, 'Rosa, you need to tell me who – who's responsible for your death. Please.' There's no reply. 'Was it the man you were with?' he demands. 'The one with the stiff neck?'

NO

'Then who?' No reply. 'Rosa! Who?' Just when he's sure she's gone, the pointer moves again.

H-U-B-B-A-R-D

Charley is struck momentarily speechless again, this time
with astonishment. 'But that's— Are you—?'

I MUST LEAVE

'No, wait! Just—'

GOODBYE

There's a moment of strained silence, then Mrs Joliffe says,
'Oh, my. Was she a friend of yours?'

Charley nods.

'And she was murdered?' asks Miss Treville.

'Yes.'

'She said it was someone called Hubbard. Do you know who
she means?'

He nods again, then says, in a choked voice, 'I'm sorry, I'm
going to have to excuse myself. Please go on without me. I'll
see myself out.' The housekeeper hands him his greatcoat; he's
so anxious to leave that he doesn't even take the time to put
it on.

Charley has seen mediums produce all sorts of eerie effects,
from automatic writing to violins that play themselves, but he
never supposed they were anything more than illusions, like
those created by stage magicians. This is something else. Even
if Sledge was somehow controlling the spiritual telegraph – and
it's hard to imagine how – and even if he learned of Charley's
connection with Rosa and her daughter, how would he know
about the cameo? And why on earth would he link Rosa's
murder to one that happened . . . how long ago?

He pulls out his list of criminals still at large and flips to the
entry on William Hubbard. 1838. So, fifteen years ago. Though
he'd lost track of the exact date, he remembers every other
detail of the Eliza Grimwood case, right down to the color of
her dress – yellow, beneath all that blood.

Perhaps it was the brutality of the crime that made it so
indelible: the poor girl – so lovely and well-mannered that one
might take her for a society lady and not a prostitute – was
stabbed multiple times and nearly beheaded. Or perhaps it was
the fact that, as with Rosa, Charley knew the victim – not as a
client, just as a copper. Or maybe because he worked so long
and so hard to prove with evidence what he knew by instinct
– that Hubbard, her cousin and probable pimp, was the culprit

– only to watch helplessly as the courts set him free. After all this time, Charley's failure still rankles him.

Mr Dickens brought Hubbard to poetic justice, at least, by using him as the basis for the despicable Bill Sikes in *Oliver Twist*. Though Sikes, like Bucket, is a household name, Hubbard is all but forgotten. Few besides Charley would even recall the man's name, let alone accuse him of another murder – especially since, shortly after he was acquitted, Hubbard hopped a boat bound for America.

But they say, don't they, that the departed know things we, the living, cannot. If Rosa's spirit is to be believed, the bastard is back.

EIGHTEEN

C harley doesn't give up the pursuit of Neck altogether; after all, the cove is guilty of so many other things, and even if he's not directly responsible for Rosa's death, he may still have had a hand in it. But now Charley has a new suspect, perhaps one who will prove less elusive.

It could be a while before the Pillbeam connection lands him any clients; for now, he's free to roam about the city, consulting his network of informants. Well, not totally free; he did promise Rosa – presuming it actually *was* Rosa – that he'd check on the welfare of her daughter. And even if it wasn't Rosa's idea, it's still a good one. He pays a visit to Mrs Bramble's, where he collects the cameo, then heads for the Priestley Orphans' Asylum.

The asylum lies in Lambeth, just across the River from Millbank, so he also makes a stop at his wife's house, meaning to have Hanora wrap up some of the remaining Christmas treats. But it's the house girl's free afternoon, and she's just leaving. 'Off to visit the family?' asks Charley.

'Sure, and I am!' she says brightly, then leans in to whisper, 'not! The truth is, I'm after meeting Young Lochinvar. You won't tell, will you?'

'Not I. Could you give him a message for me? Ask him whether there's been anything in the route-papers concerning a fellow named William Hubbard. I think he may have been involved in the murder of – of a friend of mine.'

'Rosa, you mean.'

'Yes. How did you—'

'Lochinvar told me. I hope you don't mind.'

Charles shakes his head sadly. 'I suppose not. You will ask him about Hubbard?'

'Yes, sir. Just so's I don't forget, I'll think of Old Mother Hubbard.'

'One other thing, Hanora: Do you happen to know where Mrs Field has stowed my old walking stick?'

'I do, sir. 'Tis in the wardrobe, in your room.'

He actually prefers the old stick, a gnarled, unadorned length of ash, to the more elegant one, which he lost at Ah Choy's – and which was, of course, a present from Jane. He fetches the stick, rounds up some raisins and nuts and oranges, and manages to escape without inciting a single argument or enduring any sort of lecture.

When I say orphans' asylum, you may picture something along the lines of Wanstead's impressive institution, which resembles one of those sprawling stone country houses of the landed gentry – the sort of folk, in fact, who furnished the funds to build the place. Reverend Priestley's asylum is considerably more modest. In fact, the premises was once a brewery, and a faint, musty bouquet of yeast and hop dust still issues from the bricks – this in addition to the vapors from Beaufoy's Vinegar Yard, which lies only one street away. Well, there are certainly worse smells, and worse places for an orphan girl to end up.

Priestley has no wealthy patrons, only a few dozen subscribers – including Mrs Bramble – who have been wheedled or, just as often, shamed into donating a paltry ten shillings per year, renewable upon the occasion of more wheedling. The Reverend and his small staff do the best they can with these limited resources. The orphan girls, ranging in age from five to ten years, are clothed in gray shifts that are unflattering but at least warm, and they're fed two meals a day that are uninspired but at least filling.

Charley conceals the bundle of treats inside his greatcoat –
unfortunately, there's not nearly enough to go around – and
gets directions to the Reverend's office from one of the matrons.
The office and, in fact, the man himself are as modest in appearance as the rest of the place. Priestley looks pretty much the
way you'd expect, given his name. He's not an actual priest, of
course, but he is a man of the cloth, and the cloth is black and
a bit shiny at the knees and elbows. He appears serene and
patient and good-humored, just the sort of fellow you'd be
tempted to confess your sins to if he were a priest – and if you
were the sort of fellow to make confessions, which Charley
isn't, though god knows he'd have more than enough material.
The Reverend rises from his well-worn, well-organized desk to
shake hands. 'Good afternoon, Inspector.'

'Have we met before?'

'Not formally. Your wife is one of our subscribers, and I've
seen you in her company.' That must have been some time ago;
Charley can't recall the last time he and Jane were out together,
nor does she keep him abreast of what charities she contributes
to. 'What can I do for you, sir?' asks Priestley.

'You have a new girl here, Audrey MacKinnon. I'd like to
visit with her, if I may.'

'Audrey? Oh, the daughter of the unfort'n't who drowned
herself?'

Charley bristles, and it's all he can do not to protest. But
what's the point? Though suicide is good for a shudder or two,
what really fascinates people is murder – as evidence the plethora
of penny bloods – and if he reveals Rosa's true fate, the other
girls and the staff will surely bombard her daughter with morbid
questions. He simply says, 'Yes.'

'Actually, I believe we've found a family for her.'

'Family? I didn't know Rosa had any.'

'An adoptive family, I mean.' Priestley opens a cloth-bound
ledger and runs a finger down the pages. 'Yes, here we are.
December 30th. She was taken by a couple from Lancashire.'
He glances up from the ledger. 'You seem surprised, Inspector.
We do our best to find good homes for our girls.'

'It's just that – well, it happened so quickly. She'd been here
only a few days.'

'Yes, but she's a healthy, outgoing young girl. So many of those we take in, I regret to say, are rather sickly – physically or mentally, or both.'

'Are you sure these people don't just want her as unpaid servant?'

'Quite sure. They're a very respectable man and wife who are unable to have children of their own. I'm confident she'll be very well looked after.'

'Do you mind if I make a note of their name and where they live?'

Priestley closes the ledger. 'I'm sorry, but that's against our policy. Sometimes a mother will give up a child, you know, and then come back for her later. That's not fair to the adoptive parents, I think you'll agree.'

'I have no claim on Audrey. I'm just looking out for her welfare.'

'As are we, Inspector, trust me.'

'I'm trying.' Charley sighs. 'I just hope you're right about this couple.' He places his hands on the desk, leans in, and says, almost amiably, 'If I find out otherwise, Reverend, I won't be pleased.'

If Priestley catches the implied threat, he shows no sign, only smiles serenely. 'You won't. Find out otherwise, I mean.'

Charley takes out his little bundle of treats and places it on the desk. 'Those were meant for Audrey. You may distribute them however you see fit.' All he can do with the cameo is hang onto it, in hopes that he'll see Audrey eventually.

Though he's still not completely certain that he communed with Rosa's spirit, he feels he owes it to her to try contacting her again; if she is out there somewhere, she'll want to know that her daughter is, as Priestley puts it, well looked after – even though Charley's not completely sure of that, either. When young Wink, the porter, turns up at his office the following day, bearing Mr Poppy's generous gift of gratitude, Charley has the boy carry a message to Professor Sledge, asking when he can sit in on another séance. The medium takes his time in answering; a week later a reply comes by post, saying that the next few sessions are completely full, but he'll certainly let Charley know as soon as there's a vacancy.

Luckily, the detective has a number of new cases to keep him occupied and quell his impatience – and pay his rent. Mr Pillbeam's connections have begun to pay off at last. Unluckily, most of them are of the usual uninspiring sort: collecting debts, recovering stolen property, evicting tenants – and, though it's not really part of the job, sometimes helping them find new lodgings. None offers much of a challenge, but several at least have the virtue of novelty.

One of the clients is a wife who suspects her husband of infidelity and has him followed; another is a husband who hires Charley to spy on his faithless wife. Neither assignment would be particularly unusual or interesting – except that the two are married to each other.

The only truly intriguing case involves a prominent merchant who, despite the wintry weather, regularly wanders about the dark streets in his nightshirt and bare feet, accosting women. Though he's been arrested several times, he always disavows any knowledge of his actions. Deducing that the incidents always take place during a full moon, Charley lies in wait one lunar-lit night and nabs the fellow – who is, of course, walking in his sleep, like the poor protagonist of *Sylvester Sound, the Somnambulist*.

He wraps up all these cases successfully, and is well-paid and much praised, but he can't help feeling a failure, for the one he actually cares about is no closer to being solved. It's not for want of trying. In between those other assignments, he puts in so many hours pounding the cobbles, he sometimes he feels as if he's back on the force. He'd almost forgot how much of his time as a sergeant and detective inspector was spent simply slogging about the city, looking for leads, questioning merchants and miscreants and madams and, most of time, getting nowhere. And he no longer has as much stamina as he did then. But at least his ribs have finally stopped hurting.

He does manage to turn up a few coves who remember the name William Hubbard, but no one has heard it lately. The whole tedious and tiring process is made even more unpleasant by the fact that, if he wants a cup of coffee – and he does, quite often – he has to settle for the sickly stuff sold in coffee stalls and chop houses.

Well, as Mr Dickens pointed out, there's a case worth solving. The fact is, he's more or less solved it already; it's just a question of bringing the adulterers, if they may be called that, to justice – or at least enough of them to throw a scare into the rest. Armed with the results of the Scarecrow's tests, he pays a visit to the offices of *Household Words*, which occupy the second floor of a town house in Wellington Street, quite near where he dropped off Miss Fairweather a few weeks ago – no, hard as it is to believe, it's been over a month, now. If only he could be as relentless as time, perhaps he'd accomplish more.

When he calls on Mr Dickens, he finds the Great Man at his desk – unfortunately. Charley was rather hoping to catch him in his apartment, which takes up the entire third floor; he'd like to have a look at the place. No doubt it's a good deal grander than his own little bachelor diggings; apparently there's even a housekeeper. As far as that goes, Dickens' office is nothing to sneeze at – nicely carpeted, comfortable armchairs, artwork on the walls. Charley is gratified to note, however, that the man's desk isn't nearly as large or impressive as his own.

It's also gratifying that, despite his busy schedule, Mr Dickens takes the time to carefully look over Charley's findings concerning the adulteration of coffee. 'Yes, yes, this is excellent; it'll make for a very provocative piece. I see you've even recorded the source of each sample. I think it's best, though, if we don't divulge actual names or locations at this point.'

'You may be right. We could say that, if they don't change their ways, then we *will* name names.'

'Exactly. We're too late for this week's issue, but I'll try to get it in next week. I'll put one of my best men on it.' Turning away, he calls out, in his best stage voice, 'Mr Mumchance! Come here, please!'

'Is this Geoffrey Mumchance, the *poet*?' asks an astonished Charley.

'I believe he's given up poetry,' murmurs Mr Dickens. 'Thank god.'

Apparently he's also given up his attempts to appear Bohemian. His formerly unruly hair and beard are now quite ruly, his clothing is subdued, his sturdy boots have given way to brown lace-ups. He doesn't seem nearly as melancholy, either;

even his handshake has more ginger to it. 'Inspector! It's good to see you!'

'Likewise,' says Charley. 'How's that girl of yours? Emmeline, was it?'

The ex-poet gives a broad, embarrassed grin. 'Yes, though in fact it's now Mrs Mumchance.'

'Well done, lad.'

'It's all due to Mr Dickens hiring me on here. Emmeline's parents are great admirers of his work.'

'Speaking of work,' says Mr Dickens gruffly, 'may we get back to it? Mr Field has proposed that we do a piece on the deplorable state of Mocha – the beverage, that is, not the city. He's provided the information; you will write it up. Does that suit you?'

'Does it? I've been complaining about the swill they call coffee ever since I landed in London!'

'Good.' He hands Mr Mumchance the notes Charley has compiled. 'Before you begin, why don't you see if you can find us some swill that's halfway drinkable?' When Mumchance is gone, Mr Dickens says, 'I hope you don't mind my putting him on the story. It just occurred to me that you might have meant to write it yourself.'

'No, no, I'm no good with words.'

'Oh, come, Charley; you've told me some fascinating tales of police work – for example, the one about Fikey the Forger. I still recall what he said when you collared him: "Well, burn my body, if this ain't TOO bad!"' Mr Dickens is so amused, he has to dab tears from his eyes.

Charley shrugs. 'Oh, I can talk all right, I suppose; it's putting things down on paper that gets me. I don't know how you do it.'

'To be honest, Charley, neither do I. It's a mystery. But you have your own talents, and your friend the Scarecrow has his, and Miss Fairweather has hers. Which reminds me—' Mr Dickens pulls out his fat wallet. 'I promised you a bonus if you foiled her evil plans.'

'I didn't, though; she completely fooled me.'

'Even so, you ushered her out before things got too out of hand.' He holds out a pound note. 'Go on. You earned it.'

Charley gives a sheepish smile. 'Well, the truth is, I collected my bonus already – from Miss Fairweather herself.'

'Why, you cad! Well, you can use this to pay her back.'

'All right, then. I expect she can use it. I don't think she's had much work lately, ever since—'

'Ever since I put her company out of business; I know. And I don't regret doing it. Trust me, they had no right to inflict themselves on unsuspecting theatregoers. I do regret, however, that Miss Fairweather had to suffer in the process. She deserves better. And do you know what?' Dickens pauses dramatically, his eyes wide. 'She shall have it, and very soon! I've prevailed upon my friend Mr Elton to cast her in his latest theatrical spectacle, *Faust and Marguerite*! They begin rehearsing next month, at the Princess!' He claps his hands together as if applauding his own performance.

When the following week's issue of *Household Words* appears, Charley wastes no time in purchasing a copy. It's hard to imagine that anything very compelling could be made out of the Scarecrow's tables of facts and figures, but Mr Mumchance has done it. There on page 570 is quite a lively essay titled 'Foreign Matter.'

The first sentence reads, 'Despite the pounding it has taken over the years from violent criminals and bare-knuckle boxers, the nose of our good friend Inspector Bucket is still one of the sharpest in the city, and if he smells a rat, you don't question him, you don't hesitate; you put out the rattraps.' The lad has recovered nicely from his weakness for poetry. Grinning, Charley tucks the journal into his coat pocket and heads for Isam Jones's studio; it's only fair that they read the piece and gloat over it together.

As it turns out, Charley is forced to read it aloud, for 'Sam is having one of his bad days – sweating, coughing up blood, unable even to muster the strength to rise from his worn and faded fainting couch. But before he's got through a single paragraph, the photographer interrupts him. 'Charley?'

'Yes?'

'What in god's name are you wearing?'

Charley pulls open his frock coat to reveal a bright blue silk waistcoat embroidered with complex circular Chinese designs. 'It's a gift from Mr Poppy, the opium master. He claims it has special powers that protect the wearer from harm. Unfortunately, it also makes me look a bit puffy.' He fingers the fabric, which is a good half-inch thick. At the same time, the garment is incredibly light – no more than a pound or so.

'Come closer,' says 'Sam. He rubs the silk between his hands. 'The devil take me. I've read about these.' His words are punctuated by a series of coughs, which he tries to control, with little success. 'They say the Mongols wore them, centuries ago. They're made of twenty layers of tightly woven silk. According to legend, they were actually able to deflect an arrow or a sword blade.'

'Hmm. I'm not sure I believe that. But perhaps it'll bring me luck, so I'll wear it, anyway. Not around Jane, of course; I'm sure she'd consider it *vulgar.* Now, if you're done admiring my waistcoat, I'll finish reading the essay.'

The piece brings a smile to the Scarecrow's gaunt face. 'Well, now. That should make those damned coffeehouses sit up and take notice.'

'I hope so,' says Charley. He doesn't really expect their exposé to make any great difference. Though the better coffee shops have a selection of reading material, he's never seen the proprietors or the waiters pick up a book or a magazine; as for the owners of coffee stalls, he'd be surprised if very many of them have even learned to read.

What he fails to consider is that it's not the proprietors who will peruse the piece and conclude that something must be done; it's the customers. The fact is, Mr Dickens' little journal sells in the neighborhood of 40,000 copies each week, and each of those copies reaches the hands of at least three or four readers, a good half of whom are habitual consumers of coffee, not to say addicts. Tamper with a man's Mocha, and you've made a formidable enemy.

A fortnight after the article appears, Charley once again makes the rounds of coffee shops throughout the West End, collecting samples, even venturing to take a few sips. Though none of them holds a candle to the stuff he grinds and brews for himself, there's no denying that, in almost all the shops, the quality has increased considerably. As you might expect, so has the price, but usually only by half a penny.

Charley doesn't bother to check the ramshackle coffee stalls that are scattered about the streets. He knows well enough that his crusade will have had no effect there; if such places raise the quality and the price of their coffee, the bulk of their customers – the working poor – will have to do without. To improve that situation, a far more ambitious campaign is needed, one that will force employers to pay their workers a reasonable wage. Well, perhaps that battle will be fought and won some day, somewhere, but not here and not now.

NINETEEN

Though all this meandering about, collecting coffee and information – a great deal of the former, precious little of the latter – can get wearisome, Charley doesn't really mind it so much. Certainly it's far better than being shut up in his wife's house, or even in his little office – especially when the weather is mild, as it has been lately.

After winter missed its cue and came on so late, you might expect it to overstay its welcome, blustering and capering about like a bad actor trying to milk the audience. But no, in mid-March it begins making a timely and graceful exit. The gray slush slowly disappears and the streets return gradually to their natural state – a shallow swamp of dirt, horse manure, and unclassifiable matter swept from stalls and pavements.

Late one afternoon, thanks to a bit of hearsay pried out of an unwilling informer, Charley finds himself in Oxford Street, not far from Soho Square. Though this trail, like all the others, comes to a dead end, at least it has brought him to an interesting spot: just down the street lies the Royal Princess's Theatre, where, according to Mr Dickens, rehearsals of *Faust and Marguerite* are in progress.

The last he heard, his old sparring partner, Perky Grimes, was working backstage, hoisting scenery, mopping floors, keeping overzealous admirers at bay. As we've seen, Charley is quite zealous in his admiration of Miss Fairweather; still, he's not about to thrust himself upon her. (And what, he wonders, would she make of that rather suggestive phrase?) He'd just like to sit in some out-of-the-way spot and watch a little of the proceedings, see how a real play comes together – or at least that's what he tells himself.

The theatre has always held a certain fascination for him, ever since he saw his first *Punch and Judy* show; who knows, it may have been the doggedness with which the Beadle pursued the sadistic Punch that, years later, led him to join the force. He's trod the boards himself a few times, but only in those police pantomimes. And in the course of his career he's played all sorts of parts, from a match seller (or 'timber merchant,' as he so amusingly called himself) to a blueblood. Wouldn't it be fun if he were to take on the role of The Inspector in some mystery melodrama? Well, perhaps not. But at least he'd be guaranteed to always get his man – something you certainly can't say about real life.

As it turns out, he is, in fact, called upon to play The Inspector. Perky Grimes is long gone, replaced as assistant stage manager by another of the horde of barely post-pubescent youths who appear to be taking over the world. Charley convinces him that he's on a case – never mind what sort; that's confidential – and that the lad would do well to cooperate. And so it is that when Madeline, played by Miss Fairweather, scampers off stage left, calling 'Goodbye, dearest Margaret!' she collides with Charley, who's lurking in the wings.

'Inspector Bucket!' she gasps. 'What are you doing here?'

'Ssssh!' says Charley. 'I'm incognito.'

'You don't mean you're investigating a crime?' she whispers, almost in his ear. Her breath somehow contrives to smell of bergamot, rather like Grey's tea. 'How thrilling! It's not a murder, is it?'

Her closeness makes Charley feel slightly dizzy, as if he's being chloroformed, and he draws back a little. 'No, no.'

'Oh, good. There's enough of that going on already.'

'How do you mean?'

'I mean the actors murdering their lines. But you watch; Mr Elton will tell them they're all doing wonderfully.'

She's right on both counts. Charley is fairly sure he could acquit himself as well as most of the players out there, or better. And yet when the rehearsal ends, the company manager, who is also playing Mephistopheles, has nothing but praise. Miss Fairweather sighs and shakes her head. 'I need a drink.'

'Is there a place nearby that serves women?'

'As one of the menu choices?'

'Well, no, I meant as in—'

'I know what you meant; I just wanted to see you blush. Yes, the Horse and Groom kindly permits us ladies of the stage to imbibe – provided we're accompanied by a man.'

'I'd be happy to escort you.'

Miss Fairweather flashes her stunning smile and takes his arm. 'Of course you would.' As they exit the theatre and head up Winsley Street, she says, 'You haven't told me yet how brilliantly I played my part – all nine lines of it.'

'Hmm. Well, no doubt you'll do better in the actual performance.'

'Oh, not pulling any punches, are we?'

'Just being honest.'

'Well, there's an unusual approach – honesty. Guaranteed to win a lady's heart. I'm surprised more men don't try it.'

'Is that sarcasm, Miss Fairweather? I can't quite tell.'

'No? Well, perhaps I'll get it right in the actual performance.' Her sour mood doesn't last long; a moment later, she says brightly, 'You also failed to tell me what it is you're investigating.'

'Investigating?'

'At the theatre!'

'Oh. Nothing, actually. I lied to the boy so he'd let me watch the rehearsal.'

'So you could watch *me*, you mean.'

Well, yes, but Charley doesn't care to admit it. 'I could hardly help it, could I, since you were onstage.'

As they near the Horse and Groom, a cheerful clamor reaches their ears – raucous voices raised in song. 'Oh, damn,' says Miss Fairweather, startling Charley a little; though he's heard far worse words from women, it's usually doxies and drunks, and Miss Fairweather is neither – as far as he knows. 'I forgot, it's Free and Easy Chappy Hour.'

'So? You said yourself, you're an old hand at music-hall ditties.'

'Yes, but they won't be content to let me just sing along; they'll want me to get up and perform. I do quite enough of that.'

'I could just fetch you something and you can drink it as we walk. Or as you walk by yourself. Or ride. Or whatever you plan to do.'

'I was planning to take a cab, but if you wouldn't mind walking with me . . .'

Charley shrugs. 'I don't mind.'

'Oh. Very well, then. Since you're so wildly enthusiastic about the prospect. And you won't mind paying for my drink either, I'm sure. Brandy, please.'

'All right. Oh, and speaking of paying . . .' He fishes a sovereign from his pocket and places it in her palm, using the transaction as a flimsy excuse to take her hand. 'Mr Dickens paid me my bonus, so you're off the hook.'

'Thank you. Perhaps you're something of a gentleman after all.'

'I wouldn't count on it.'

When Charley emerges from the tavern with his pocket flask full of *eau de vie*, the Free and Easy crowd are belting out 'The Bill Sticker,' and Miss Fairweather is singing along softly:

> Holloway's ointment and Paris pills,
> The last a great reformer,
> I plastered to Miss Kemble's tail
> The first night she played *Norma*.

'Do you know Miss Kemble, then?' asks Charley.

'Why, yes, of course,' replies Miss Fairweather haughtily. 'Both Misses Kemble, in fact.' Then, true to her mercurial nature, she changes moods and gives him a sly sidelong glance. 'Oh, that's right, we're being honest, aren't we? Well, honestly, Fanny Kemble wouldn't know me if she fell over me. Her sister, however, once did.'

'What? Fell over you?'

She smiles and nods. 'I was in the chorus of *La Sonnambula*;

I forgot my blocking and flitted in front of her just as she was making her grand exit. She went off limping rather badly, I'm afraid. But at least it got a good laugh from the audience.' With a laugh of her own, she takes a swig of brandy directly from the flask. 'Of course,' she adds, more soberly, 'the next day, they gave me the heave-ho.' She passes the flask to Charley and then, to his delight, links her arm with his again. 'I'm afraid I'm taking you out of your way.'

'Honestly, nowhere is out of the way for me at the moment. I'm in the midst of scouring the city for a fugitive.'

'Ooh, a *fugitive*! What has he done, then? Performed poorly in rehearsal?' To make her little dig more emphatic, she pokes her elbow into his ribs.

Charley is not amused. 'He's killed at least one woman,' he replies irritably, 'and probably a second.' Ordinarily, he can take a good deal of joshing, but she's struck a sore spot – not literally; even though his ribs are still tender, he barely felt her jab, thanks to Mr Poppy's protective vest. No, it's the canker of guilt that he's carried about ever since Eliza Grimwood's murder and that has flared up again with Rosa's death.

He expects Miss Fairweather to be put off by his peevishness, but she actually seems concerned and contrite. 'I'm sorry, I didn't mean to make light of it. I didn't imagine that private enquiry agents actually investigated such things; I thought it was the job of the police.'

'Well, when the first murder was committed, I was with the police. I should have put the killer away back then.' Just thinking about it, he needs another healthy dose of brandy.

Miss Fairweather gives his arm a sympathetic squeeze. 'I'm sure you did your best, Charley.' It's the first time she's called him Charley; although it's a perfectly mundane sort of name, it doesn't seem that way when she says it.

'Maybe. But I'll have to do better. I can't let him get away with it this time.'

'You make it sound as though it's personal.'

'It is.' Despite his determination not to talk about the case, somehow the details just spill out of him. He's seen that happen with criminals; they so often feel compelled to confess their deeds, as if that will somehow exonerate them. One thing he deliberately fails to mention is the séance; if he tells her that his search for William Hubbard was set in motion by a message from the spirit world, who knows what she might think of him? And isn't that a curious thing for him to worry about – what someone thinks of him? It's never bothered him much before.

'I'm sorry about your . . . your friend,' says Miss Fairweather. 'Prostitution is such a dangerous trade.'

'She meant to get out of it; she was saving up to start a millinery shop.'

'Perhaps I should consider that. When my face and my figure go, I'll have to make a living somehow.' She takes her turn with the brandy flask; she doesn't seem to mind swapping saliva with him. Charley's fine with it, too; though it may not be very hygienic, there's something intimate, even sensual about it.

'You could always marry one of those many admirers you mentioned.'

'Oh, dear me, no. Don't you know, actresses aren't for marrying? They're for playing around with. Just ask your friend Mr Dickens; he can tell you all about it.'

Charley chuckles. 'Yes, he does have an eye for the ladies. I don't think it ever goes beyond that.'

Miss Fairweather laughs, too, but there's little humor in it. 'Perhaps you should re-examine the evidence, Inspector – question a few witnesses.'

'Oh? Has he made advances to anyone you know?'

'Someone I know quite well, in fact.'

Charley is about to ask who, but he sees the answer in her dark eyes. 'Yourself.'

She shrugs and takes another sip of brandy. 'Why do you suppose he raked our acting company over the coals as he did?'

'I don't know.' He's naturally hesitant to say, *Because they were terrible actors?*

'Well, I do. It was his way of getting back at me. "Heaven has no rage, like love to hatred turned, Nor Hell a fury like a man scorned."'

'Well, he mustn't be carrying much of a grudge, or he wouldn't have got you this acting job.'

Miss Fairweather stops in her tracks and gapes at him. 'It was *his* doing?'

'I'm sorry, I thought you knew.'

'No! I was foolish enough to think it was because I'm such a marvelous actress. Why would he do that for me, especially after I tried to ruin his show?'

'He's a generous man. I'm sure he thought you'd be grateful to have the work.'

'Oh, I am. But I'd rather have got it on my own merits, and not because Mr Elton had his arm twisted.' Miss Fairweather finishes off the brandy and gives a delicate burp. 'I believe I'm just a little tipsy. Luckily, I'm almost home.' She returns his flask and unlinks their arms. 'I'll be fine from here. I think I can at least do *that* on my own.'

'Are you sure? It's safer if I see you to your door.'

'No,' she says. 'It's more dangerous, actually.'

'Why is that?'

'Because. Then you'd know where to find me.'

'I won't plague you with unwanted attentions, if that's what worries you.'

Miss Fairweather laughs softly, ironically. 'It's not. What worries me . . . what worries me is that you'll see what I'm like when I'm not putting on a performance.'

'But I already have.'

'Have you?'

'You can't tell me that the whole time we've been together, you were playing a part.'

She sighs, as if he's being hopelessly naïve. 'It's what I do, Charley. Actresses are no different from whores, really. We're continually making ourselves over, into whatever our audience desires.'

'How do you know what I desire?'

'I see it, every time you look at me. You think detectives are the only ones who can read faces?' She's so near him now that her breath, turned to fog by the brisk evening air, mingles with his. For an unbearable second or so, he's sure that their lips, too, will mingle. But in that small space of time, she undergoes yet another change. Backing off a step, she says wryly, 'You're easily satisfied, Inspector, I'll give you that – all it takes is a bit of sympathy, a bit of sweetness, with a touch of sauciness thrown in to spice things up. I wish all men were content with so little.' She shivers slightly and pulls her cloak about her. 'You can come and see me at the theatre any time, Charley. But for now, just go on home, all right?'

There's nothing Charley can say; he simply nods.

'Promise you won't follow me.'

'I promise.'

And, though it's difficult, he keeps his promise. He walks away without looking back. He doesn't head home, though, not to the Holywell Street house. He goes only as far as his office, where he brews up a cup of strong coffee to console himself. Though he knows it'll keep him up half the night, it scarcely matters; he would have lain awake, anyway, brooding about his scene with Miss Fairweather, wishing he'd played it differently somehow. But what's the use? No matter how many chances he got to do it over, he'd never get it right.

As he's undressing for bed, removing the silk waistcoat, in spite of his gloomy mood he can't help chuckling a little. According to Poppy, the gift was supposed to protect him, but apparently that applies only to arrows and swords, not to the subtle blows delivered by women and aimed at the heart.

Despite all the Mocha and the misery, Charley is at some point visited by good Queen Mab, who brings him blessed sleep. At some much later point, another visitor arrives to disturb his slumber. When he first hears the sound of knocking, he can't quite sort out the source of it. It seems to belong not to the real world but to the dream he's having.

In the dream, he's attending another séance, conducted not by Professor Sledge but by Miss Fairweather. There's no spiritual telegraph, either; the spirits communicate by rapping on the tabletop – once for Yes, twice for No. Supposedly it's Rosa's spirit doing the rapping, but this time Charley is certain that it's no such thing; it's clearly just Miss Fairweather putting on another performance.

Then, to his surprise, the spirit calls out to him: 'Inspector Field! Are you there?' Oddly enough, the voice sounds like that of Constable Mull. Well, not so odd, really, since that is, in fact, who's calling him, not from the spirit world but from right outside his office door.

Yawning, Charley wraps himself in his slightly shabby plaid dressing gown – which is far more comfortable and practical than that damned smoking jacket – and allows Young Lochinvar to enter. 'I should have taught you how to pick locks, lad; you could have let yourself in, without all the racket.'

'I'm sorry to wake you, Inspector. I had no idea you'd still be abed.'

'It's all right. Only you might have brought me a bit of breakfast. Sit down, and I'll make us some coffee.'

'You brew your *own*?'

'You needn't act so surprised.'

'Sorry, sir.'

'Perhaps I'll teach you that skill, as well. It'll make you a very popular fellow at the station house.'

'Eh, that would be a welcome change.' The constable shakes his head and sighs. 'How I wish I could solve some baffling case, or bring in some desperate criminal, and show them all.'

'That'll happen in time, lad. Be patient.'

Lochinvar looks anything but patient. In fact, he looks as though he can barely sit still. 'I don't suppose there's a case you'd be needing help with? 'Tis my day off.'

'I'm afraid not. Most of my time is spent – wasted, I might better say – trying to track down Mr Neck and Mr Hubbard.'

'Hanora said I should ask around about Hubbard, and I've done so, but I've turned up nothing. You think he's the one he's responsible for Rosa's death?'

'It seems unlikely. But, despite what William of Ockham may think, the most likely solutions aren't always the right ones.'

'You know about Ockham's razor?'

'I have read a book or two in my time, you know.'

'Yes, sir. I didn't mean to—'

'Never mind. You know, you might do worse with your day off than to call on Hanora. No doubt I can convince Mrs Field to spare her for an hour or two. A fellow doesn't need to be a detective to deduce that she's fond of you.'

The constable blushes and ducks his head. 'She's told me as much. And I like her, too. It's just that – Well, I seem to have forgotten how to just relax and have a bit of fun. Even when

I'm not on duty, I feel as though I mun be *doing* something, do you know what I mean?'

'I do,' says Charley. He remembers that feeling well, from his early days on the force – the awareness that somewhere out there crimes were being committed and wrongs being done and that he should be out there, too, doing his best to prevent them. 'I wish I could tell you that that, too, will change in time. But it doesn't, I'm afraid. Just don't let your whole life revolve around policing, lad, or it won't be much of a life.'

The constable stays only long enough to drink his coffee. 'Eh, if you've nothing I can help with, I'll be up and off. Perhaps I can manage to see Hanora on her free afternoon; we'd have more time, then. For now, I believe I'll just do some—'

'Some poking about?'

'Yes; some poking about.'

'All right, lad. Only be careful, will you? Poking about can be dangerous, if you poke the wrong people.'

TWENTY

C harley feels no great urge to do time at the Holywell Street house, but he can't think of any excuse not to. Besides, it's his duty, he supposes, to put in an appearance now and again, and no one has ever accused him of shirking his duty.

Though the day outside is sunny, within the house the climate is even more bleak than usual, for the mother has fallen ill with some unspecified ailment just severe enough to keep her in bed, lounging regally on a throne of pillows, but not enough to keep her from issuing royal commands with astonishing frequency, most of which are carried out by Hanora. At least Charley brings a smile to the poor girl's face by conveying Young Lochinvar's best wishes.

There is one thing to be said for his wife's home: there's always plenty of good food and drink – excepting coffee, of course, but he's consumed enough already to see him through

most of the day, and if need be, he can always fetch a cup of
something resembling Mocha from the slap-bang down the
street. As he's tucking into a plate of deviled kidneys, Jane
appears and, sitting across the table from him, pours herself a
cup of tea. Charley steels himself, anticipating a minutely
detailed account of the mother's complaints. Instead, his wife
says, 'Have you been on a – what do you call them? A case?
An enquiry?'

'Either one. Yes, I have. Though I'm afraid I'm not at liberty
to reveal any details.' Particularly those details involving Miss
Fairweather.

'Oh,' says Jane, sounding slightly put out, it seems to him.
But then she so often sounds that way; perhaps it's just from
old habit. Charley assumes that will be the end of the discus-
sion, but to his surprise, she keeps it going. 'You've been getting
quite a lot of cases lately, haven't you? I suppose it was your
advertisement in the newspapers that made the difference?'

Perhaps he's being unfair, but Charley can't help wondering
what her game is, why she's suddenly so interested in his work.
He also can't help feeling a bit resentful; the enquiry business
is his territory, and he doesn't much want her trespassing on it.
After all, he never interrogates her about the way she runs the
household. 'Yes,' he says dryly. 'People would much sooner
consult Inspector Bucket than Detective Field.' Before she can
question him further, he beats her to the punch. 'Have you
called in a doctor to examine your mother?'

'Yes; apparently it has something to do with her heart.'

Charley is tempted to say, *Oh, she does have one, then?* but
he restrains himself. 'Did he prescribe any sort of treatment?'

'Bed rest, mainly. Oh, and you'll be gratified to know, he
suggested she drink several cups of coffee a day, as a diuretic.'

Charley barely suppresses a grin. 'You don't say? Do you
think she'll actually do it?'

'I'll make certain she does.'

'Well, be sure to put in lots of cream and sugar; that takes
the edge off. Who knows, she may even come to like it.' They
glance at each other, shake their heads, and say, with one voice,
'No.' Charley can't recall the last time they actually agreed on
anything; it's a strange feeling. Though it takes them even deeper

into his private territory, he feels obliged to offer the use of his grinder and biffin. He doesn't know whether to be offended or relieved when she declines.

'Oh, we don't want the whole house smelling of the stuff; Hanora can bring it in from the dining house down the street.' A grand title for such a run-down place, but of course she would never be caught uttering so vulgar a term as *slap-bang*.

Back when he was still a Runner, Charley began to notice that criminals, like farmers, are governed to a surprising extent by the seasons. As Chaucer observed, in spring folk longen to goon on pilgrimages, but it seems they also longen to commit fraud, burgle homes, and beat their wives and mistresses. And when the police aren't willing or able to help, the defrauded and burgled and beaten turn to Charley and his colleagues – to use the term loosely. In truth, the world of private enquiring is a very small one, and so the agents are more in the nature of rivals than colleagues.

Charley has a leg up, however; thanks partly to Mr Pillbeam, but even more to Mr Dickens and Inspector Bucket, he's quickly acquired a reputation as a clever and conscientious detective. For the month or so that follows, he has more work than he can handle. Though he's grateful for the money, it's vexing to have so little time for pursuing the lawbreakers on his list. It looks as if he'll have to give up on Neck, at least for the moment. His top priority is the villain who did Rosa in, and if Rosa's spirit spoke true, it wasn't Neck at all, but William Hubbard.

Charley doesn't have much time to spend at the Holywell Street house, either, but his sense of duty compels him to look in every few days to see how Jane and the mother are getting along. He always brings with him an extra cup of Mocha and, however much she may grouse about it, the mother always forces it down. Though she distrusts people in general, she has an almost childlike awe of doctors, and will follow their instructions to the letter. Unfortunately the coffee appears to have little effect, beyond obliging her to use the bedpan a dozen times a day. Each time Charley visits, she seems to have slid downhill a little, in the general direction of the graveyard.

All in all, it's a sad and stressful situation, but as far as he can tell, Jane is coping fairly well. She's always been at her best when called upon to help those in need, whether it's the orphans at the asylum or a tramp looking for work, a starving stray cat or a bird with a broken wing – and once, twenty years ago, an unruly, uncultured, and underfed young police sergeant.

Not only is she as patient as Job in tending to her mother, she continues to be more civil than usual to Charley. Though he has more than enough mysteries to solve already, this one needs some investigating. He begins by interrogating the house girl.

It's always best to approach these things in a casual, offhand way – preferably while the subject is occupied with some other business, so he or she is off guard and more likely to let something slip. Hanora is simultaneously chopping vegetables and reading the evening edition, which seems a bit risky to Charley, but apparently her hands are so used to such tasks that they can operate independently of her brain. No doubt it would be even riskier if Jane were to find her idly perusing the paper; after all, what need does a servant have to know the news?

'Have you noticed,' says Charley, between bites of his gargantuan beef sandwich, 'that Mrs Field is being more . . . more tolerant lately?'

Hanora gives him a puzzled glance. '*Tolerant*, sir?' Charley's sure she knows the meaning of the word; it's probably just that she's never heard it applied to Mrs Field before. 'Not particularly.'

'Well, not with you, perhaps, but with me. I mean, I may be wrong, but it seems to me that . . . well, if she shows any interest in what I'm doing or what I want, it's usually because there's something *she* wants. Do you have any idea what that might be?'

Hanora ceases chopping and nibbles thoughtfully on one of the carrot slices. 'Are you after asking my unvarnished opinion, sir?'

'Please, spare the varnish.'

'Well, sir, I expect she's beginning to realize that her mam won't be around forever, and maybe she's fearful of finding herself all on her own.'

'Ah. So you think she's trying to bridge the gap between her and me?'

'I would say so, aye.'

'Thank you. We detectives are good at figuring out *who* did something, and *how*, but not always so good at guessing why.'

Hanora smiles a mischievous smile. 'Perhaps the police should consider hiring some women, sir. We're good at that.'

A few months ago, Charley wouldn't have thought it possible, but he's getting a bit weary of solving cases. He can barely recall the last time he did anything purely for his own amusement, aside from downing a few pints at a tavern and swapping stories with his drinking companions, but a fellow gets weary of that, too. When he spots an announcement in the *Daily News* that *Faust and Marguerite* is being presented nightly at the Princess's Theatre, it's like stumbling upon an oasis in the middle of the desert.

But in order to reach the promised land of Miss Fairweather's play, he has to endure an hour's trek through something called *Married Unmarried*, a rather smarmy piece that has the audience unaccountably laughing itself into stitches. Actually, Miss Fairweather has a small role in that one, too, and doesn't look terribly thrilled about it.

When she comes onstage in *Faust and Marguerite,* she still looks somehow out of sorts. She's clearly making an effort to be her usual scintillating self, but not quite succeeding. Each time she's called upon to laugh or smile, it seems as though it pains her. Though it's quite possible that the rest of the audience doesn't even notice, Charley certainly does, and it makes him uncomfortable.

He was uncomfortable enough already. Like Constable Mull, he's feeling the need to be *doing* something, specifically something that will put him closer to finding Rosa's killer, instead of sitting here enjoying himself. There's a double irony at work, there. First of all, he has no leads. Second of all, he's not really enjoying himself; he can't appreciate Miss Fairweather's performance when he's wondering what her problem is. Just what he needs: another mystery to solve.

According to the playbill, she's been spared a part in the

third offering of the evening, *A Storm in a Teacup*. Charley decides to spare himself, too. He slips out of the theatre and takes up a post outside the stage door. He's used to standing by while a woman puts on her clothes and her face – at least he once was, back when he and Jane still went out together occasionally – and he's prepared to wait for twice as long as it could conceivably take.

He's quite astonished when, a mere quarter of an hour later, Miss Fairweather emerges. She shows no sign of astonishment at finding him there, or even mild surprise, though it's hard to be sure, since the broad-brimmed bonnet she's wearing casts her face in shadow. Neither does she show any sign of being particularly pleased. In fact, she barely glances his way. She does deign to say, 'Hello, Charley; did you enjoy the show?' as she glides past him.

Charley falls into step with her. 'Not very much. It didn't look as though you were enjoying it, either.'

'Oh? I thought it went quite well!' she replies, almost brightly enough to convince him that nothing's amiss after all.

'Well, except for the stage manager being stabbed to death.' Perhaps he should be on the boards after all; his timing is perfect. Just as she turns to him and cries 'What!' they pass beneath a street lamp and her face catches the light. Though she's tried hard to hide it with makeup, the bruise on her cheekbone is too dark and too swollen to be covered up altogether.

Miss Fairweather is a clever woman, and it takes her only an instant to realize that she's been gammoned. Scowling, she delivers a surprisingly solid blow to his chest. 'Damn you, Charley!'

'I could see there was something wrong, even from the audience. You can't blame me for wondering what it was.'

'Yes, I can. It's none of your business.'

'Perhaps not. I just thought we were friends.'

'Are we?' she says coldly. Then abruptly her tone changes, becomes almost pleading. 'If you *are* my friend, Charley, you won't ask me any questions; you'll just let it go.' She reaches out with the hand that, a moment ago, was a fist, and closes it around one of his. 'Promise me?'

She doesn't know what she's asking; she's asking the ferret

to loose its dogged grip. But he's seen too many women brutalized by husbands or lovers to shrug it off. A man who will strike his wife or mistress once will seldom stop at that, any more than a detective with one clue will give up the case. He can't promise what she wants; he can only sigh and say, 'Well, for now, anyway.'

'Thank you.' They've come abreast of the cab rank – and rank is a good word for it. The rigs and drivers that serve the theatre crowd tend to be, like many of the theatregoers themselves, somewhat on the shabby side, and the watermen are generally not overzealous in keeping the area tidy. There are sodden piles of hay strewn about, and puddles of muck in the vicinity of the pump, not to mention the inevitable heaps of horseshit.

'Let me get a cab for you,' says Charley. Seeing her dubious look, he hastens to add, 'Not to worry; I won't be sharing the ride.' Well, not in the usual sense, at any rate. But once the cab has pulled forward to a less sloppy spot and he's helped Miss Fairweather into her seat, he circles around to the rear, where he puts a finger to his lips and a shilling into the cabbie's gloved hand. Then he steps onto the metal rail, swings himself up next to the driver, and clings there, like a footman on a countess's carriage, as they set off for Covent Garden.

Instead of dismounting in front of the Royal Theatre as before, Miss Fairweather calls out an address to the driver. Charley doesn't quite catch it, but it's safe to assume that they'll end up in one of the sorry little low-rent areas to the north and east of the Opera House. But no; they turn south instead, toward the Strand.

A few minutes later, the driver makes pointing motions to signal that their destination is just ahead, then makes further motions in the direction of the pavement. Charley nods; the moment the cab begins to slow, he hops down, stumbles and nearly falls on his face, then recovers and heads for one of the trees that line the street. Concealed behind its trunk, he watches as Miss Fairweather climbs out and gracefully ascends the stone steps of a three-story terraced town house.

TWENTY-ONE

O nce the cab and its passenger are safely out of sight, Charley crosses the cobbles and stares up at the brick building. It's completely contrary to the mental image he had of Miss Fairweather's lodgings. Though it's what's called a third-rate town house, that refers only to the size; it's still plenty impressive. You don't get a residence of any sort in this neighborhood for nothing; the rent must be at least double what Jane pays on the Holbrook Street house. How can Miss Fairweather possibly afford such posh digs on an actress's earnings? Either there's a family fortune she hasn't bothered to mention, or . . . or she's being provided for by one of those wealthy admirers they've been bantering about.

As he stands there, gawping, voices drift down from an open window on the second floor; though he can't quite make out the words, there's no missing the harshness with which they're spoken. One voice is unmistakably that of Miss Fairweather; the other is surely a man's, though it's higher pitched than most. Then comes another, more startling sound – the shattering of glass is Charley's guess – and a moment later the window sash is slammed shut by some figure made indistinct by the billowing curtains.

This is probably none of Charley's business, either – not that he's ever let that stop him, not when he's convinced that there's mischief brewing. Perhaps Miss Fairweather and her friend are just having a bit of a quarrel, the sort that happens in every relationship. But that may well be what Eliza Grimwood's neighbors told themselves, too, when she cried out as she was being stabbed to death by William Hubbard.

Charley glances about to be certain the street is empty, then scurries up the steps and tries the door. No need to resort to his picks and rakes; it's open. He slips inside and closes it softly behind him. Though he can hear someone bustling about in the kitchen, he ignores that and focuses on the sounds coming from upstairs. The voices are still at it, but they're a bit more subdued now.

He's tempted to just make a quick and quiet exit; Miss Fairweather won't thank him for sticking his much-broken nose into her affairs – or her affair, singular. But then there's an alarming crash and a resounding thud, as of a body hitting the floor. Charley pounds up the stairs to the room from which the noise came and bursts through the door.

As a copper, he developed early on the ability to size up a situation in a single glance; it's saved his life more than once. The situation in the sitting room does not look good. In the middle of the floor is a coffee table with a broken leg; its marble top has been smashed to pieces. Miss Fairweather is standing next to it, white-faced and trembling. Looming over her is a tall, thin cove in an oriental-looking red dressing gown; his face is flaming red, from anger or drink or both. In one hand he grips a nearly empty glass of whiskey; the other is clamped onto her collarbone, as though he's been shaking her, or means to strangle her.

Charley crosses the room in three strides, thrusts Miss Fairweather aside, and delivers a fierce right cross to her assailant's jaw. The man goes down as easily as a fighter who's been paid to take a fall. He makes no attempt to rise, just sprawls there, his face a picture of astonishment and agony – far more than is warranted by a single punch. Someone seizes Charley's arm and he whirls about, his walking stick raised. But it's not some confederate, as he feared; it's only Miss Fairweather. She doesn't look the least bit relieved or grateful; in fact, she looks furious.

'What do you think you're *doing*?' she demands.

Baffled, Charley stammers, 'I – I thought I was saving you.'

'Well, you thought wrong!' She kneels next to the faux foe and takes his hand. 'Oh, Monty, I'm so sorry. Are you hurt?'

'My pride certainly is,' he murmurs.

Miss Fairweather glares at Charley. 'Don't just stand there like a lummox; help him up!'

Wordlessly, Charley extends a hand. The man grasps it and rises unsteadily, painfully to his feet – or to one foot, at any rate; he seems unable to put any weight on the other one. Miss

Fairweather wraps an arm about his waist and, despite his protests, supports him as he lurches into the nearest armchair.

Charley finally finds his voice. 'I apologize, sir, if I misread the situation. It certainly looked as though you were threatening Miss Fairweather.'

'Well, he wasn't!' snaps the actress. 'He – he lost his balance, and I was helping him regain it, that's all!'

'Julia, please,' says the man. 'I may not be able to walk, but I can speak for myself, at least.' He grasps Charley's hand again, this time in order to shake it. 'You're the famous Inspector Bucket, I suppose? I'm the obscure Montgomery, Lord Bainbury. But anyone who has knocked me down is entitled to call me Monty.' He turns to Miss Fairweather. 'Would you mind fetching me another robe, my dear? This one's drenched in whiskey, I'm afraid.' He shakes his head ruefully. 'Such a waste of good Scotch.' Judging from the way he's slurring his words, the rest of the bottle has been put to good use. And judging from the way he's gripping his right leg with a white-knuckled hand, the whiskey is not doing much to relieve the pain.

Charley nods toward the injured limb. 'Was it a rifle ball? Or a kirpan?'

'How do you know about kirpans? Were you in India?'

'No, but a former colleague of mine fought the Sikhs, and he brought home one of their swords as a souvenir. It was so sharp, he used to shave with it; it impressed the new recruits no end.'

'No doubt. But how did you know *I* was over there?'

'Your dressing gown, for one thing; we don't have dyes like that in England. For another, the shade of your skin; malaria, I assume? And of course—' He gestures toward the far wall '—that portrait of you in uniform. 14th Light Dragoons, were you?'

'Good god, man; you don't miss much, do you?'

'No. I have been known to mis*interpret,* however.'

Monty holds up a hand, as if in benediction. 'A natural mistake. No harm done – or at least very little. To answer your question, it was a Minié ball. *Is,* I should say, since it's still in there somewhere.' When it comes to relating the history of their wounds and scars, soldiers are worse even than coppers. Monty would likely recount the entire battle of Chillianwala in detail except that Miss Fairweather returns just then with the robe he requested and a bottle of laudanum he didn't request. Nevertheless, he obediently swallows the several spoonfuls she feeds him. 'You sit there, now,' she says, 'while I show the inspector out.' She picks up Monty's cane – a beautifully carved piece of Indian mahogany – from the floor and props it against his chair arm. 'I'll put that there, but don't use it unless you absolutely have to, understand?'

Lord Bainbury nods meekly. If anyone is doing a bit of bullying here, it's clearly not him. And yet there's the matter of the bruise. Before he can bring it up, Miss Fairweather beats him to it. As they're descending the stairs, she says softly, 'I know what you're thinking: If he doesn't actually mistreat her – and he doesn't, I assure you – then how did she get the bruise?'

'Well, yes, the thought had crossed my mind.'

'Promise me you won't breathe a word of this to anyone.'

'Haven't you seen my business card? "The utmost discretion and confidentiality." Is that an actual word, by the way?'

'I believe so.' They emerge onto the stone steps, where she takes a seat and motions for him to do the same. 'Though Monty would never admit it to anyone but me – and it was difficult for him to do that – his leg is not the only part of him that bears the scars of that battle.'

'His mind, you mean.' Charley has encountered broken soldiers before, begging for alms – or dangling from rafters.

'Yes. After four years, he still relives it in his dreams. He cries out and thrashes wildly, as though fending off some invisible enemy; I try to comfort and soothe him, and sometimes it works, but other times he takes me for the enemy.' She touches the bruised cheek gingerly.

'I understand.' Perhaps Monty wouldn't have told him all about the battle after all; no doubt he'd prefer to forget it.

'*Now,*' says Miss Fairweather, in a voice that would give any sword-wielding Sikh second thoughts. 'Would you like to tell me how you managed to track me down?'

'I'm sorry,' says Charley, 'I never reveal my methods. I won't do it again, I swear. I was concerned about you, that's all – especially after I heard raised voices and smashing glass.'

He's expecting a heated lecture, but Miss Fairweather, as usual, proves unpredictable. She actually smiles and lays a hand on his arm. 'That's sweet of you, Charley, really it is. But I can handle myself; heaven knows I've had plenty of practice. As for the argument you overheard, it was nothing – or at least nothing new. He was complaining as usual about my "making a spectacle of myself" upon the stage, and I was protesting as usual that it's my *career*, to which he of course replied that I don't *need* a career, he can provide for me perfectly well, to which I of course replied that I can provide perfectly well for *myself*, and – well, you get the idea. The smashing glass was just that – he flung his whiskey tumbler into the fireplace. But you noticed that, I'm sure.'

'Yes, I did. And again, I apologize for jumping to conclusions. But, you know, there's still one thing I don't understand.'

'What's that?'

'Why you didn't want me to know where you actually live.'

She heaves a sigh, as if he's opened a box she'd really rather not open but has known all along she'd have to, eventually. 'What I said before, about providing perfectly well for myself – it's one of those things that we're always telling ourselves and other people, and that we very much wish were true. Unfortunately, it's not. I tried to prove otherwise by forming my own acting company, but all it took was a couple of paragraphs from Mr Dickens' pen to remind me how dependent we are on the generosity of men. Well, not just their generosity; their *approval*.

'I feel sometimes as though I'm still that little girl performing songs and dances for my daddy – on those rare occasions when I actually saw him. It was the only way I knew of to make him actually notice me. It was no good just being myself; that was far too ordinary.'

'For what it's worth,' says Charley, 'I think you're quite extraordinary.'

Miss Fairweather inclines her head until it's resting lightly on his shoulder. 'I know. But you're wrong, you see, because it's all just another song and dance.' She sighs again and gets to her feet. 'He'll be wondering where I am. Really, Charley, don't waste your time worrying about me. I'm better off than I have any right to be. He treats me well; I have a roof over my head – a very elegant one; I dress and dine in style; and every so often I get to show off on the stage. What more could a woman want?'

It's a rhetorical question, of course, but even if it weren't, Charley has no idea what the answer might be. That's a mystery he gave up trying to solve long ago.

He can't bring himself to spend the night at the Holywell Street house. Not that there's much chance of him encountering either Jane or the mother; it's long past their bedtime, and in the morning he could easily get away before they arise. It just seems somehow unfair for him to go there after having spent the evening with another woman, even though he's done nothing to be ashamed of – unless you count flattening a wounded war hero. In some odd way, it seems unfair to Miss Fairweather, too; it suggests that he can change women as carelessly as clothing, with as little thought as he might give to leaving one public house and repairing to another down the street.

Charley does, in fact, repair to the tavern down the street, but only for a single pint; then he makes his way to his office in Ebury Square. As usual, the post contains several appeals from prospective clients, but there's also a note from, of all people, Miss Treville, the attractive young woman who held his left hand so tightly at Professor Sledge's séance. She'd like to meet with him at his earliest convenience. Well, the earlier the better, by Charley's lights. His smile fades as he examines the last piece of mail. The envelope is familiar-looking and the hand-writing is even more familiar. The message it contains is as terse as a telegram: *Mother dying. Please come at once.*

Charley isn't unduly alarmed. Jane does have a penchant for exaggeration and a flair for the melodramatic, so he takes the message with a grain of salt. 'Dying' no doubt means that the mother is complaining more than usual. And he takes 'at once' to mean 'sometime today,' so he doesn't bother with a cab.

The trouble with chronic exaggeration, of course, is that when the situation truly is dire, you have no way of conveying that fact. By the time Charley arrives at his wife's house, it's well

past midnight, and her mother is already gone. He can't pretend
to be devastated by her death, but he realizes that Jane must
be, and he's had enough experience dealing with the families
of suicides and murder victims to at least put on a convincing
show of sympathy.

Though it's little enough in the way of comfort, it seems to
be all that Jane needs. She doesn't chastise him for taking his
sweet time in getting there, nor does she remind him of how
unkind he was to her mother, and how it's too late to beg her
forgiveness. She just wraps her arms around him and buries her
head in his chest. Awkwardly, he pats her shoulder and murmurs,
'There, there.' He can't recall the last time they embraced.
Though she's not a strong woman, he feels almost the way he
felt in the clutches of the Chinese Colossus – as though all the
breath is being squeezed out of him.

The next few days are even more awkward and suffocating,
but he does his best. Aside from the occasional pipe-smoking
break or trip to the slap-bang for coffee – theirs has improved
noticeably, too – he can't possibly desert his post until after the
funeral, and even then it's not easy. 'I'm sorry, my dear,' he
says, the morning after they put her mother in the ground, 'but
I have cases that demand my attention; some of them are quite
urgent.'

'More urgent than being with your family at a time of
mourning?'

'Well, you know, if your mother had been murdered, I'd do
everything in my power to find her killer. But she died of natural
causes, Jane; there's nothing I can do for her. There are people
out there, however, who *do* need my help.'

'And what about me? What if *I* need your help, to get through
this?'

'You have your friends,' he says – quite reasonably, it seems
to him. 'I'm sure they can offer you much more than I can.'

Jane fixes him with a glare so accusatory that he, who has
faced down a hundred hardened criminals, is forced to look
away. 'Yes,' she says, coldly. 'Perhaps they can. Perhaps they
won't have more important things to do.'

Charley doesn't reveal, of course, that one of his urgent tasks
is to meet with the charming Miss Treville. He's already replied

to her note, suggesting a time – this very morning, in fact – and a place. It's a tricky business, arranging a tête-à-tête with a young lady. He could hardly have her here, even under the best of circumstances; Jane would never let him hear the last of it. There's always his office, but it wouldn't be quite proper without a chaperone, and she didn't mention that possibility. For a respectable woman, a coffeehouse or an ordinary is out of the question. The forecourt of the British Museum is a popular meeting-place, but not very convenient for Miss Treville, who lives in the southern suburbs. Finally, he settled on the Crystal Palace, which has recently reopened at its new site in Sydenham.

Or at least he thought it had. The Palace has indeed been relocated but, though construction seems to be complete, for some reason it's not yet open to the public and won't be until June, according to a sign stuck in the newly laid sod. It's hardly a catastrophe, but it certainly is unfortunate, particularly since it's begun to drizzle. 'The devil take me,' mutters Charley. Spotting Miss Treville huddled near the un-enter-able entrance, he adds, 'And he can take the bloody Crystal Palace, too.' Well, at least she had the foresight to bring an umbrella.

She waves cheerily to him, then points to a wooden shed that stands nearby – a temporary haven for the construction crew and their tools, no doubt. They both scurry toward the shelter. Miss Treville gets there first, to her obvious delight. 'I win!' she cries, jumping up and down like a child who's crossed the finish line first in a sack race.

'You had a head start,' growls Charley good-naturedly, as he shakes the water from his frock coat. 'I don't understand why we can't get in. The grand opening was to have been on May Day.'

Miss Treville stares at him, wide-eyed. 'Oh, haven't you heard?'

'Heard what?'

'The reason for the delay!' She puts a hand to her mouth to stifle a giggle. 'It's because of the statues.'

'The statues?'

'Well, not all of them. Just the male ones. Well, not all the male ones, either. Only the *unclothed* male ones. Someone – no one seems to know exactly who – declared them indecent. Apparently they plan to chisel off the offending parts.'

'Good lord,' says Charley, wincing in empathy. 'Wouldn't fig leaves do the trick?'

'Perhaps reason will prevail – though I doubt it.' In lieu of a chair, she boosts herself up onto a workbench. 'But we didn't come here to discuss fig leaves, Inspector.'

'I'm glad to hear that. What *are* we here for, Miss Treville? Your note gave me no clue.'

'We're here,' she says, confidentially, 'because I have some interesting information to share.'

'Information? About what?'

'About Professor Sledge and his spiritual telegraph. It appears the device is a fake.'

TWENTY-TWO

'**B**efore we get into that,' says Miss Treville, 'I should explain that I'm not what I appear to be: A spoiled young socialite with nothing better to do than attend garden parties and spirit manifestations.'

'I never imagined you were.'

'Of course you did. But the fact is—' She leans into him, as if to divulge some dire secret. 'I am a newspaper reporter.'

'Are you? If you'll pardon my ignorance, I didn't know there was such a thing as a female reporter.'

'There isn't; not officially, anyway. But I convinced my editor that some stories may be covered more successfully by a woman. Say, for example, he wants someone to write up a series of pieces about spiritualism and whether or not there's any truth to it. No offense, Inspector, but men are by and large not very good at deception. If he sends in one of his worldly wise male reporters, the medium will likely spot him as a ringer right away. But who would suspect an innocent ingénue of being after anything more than a harmless bit of titillation? Naturally, I'll have to write my stories under a *nom de plume*, as the

Brontës did; we don't want to send our readers into a state of shock. I thought I might call myself Cesario. What do you think? Too obvious?'

Charley isn't all that keen on Shakespeare, but he did see a production of *Twelfth Night* a few years ago. He's even kept the playbill, for, curiously enough, the part of Viola/Cesario was played by none other than Miss Fairweather. How can anyone take Mr Dickens to task for relying too much on coincidences when the world is so full of them? Dressed in men's clothing, the actress looked quite fetching.

'I didn't learn much at that first séance,' says Miss Treville. 'I thought I'd just sit tight and see what you came up with. Like you, I assumed that Sledge was controlling the spiritual telegraph somehow, and when it operated independently of him, I was set back a bit. Obviously, you were, too – especially when it seemed that your friend's spirit was speaking to you.'

'*Seemed*? You don't think it was genuine, then?'

She lays a sympathetic hand on his arm. 'I'm sorry to say so, Charley, but I'm sure it was just another of the Professor's tricks. You see, after the séance, I did some investigating. You remember Mrs Morley, the woman who believed her dead husband was communicating with her? Well, I talked to several of her friends, and it turns out that, a few days earlier, one of them – the neighborhood gossip, I gather – was contacted by a man claiming to be an old sweetheart of Mrs Morley's. He didn't want to intrude upon Mrs Morley, he said; he only wanted to know what had become of her, whether she was happy and so on. The woman was glad to give him an earful.'

'Clever. Naturally he asked her to say nothing to Mrs Morley.'

'Right. And naturally her description of the "sweetheart" matched the Professor's, right down to the Scots accent. So, now that I had evidence that he was a sham, I tried to get a seat at another séance. It wasn't easy.'

'I know,' says Charley. 'I tried, as well.'

'Apparently the Professor doesn't like repeat customers. After all, once that initial sense of awe has worn off, a person might start asking questions. But I kept pestering him until he gave in. Now, here comes the interesting part. There was one other repeat customer besides me. Who do you suppose it was?'

'Mrs Morley?'

She shakes her head. 'Mrs Joliffe.'

'The sweet old lady who seemed so flustered?'

'That's the one. I got to wondering whether she was a regular, and if so, whether *she* might be the one running the telegraph. In order to get a better look at the mechanism, I accidentally dropped my handkerchief and spent a good thirty seconds retrieving it from beneath the table. For some reason that setup with the wires and the weights put me in mind of a sewing machine treadle, and how you operate it by pressing with your feet. And then I noticed that the weights had small holes near the bottom of them.'

'Hmm. I saw that, too. I didn't think much of it at the time, but I suppose if a person had, let's say, little hooks in the toes of their shoes . . .'

Miss Treville grins broadly. 'Exactly! So clumsy me, while we were having tea I dropped my spoon, right at the feet of sweet old Mrs Joliffe. And guess what? Her practical shoes turned out to be far more practical that anyone could have guessed.'

'They were equipped with hooks.'

'They were. Very tiny ones, to be sure. It must have taken a good deal of practice to master the technique of snagging those weights. I'm afraid that, as the séance got underway, I did something even clumsier.'

'Oh, dear,' says Charley, tongue in cheek. 'Don't tell me: you knocked over the candle.'

'I did – right onto the carpet. Naturally, I lunged for it and, in the process, got a good look at what was going on beneath the table. Mrs Joliffe was frantically trying to unhook her shoes, but she wasn't quite quick enough.'

Charley guffaws and claps his hand appreciatively. 'Well done, Miss Treville!'

She smiles and gives a modest shrug. 'I'm sure that, if you'd had a second go at it, you'd have figured it out. Speaking of which, have you learned anything more about your friend's murder?'

He shakes his head ruefully. 'Nothing. But of course, if the message from Rosa was a fake, then so was the business about Hubbard, and I've been chasing after a wild goose all this time.'

'Where do you suppose Sledge learned about him, and about your friend – what was her name? Rose?'

'Rosa. I don't know,' says Charley. 'But I'm about to find out.'

It would be useless, of course, to ask Sledge for a seat at another séance. Charley's best bet is to just barge in on the man and demand an explanation. As it turns out, there's no barging or demanding necessary; apparently he's expected. The Professor hasn't even bothered telling the housekeeper to say that he's not at home. Charley finds him in the parlor, dismantling the spiritual telegraph. Without even looking up, Sledge says, 'Good afternoon, Inspector.'

'Not so good for you, it looks like.'

'Nae, I'm afraid that, once Miss Treville's story appears, my credibility will *dis*appear, along with my clientele – except for the ones who take me to court, of course, in an attempt to recover the money they donated.'

'Donated?'

'To the Foundation for Spiritual Research.'

'Ah. I wondered what was in it for you.'

The Professor sighs and turns away from his task. 'You may consider me a mountebank, Inspector, but I assure you, my intentions were good. I've spent half my life working to further our knowledge of the spirit world and how to communicate with it, and I've had some success. But "some success" is never good enough, is it? Look at it from your perspective: If someone hires you to take on a case, they dinna want you to find a clue, or to offer a theory, do they? They simply want you to solve the case. By the same token, very few people are content to sit silently for hours, waiting – usually in vain – for a spirit to make its presence known. They want results, and they want them now.'

'Even if it's a lie?'

'Dinna tell me, Inspector, that you've never lied to a client, told them what they wanted to hear?'

Only a hundred times or so – not as a private enquiry agent, perhaps, but certainly when he was a copper. It went with the job. What wife, after all, wants to hear that her beloved husband succumbed to his heart attack while in the arms of another woman? What mother wants to know that her daughter died, not as the result of a miscarriage, but as the result of a botched abortion? What son would have you tell him that his father, the constable, was knifed not by a criminal he was apprehending but by a fellow card player who caught him cheating?

Charley says none of this, of course. 'You invited me to that séance,' he says, 'in order to prove you were legitimate. Or so you said. I take it that was a lie, too.'

The Professor considers a moment, then reluctantly nods.

'In reality,' says Charley, 'you brought me here to feed me false information about Rosa's murder. Now, that may have been just a trick on your part, a way of convincing me that we were communing with the spirit world, but I don't think so. I think someone paid you to do it – someone who knew details about Rosa and her daughter. Someone who was aware of Hubbard, and my connection to him. Someone who wanted to get me off his tail for good and all, send me in another direction altogether. There's only one cove I can think of who fits the bill. I don't expect you to give me his name. In the first place, it's probably not his real name. In the second place, if you do tell me, and he finds out, he's likely to come after you.'

'He may have a wee bit of trouble finding me,' says Sledge. 'I'm off to Europe, to try my luck there. In any case, he never said his name. But nae doubt you know him by his appearance – a tall, thin skyte with black hair and bulging eyes and something wrong with his neck.'

Always before, when the law began breathing on him too hot and heavy, the nasty Mr Neck just hooked it for some other shire where his face and reputation weren't so well known. Since Charley has had no luck at all locating him, he assumed that the villain used that same strategy again, that after the narrow escape at Mrs Bramble's he went off somewhere safe to lick his wounds.

But if he's gone to all this trouble and expense to throw Charley off the scent, it must mean that he's still hanging about London. The scheme he so rashly spoke of to Rosa must be profitable indeed, to be worth that much risk. It's unlikely that he's just engaged in the same sorts of mischief and mayhem that have been his specialty all along – burgling, mugging, fraud, arson; Charley's informants would surely have got wind of those. He must have ventured into new territory. Apparently he's found himself a new hidey-hole as well, somewhere very out of the way, somewhere Charley would never think of looking – a church, for example, or maybe a monastery. Well, no; even Neck would never stoop to that.

Inspector Bucket's Private Enquiry Agency still has a bit of a backlog, but the jobs are all pretty mundane and minor; he should be able to make time for some more pavement pounding. That's the plan, anyway. But, as everyone knows, making a plan is like making a pie crust; it's always stickier than it should be and very often it falls apart altogether. The very next day, he's presented with a case that can't be postponed or refused or solved with one hand tied behind his back.

He almost wishes he *could* refuse it. When investigating a crime, he's always done his best to remain detached, objective, to assess the situation in an unbiased, clear-eyed fashion. Rosa's murder, of course, is the exception; he has a personal stake in that one, and he suspects that it's clouded his judgment, made him overlook some crucial bit of evidence, made him snatch at straws such as the phony spirit message. He certainly doesn't need another case like that one.

But whether he wants it or not, he's stuck with it. As he'd be the first to admit, he does have a certain tendency to play Sir Galahad; he'd have a hard time turning down a plea for help from any woman at all, let alone from the enchanting, perplexing Miss Julia Fairweather. To make it even harder to say no, she doesn't present her appeal through the post, or by ticket porter. She shows up at his office in person.

It's late in the day, and Charley is debating whether to do his duty and spend the evening with his wife, comforting and consoling her insofar as he's able, which isn't really very far. Well, even Galahad was a bit lacking in that department; a suit of armor is all very well for rescuing maidens, but when consoling is required, it gets in the way. Just as Charley has resigned himself to his fate and is heading for the door, it flies open and Miss Fairweather makes a dramatic entrance. For once, though, it's obvious that she's not playing a part. She has the distracted, desperate look of someone who's seriously troubled, or *in* trouble, or both.

'Oh, Charley!' she cries. For the second time in the space of three days, a woman wraps her arms about him and buries her face in his chest. Though he feels guilty admitting it, Charley enjoys this embrace a good deal more than the last.

'What is it? What's happened?'

'It's Monty! He's had an accident!'

'What sort of accident?'

'He lost his balance on the stairs, and – and—' She breaks off, sobbing.

'He fell? Good lord. Did you call a doctor?'

She moves her head slightly – a nod, Charley supposes, though it's hard to be sure, with all those layers of silk waistcoat between them. 'It was no use. He said – he said Monty's neck was broken. And then – and then he called a constable.'

'Oh. Well, that's not unusual, if there's any chance . . .' He trails off.

She looks up at him, her dark eyes wide and filled with tears. 'If there's any chance it *wasn't* an accident. That's what you were going to say, isn't it?'

Charley doesn't reply. He doesn't have to; he's certain she can read the answer in his face.

'They think . . . they think that I caused it somehow, don't they?'

'They may think it, but they can't accuse you or detain you, not unless there's some evidence, some clear *motive*. You certainly had no reason to want him dead; after all, you depended – that is—'

'Go ahead and say it, Charley; it's the truth. I depended upon him, for everything I had.' She leans her forehead against his chest once more. 'And what in god's name am I going to do *now*?'

TWENTY-THREE

When Charley returns to the town house with Miss Fairweather, Lord Bainbury's body is gone. There's nothing mysterious about the fact; the doctor and the constable have simply laid him out the coolest spot available – the cellar – where he will await a viewing by the coroner and his jury, a process that's unlikely to happen for a day or two. It's the house girl's night off and, as most people would be, Miss Fairweather is spooked by the prospect of sharing the house with a corpse. 'Would you stay with me?' she begs Charley.

Now there's a proposition that's difficult to refuse. There's nothing he'd like better, of course, and yet it doesn't seem entirely proper. 'Hmm. I'm not sure that—'

'Please, Charley. I'm asking as a friend, but I'm also asking as a client.'

'A client?'

'Well, I thought that if you did a bit of – what do you call it? Poking about? – you might be able to prove that it was an accident.'

'Oh.' Though he would have preferred to be cast in the role of friend rather than detective, he's ready and willing to help however he can. 'I'm not sure it'll do any good, but I'll give it a go.' He takes out his notebook. 'First, I'll want to ask you some questions, if you're up to it.'

'I think so – if we do it over drinks.'

It's brandy she has in mind, but Charley settles for tea; he doesn't want his objectivity compromised any more than it already is. 'All right. First off, I'm assuming that, when the accident happened, the house girl was already gone?'

'Yes. In fact—' Miss Fairweather seems close to breaking down again, but she takes a deep, ragged breath and starts over. 'In fact, if she had been here, it might – it might never have happened.'

'We don't have to do this now, Julia, if you'd rather not.'

'No, no. I want you to get it all down in black and white, in case they try to force a confession out of me later.'

'I won't let them,' he assures her. 'Go on.'

'Monty was always trying to do things for himself; he didn't like feeling helpless. When we dined together, he insisted on coming down here – it's more civilized, he said. He wouldn't let me help him on the stairs. I always walked ahead of him, though, so that, if he did stumble, I could catch him. But this evening, I was . . . I was reading to him, and I – I fell asleep in my chair. I suppose he got hungry and didn't want to wake me, and he couldn't ring for the maid, so he . . .'

'I understand. I'm sorry if it seems rude to ask, but had you given him his dose of laudanum?'

'No. He always took it as late in the day as possible; he said it spoiled his appetite, and he was afraid that, if he didn't eat well, he'd lose what little strength he had.'

'But he'd had a drink or two, I'm guessing.'

She nods. 'Lately, he was never without a drink in his hand. It didn't help much with the pain, he said; it was more just to calm him, to help him forget.'

'Forget?'

'The horrors of that battle. He seldom spoke about it, but I know it tormented him.'

'Again, I apologize, but I have to ask this: You don't suppose it could have been a . . . well, a *deliberate* accident?'

'You think he might have done it on purpose?'

'Perhaps not consciously. But sometimes when people are careless, it's because they *don't* care; it doesn't matter to them whether they live or die.'

'I suppose it's possible. I did my best to make him happy, Charley, but it got more and more difficult with each day that passed.'

'I'm sorry it turned out this way.' Charley closes the notebook. 'Well, I'll do my poking about now; there's no need for you to come. Just sit there and try to calm yourself; everything will be all right.'

'You promise?'

Charley turns away, pretending not to hear; he doesn't like

making promises he's not certain he can keep. Donning his
spectacles, he goes over every inch of the stairwell, like a miser
searching for a dropped farthing. But even before he does that,
he's discovered his first piece of evidence: Monty's whiskey
glass, which somehow survived the tumble down the stairs and
came to rest against one of the walls in the entryway. It's empty,
of course, but by sniffing about in bloodhound fashion he deter-
mines where it fell; there's no mistaking the peaty scent of a
good Scotch whiskey. The spot is only four steps from the top,
which means Monty had the glass in one hand as he started
down the stairs – not the best idea even with two good legs.

When Charley examines the bannister, he notices that the
glossy finish has been scraped by something hard, and recently,
too, judging from the tiny flakes of varnish that still cling to it.
Whatever made the scratch left behind a trace of something
dark red. No, it's not dried blood. Charley's guess is that it
came from the Indian mahogany cane he saw on his previous
visit, leaning against Monty's armchair. So: The man has a bum
leg; he's under the influence; he has a cane in one hand and a
whiskey glass in the other, which means he's not holding onto
the bannister, at least not tightly – it would have been remarkable if he *hadn't* fallen.

Unfortunately, Charley can't seem to find the actual cane.
Nor can Miss Fairweather. 'Well,' says Charley, 'that's curious.
Perhaps the constable took it, as evidence. I don't suppose it
matters, in any case. It's pretty obvious what happened.' He
only hopes it'll be as obvious to the coroner and the jury.

Charley gets very little sleep that night – not because he's
concerned about how the crowner's quest will go, nor because
he's curled up in an armchair in the sitting room, nor even
because of the corpse in the cellar. Dead bodies don't bother
him particularly; it's the thought of the live one lying only one
room away that keeps him awake.

She's left her bedroom door ajar, and each time she tosses
about or mutters in her sleep, he hears it and can't help imagining
that she's calling softly to him, or that she's rising restlessly from
her bed and will appear in the doorway at any moment, wearing
only a nightgown and beckoning him.

She doesn't, of course – which is probably just as well. To

add to the aches and pains that are the natural result of trying to sleep in an armchair, he's experiencing the occasional twinge of guilt; he probably should have at least let Jane know that he wouldn't be coming home. He's never worried much about that in the past, nor did she, but things are different since her mother died. Jane seems more fragile, somehow, as if, like Monty, she's been wounded and needs someone to lean on.

He assumed that the house girl would return from her day off at some early hour and prepare breakfast for them; when that doesn't happen, Charley finds a coffee stall and brings back muffins and Mocha. The muffins are delicious; the coffee is swill, but at least it's hot swill. 'I don't understand,' says Miss Fairweather, 'why Arly isn't here by now. I hope nothing's happened to her.'

'So do I,' says Charley. Actually, he's wondering whether there could be some more sinister reason for the girl's absence. Perhaps he's being unnecessarily suspicious, but that's one of the hazards of the detective business. 'How long has she worked for you?'

'She was here when I moved in, nearly a year ago. Apparently she'd been a maid before that, at the family's country house, but Lady Bainbury didn't like her, so when Monty leased this place, he brought her here.'

'Pardon me for asking, but was she . . . well, was she anything *more* than a house girl, do you think?'

Miss Fairweather gives him a wry glance. 'You don't have to worry about my sensibilities, Charley. I'm in the theatre, remember? You mean, was she his mistress? Very likely.'

'She must have resented it, then, when you came on the scene.'

'Probably. If so, she kept it to herself. If she hadn't, she'd have risked losing her position. An attractive young woman can always get a man; jobs are harder to find.'

'Hmm. I don't know much about women, I'll grant you, but it seems to me they seldom forgive a hurt or an insult, or forget it.'

'What are you saying, Charley? You think she's somehow responsible for . . . for what happened?'

'I don't see how she could be. But I'm not going to rule it out.'

'And are you ruling out the possibility that *I'm* responsible?' Though her tone says she's only joking, the look in her eyes suggests otherwise.

Charley sips at his coffee and says, with studied nonchalance, 'I can't imagine that, either. But it's my job to consider every possibility until the evidence provides a solution.'

'Ah. We're being brutally honest again, are we? Well, as you say, that's what I hired you for.'

'I don't expect to be paid, you know.'

'Good. Because I can't afford it – or anything else, including rent. They'll be throwing me out of here soon, I'm sure.' She gives a grin that manages to be both rueful and mischievous. 'How do you suppose Jane would feel about my moving in with her?'

Charley smiles, too, and shrugs. 'Who knows? She might be glad of the company.'

The house girl doesn't turn up at lunchtime, either. Miss Fairweather – who has mimed cooking meals onstage, but otherwise has no notion how it's done – puts together a platter of cheese, cold cuts, and bread. Meanwhile, Charley conducts a full-scale investigation of the kitchen and uncovers a bag of coffee and a grinder, but no apparatus for brewing. He's forced to resort to the method he learned long ago, while living at the station house: Add the grounds to a pot of boiling water and throw in a couple of eggshells to settle them.

After lunch, he turns his attention to Arly's room, hoping to discover something – old love letters, keepsakes, legal documents – that will either incriminate the girl or exonerate her. He finds none of those things, but what he does discover is nearly as revealing. The chest of drawers and the wardrobe are surprisingly well-made and in good condition – more befitting a mistress than a domestic. They're also practically empty. The only items in the wardrobe are two maid's uniforms and a pair of shoes. It's beginning to look as though her disappearance was not unexpected at all, but planned.

He decides to hold off on mentioning any of this to Miss Fairweather; better to wait and see whether she brings it up. No doubt he should give her room a going-over, too, but he doesn't want to make her feel as though she's a suspect, for she isn't. Not just yet, anyway.

But an hour or so later, the situation takes an unexpected turn. Charley is down in the cellar, checking the corpse for anything out of the ordinary, when the front doorbell chimes. Miss Fairweather calls, 'Could you please get that, Charley? I don't want to see anyone.'

Whoever is at the door, he or she is an impatient blighter; before Charley can answer it, the bell has rung four more times. To his surprise, the caller is familiar to him, though it takes him a moment to recall from where and when. The man has gained a few pounds and a set of mutton-chop whiskers. No doubt the latter is calculated to make him look more authoritative and mature; he can't be more than twenty-five, after all. Further evidence that the world is falling into the hands of children. Even if they hadn't met, Charley would have made him as a copper easily enough. In his plain clothing, he might almost pass for a banker or a barrister, but the standard issue seven-league boots are a dead giveaway. 'Dolly Williamson,' says Charley.

'Inspector!' The detective sergeant thrusts out a pudgy hand. 'You've beaten me to the punch yet again!'

'It's good to see you,' says Charley, and for the most part he means it. Though Adolphus Williamson joined the force only two years before Charley left, he quickly proved himself a very likable, dedicated and resourceful fellow, not to mention a pretty fair sparring partner. Still, Charley would be a lot happier *not* to see him; his presence here means that the Detective Branch has suspicions of some sort. 'Are you conducting an investigation?'

'Not exactly.' Dolly grins good-naturedly. 'I'm sure you've taken care of that for us, eh? No, I'm here to remand Miss Fairweather into custody, until the coroner's inquest.'

Charley doesn't invite the sergeant in; instead, he steps outside and pulls the door closed behind him. 'Why? Is she accused of something?'

'Not accused, just suspected.'

'As far as I can tell, Lord Bainbury's death was an accident, nothing more.'

'Well, that's what I figured, too . . . until about an hour ago, when I talked to his solicitor. It seems that Bainbury recently changed his will; it now says that, in the event of his death, this property here goes to Miss Fairweather.'

Charley can't help wincing. That's not going to play well at the inquest; it sounds too much like a motive. 'But that's hardly some great windfall for her; she couldn't possibly make the payments on it.'

'She won't have to,' says Williamson. 'The lease is already paid up. For the next thirty-three years.'

Charley puts a hand to his forehead and mutters, 'The devil take me.'

'I'm sorry, Charley. Don't be blaming yourself; we all get it wrong now and again.' Williamson puts a sympathetic hand on his shoulder, but Charley shrugs it off.

'Have they scheduled the inquest yet?'

'Seven this evening, at Offley's.'

Charley groans. 'That's not much time. Could you do me a favor, Dolly? Don't run Miss Fairweather in; just keep her here, will you? If word of this gets out, it'll surely hurt her career. Notoriety is one thing; being accused of murder is another.'

'All right. I'll tell the Branch that I'm investigating. I'll need to be here for the viewing, at any rate.'

'Thanks. You're a good man. Is it all right if I speak with her?'

'Be my guest. I'm not eager to break the news to her.'

Charley starts inside, then turns back. 'What prompted you to visit Bainbury's solicitor, anyway?'

'It wasn't a what, it was a who: Lady Bainbury. She practically demanded Miss Fairweather's head on a platter.'

Charley shudders at the thought. 'You think Her Nibs will turn up at the inquest?'

'And mingle with the hoi polloi? I doubt it.'

Charley finds Miss Fairweather curled up in the same armchair in which he spent the night, a fact that creates a disturbing sense of intimacy. When he clears his throat nervously, she glances up from the script she's perusing.

'Sorry. Just going over *Henry VIII*. Elton's doing it next, and he's offered me a role. Who was at the door?'

'Um . . . a detective, actually.'

'Damn. What did he want?'

Charley doesn't reply. He pulls up a footstool close to her chair and sits. 'I need you to tell me the truth about something, Julia.'

She gives him a bright smile. 'Don't I always?' When he again fails to reply, the smile fades and she shrugs a bit sheepishly. 'That's a silly question, isn't it? Of course I don't. Well, I'm not very good at honesty, but I'll try.'

'Try very hard. It's important.' He stares straight into her dark eyes, and she doesn't look away. 'Were you aware that Monty left this place to you in his will?'

Her eyes blink and grow wide; her mouth drops open slightly. Either she's genuinely surprised or she's an even better actress than he thought. '*What*?'

'He never mentioned it to you?'

'Not a word. Not even a hint.' She looks about the room in a dazed fashion, as if trying to grasp the notion that it belongs to her. 'Are you sure?'

'So says his solicitor.'

'My god. I had no idea.' Her expression changes yet again, as she realizes the implications of this. 'Will the coroner and the jury be told?' When Charley simply nods, she groans and puts her head in her hands. 'It'll seem as though I had a reason to . . . to want him dead.'

'I'm afraid so.'

As with most of her moods, her despair doesn't last long; when she raises her head a moment later, there's a hopeful look on her face. 'But what if someone were to vouch for me? To verify that I knew nothing about the will?'

'You have someone in mind?'

'Yes,' she says, 'I do.'

Five minutes later, Charley is in a cab, heading for the Princess's Theatre. Though it's only a half hour away on foot, he can't afford to waste time. He only hopes that the acting company will be around this far in advance of the evening curtain. Luckily they've already begun rehearsals for *Henry VIII*, without Miss Fairweather. Charley doesn't wait for the troupe to take a break;

he pushes past the boyish assistant stage manager and strides onto the set as though this is not Shakespeare they're doing, but a second-rate murder mystery in which he's been cast as The Inspector.

Mr Elton is, of course, playing the much-married monarch himself, and the part seems to have gone to his head. He gives the intruder an imperious glare and indignantly demands, 'Who the devil are you, and what do you want?'

Charley has learned from long experience when a situation requires subtlety and tact, and when a more direct approach is called for. Elton is used to being in charge; he needs to be disabused of that notion right away. Seizing the astonished director by the front of his frilly shirt, Charley drags him downstage, away from the others. 'I'll tell you who I am,' he says in a voice that's like a knife – quiet but deadly. 'I'm the cove who's going to knock your bloody teeth down your throat if you don't cooperate. Is that clear?' When Elton, who has been struck dumb, nods fearfully, Charley releases him. 'Good. I'm Inspector Field, and I need to ask you some questions. Can we go somewhere private?'

Elton straightens his clothing and puts on a strained smile. 'Of course, Inspector. We're always happy to assist the police.' He conducts Charley to the property room, where they seat themselves on a couple of steamer trunks.

'Now, tell me: How well do you know Miss Fairweather?'

'Julia? I – she's acted in several of my shows. I'd say we're friends, but not close friends. Why?'

'Has she ever said anything to you about her . . . living arrangements?'

Elton momentarily regains some of his haughtiness. 'I don't think it would be proper to discuss such matters without Miss Fairweather's consent.'

'I don't care what you think,' growls Charley, 'and I don't care whether it's proper or improper. Just answer the question.'

'Uh, well, I don't suppose it's any great secret that she's being . . . provided for.'

'Has she told you that herself?'

'Not in so many words. But a few days ago, she came to me in tears. She said that Lord B— That her benefactor—'

'Lord Bainbury, I know. Go on.'

'Well, she said that he's been very ill, and she's afraid that, if anything happens to him, she'll have nowhere to go. She asked me – practically begged me – to cast her in another play, so she'd have a little income of her own. And, well . . . I obliged.'

'Very generous of you.' Elton may be able to carry off Henry VIII, but he's not very convincing in the role of beneficent theatre manager. He's concealing something, most likely something he's a bit ashamed of. 'And in return?'

The director shifts uncomfortably on the trunk. 'What do you mean?'

'You agreed to give her a role; what did she agree to do for you?'

'Why . . . just to appear in the play, that's all.'

'I don't believe you,' says Charley. 'However, I'll let it go – for now.' Elton looks distinctly relieved – at least until Charley adds, 'Provided, of course, that *you* agree to do something for me.'

TWENTY-FOUR

When Charley enters the long gallery above Offley's Tavern with his witness in tow, the inquest is already underway. Mr Mallett is seated at his bench, which has been jury-rigged – literally, by several members of the jury – from two sawhorses and a discarded door. Charley has known Mallett ever since joining the force. The coroner seemed ancient even then; now he looks as though he might be the subject of an inquest himself, any day.

The jury is a small one – only fourteen men – and one of them seems to have no idea why he's here; no doubt they've recruited him from the tavern just to avoid having an unlucky number. There are more spectators than is usual at an inquest – probably because the deceased is high born; working folk are always curious about the affairs of the rich and titled. But they're

also more subdued than normal, perhaps in deference to Miss
Fairweather, who sits all alone, looking quite forlorn and quite
beautiful. When Charley catches her eye and nods, she seems
to relax a little, but otherwise maintains her melancholy mien.

Dolly Williamson stands before the bench, recounting what
Lord Bainbury's solicitor revealed to him about the will, and
doing so with obvious reluctance; no doubt Miss Fairweather
has won him over in the short time available to her. The information causes such a stir among the jury members and spectators
that Mr Mallett must rouse himself and call for order, so feebly
that Williamson is forced to relay the message. 'Ladies and
gentlemen!' he says, in a voice that's far from feeble. 'Quiet,
please!' He turns back to the coroner. 'That's all I have for
now, Your Honor. But I see that Inspector Field has just arrived;
I'm sure he will be able to enlighten you further.'

Charley's done this sort of thing a hundred times, and he
knows how to work a jury. Not that he would lie to them,
exactly, or even deliberately mislead them. But he doesn't want
to confuse them either, so he tells tell them only what they need
to know. For example, there's no point in mentioning the cane,
since he doesn't yet know what became of it. Nor does he bring
up Arly, the house girl, and his vague suspicions about her. He
can follow up on those later on; for now, the important thing
is to establish Miss Fairweather's innocence.

Slowly and in great detail, he lays out the evidence for them;
he emphasizes the fact that Lord Bainbury drank heavily, that
he'd taken another fall very recently, that he was always trying
to do things he shouldn't. Once he's sure they've taken all that
in, he broaches the subject of the will. There's no point dancing
around it; he readily admits that, at first glance, it may seem
to incriminate Miss Fairweather. This gets the men of the jury
worked up again; some seem to be objecting, some agreeing.
'But!' Charley continues, over the babble, 'that would be true
only if she *knew* about the will! Which, as Mr Elton will make
clear, she most certainly did not!'

He's been hoping all along that Elton, like any actor worth
his salt, will make the most of his moment in the limelight, and
the man doesn't disappoint. He approaches the bench like Henry
VIII making his grand entrance in Scene II. The murmuring

swells again, even louder, and not only from the jury but from the audience. Surely a substantial number of them have seen the celebrated actor looming larger than life upon the stage, and now here he is, gracing them with his presence – as if a dead lord and a beautiful woman in distress weren't enough.

In well-rounded tones and with great feeling, Mr Elton recreates his dialogue with Miss Fairweather; in his hands, it becomes a full-fledged dramatic scene, and when he's done, a few of the spectators actually applaud.

The coroner has a question. Charley catches it but, knowing he may be the only one, he repeats it. 'His Honor would like to know when this conversation took place.'

'The day before yesterday, Your Honor,' says Elton.

Mr Mallett turns to Dolly Williamson and croaks, 'Did you happen to note the date of Lord Bainbury's will?'

'I did, Your Honor. April 14th, of this year.'

'Nearly two months ago, then. So Miss Fairweather clearly knew nothing about the will – unless Lord Bainbury told her sometime in the past two days.' For the first time, he addresses the lady herself. 'Did he, Miss Fairweather?'

'No, Your Honor. And even if he had, it certainly would not have caused me to – to—' She begins sobbing softly into her lace handkerchief. For a moment, Charley fears that the audience will break into applause again, but they don't. Instead, the gallery is as hushed and still as a Friends' meeting house. He spots several of the female spectators pulling out their own handkerchiefs.

Though Mr Mallett seems barely able to lift his gavel, he manages to bang it hard enough to startle everyone. 'Gentlemen of the jury, will you please gather at the other end of the room and discuss this amongst yourselves? And would someone please bring me a pint of mild?'

Mr Elton, Sergeant Williamson, and Charley all converge on Miss Fairweather and ask, almost in one voice, whether she's all right. 'Yes,' she says, sniffling, 'just a little shaken, that's all. Mr Elton, I'm so grateful to you for speaking out on my behalf. I don't know how to thank you.'

Judging from Elton's subtly salacious smile, he's already thought of several possibilities. But he says, with an air of magisterial munificence, 'I'm only too happy to be of help, my dear.'

Of course, there's no guarantee that his testimony will, in fact, prove helpful; Charley is about to point that out when there's a sudden flurry of activity at the far end of the gallery. The jury has already come out of its huddle and the foreman, a burly cooper, is approaching the coroner's bench. Mr Mallett regards the group with surprise and a touch of disapproval; he hasn't even had his pint of ale yet. 'What is it?' he asks, no doubt assuming they have further questions.

'We've arrived at a verdick, Your Honor,' says the foreman.

'Already? You arrived almost before you left.'

'That's as may be sir, but we've talked it over, and 'tis our considered opinion that Lord Bainbury's death were a accident, plain and simple.'

Miss Fairweather responds with a very gratifying display of tearful joy. Almost instantly, she and Mr Elton are surrounded by spectators and jurymen, some offering congratulations, some just wishing to touch the hems of their garments, as it were. And of course there are the inevitable newspaper reporters looking for a quote from the dead man's mistress, one that they can completely reword to suit their purposes.

Charley wants none of it. He's done his job; it's time to go. Well, as soon as he's visited the bar downstairs for a glass of grog, anyway. He should feel a sense of satisfaction, he supposes; things could hardly have turned out better – except for poor Monty, that is. But for some reason, the whole business seems unfinished.

He still can't help wondering what became of the house girl. It's unlikely that she'd suddenly just slope off with no notice at all; as Miss Fairweather said, jobs are hard to find, and even harder without a reference. In his experience, there are two main reasons why people unaccountably disappear: Either they're guilty of something, or they're afraid of something. Of course, there's always a third possibility, but he doesn't like to consider it. There's been entirely too much dying going on.

When he's mulling over a case, Charley likes to keep a clear head, but it doesn't seem be doing much good. Besides, he could use another drink; he's feeling a trifle sorry for himself, a bit unappreciated. He didn't expect Miss Fairweather to fall all over him, but she might at least have said thank you. She certainly made a point of thanking Mr Elton; it wouldn't surprise Charley if, after the inquest winds down, she shows her gratitude in some more intimate fashion. No doubt that sort of thing is commonplace in the world of the theatre. Perhaps he should have been an actor and not a copper, after all.

By the time he's walked all the way to Millbank, it's going on eleven. Jane will surely have given up on him and gone to bed long ago. Just as well; he's not really in a mood for talking or, more likely, being talked at. What he's really in the mood for is a late supper. With any luck, Hanora will have left a plate of something for him.

When he shuffles into the kitchen, he's taken aback to find Jane sitting at what she calls the servants' table – as with *servants' entrance*, it implies that they have more than one – sipping a cup of tea. Charley recovers quickly and says, half joking, 'Aren't you afraid that'll keep you awake?'

'It doesn't matter,' she says. 'I haven't been sleeping well lately, in any case.'

'I'm sorry to hear that, my dear. Can I fix you a sandwich?'

'No, thank you. I haven't had much appetite, either.'

Well, he's not about to coax her; she knows her own mind. As he assembles his repast, he softly whistles 'Under the Greenwood Tree.' He's not about to volunteer any excuses or apologies, either. Maybe it would have been more thoughtful of him to send her a message, explaining where he was and what he was up to, so she wouldn't worry, but he didn't, and that's that, and if she wants to take him to task for it, so be it.

'I don't mean to be critical,' she says, and Charley's whistling trails off. *Oh, here we go.* But she doesn't go in the direction he expects. 'It's just that Hanora seems a bit . . . distracted lately. Do you suppose there are problems with her family, or something of that sort? Has she said anything to you?'

'No. Nothing.' If you don't count her rhapsodizing about Young Lochinvar, who is very likely the cause of her distraction. 'Why don't you ask her?'

'Well, I don't want to seem as if I'm prying.' There's a

sentence he doesn't recall ever hearing her use before. What's come over her?

'I'll bring it up tomorrow, if you like.'

'Would you, please?' She finishes her tea, dabs her mouth delicately with a napkin, and rises. 'I hope you had a good day, and solved lots of cases.'

'Well, only one, but it was an important one. I helped prevent a—' Better not to say a *young* woman; that might lead to more questions – 'a woman from being charged with murder.'

'She was innocent, I hope?' Her tone sounds almost teasing – something else Jane doesn't ordinarily do much of.

'Yes,' says Charley, and adds, under his breath, 'I hope so, too.'

She yawns discreetly, one hand covering her mouth. 'I suppose I may as well go to bed, even though I probably won't be able to sleep for hours yet.' Is it his imagination, or is there something slightly suggestive in the way she says that? When Miss Fairweather makes a risqué remark, it's hard to miss her meaning; of course, she's had far more practice. 'Perhaps you should come to bed, too; you look tired.'

'Uh, no, I'm fine. I think I'll stay up for a while yet. I need to make some notes about this case, while it's fresh in my mind.' As he bites rather emphatically into his sandwich, Charley fancies he hears a faint sigh of disappointment or resignation from her.

'Of course,' she says. 'Well. I believe I'll read the Brontë book you gave me at Yuletide.'

Perhaps Jane was exaggerating about her inability to sleep. When Charley arises early the next morning and passes her room, he can hear her snoring softly. Hanora is up already, simultaneously shelling peas and scanning the *Daily News*. She gives him a cheerful grin. 'Good morning, sir. Can I fix something for you?'

'A nice cup of Mocha wouldn't be amiss. Since Mrs Field is in such an accommodating mood, perhaps she won't mind if I bring my grinder and biffin into her house.'

'I'm not sure she's quite *that* accommodating just yet. I'd give her a bit more time.'

'Hmm. I don't suppose she's ready for pipe smoking, either?'

The house girl shrugs. 'It wouldn't hurt to try.'

'It might.' He nods at the paper. 'Any news of interest?'

'Oh, aye. Here's a fascinating story about the coroner's inquest into the death of Lord Bainbury. Would you care to read it?'

'No, thank you. I'm sure *story* is the proper term for it; they'll have made up most of it.'

'You mean you didn't actually say "Once again, gentlemen, the English system of justice has shown itself to be the most efficient, most thorough, and most unbiased in the civilized world."?'

'Does it sound like something I'd say?'

'Maybe. If you were delirious, and imagined you were Mr Disraeli. Oh, and here's another bit of invention. It says that Lord Bainbury's house girl has mysteriously vanished.' Hanora gives a snort of derision. 'I happen to know that he *dismissed* her, with no notice at all. She went home to County Clare.'

Charley, who has discovered the still-warm oatcakes Hanora baked earlier, pauses in the middle of eating one to gape at her. 'Are you certain?'

'Aye. My friend Mary knows her well; she helped her pack and all.'

'When?'

'Two days since.'

Charley puts aside the half-eaten oatcake and turns away, not caring to let Hanora see how disturbed and how baffled he is by this information. It's better if she has no notion that anything is amiss. Once people get it into their heads that someone has committed a crime or been the victim of one, it colors their perception; they begin to remember things differently.

Why, he wonders, wouldn't Miss Fairweather tell him that Arly had been let go? Did she not know? Hard to imagine that Monty wouldn't at least discuss it with her. And why dismiss the girl so abruptly? Because she'd done something wrong? Threatened him somehow, or demanded something from him? Charley takes a deep breath and puts on a neutral face, then turns back to Hanora, meaning to determine, very calmly, what else she knows. But before he can say a word, she gives a startled cry and claps a hand to her mouth. Her wide eyes stare incredulously at the newspaper. 'Saints preserve us!' she gasps.

'What? What is it?'

Wordlessly, she hands him the paper, pointing with a shaking finger at a brief item in the lower right corner of the page. While the headline – 'CONSTABLE BRUTALLY BEATEN' – is certainly upsetting, it's hardly startling or unexpected. There are over five thousand men on the force, after all; hardly a month goes by without one of them suffering injuries in the line of duty. Charley certainly suffered his share.

And then he reads the text of the piece: *Last evening, a policeman walking his beat near the Oval in South Lambeth came upon the unconscious, nearly lifeless form of a fellow constable. The unfortunate officer, who had been severely beaten over his entire body, was identified as Constable Lochinvar Mull, a recent recruit to Scotland's Yard's Chelsea (B) Division. He was conveyed at once to Westminster Hospital where, at last word, he was in critical condition; doctors there hold little hope for his recovery.*

TWENTY-FIVE

Westminster Hospital was built only twenty years ago as a refuge for the ill and injured who can't afford a private physician's care. That unfortunately includes constables, whose weekly wage is scarcely more than that of a good chimney sweep or a bag maker. The hospital's modern design – a series of small rooms rather than a single large ward – was meant to minimize the spread of infectious diseases. It hasn't worked very well, for the sheer volume of patients – some 20,000 a year – is such that half a dozen or more must be crammed into each room, like animals at a slaughterhouse awaiting their turn to be pole-axed and bled out.

Being a copper does have its advantages, though; an officer

injured in the performance of his duty is, after all, a kind of hero, and heroes should not be treated as cavalierly as ordinary patients. Constable Mull has been placed in a room that contains only three other men. It's even possible to walk between the beds.

For once, the newspaper wasn't exaggerating; the poor fellow is in bad shape. His left forearm is encased in a gypsum roller bandage; his face is as swollen and purple as an overripe plum; his scalp has been stitched up in half a dozen places; bloody gauze encircles his abdomen like a gruesome sort of cummerbund. 'Oh, Lochinvar!' whispers Hanora. 'Just look at you!' She sits on the edge of the painted metal bed and takes one of the lad's mangled hands in her own; he doesn't respond at all. Charley remains standing, partly because he's not sure the bed will hold another person's weight and partly because hospitals, like prisons, make him nervous; he likes to stay on his toes, just in case – in case of what, he's not quite sure. As his mother was fond of saying, 'You just never know.'

After an hour or so of silence from Mr Mull and a unceasing chorus of coughs and groans from his roommates, a nurse turns up to check on the patients. Before the woman can get away, Hanora corners her and demands to know about her friend's condition. Apparently the surgeon who sewed him up and set his arm is convinced that one of the lad's internal organs was ruptured by the beating – most likely his spleen. Since no one has ever removed a ruptured spleen, at least not without killing the patient, their only hope is that it will heal on its own – a rare occurrence, but not unheard of.

And their only hope of finding out who attacked him may be to ask Mull himself. Charley does pay a visit to the Walton Street station and, over the objections of his old foe, the flat-nosed sergeant clerk, questions every constable there. But not a man among them has any notion of what Lochinvar was doing so far from B Division during duty hours. Mere constables don't ordinarily go chasing down culprits in some other part of the city; that's the job of a detective inspector. Could someone have beaten him senseless in his own territory, then, and hauled the body to South Lambeth? It would be possible, of course, but it would also be very stupid. Not that there's any shortage of stupid criminals; for the most part, though, they don't take any more risks than they have to.

Charley has a pretty good understanding of how Lochinvar's mind works, since the lad is so much like he was himself at that age. So, when he was a young copper pounding the pavement, what would have prompted him to break the rules and abandon his beat? Though it may seem a hypothetical question, actually it's not, for Charley did that very thing, not a month after he joined the force.

Of course, he wasn't a total novice, like Lochinvar; he'd already done a year's duty as a Bow Street Runner, and he'd learned a few things about thief-taking. One of those things was that, contrary to what the copper's *Book of General Instructions* says, it isn't wise to patrol your beat in a regular fashion, always taking the same streets in the same order, completing each round in the recommended time. It doesn't take long for a burglar to catch on, to know that he has a guaranteed grace period of twenty or thirty minutes in which to jump a crib – that is, climb through a window – fill his booty bag, and be gone.

Constable Field ignored the instructions and took a different route each night; sometimes he even doubled back. And that's how he happened to catch a man in the act of cutting lead sheets from the roof of a town house. Charley hadn't yet learned to keep a sharp eye on the roofs of buildings, and might have passed by without noticing anything wrong, only the lead-stealer was a clumsy cove. He dropped his shears, which bounced off Charley's reinforced chimney-pot hat.

The thief scrambled down a drainpipe at the rear of the house and could have easily made his escape except that, in addition to being clumsy, he was stubborn; he refused to give up his hard-won roll of roofing. But Charley was even more stubborn, plus he had a bare-knuckle boxer's stamina. You had to hand it to the culprit, though; he made it nearly all the way to St Giles before he collapsed from the weight of all that lead.

Maybe it wasn't the smartest thing to do, pursuing that fellow; after all, it left his beat at the mercy of every other thief and burglar in the vicinity. But, though his superiors insisted that the force's role was to discourage criminals, not capture them, to tell Charley that was like telling a dog not to chase a rabbit. He's almost certain that, in a similar situation, Constable Mull would have done the same thing – and perhaps did.

By the time Charley is done questioning the constables at the station house, the sullen sergeant clerk's shift has ended; his replacement is an old chum of Charley's, Stanley Smoak, who doesn't mind at all if Charley peruses the previous day's route-paper. 'Hmm,' says Charley. 'That's interesting.'

'What is?' asks Stanley.

'It says here you brought in a Reginald Hoggles and charged him with the theft of Lord Belliveau's carriage. Am I right in thinking that's the rascal we called Neckless?'

'One and the same. Belliveau's driver said he could identify the thief, but between the time he said that and the time he come face to face with our man, something happened; suddenly, he looked very scared. My guess is, one of Neckless's cronies got to him, told him if he didn't keep his mouth shut they'd shut it for him, or something of that sort.'

'Any idea who Mr Hoggles works for these days?'

'Not a clue.'

'I can't help wondering: why steal a carriage? And such a fancy one at that? It'll stick out like a tippler's red nose.'

'Oh, they'll strip it and repaint it, probably sell it to some country squire.'

'I suppose. So, you released the blighter, then?'

Stanley shrugs. 'We had to.'

'Were you behind the desk at the time?'

'I was.'

'Do you happen to recall whether Constable Mull was around?'

Stanley checks his Beat Book. 'He was on the night shift, so he would have been just going on duty.'

'But I'll bet any amount that he *didn't* go on duty. I'll bet that he tailed Neckless, instead, the young fool.'

'Why would he do that?' asks Stanley.

'Because,' says Charley, 'I told him to.'

Not in so many words, of course. All he'd said was for Lochinvar to keep an eye out for the man and his sometime partner, Neck. But the young constable is so deuced eager to prove himself a good copper; Charley should have known that

if he spotted either man, he wouldn't be content to just
report it. He'd want to collar the cove, or at least tail him and
find out where his hidey-hole was.

It's reasonable to suppose, then, that he followed his man all
the way to Lambeth before Neckless was aware of it. Or it
might be that Neckless *was* aware of it, but didn't let on, just
played him along until they were in some dark, deserted street
more suitable for an ambush. No, that doesn't seem quite right,
either. Though Neckless is no angel, Charley has never known
him to be unduly violent; he's not really the sort to bludgeon
a copper so savagely, for no good reason. However, Charley
knows someone who is. If he had to guess, he'd guess that
Neck and Neckless have joined forces again.

The newspaper article didn't say exactly where Lochinvar's
unconscious body was found, but the route-paper does: Fentiman
Road, next to Beaufoy's Vinegar Yard. Well. Things are getting
more interesting all the time. As it happens, Beaufoy's is only
a stone's throw – well, for someone with a good arm, anyway
– from Priestley's Orphan's Home.

Charley concluded long ago that Neck must be holed up
somewhere that no one would ever think to look for him; an
orphans' home seems an even more unlikely spot than a church
or a monastery. But, to quote his mother again, 'You just never
know.'

If he were still a copper, he'd have to do things by the rules,
all open and aboveboard. He'd need to ask a magistrate for a
search warrant and would no doubt be refused – after all,
Reverend Priestley is a well-respected citizen, and Charley has
no real evidence. His only recourse, then, would be to pay the
Reverend a friendly visit and question him politely and learn
nothing – in other words, show his hand before he'd even seen
for himself what cards he was holding.

Not that Charley didn't bend or break the rules from time to
time in his policing days, when it suited his purpose; usually
he had something more to go on, though, than just a hunch,
which is all he has now. But the beauty of being a private
enquiry agent is that you can play your hunches and make your
own rules – provided you don't get caught.

If, by some far-fetched chance, Charley is right and Priestley has been harboring a wounded fugitive all this time, he must have had some compelling reason. Did Neck threaten to harm the man or his orphan girls if he didn't cooperate? Or is there some more complicated relationship between the two of them? Are they family? Lovers? – well, perhaps not, considering how Neck likes the ladies. Colleagues, then? That seems more likely. After all, Neck's shattered shoulder blade must have healed months ago, and yet he hasn't decamped to some safer stamping ground; something's keeping him here. Suppose the lucrative enterprise he's been boasting about somehow involves the Reverend?

One odd fact has been nagging at the back of Charley's mind ever since his previous visit to the orphans' home – a very small fact, to be sure, and yet sometimes those are the most significant. It was the way Priestley refused to reveal the name and location of the family who took Audrey in. Charley didn't make much of it at the time; he had no call to, and Priestley's explanation seemed reasonable enough. But now he can't help wondering whether the man was hiding something – something more than just a fugitive.

Well, there's only one way to find out, and it's not by inter-rogating him. Charley whiles away an hour or so in a chop house over a plate of chicken curry – as fond as he is of beef, he sometimes likes a change, and the stuff isn't bad. Neither, he's gratified to discover, is the coffee. The bread is a bit chalky, though; no doubt it's been bulked up with sawdust and plaster and whitened with alum. His campaign to improve the quality of Mocha was so successful, maybe he should tackle the adul-teration of bread next – or adultery, as Miss Fairweather likes to call it. And, speaking of Miss Fairweather, there's yet another situation he needs to do something about. But one thing at a time.

Armed with a bull's-eye lantern borrowed from the Lambeth station house, Charley conceals himself outside the orphans' home at dusk and watches. Though he's borrowed a set of handcuffs as well, he probably won't get to use them. There's very little chance that he'll find Neck or Neckless here; you don't maul a police constable and then hang about waiting to be caught. He could easily nab Priestley, who is closing up his office for the night, but what would be the point, since he has nothing on the man?

Once it's totally dark and all the orphans are abed, Charley puts to use another lesson he's learned: if you're somewhere you're not supposed to be, act as though you belong there. As he's strolling casually across the courtyard, two young women – cooks or cleaning girls, no doubt – emerge from the kitchens. He smiles, tips his hat, and bids them good evening; giggling, they go on their way.

The lock on the door of the Reverend's office is no match for Charley's tools and expert touch. Perhaps he and the Scarecrow should put their heads together and devise a pick-proof lock; they'd make a fortune. Once inside, he lights the bull's-eye lantern and adjusts the slide so it emits only a narrow beam.

The bound ledger still sits atop the neatly organized desk, in the exact position it occupied on his previous visit. As with so many men of the cloth, Priestley's notion of Paradise seems to be a world in which everything and everyone has a place and is kept in it. Charley turns to the page labeled DECEMBER and holds it up to the light. Audrey's name appears on the 30th of the month, just as Priestley said, followed by the name of the couple who took her in: Mr and Mrs Stinson of Lancashire.

Charley jots this scanty information in his notebook, then scans the other entries on the page. There are a surprising number of them – half a dozen in January alone. How on earth does Mr Priestley manage to place so many of his orphans in what he likes to call 'good homes'? Are there that many good homes available? Or are some of them not actually all that good? Is it possible that the girls are not being adopted so much as apprenticed, or indentured?

The entries themselves don't tell him much: On January 10, Sarah Fowler was sent to live with a Mr and Mrs Quentin of Derbyshire; a fortnight later, Alice Ford was taken by Mr and Mrs Phoenix of Cheshire, Mary Godwin went off to Lancashire with Mr and Mrs Shipley, and so on. It all looks simple and straightforward enough – at first glance. But Charley is seldom content to glance at things just once; he's found that, if you examine almost any series of events closely enough, a pattern emerges.

This one is no exception. When he turns the page, he discovers that the entries there follow the same pattern: the adoptive families are spread about somewhat, but not nearly as widely or as randomly as you'd expect. The fact is, by far the greatest number are located in the North West counties.

And here's another fact that, though it may be totally coincidental and irrelevant, is nonetheless intriguing: The surnames of the families from Cheshire all begin with the letter P, and the Lancashire ones with either an S or an L. But what's truly bizarre is that the Derbyshire couples all have names starting with a Q. If that's not a pattern, Charley will eat – well, perhaps not his hat, but a loaf of plaster-and-alum-laced bread, at any rate. They're clearly not genuine names; Charley's guess is, they're part of a code of some sort. The question is, what do they stand for?

Charley once told Young Lochinvar – the poor, battered lad – that the most obvious answers are not always the right ones, or words to that effect. But it generally pays to start at the top of the scale of obviousness, at least, and work your way down. What's the first thing that comes to mind when a person thinks of Derbyshire or Lancashire or Cheshire? Cotton mills, of course. Thousands of them.

As anyone who has read *Michael Armstrong: The Factory Boy* or *Helen Fleetwood: A Tale of the Factories* is well aware, those mills have a long and dark history of employing children as young as five or six to perform the most dismal and dangerous tasks, working them to exhaustion and paying them next to nothing. But we allow ourselves to imagine that, with the passage of Fielden's Act and the Factory Act, all that magically changed.

Charley knows better. Though it may be true that sending government inspectors into the mills has improved conditions overall, the blokes naturally expend most of their time and effort on the big conglomerations of factories in Manchester and Bradford and Leeds. The relatively small and scattered rural mills find it easier to skirt the law; they tend to have fewer child workers, anyway, since wages are better in the cities.

When he was still with the force, Charley was sent to a

village in Gloucestershire to help solve the murder of a mill owner. The man was so universally despised that practically every person in the parish was a possible suspect, but it turned out he'd been shot by the father of a ten-year-old boy who was killed in an accident a few months earlier.

Ordinarily, the minders briefly shut down their machines, which are called spinning mules, every hour or so to allow the scavengers – invariably young children, because of their small size – to crawl beneath the thread sheets and gather up the loose cotton fibers. But of course lost time is lost money, so the owner had forbidden his employees to shut down, even for a minute. The unfortunate lad, apparently startled by a rat, made the fatal mistake of lifting his head a bit too high; it was caught between the roller beam and the carriage, and crushed.

Charley learned from the gaffer in charge of the floor that, though it was certainly the most gruesome accident in recent memory, it was hardly the only one. There had been six incidents so far that year, most involving lopped-off fingers or hair pulled out by the roots, and nearly all involving children. None had been reported to the Factory Act inspectors.

Since a boy or girl with missing fingers isn't much use when it comes to piecing broken threads, they were let go, as were the ones who fell sick from typhus or bloody flux, or from breathing in all that cotton fly. Between injuries and illnesses and the exodus to the cities, the rural mills suffered a continual shortage of young workers. Adults just aren't as useful; aside from the fact that their bodies are too big for scavenging and their fingers too thick and clumsy for piecing, they have an annoying tendency to complain, or even quit, if worked too long and hard. Unlike domestics, factory workers have little difficulty finding a job.

As the number of mills has increased and more and more country folk have fled the countryside, the shortage has become even worse. So, if Charley were a mill owner – now there's a sobering thought – how would he deal with such a dilemma? Mrs Bramble's maxim comes to mind once again: Doan't thou marry for munny, but goa wheer munny is. By the same token, if you want children, you mun goa wheer children are.

TWENTY-SIX

C harley has known a number of finicky people – in fact, he's married to one – and he can't imagine any of them being content with such a sparse and sketchy system of record-keeping. But perhaps Priestley keeps this ledger just for show, to reassure his benefactors that the orphan girls have a good chance of being placed in a real home. Unless Charley has seriously misjudged the man, somewhere in his well-ordered personal paradise is a more thorough account of those transactions.

Picking the lock on the office door was mere child's play; Charley can't even think of a metaphor that describes how easy it is to break into the desk drawers. But alas, they contain nothing that's the least incriminating, unless you count the flask of what smells suspiciously like sherry, or the small, poorly rendered sketches of young girls – is Priestley a frustrated artist, or merely a man with secret and unnatural desires? – or the lock of brown hair tied with a faded pink ribbon – no telling whom that might belong to. If Priestley keeps a more detailed history of some sort, he clearly doesn't keep it here.

Cursing softly, Charley locks the drawers and turns his attention again to the ledger. If only he had a better knowledge of the mills in the North West counties and precisely where they're located, or if there were someone among his wide network of informants and acquaintances who had such knowledge, but . . . But perhaps there is. Didn't Mr Mumchance once say that his 'old man' owned a woolen mill in Gloucestershire? In fact, Charley got the idea that young Geoffrey was employed there for a time, before his conscience got the better of him and he settled on being poor and poetic instead.

He has no idea where Mumchance and his new bride reside – surely not in the vicinity of the glue and bone works, still? It's just possible, however, that he may be able to catch his man at the offices of *Household Words*. It's late in the day, but this close to publication the staff will likely be burning the midnight oil – well, the ten o'clock coal gas, at least.

Though Shrewdness and Persistence have been the main contributors to Charley's success, he's well aware that Luck has played a major role. Like an old trouper, it enters now, right on cue. Not only does it provide a cab for him to hail, it ensures that Geoffrey Mumchance remains at his desk, making last-moment adjustments to his latest article – which concerns the lack of decent drinking water in certain areas of the city – until the inspector arrives.

As Charley hoped, Mr Mumchance, having spent most of his young life in and around woolen mills, knows the most profitable ones, at least, by name and by reputation; they were, after all, his father's main competitors. It takes only a few minutes of perusing Priestley's ledger for him to confirm that the names of the 'adoptive parents' likely constitute some sort of code. 'See here,' he says, eagerly, clearly glad to be of help to the man who has helped him so much. 'Most of the supposed families in Cheshire have names beginning with a P. I'll wager that stands for the biggest mill in the county – Pembroke. And all those Q's in Derbyshire; what could they mean but Quarrington's?'

Charley points his crooked index finger at the entry claiming that Audrey was taken in by the Stinsons of Lancashire. 'What about this one?'

'Stubbins Mill, no doubt. And the names with an L, they'll be Levenside.'

The entries in the ledger are so brief and matter-of-fact, and what they represent – helpless orphans sold into slavery, in effect – is so beastly that Charley is overcome by that stunned, sick feeling again, as if someone has knocked all the wind out of him. He's tempted to set fire to the book, as people burn the infected clothing and possessions of a cholera victim. But the coppers will need it as evidence when Priestley is brought up before a judge – and Charley will make sure that happens. He also intends to see that the bastard doesn't slip the noose, the way Hubbard and Neck and Lord Starkey did.

There's no great hurry to nab the Reverend, of course. He's

not likely to go anywhere. Charley returns the ledger to its
accustomed place that same evening, so Priestley will have no
idea that Charley is onto him. Besides, there are far more
important matters to attend to.

You might assume that the inspector's primary concern is
tracking down the villains who gave Mr Mull such a beating–and
who, presumably, are doing Priestley's dirty work for him. But
no, he's been on their trail for years; they, too, can wait another
day or two. At the moment, all he can think about is finding
Sarah Fowler and Alice Ford and Mary Godwin – and, above
all, Rosa's daughter, Audrey – and taking them home, before
they're taken to some potter's field in a pasteboard coffin. Should
he stumble upon Neck or Neckless in the process, so much the
better.

If there were any quick and practical means of getting to
Lancashire other than the London and North Western Railway,
Charley would surely take it. He doesn't care to be reminded
of Miss Fairweather and their journey together – or anything
else they've done together, for that matter. He needs to concentrate on the task at hand. Miss Fairweather has always had a
way of destroying his concentration, and the whole unsettling,
unsettled business with Monty's death and the maid's disappearance has his mind in even more of a muddle.

Charley likes to know as much as possible about whatever
situation he's walking into, so he's brought along the only book
about cotton mills that he could find on such short notice: His
wife's copy of *North and South* by Mrs Gaskell. Since one of
the main characters runs a mill, Charley assumed it would
contain some useful information. And so it does – but only if
he were looking to learn about thwarted love affairs, which he
certainly isn't. Instead of describing working conditions at the
mill, Mrs Gaskell prefers to tell us about the workings of
the heart:

> *Mr Thornton stood by one of the windows, with his back
> to the door, apparently absorbed in watching something
> in the street. But, in truth, he was afraid of himself. His
> heart beat thick at the thought of her coming. He could*

not forget the touch of her arms around his neck,
impatiently felt as it had been at the time; but now the recol-
lection of her clinging defence of him seemed to thrill him
through and through, – to melt away every resolution, all
power of self-control, as if it were wax before a fire. [. . .]
    Strong man as he was, he trembled at the anticipation
of what he had to say, and how it might be received. She
might droop, and flush, and flutter to his arms, as to her
natural home and resting-place. One moment, he glowed
with impatience at the thought that she might do this, the
next, he feared a passionate rejection, the very idea of
which withered up his future with so deadly a blight that
he refused to think of it.

'Bloody fool,' Charley mutters, and flings the book aside.
It's going to be a long trip. He should have brought *The History*
of Rome, or a few issues of *Household Words*. Back when he
was walking a beat, he'd pass the time by humming music hall
tunes or singing them under his breath – it wouldn't do to belt
them out and tip off the thieves. He tries that now, but it, too,
puts him in mind of Miss Fairweather. He's even more of a
bloody fool than Mrs Gaskell's hero.

At least he has his pipe, and the compartment all to himself.
Luckily, though it's well past sunrise, the conductor hasn't yet
extinguished the oil lamp, so it's easy enough to light up. Then
he takes out his notebook and reviews the information he copied
from Priestley's account book the night before. He didn't think
it wise to make off with the actual ledger; if the Reverend
noticed its absence, it might spook him. The first place he'll
investigate is Stubbins Mill in Blackwater. It's been over four
months since Audrey was 'adopted;' he can only hope that she's
still there and still safe and sound. She's a sturdy girl, and a
clever one, but those qualities are no proof against accidents or
abuse or disease.

Though he took a morning train, by the time he finally reaches
Lancaster, it's nearly dusk. Two more hours are taken up with
hiring a gig and navigating the muddy track that leads to
Blackwater. A more fitting name for the place would be
Backwater. Judging from the buildings, which include a decrepit

iron foundry, it must once have been a fairly prosperous village
– a hundred years ago or so, when being situated on a fast-
flowing river counted for something. But the advent of the
coal-fired steam engine had the same effect on industry that it
had on transportation – an even greater effect, actually. Horse-
drawn wagons still have a place in the world, at least for the
time being; water-powered factories are all but obsolete.

Of course, so are bare-knuckle boxers, but a few of them are
still in business, and so it is with water mills. Mr Stubbins is
apparently either very conservative or very stubborn; instead of
investing in what the Luddites termed 'the iron monster,' he's
increased his so-called horsepower by adding on new and larger
water wheels, one after another. So far, he has a total of ten,
which power sixty spinning mules, not to mention carding
machines, drawing frames, and slubbing frames.

At the moment, most of the machinery is silent. The spinning
mules are run only during daylight hours. Though mill owners
may be tyrants and money-grubbers, they're not fools; they
know well enough – some of them by experience – how disas-
trous the combination of cotton fly and gas lighting can be. The
only devices operating now are the half-dozen weaving looms
that Stubbins installed recently, in an attempt to breathe new
life into his ailing enterprise.

The looms create more than enough noise to cover the sound
of Charley's horse and carriage. Nonetheless he leaves the rig
tied up beneath a tree and approaches the place on foot. A dozen
yards from the mill itself are two low, shed-like buildings with
no ordinary windows, only skylights – dormitories is Charley's
guess, and as usual it's a good one. From the larger building
comes the sound of adult voices, barely audible over the racket
from the looms. There's none of the carousing or singing or
laughter you'd expect from workers who have shrugged off the
day's yoke and may do what they please, for a few hours,
anyway. The voices sound sad and weary and subdued.

The second building is completely quiet. So is Charley, as
he moves to the door, which is barred from the outside. He
lifts the bar, opens the door hardly more than a crack, and slips
inside. The shed smells of unwashed bodies and unwashed
chamber pots. It's lit only by the moon, which is nowhere near

full; still, Charley can make out three rows of beds, each consisting of an upper and a lower bunk. Each bunk is occupied by two small forms huddled beneath a single blanket so thin and scanty as to be hardly deserving of the name; you'd think a cotton mill, of all places, could at least provide decent blankets. Now that he's within, the place is not as quiet as it seemed; there's a continual soughing, almost like that of the wind or of waves, but composed of coughs and sniffles and sighs.

Charley wishes he'd brought the bull's-eye lantern. As it as, his only means of locating Audrey is to weave his way among the bunks, calling her name softly. A few pale faces turn toward him, but most of the children pull the blankets over their heads, as though fearing he's some bogeyman come to claim a victim; if he can't find poor Audrey, he may decide to settle for them instead. Only one child, a strapping girl with a hoarse voice, is brave enough to speak. 'Who are you?'

'Inspector Field,' whispers Charley. 'From London. I'm looking for Audrey MacKinnon. Do you know her?'

'I know a Audrey; I dunno her last name. She's in the hole.'

'The hole?'

'The little building behind this 'un. 'Tis where they put them as tries to run off.'

'Thank you. You're from Lancashire, I'm guessing?'

The girl nods.

'Are you an orphan?'

'I wasn't when I left home. 'Twas my mam sent me here. Said she had too many mouths to feed.'

'How long ago was that?'

'I've lost track. Four years, maybe.'

'Have you ever tried to escape?'

She shrugs. 'If they don't want me at home, where would I go?'

Charley wishes he could take this child and all the others with him, this very night. It's impossible, of course. What he can do, though, is report on the conditions here to the Factory Act inspectors and make sure they pay the place a visit. He can also give an account to Mr Dickens or to Miss Treville, the lady reporter; no doubt her paper would love to print a series of sensational exposés. But first he has to find Audrey.

The hut known as the hole is about the size of a jail cell, but is even more dismal, for it has no windows at all, not even barred ones. The narrow door is secured with a lock, against the unlikely event that one of the prisoner's chums should try to set her free. Luckily, Stubbins is either too ignorant or too miserly to invest in a really secure device; the cheap Willenhall yields as readily as a streetwalker.

The moment he opens the door, a child's voice says, 'Could you let me go to the privy, please? I promise I won't try to run.'

'Sssh, now. It's me, Charley Field. I've come to take you home.'

There's a brief silence, as though Audrey can't make sense of this outrageous claim; she can't see him, after all. 'Is this a trick?' she says at last.

'No, it's really me, I promise.'

'Prove it.'

'I gave you a doll for Christmas. You named it Charlene.'

There's another pause, and then the child propels herself into his arms like one of the baby monkeys at the Regent's Park Zoo. 'Oh, Inspector! I'm so glad to see you!'

'Sssh!' cautions Charley, again. 'We mustn't let them hear us.'

'Sorry. Are you going to arrest them?'

'Not just yet. First we have to get you away from here.'

He tries to set her down, but she clings to him like that monkey baby. Noticing how prickly her hair feels against his chin, he runs a hand over her head. Damn them; they've cut off all her lovely wine-colored hair – no doubt as a punishment for trying to escape. To add insult to injury, they've likely sold it to a wig-maker.

Charley locks the door when they leave, to avoid arousing suspicion, then carries Audrey pig-a-back to where the concealed carriage waits. He's about to lift her into the seat, when she says, 'Can I do my business in the bushes first?'

'Of course, my dear. Just don't stray too far, will you?' As Charley is untying the horse, he hears a rumbling, crunching sound – the wheels of another carriage. Cursing, he draws his own rig deeper into the shadows just as the newcomers hurtle recklessly past, far too quickly considering how dark the night is and how rough the road. They've clearly failed to spot him, and for a moment, he congratulates himself. Then, over the clatter of the carriage, he hears a voice – high-pitched yet unmistakably a man's – shout, 'Can't you slow it down, just a little?'

The driver lets out a raucous laugh that resembles a strangled cough, then says, in a rasping voice, 'Don't be such a damned poof, Reggie!'

'The devil take me!' mutters Charley. Alarmed, he turns to call to Audrey, but she's already standing next to him.

'It's him, isn't it?' she whispers. 'The man with the broken neck.'

'I'm afraid so.' Charley crouches next to her. 'Is he the one who brought you here?'

'Yes. Only we came on the train. He said I was going to live with a nice family. He said they had a dog, and a boat, and everything.'

Back when Charley was a copper and came upon Neck setting fire to that boot shop, he knew he could either capture the villain or put out the flames, but not both. He's in the same sort of fix now, torn between rescuing Audrey and collaring the coves who occupy the two top slots on his most-wanted list. 'Listen,' he says quietly, 'if you want to be an inspector some day, the first thing you have to do is learn to follow instructions; you understand?'

Audrey nods soberly. 'Yes, sir.'

'Good. Here's what I want you to do: Stay hidden here until I return, even if it takes a while. Can you do that?'

She nods again, more eagerly. 'I'll burrow into the underbrush, like a rabbit.'

'You won't be frightened?'

'No.'

'You won't come after me, and you won't run off?'

'Cross my heart,' she says, and makes the appropriate motions.

'All right, then. I'm counting on you, Constable Audrey.'

'I won't let you down, sir.'

'I believe it,' says Charley. He only hopes that he won't let *her* down.

Keeping to the shadows, he approaches the mill again. The newly arrived carriage sits just outside the low wooden structure that Stubbins has tacked on to the mill to house the looms. The rig matches the general description of the brougham that Neckless was accused of stealing a few days ago, though it's clearly been repainted and the rightful owner's coat of arms removed.

At the moment, there's only one figure sitting in the dickey box and, judging from the squat shape, it's Mr Reginald Hoggles himself. There's no sign or sound of Neck; he must have gone inside. Charley creeps up from the rear; as he carefully circles the carriage, a child's face appears at the side window – a boy; so, Priestley's is not the only orphans' home from which Neck is stealing children. The inspector puts a finger to his lips, and the wide-eyed boy nods to show he understands.

Placing one foot on the passenger's step, Charley grabs hold of the side lantern and swings himself upward; the motion sets the spring-suspended carriage swaying. When Hoggles jerks his pumpkin-like head around to see what's up, Charley plants a fist in the middle of the man's face. Before he can recover, Charley seizes him by the shirt collar and yanks him sideways; he hits the ground with a thump, like a letter bag thrown from a mail coach.

As quick as gunpowder, Charley has his borrowed handcuffs out. He clamps one end to Neckless' thick wrist and the other to a spoke of the wheel. Fishing his bandana from the pocket of his frock coat, he hands it to Hoggles so the man can stanch the blood bubbling from his nostrils. Then he opens the door of the brougham and peers inside.

Two girls, aged eight or nine, cower on the upholstered bench seat. Perched on the foldaway seat is the boy, who is likely a year or two younger. 'Don't be afraid,' says Charley. 'I'm a policeman.' Well, almost. 'I'll get you out of here as soon as I can. I just need to catch the other fellow first, right? Stay here and don't move. That's an order.'

He bends over his prisoner and says softly, 'Now. Where's your partner got to?' Hoggles flaps the red-stained kerchief toward the sound of the looms. 'I hope for your sake you're telling the truth,' says Charley. 'I'm going after him, and I would advise you to keep your bloody mouth shut, or it's likely to be a lot bloodier, and with a lot less teeth.'

The inspector scrambles across the open yard and crouches down next to one of the lighted windows. Though the shed could easily hold twenty power looms, Stubbins has apparently decided to start small and work his way up. Lined up at one end of the gallery are six iron-frame Lancashire looms; they rather resemble printing presses, or perhaps pump organs with the woodwork removed. The young women who stand before them wear dresses that are almost scandalously short and close-fitting – not because the girls are trollops but because the less fabric there is the less likely it is to be caught in the belts and gears. For the same reason, their hair is tightly braided or covered by a cap. Next to the weavers are their assistants – girls so small that they have to stand on bricks in order to reach the warp threads and feel for any broken ones.

At the near end of the room stands Neck, conversing with a portly cove wearing a frock coat, waistcoat, and trousers all of the same gray broadcloth. Though Mr Stubbins' mill may belong to an earlier age, when it comes to clothing no one can accuse him of being out of fashion. The two men are obliged to shout in each other's ears in order to be heard over the clattering of the looms. That's good. With any luck, they won't hear him coming.

TWENTY-SEVEN

He wishes he'd brought his walking stick, or at least a second pair of handcuffs. Neck isn't going to let himself be taken without a fight. Well, Charley will just have to make do with his fists. He'll need to be quick about it, though; the last two times he caught up with Neck, the bastard had a revolver.

He'll also have to be quick about making his entrance; no dilly-dallying outside the door, gathering his nerve, or his eyes will adjust to the dark again, and the gas lights inside will blind him. Now's the time, now that Neck is turned with his back to the door. No need to break the thing down; they'd have no reason to lock it. Just turn the handle, fling it open, and plow right in, like a boxer coming out of his corner, getting the jump on his opponent.

Stubbins sees him first; the man's jaw drops and he utters something unintelligible, some combination of *Who?* and *What?* Unable to turn his head properly, Neck swivels his entire body around. His hand reaches for the bulging pocket of his coat, but he's too slow; Charley is already upon him, seizing the man's shirtfront with one hand and, with the other, knocking the revolver from his grasp. The hammer of the Colt's painfully gouges Charley's knuckles, but he ignores it. 'Mr Tufts,' he hisses, through clenched teeth, 'I've been looking for you.'

Neck gives a ghastly grin and says, in his coffee-grinder voice, 'Whatever for?'

'I wouldn't know where to begin,' says Charley. He notices Stubbins eyeing the gun, which lies on the floor a few feet away. 'No, no. You don't want to do that, believe me.' Best not to leave it there to tempt him, though. Giving Neck a shove to put him off balance, Charley bends, scoops up the revolver, and shoves it in his pocket; he can keep the prisoner in line well enough without it.

Or so he thinks. But once again, he's underestimated the villain. From somewhere on his person, Neck has, magician-like, made a Philadelphia Deringer pistol appear. Unlike the evildoers in those penny bloods, he wastes no time gloating or explaining himself; he just points the thing at Charley's chest and fires.

There's no pain at first, only the sense of being struck by something far more powerful than any bruiser's fist, probably even that of the Chinese Colossus. Charley doubles over, clutching his ribs, groaning, gasping for breath. And yet somehow he manages to stay on his feet, to force himself almost erect, to take a lurching step forward, then another. Neck flings the useless one-shot at him; Charley bats it aside and advances, halting but relentless, still not bothering to reach for the Colt's in his pocket. He doesn't want to shoot the blighter; he wants to close his hands around that stiff, scrawny neck.

Step by step, his quarry backs away from him and, for the first time that Charley can recall, he looks worried – panicky, almost. He's clearly thinking the same thing Charley thought as he watched Neck scramble across that snowy rooftop and make his escape: *Good god, the man is indestructible.*

Neck doesn't dare turn to survey the room; it's such a slow and awkward process for him, Charley is sure to close the gap between them. All he can do is keep on backing up, heading for the only other exit, which lies at the far end of the shed, beyond the looms. The weavers and their assistants, unwilling to flee and risk being consigned to the hole, flatten themselves against the wall, leaving a clear path for Neck to navigate. Well, almost clear. They haven't bothered to move the bricks on which the girls were standing, and it's one of those that proves to be Neck's downfall.

His heel catches on it; he stumbles, does a quick shuffle step in an effort to regain his balance, and doesn't quite succeed. Like a man with too many drinks in him, he staggers sideways and knocks one knee into the nearest loom, which brings him even closer to falling. He thrusts out an arm to catch himself but, instead of connecting with the frame or something equally solid, he lands on the fiercely spinning leather belt that transfers power from the drive spindle. Snagging the sleeve of his frock coat, the belt drags his arm into the massive gears and severs it from his body, as effortlessly as a drumstick is yanked from a Christmas goose.

There's no point in trying to bandage Neck's wound; within a very few minutes, he's bled out. Once again, he defies the conventions of the penny bloods by failing to utter a few final words of remorse at having devoted himself to a life of crime. He dies unrepentant and blessedly unaware. Doesn't Death have a keen sense of irony, though? After foiling all attempts to dispatch him deliberately, by means of nooses, scalpels and revolvers, the man is done in at last by a stupid accident.

But what about Charley's wound? Surely it needs bandaging, perhaps even surgery. Well, the fact is, he hasn't suffered an actual wound. Oh, he'll have to put up with aching ribs for the next week or so, but that's nothing new. How, you may wonder, is that possible? After all, he was shot by a .41 caliber pocket pistol at close range.

If this were a certain sort of novel, it would turn out that he was carrying a Bible in his coat pocket, and that the lead buried itself in the plethora of pages. But Charley doesn't even own a Bible. And, though Mrs Gaskell's book would surely stop a bullet, he left it on the train. He is, however, wearing a Mongol vest made of twenty layers of tightly woven silk, and it has lived up to its reputation; not only can it turn aside a sword or an arrow, it can deflect a ball from a Deringer.

There's no point, either, in trying to settle the score with Stubbins just now; the factory inspectors will deal with him. Charley lets him go for the moment, but not before he's issued a warning: If the man keeps up his practice of enslaving and abusing children, Charley will come back and burn his mill to the ground, preferably with Stubbins in it.

He transfers the three newly arrived orphans to his rented gig, along with Audrey; true to her word, she never budged from her hidey-hole. He loads Neck's corpse, swathed in some of Stubbins' newly-woven fabric, into the brougham, then seats the dead man's partner in the dickey box, handcuffing him to the wrought-iron side rail. 'Mr Hoggles, you may lead the way. I'll be watching your every move, of course.'

'What if I 'ave to piss?' Curiously enough, Hoggles feels compelled to say this in a whisper, as if afraid of offending the children's tender ears.

'If you're that modest,' says Charley, 'I'll look the other way.'

'No, I mean you'll let me get down, right?'

'I'm afraid not. Just drive quickly; the breeze will dry you out in no time.'

Charley is so weary that he can barely hold the reins of the gig. Fortunately – well, in a way – the pain from the gunshot keeps him awake; just to be safe, he lets Audrey share the driver's seat, so she can pinch him if he nods off.

Once they've left the mill far behind, she says, in a voice that's barely audible over the chattering of the wheels, 'I'm sorry about Charlene. I tried to bring her with me, but Mr Priestley took her away. He said I was a big girl now, and shouldn't be playing with dollies.'

'I'm sorry, too,' says Charley. 'I should have visited you sooner at the orphans' home. Maybe I'd have figured out what was going on.'

She places a hand lightly on his sleeve. 'It's not your fault,' she says. 'And besides, you did rescue me, just like a Knight of the Round Table.'

Though Charley is, for some reason, feeling quite choked up, he manages say, 'You sound like your mother.'

The ride back to Lancaster seems to take twice as long as the trip out. It's nearly dawn by the time they pull up in front of the constabulary, and then they're obliged to wait another hour before the deputy chief constable can be roused from his bed. He's almost as baby-faced as Mr Mull and eager to be of assistance to the fabled Inspector Bucket, whose name is well known in these parts, too, perhaps better than those in *The Book of Saints*. He's been trying to get the goods on Mr Stubbins for years, he says – though that would mean he must have started around the age of fifteen – but the chief has always put obstacles in his path. He rather suspects that the Old Man has struck a deal of some sort with the mill owner.

'I struck a deal with Stubbins myself,' says Charley. 'We agreed that he'd either improve the conditions at his mill, or else turn it into a coffee roastery.'

'A coffee roastery?'

'Yes, indeed. Those old oak boards should give the beans a nice smoky flavor.'

Charley turns the stolen brougham and its gory contents over to the deputy chief constable and obtains a voucher that entitles him and his prisoner and his young charges to free passage on the next London-bound train.

For the first half hour or so of the trip, Hoggles is unexpect-edly chatty, given the circumstances. Except for the handcuffs, anyone would think he'd been rescued as well – and in a way perhaps he has. He seems quite glad to be rid of his sometime partner and expresses no regrets or ill feelings about Neck's death. In fact, he sounds more concerned about the fate of Young Lochinvar. 'It weren't my idea to beat 'im up that way, y'know.' He leans in close to Charley and murmurs, almost in his ear,

'And it weren't my idea to do that one's mother in, neither.' He nods in the direction of Audrey, who is curled up on the seat, peacefully asleep.

The temptation to shove his fist into the man's face again is almost too strong for Charley to resist. He takes a moment to collect himself, then he says, 'You remember what I told you before, about what would happen to your mouth if you didn't keep it shut?'

Hoggles nods dumbly.

'Well, that was me being polite.'

After he's handed Neckless over to the authorities – who are delighted to have him at last – and left the children in the care of Mary and Mrs Bramble, Charley heads straight for the Priestley Orphans' Home, without even stopping at the Holywell Street house to refresh himself. Perhaps he could trust the coppers to haul the Reverend in, but then again, maybe not. They're always reluctant to arrest anyone well-born or well connected, especially for such a nebulous sort of crime. After all, the Reverend hasn't killed anyone – not directly, anyway – or stolen anything, except perhaps innocence.

Clearly, that's the way Priestley himself sees it. When Charley shows up, brandishing the cuffs, the man seems genuinely surprised – almost amused, in fact. 'Are you remanding me to custody, Inspector Bucket?'

'I am.'

'Do as you like, but I guarantee you they won't keep me for long. What's more, your wife is going to be very upset.'

'And why is that?'

'Haven't you heard? Several weeks ago she joined our board of overseers – said she needed something worthwhile to keep her occupied. She and all the rest of the board members – some of whom are *very* influential – are going to be quite unhappy if you try to put their director behind bars.'

Charley scowls and lowers the cuffs. 'I see. Well, that puts things in a very different light, doesn't it? I suppose I have no choice but to let you go.'

'Now you're being reasonable. No hard feelings, I hope?'

'No, no; they say the coppers always get their man, but it's not true, of course.' He extends a hand and the smugly smiling Priestley clasps it. The smile quickly changes to a grimace as Charley tightens his grip. While the Reverend squirms and gasps, Charley claps one end of the cuffs on the man's bony wrist and the other on his own brawny one. 'That, Mr Priestley, is what's known in the bare-knuckle boxing trade as a *feint* – you pretend to go in one direction and then go another way altogether.'

But the Reverend isn't down and out just yet; after all, he bargains daily with a far higher authority than a mere private enquiry agent. He actually manages a laugh, though it's a trifle weak and shaky. 'Oh, come now, Inspector. You're a practical-minded man. Surely you realize that we can't possibly keep this place going solely through donations from benefactors, no matter how generous they are. Even in the workhouses, young inmates are apprenticed to various trades. I know, because I was one of them. What we're doing is no different.'

'Oh, really,' says Charley. 'Tell me, Reverend: When you were an apprentice, did they work you twelve hours a day, every day, and never let you sit and rest, not for even a moment?'

'Well, no, but—'

'Did you sleep alongside twenty other children – most of them sick – on a moldy, bug-infested mattress, with only a bucket to shit and piss in?'

'Really, Inspector—'

'If you tried to escape, did they cut off all your hair, lock you in a windowless cell, and feed you bread and water?'

'Well, I never actually—'

'Did you live in constant fear of having your fingers crushed, or your hand, or your head?'

'N – no, not exactly, but—'

'Then don't try to tell me that what you're doing to these children is no different, goddamn it!'

In the cab on the way to Lambeth station house, the Reverend tries yet again to get through to Charley. 'You're going to look very foolish, Inspector, when they release me. I'm a well-respected citizen, and, whatever you may think, apprenticing children is not a crime. No judge will ever convict me.'

Charley nods thoughtfully. 'You know, Reverend, you may

be right . . . or rather you *might* be, except for the fact that you've also harbored a notorious murderer and hired his friend to steal the carriage of an even *more* well-respected citizen: Lord Belliveau.'

Priestley gapes and then groans, 'Oh for god's sake! I never meant—' Realizing how incriminating this sounds, he breaks off abruptly.

Charley finishes for him. 'You never meant for him to rob anyone quite so important. Well, you know what they say: If you run with the dogs, you'll surely get fleas. My guess is, that'll earn you at least two years in quod – where I doubt your social standing will be worth very much.'

Though Charley is in no hurry to face Jane, he can't possibly stay on his feet much longer, and her house is his nearest haven. He's too played out even to stop at a tavern or a coffeehouse for a bracer. His weariness makes him a bit ashamed, really, a bit betrayed by his body; there was a time when he could chase a criminal for days on end with little or no sleep and barely break his stride. But as he climbs from the cab, his ribs remind him that, oh, yes, he's been shot. Well, all right, then; his body is forgiven, just this once.

He can only hope that Jane, too, is in a forgiving mood. Perhaps he shouldn't even bother telling her about Priestley; let her read it in tomorrow's paper. But no, that'll give her even more reason to chastise him. Better to have it out now, and be done with it.

Jane is tucked up in her favorite overstuffed chair, book in hand; ordinarily she's blind and deaf to the real world at such times, but to his surprise, she actually notices his entrance. 'How did it go?' she calls. 'Did you get your man?'

Charley pours himself a glass of rum and downs half of it before replying. 'Yes, I did, my dear. All three of them.'

'Three? Oh, my. I hope they didn't give you any trouble.'

'Not really. I think Mr Priestley was the worst of the lot, actually. He tried to talk me to death.'

She turns to stare at him over the back of the chair. 'Mr Priestley of the orphans' home?'

There's no turning back now. He slumps down on the squab

sofa and recounts the whole sorry tale – well, most of it, anyway. She won't want to hear the nasty details of Neck's demise, of course, But, however much it may offend her sensibilities, she needs to know what sort of existence those children lead if she's to understand why Mr Priestley must be brought to justice.

And she actually does appear to understand. In fact, she's so moved by his account that she dabs at her eyes with a hand-kerchief. Well, she always has had a soft spot for the helpless and downtrodden. 'How many of them has he sent off to the mills?' she asks, in an unsteady voice.

'Dozens,' says Charley. 'He's listed them all in a ledger. I'm hoping I'll be able to rescue at least some of them. Do you think can we find places for them in other orphanages?'

Jane frowns and shakes her head dubiously. 'It won't be easy. They're all so overcrowded as it is. I suppose we overseers can keep our home going for a while, until we find a new director.'

'Good, good,' says Charley. He's far too muddle-headed with exhaustion to be discussing anything of importance, but the sooner he speaks what's on his mind the better. She'll surely need some time to get used to the idea. He clears his throat uncomfortably and says, 'I'd like us to take in one of the girls ourselves.' It's been some time since he spoke of Jane and himself as 'us,' or even thought it. The words don't come easily. But he can't let it sound as though this is her decision alone, or her sole responsibility.

Jane blinks in surprise. '*Here*, you mean?'

'Yes. Audrey's a very pleasant and very resourceful child; she'll be no trouble at all. I'm sure Hanora will gladly help take care of her – not that she'll need much taking care of, mind you – and I'll . . . I'll try to spend more time here myself, so she won't be a burden on you.'

She studies his face curiously, as if searching for some sign that he's joking, or perhaps going mad. 'What is this girl to you?' she says. 'I mean, what makes her different from any of the others?'

Charley sighs. He's known all along that the question would come up, and yet he still doesn't have a satisfactory answer. 'Her mother was . . .' He was about to say *One of my clients*, but that seems unfair to Rosa. 'Her mother was a friend – a milliner and an artist. She was murdered by the same coves who did Priestley's dirty work for him.'

Jane is an intelligent woman; the real meaning of the term *friend* is surely not lost on her. No doubt she's been aware for many years that Charley had women friends – though of course she'd never have broached so vulgar a subject. Nor does she now. 'I see,' she says. 'And you feel it's your duty to look after her daughter?'

'You might say that.'

She gives a small, humorless laugh. 'Well, god knows you've always been a man who tries to do his duty.' She picks up her Brontë book again. 'Let me think about it, Charley, all right? You look worn out. Go to bed.'

TWENTY-EIGHT

Making promises to Jane is a dangerous thing, almost as dangerous as injuring her feelings; she never lets you forget either one. Charley knows how difficult it will be, making good on his vow to spend more time in the Millbank house. But he also knows that, if he wants something from Jane, he has to be prepared to give something up – in this case, a certain amount of freedom.

He can't just ignore the demands of his private enquiry business, of course. There may be half a dozen urgent cases awaiting his attention, not to mention the rescue of those other orphans – and let us not forget the tricky matter of Miss Fairweather. Ordinarily, he would just slip away to his office the next morning before Jane rises, but he forces himself to stick around long enough to let her know where he's off to.

Predictably enough, she seems peeved but, unpredictably, she says, 'Well, no matter. I'll be gone much of the day, anyway.' She holds up a card that arrived in the early post. 'The overseers have called a meeting, to determine how to proceed.'

Charley is tempted to ask whether she's considered his proposal to take in Audrey, but restrains himself. Wives, he's learned, are

much like informers; if you push them too hard, they're likely
to turn on you.

That afternoon, as Charley is at his massive oaken desk going
over Mr Priestley's ledger and considering where and how to
begin his rescue efforts, there's a soft rap at the office door.
'Enter!' he calls, distractedly, and the visitor obliges. 'Just
give me a moment,' says Charley. Though he prides himself
on his acuity, when he looks up from his task he almost doesn't
trust his eyes. 'Jane? Audrey. Where did you— How did
you—?'

'May we sit down?' asks his wife.

Flustered by this sudden collision of what have until now
been separate worlds, Charley gets clumsily to his feet, holding
his aching ribs. 'Of course. I'm afraid I have just the one chair,
unless—' He tries to maneuver his own chair around to the
front of the desk; it's like trying to pass a costermonger's cart
in Paternoster Row.

'It's all right,' says Audrey. 'We're small enough to share a
seat.'

Jane clearly takes this as a compliment and rewards the girl
with a slightly stiff smile. Still, it is a smile. 'Just as I was
returning home from my meeting,' she says, 'a very nice and
rather elegant lady named Mrs . . . what was it, dear?'

'Mrs M'Alpine,' says Audrey.

'Mrs M'Alpine came by. She said that you had left Audrey
in her care, but that the child had been asking to see you. So
. . . well, as you can see, I brought her here.'

'I hope you don't mind, Inspector.' Audrey tugs at the bonnet
she's been given to cover her shorn head. 'I know you're busy
with cases. I just . . . I didn't feel quite safe, that's all.'

Charley circles the desk and crouches next to her. 'Of course
you don't. After all you've been through, it'll take some time.
In the meanwhile, you can come and see me whenever you
want, for as long as you want.'

Jane clears her throat, as if preparing to say something
difficult. 'As a matter of fact, we've been thinking that . . . that
if you'd like, perhaps . . . perhaps you might come and live
with us for a while.'

Audrey regards her with something like disbelief. 'In your house?'

'Yes. It's quite large, you know; you'd have your own room. I'll be working at the orphanage most days, but you could come with me. That way you could see your little friends.'

'But I wouldn't be living there?'

Jane glances at Charley as if to say, *Why doesn't she understand?*

Because, Charley wants to reply, she has no notion what a real home is, only a shabby one-room flat or a brothel or an orphanage. 'No,' he tells the girl, 'as Mrs Field says, you'd live with us. Do you think you'd like that?'

Audrey considers this a moment, then nods gravely. 'Yes,' she says. 'I'm quite sure I would.'

'Well, let's go home then,' says Jane, 'and let the inspector get back to work.' She glances at the open ledger containing the names of all those condemned children waiting to be set free. 'No doubt he has important cases to see to.'

'I do, in fact. But before you go, what's this about working at the orphanage?'

'Well, I told the other overseers everything you told me, and they agreed that we should find a new director, and I said that I felt I could handle the job, and they seemed amenable to the idea – especially when I said I wouldn't require a salary.'

'Oh. Well. That's . . . that's good.' He leans in closer to her and says softly, 'Are you sure you want to do this?'

She bristles a bit. 'You don't think I can?'

'No, no, I don't mean running the orphanage. No doubt you'll manage that perfectly well. I meant . . .' He glances toward Audrey, who is examining his coffee-making paraphernalia.

'Yes, I think so. As you said, she's a very pleasant child, and very little trouble. And . . . well, she needs a family of some sort, doesn't she?' A family of some sort; that's as good a way as any of describing what he and Jane have. She glances again at the ledger. 'Charley,' she says quietly, 'I know you promised to be home more, and I appreciate that. But don't you feel it's more important just now to find those other children and bring them back? Every day you delay is another day of misery for them.'

'Of course. I just thought that – well, I didn't want to—' He gestures awkwardly in Audrey's direction.

'Between Hanora and me, she'll be well taken care of.'

'I know. I just feel—' There's no way he can explain to Jane how he feels, the guilt he still carries over Rosa's death. He knew she was afraid of something and he failed to protect her. Though Audrey is in no real danger now, he can't bear for her to think that he's abandoning her, the way he did her mother. But neither can he bear to think of all those other orphan girls, whose lives truly are in danger. Charley can't recall Sir Galahad ever being faced with such a dilemma – having to choose which maiden to rescue. 'Well,' he says, 'let's give it a few days; once she's settled in perhaps she'll feel safer.'

None of the appeals that have arrived by post, addressed to Inspector Bucket, is particularly dire or urgent. He has no trouble turning them down. But there are two other, more difficult matters that he really can't ignore. He'll just have to attend to them in the evening, when Audrey is soundly asleep.

The first is a trip to Westminster Hospital to look in on Lochinvar Mull, something Charley has been dreading. Though the lad is still hanging on, Hanora, who visits him daily for an hour or so, hasn't seen any real improvement in his condition. Nor does Charley, when he approaches the constable's bedside. Beneath all those bruises and lacerations, Mull's face is ashen; his forehead is covered in beads of perspiration. Charley sits on the edge of the bed and, taking out his new bandana, gently pats the boy's brow with it.

He's always considered bandanas to be a very useful accessory, but he never suspected they had restorative powers. No sooner has he finished soaking up the sweat than Young Lochinvar's eyelids flutter, then struggle open a little, like the cocoon of an emerging butterfly. The boy's dry, cracked lips do the same, and a word comes forth: 'Jesus.'

'Not just yet,' says Charley. 'It's only me.'

'Jesus,' the constable says again. 'I hurt.'

'If you keep trying to talk,' says Charley, 'you're going to hurt a lot more, because I'm going to throttle you. Just lie still, now, and let me do the talking.' He proceeds to give the lad a quick summary of the events of the past few days – well, as quick as is possible, anyway, given all that's happened.

When he's wrapped up his tale, Lochinvar speaks again. 'I'm sorry,' he says.

'Sorry? For what, lad?'

'I should never have . . . gone after Neckless.'

'No. You shouldn't. But if you hadn't, I might never have thought to investigate the orphans' home.' He pats the young constable's shoulder gently. 'If you want to know the truth, I'd have done exactly the same thing.'

Mull gives a weak smile. 'But I'll wager . . . you'd have given them . . . more of a fight.'

'Well, when you get back on your feet,' says Charley, 'I'll give you a few lessons.'

As he's leaving the hospital, the bells of St Margaret's are tolling ten o'clock. There's still time, then, to accomplish his second task. He doesn't relish it any more than he did his visit to Young Lochinvar. But that went far better than he expected; perhaps fortune will continue to smile. He's going to need a bit of luck if he's to be in and out of Miss Fairweather's town house before she returns from the theatre. But it's a pleasant evening; maybe she'll walk home. Or it could be that after the show Mr Elton will buy her a drink or two at the Horse and Groom or, who knows, invite her to his lodgings. Though that possibility makes Charley cringe, there's no denying that it would give him more time to conduct his investigation.

Just to be safe, he catches a cab, which has him there in no more than a quarter hour. To be even safer, he circles around to the rear door, where he's less likely to be noticed while plying his picks. The interior is silent and lit only by a single sinumbra lamp, turned low. He carries it with him up the stairs. He's already searched the cellar, the sitting room, and the maid's room. All that remains is Miss Fairweather's bedroom.

Charley isn't certain what he hopes to find there, or hopes not to find; he's simply doing what he does best – poking about. Though most coppers – unwittingly, of course – adhere to the principle of Ockham's razor and search all the likeliest places first, Charley has always done quite the opposite. After all, a person with something to hide doesn't stick it behind the painting or in the stocking drawer, does she? Not unless she's stupid, and Miss Fairweather is far from stupid.

Nor does she necessarily have anything to hide. He can't shake the feeling, though, that there's something she's not telling him. Well, in fact he *knows* there is; she must surely have been aware that Arly, the house girl, was dismissed, and yet she said nothing about it.

It makes no sense. Of the many murders Charley has investigated over the years, a startling share involved employees who felt they were unjustly sacked or poorly paid – look, for example, at the cove responsible for spiking Dr Benjamin's Panacea with arsenic. Perhaps an even greater number were committed by jealous lovers. Both motives could, in theory at least, be attributed to Arly. The girl had plenty of reason, then, to pack her things and hurry home to County Clare. But why wouldn't Julia just tell the coppers that she'd hooked it, and let them bring her back? Charley can't think of a single reason. Unless . . . unless Julia *wants* her gone. Suppose, for example, Arly knows something incriminating, something that Julia doesn't want revealed?

Well, there's no point in conjecturing, is there? People are such complicated creatures, speculating about their motives is like betting on a horse race. Guesses aren't much good, not even educated ones. What he really needs is evidence.

And after only a few minutes of searching, he finds some, tucked away in the narrow gap between the wardrobe and the floor, at the very back, where no one but the most ferret-like of investigators would bother to look. At first, he doesn't know what to make of it. How could a stout cane of Indian mahogany simply break in two that way? But when he dons his spectacles and examines the broken ends more closely, the answer comes clear: they aren't jagged at all, as they would be if the wood had just snapped; no, the cane has been neatly cut, following the lines of one of the carvings, and then glued together so that, as soon as any weight was put on it, it would give way.

As Charley sits there, mulling over what this means, he hears the front door open and close. He makes no attempt to flee or to conceal himself; he can tell from the sound of the footfalls that it's Julia, and that she's alone. 'Hello?' she calls in a voice that he almost doesn't recognize, it's so tremulous, so different from the self-assured way she ordinarily speaks. 'Is someone here?'

Charley lifts the lamp and makes his way to the top of the stairs. 'It's me – Inspector Bucket.' He realizes how odd it must sound, identifying himself that way. But it feels right somehow, for it seems that the tables have turned and he's the one playing a role, now.

Julia appears at the bottom of the steps and gazes up at him, a tentative, puzzled smile on her face – which, even cast in shadow, is disturbingly lovely. 'Charley? What on earth are you doing here?' Though she's clearly trying to take command of the situation, she comes across like the understudy who is suddenly called upon to perform a part she's not prepared for. 'No, don't tell me. You're poking about again. And it looks as though you've found something.'

Charley has always rather enjoyed the interrogation process; it's a sort of game, really – though one in which the stakes may be dauntingly high – and over the years he's become very good at it. He's not eager to question Miss Fairweather, however, or to make accusations. Some part of him still wants to protect her, to rescue her, and it's hard to let go of that, to have Julia regard him not as a Galahad but as more of a Mordred.

As it turns out, no interrogation is necessary. Once she's had a few sips of brandy, she seems almost anxious to reveal all she knows about the cane and about the disappearance of Arly, as though those matters have been weighing heavily on her mind. 'I was very distraught after the accident, of course,' she says, and she's distraught again, just recalling it. 'And yet I couldn't help noticing how . . . how unnatural the broken cane looked. When I examined it closely, I could see it had been tampered with.'

'Then why hide it? Why not turn it over to the constable?'

She stares at him as if the answer should be obvious. 'Don't you see? It wasn't Arly they'd suspect; it was *me*! I was the one with the motive!'

It takes Charley a moment to catch up. 'So . . . so you knew all along that Monty left this place to you in his will.'

Miss Fairweather shrugs. Another question with an obvious answer. 'Of course I did. But I could hardly admit it, could I?'

'I'm sorry to be so dense,' says Charley irritably. 'No doubt you can also explain why the house girl should want her employer dead.'

'Yes, I believe I can.' Her dark eyes meet his and her face seems to soften. 'I think you were right, Charley; I think she never forgave him for transferring his affections from her to me.'

Charley feels a disproportionate degree of gratification; he got *something* right, at least. 'But if she resented you so much, why didn't she do *you* in?'

Miss Fairweather is not quite so prompt to answer this one. She stares down at her glass of brandy and reflectively puts a hand to her face – in fact to the very spot where, a fortnight earlier, she sported that ugly bruise. 'Because,' she says softly. 'Because she understood that I was not the villain of the piece. Like her, I was . . . I was a victim.'

Charley winces. 'He actually did beat you, then.'

She nods.

'And Arly as well?'

Another nod. Charley can tell that she's done talking; there's no point in pressing her any further. He rises from the dining room table. When he picks up the broken cane, Miss Fairweather gives him a worried glance. 'It's all right,' he says, 'I'm not going to turn this over to Scotland Yard. Not just yet, anyway.' Thoughtfully, he reconnects the two halves. 'What a shame; it's a beautiful piece of work. But you know, I hear they have some very clever craftsmen in Ireland; perhaps I'll take a trip over there. I may find someone who'll help me fit the pieces together.'

TWENTY-NINE

Of course Charley has no intention of traveling all the way to County Clare and confronting the house girl, at least not right away. When he mentions Ireland, it's mainly to see how Julia will react. Though she's an accomplished actress, even the most seasoned trouper may be thrown off balance by a fellow actor's 'gagging' – straying from the script and saying something totally unexpected. For the briefest of moments, her face registers alarm, even fear, before she puts on a sly smile and says suggestively, 'Well, then, perhaps I'll come with you.'

Though it's a tempting prospect, Charley knows well enough that it won't happen. Even if she were serious, he has other, more urgent matters to attend to. Besides, if he tracks Arly down, unlike Julia she might actually tell him the truth, and he's not at all certain he wants to know it. Not very detective-like of him, but there you are.

It's a long walk to the Holywell Street house, but he needs a bit of a hike in order to clear his head – and in order to prepare himself. If he's going to spend more time there, as he promised, he'll have to get used to that sense of slowly suffo-cating, to weighing every move he makes and every word he says before he makes or says it, to wearing that deuced smoking jacket – and yet being forbidden to smoke – and not wearing his vulgar Mongol vest.

Near College Gardens he stops at a cozy-looking coffee stall with a cloth-draped trestle table, a bright oil lamp, even rela-tively intact china cups and saucers. Despite some misgivings, he orders a cup of Mocha and 'two thin,' as they say. To his surprise, both the bread and the coffee are quite palatable, and he tells the proprietor so. 'Well, it's got to be, don't it?' says the man sourly. 'Thanks to Mr Dickens and his journal, most folk won't settle no more for stuff that's made of 'orse peas and plaster.'

Charley can't help smiling a little, but he hides it by turning his attention to his notebook. He tears out the first two pages, the ones devoted to Neck and Neckless, crumples them, and tosses them into the coke fire that burns beneath the tin coffee boiler. There are still half a dozen of his old nemeses at large, including Bad Hat Henry, William Hubbard, Kelley the Club, and a cove known only as Rat Man, but he's making progress – or at least he was. Now he's going to have to fill out a new page. On the first blank sheet, he carefully prints:

Name: Arly _____ *?*
Age: 30?
Description: Attractive?
Occupation: House girl
Crimes: Murder?
Last known location: County Clare, Ireland

Directly below this, he makes a second entry:

Name: Julia Fairweather
Age: 35
Description: Untrustworthy
Occupation: Actress
Crimes: Murder?
Last known location: Southam Street, Covent Garden

So much for progress. He pays the proprietor, throwing in an extra tuppence for goodwill, and trudges on. When he enters the house, all is quiet except for his wife's faint snoring. Hanora will have gone home long ago – too bad; she'll want to know that her beau's condition has improved. He looks in on Audrey, just to make sure she's sleeping peacefully, and then repairs to the kitchen to fix himself a sandwich.

It's quite a large one, and he's no more than halfway through it when a small voice behind him says, 'Hello, Inspector.' Oddly enough, the words are then repeated, by an even smaller voice.

Charley wipes the mustard from his mouth and turns to Audrey. 'What are you—?' Then he notices the doll cradled in her arms. 'The devil take me; is that you, Charlene?'

'Yes, it's me,' says Audrey, in tones befitting a porcelain doll, then adds, at her normal pitch, 'Mrs Field found her, in Mr Priestley's office. We're glad you're home.'

'You feel safer, now?'

She smoothes her rumpled nightgown and yawns. 'Yes. But that's not the reason. We've been wanting to have a talk with you.'

'Oh, dear,' says Charley. 'What have I done now?'

She snickers. 'Nothing, silly. There's something we *want* you to do.'

'And what might that be?'

She holds up her arms and he hoists her and Charlene onto his lap. 'We want you to find those other girls and bring them back.'

'I will, my dear. I promise. It may take a while, though.'

'Mrs Field says you don't want to leave because of what I said – that I didn't feel safe. That was selfish of me. I know she and Hanora will protect me. It's those girls in the mills who aren't safe. You need to go after them as soon as possible. Tomorrow. Right, Charlene?' The high, soft voice returns: 'Right, Audrey!'

Charley laughs. 'You sound more like your mother every day. She was always thinking about someone else. Which reminds me—' From the pocket of his frock coat he retrieves Rosa's cameo, which he's been carrying around for months, and places it in her hand. 'She wanted you to have this.'

'Thank you. She'd have wanted you to save those other girls, too, you know.'

'Yes, yes, I know.' He gives Audrey's close-cropped head an affectionate rub. 'All right. And if it makes you feel any better, you may soon have another protector as well – an actual police constable.'

'Really?'

'Well, he won't be much use at first; he's badly hurt. But the doctor says he'll heal faster if we bring him here, where Hanora can look after him properly. All we have to do now is convince Mrs Field.'

'Leave that to me,' says Audrey. 'I can be very persuasive.'

'You can, indeed.'

'I'll help look after him, too.'

'Good, good. I just want to know one thing.'

'What?'

'Who's going to look after me?'

Audrey lets out another little laugh. 'You don't need looking after, Inspector; you can take care of yourself.'

Charley shrugs and gives a rather rueful grin. 'I suppose you're right. Only sometimes I wish . . .'

'What? Charley? What do you wish?'

Charley doesn't reply. He's thinking about Rosa: about how

sweet she was to him; how much she enjoyed his company, or said she did; how she rubbed his aching shoulder muscles; how, after making love, they lay there, barely touching, and talked in muted voices about what he'd done that day to try to make the world – or at least his part of it, his beat, as it were – a slightly better place, and about her plans to make a new life for herself and her daughter. Sometimes they talked of nothing in particular or just lay there silent, listening to the sounds from the other rooms or from the street, and that had a soothing sweetness of its own.

Some part of him wishes it could be that way with Jane, but he knows it never will be, and really it never was, and that's all right. We can't hope to have everything we wish for, or even half of them, and that's all right, too. There are enough good things in life that come to us without our wishing for them or expecting them or likely even deserving them. We're all of us guilty of something, after all; each of us appears on someone's little list of wrongdoers, and if we got only what we deserved . . . well, life would be a pretty sorry affair. And, though you were warned at the very outset of this novel that it might not always tell the truth, that is, I promise you, the truth.

9 781847 518514